# Confessions
of a
## Courtesan

# Confessions
## of a
# Courtesan

Deborah Hale
*writing as*
# Elizabeth Charles

CONFESSIONS OF A COURTESAN

ISBN 978-0-9878051-2-6

Set in 11/13pt Adobe® Caslon™ Pro.

1 2 3 4 5 6 7 8 9   15 14 13 12 11

This book is dedicated to my sister, Cyndi, who knows all about surviving and thriving in a man's world.

And to Mike, who has supported me every step of the way.

# Prologue

*St. Anne's Hill, Surrey, July 1795*

COURTESAN. CYPRIAN. DEMI-REP. HARLOT. CALL me what you will. And think of me, according to your inclination, with outrage, pity, fascination ... perhaps even a touch of envy.

Upon hearing my cockney pronunciation, you may dismiss me as a common, ignorant creature and prefer stories of genteel whores like Perdita Robinson or Dally Eliot. That would be your mistake and your loss.

On one point, however, I believe we may agree. Whether by necessity or choice, women like me live outside the rules that govern the rest of our sex.

Rigid rules. Ridiculous rules. Rules that encourage men in conduct for which women are harshly punished. Breaking those rules can be like venturing into the back alleys of Covent Garden after dark. The price of freedom and adventure is constant danger.

To avoid the worst perils of my profession, a girl must observe the courtesan's cardinal rule – *never fall in love.*

Now I have broken that rule ... and my heart along with it.

# Chapter One

*London, Coronation Day 1760 ... a lifetime ago*

"THE AIR SMELLS DIFFERENT THIS morning." I inhaled deep breaths of it as my mother and I hurried up the Strand, part of a surging tide of Londoners on our way to Westminster.

"What did you say, Lizzie?" Mother tightened her grip on my hand, perhaps fearing the swift current of sedan chairs and coaster's barrows might sweep me away from her.

I repeated myself louder to carry above the clatter of footsteps on the cobbles, people calling to one another and street vendors crying their wares.

For an instant, Mother's gaze strayed from my little brother, who seemed to bob above the crowd ahead, carried on my father's shoulders. "It's the time of year, love. Not hot enough to make the gutters ripe but too early for the fog."

She winked at me then scanned the crowd for Patrick again. People were often surprised to discover she had a daughter rising twelve years. She looked especially young and pretty that day, in a gown of silvery green satin with a froth of lace at the elbows. It suited her rich auburn hair and slender figure so well no one would guess it was a cast-off from the actress she'd once served as a dresser.

I wore plum-colored silk with a ladder of gold bows down the bodice. My petticoats made a delightful rustle when I walked. Clever seamstress that she was, Mother had cut it down to fit

2

me for this grand occasion. For once, I looked like the princess of my most extravagant fancies.

Almost before I knew it, the Strand emptied into Charing Cross. There, our stream of traffic mingled with one from Haymarket. The combined crowd swirled around the statue of King Charles on his horse, jostling as it funneled down Whitehall.

"This way, Lizzie!" Mother tugged me after her, against the traffic. "We'd never see anything around the Abbey."

She and Father had talked of little else for the past week. They'd decided we should find a spot near the Opera House to watch the great lords and ladies on their way to the Abbey. Afterward, we would be well placed to head for Hyde Park, where there would be music, puppet shows and later fireworks.

"Excited, Lizzie?" Father asked as he lifted Patrick off his shoulders.

I gave a vigorous nod that made my curls waggle. "I told Mother the air smells different this morning. She says it's just the time of year."

"Perhaps it's all the fruit mongers, sausage sellers and pie men collected so close together." Father sniffed. "Every breath is as good as a feast!"

"It's more than that." I struggled to put my vague but insistent feeling into words. "It smells ... hopeful."

"Clever puss!" Father chucked me under the chin. "Perhaps there is a whiff of optimism in the air. We have an English-born king again, at last. A fine young fellow with a sensible head on his shoulders, from what I hear. May his reign last many years and bring England peace and prosperity!"

We did not have long to wait before a parade of splendid carriages came trundling down the Mall. Sunshine glinted off the ladies' jewels, while a faint breeze ruffled the tall plumes of their headdresses. Such wondrous sights would fuel my daydreams for months to come.

An open coach rolled past, bearing a stiff young couple who

appeared to resent being a spectacle for the crowd. The pretty girl seated opposite them seemed too wrapped up in her own thoughts to notice all the people gawking at her.

"Father." I pointed toward the man in the carriage. "Is that our new king?"

He shook his head. "The Duke of Richmond and his Duchess. The other lady is his sister. I hear the king *wanted* to wed her but his mother and Lord Bute insisted on a German princess."

I craned my neck to keep the lady in sight for as long as possible. Would she be sorry to see another woman crowned, today, in a place that might have been hers?

An intake of breath from the crowd drew my attention to the beautiful woman in the next carriage.

"Lady Lorne," said my father. "One of the celebrated Miss Gunnings, she was. They came from Ireland a few years after your mother and created a sensation at Covent Garden. Such a crowd of admirers used to flock to the stage door! They did not stay actresses for long, though. One soon wed the Duke of Hamilton and the other married the Earl of Coventry."

He glanced down at me, his brown eyes twinkling. "Are you sorry your mother settled for a poor actor with nothing but his charm to recommend him? You might have been *Lady* Elizabeth, now, riding in one of those fine coaches."

"William!" Mother gave him a playful cuff on the arm. "Don't be teasing the child. I never had any noble suitors."

A woman in the crowd nudged Father. "Who's that coming next? The gentleman has a nose as sharp as a pike, but the lady is very handsome."

"That's Lord Spencer." I could tell by the slight puff of Father's chest he was pleased to have an audience. "Cousin to the Duke of Marlborough. His Grace inherited the title, but the old Duchess gave Lord Spencer's family the fortune."

As each carriage passed, father dredged up some scrap of gossip about the occupants to entertain those around us. Being the center of attention put him in high spirits. Basking in the reflected glory, I could scarcely contain my pride.

Then two young men pushed their way to the front of the crowd. "Pray who are you, sir, presuming an acquaintance with all the aristocrats?"

"William Cane," Father replied in a frosty tone. "A play actor at Drury Lane. I boast no acquaintance, but I do recognize those who frequent the theatre."

"Never heard of you." The taller youth quizzed Father up and down. "Playacting at being a play actor, no doubt. Concocting rubbish to impress the gullible."

Father's jaw tightened and his hand clenched into a fist. But Mother whispered, "Pay them no mind, Will."

Sensing my father's humiliation, I wished I could do more than squeeze his hand and bite my tongue when I longed to ask more questions. Such as, who was the boy in the next carriage? His eyes sparkled under bushy dark brows, with as much interest in the people thronging the street as we had in him.

Catching sight of Father, he cried, "Mr. Cane!" He waved, heedless of the fashionable lady who bid him be still. "What is your next production, sir, and which part will you play? I shall come from school to see you!"

Those few cheerful words wrought such a change in my father and everyone around us, I could scarcely believe it.

"Treble in *The Provok'd Wife*." Father beamed as if the part had been Hamlet. "I look forward to seeing you there!"

When the carriage had passed, he remarked to no one in particular. "No doubt he's seen the play before. Master Charles Fox has been a regular playgoer since he was out of petticoats."

The two insulting youths retreated into the crowd, driven away by dark looks and angry muttering against them. People begged Father for more stories.

Hours later, my family wandered home from Hyde Park, agreeably wearied by the excitement of the day.

Father carried Patrick, who had fallen asleep. "What did you think of all those young lords and viscounts in the procession,

Lizzie? Will any of them do for you?"

I gave a self-conscious giggle.

"Don't encourage her, Will." Mother put her arm around my shoulders. "Her head is too full of such nonsense already."

Father shook his head. "Let us not trample on the child's dreams, my dear. Life will do that soon enough."

How right he was.

The summer after my thirteenth birthday, Father came home from the theatre one night shivering with fever. Two days later he broke out in smallpox. Mother soon caught it. Then Patrick.

Father lived, though blind and pockmarked, never able to work in the theatre again. Mother and Patrick died and went to heaven, leaving me behind ... in hell.

꧁꧂

## December 1766, Vinegar Yard, Drury Lane

My hand raw and swollen with chilblains, I gripped my father's and tugged him down the crooked alley. "It's not much farther to the chophouse."

"You hardly need to guide me, Lizzie." He sniffed the frosty air. "I could find my way by smell alone."

A savory whiff of meat made my belly growl. "Can we afford a hot meal, tonight?" I pulled my shawls tighter against the prying cold of a *London particular* – that misbegotten spawn of Thames fog and coal-smoke from a thousand chimneys. "We're already behind with the rent."

"It has been a disappointing day." Father fondled the coins in his pocket. There were too few to jingle. "Can't blame people for not wanting to stop in the cold. Still, I reckon the chophouse a good investment. We can eat and get warm in time to catch the theatres letting out."

He began to cough – a harsh, hollow racket that chilled me in a place the fog could not reach.

"I've a better idea." I warned him of the steps ahead then added, "The actors get paid today, don't they?"

"Lizzie!" Father protested as I led him through the crowded chophouse to one of the cramped booths at the back. "You know I hate begging from my old mates at the playhouse."

"We won't have to *beg*." I cleared the last diners' dirty dishes from the pitted tabletop. The owner knocked a bit off the price of our dinner if we didn't need to be waited on. "The ones who give us something can spare it. What's a few pence less to drink or gamble away? You'd do the same for them."

I saved myself an argument by bustling off to the kitchen.

"Oy, Joe!" I called. "That mutton smells so good Father claimed he could find his way here by following his nose."

"Wotcher, Lizzie!" Fat Joe popped an extra scrap of meat onto each of our plates. "Cold enough for you?"

"It's the fog." I gave an exaggerated shiver. "Sinks right into your bones on days like this."

After Mother's death, I had discovered that a smile and a bit of cheek could ease the way for Father and me. At first it came naturally, but now that I was so often hungry, cold and worried about Father's cough, I had to make an effort.

Returning to our booth, I found Father talking to Mr. Armistead, an amiable Yorkshireman who was another regular at Fat Joe's.

When he saw me coming, he rose and bowed. "Evening, Miss Elizabeth. You look rosy, tonight."

I hadn't thought my face could get any redder than the cold had nipped it, but Mr. Armistead proved me wrong. Nobody else called me Elizabeth, let alone *Miss*.

"Do you flatter all the ladies whose hair you dress?" I set a plate down before him and the other in front of my father.

"All part of the service." Mr. Armistead's blue eyes twinkled. "But I didn't mean to flatter you out of your supper."

When he pushed the plate toward me, I waved it back. "I can fetch another. You eat that before it gets cold."

"If you insist, Miss Elizabeth. Ta." He settled back down in the booth across from my father. "When you work around women, like I do, you soon learn not to argue with 'em."

"Women?" Father laughed. "My Lizzie's only a child."

A child? Had the smallpox robbed Father of his ability to count, along with his sight and his looks? I would be seventeen next summer! I was taller than most grown women and if I got more to eat I might soon fill out the bodice of Mother's old gown. Not that Father could see any of that. He probably pictured me as I'd been when he lost his sight.

The two of them were still talking when I returned to the booth, but no longer about me, thank goodness. Over supper they discussed the latest pantomime playing at Drury Lane, a recent hanging, and the high price of just about everything. Now and then, I stole an admiring glance at Mr. Armistead's well-shaped features. Though he must be all of five-and-twenty, his face still had a boyish air.

When we finished eating, Father rummaged in his pocket and handed me a meager assortment of farthings and haypennies to pay for our meal. Returning to the table afterward, I spied Mr. Armistead coming toward me.

I tried to pass him with a silent nod, but he blocked my way. "Your father doesn't look well, Miss Elizabeth."

"It's just the cold weather. Once spring comes, he'll get better. I've taken care of him the past three years, and we haven't fared so bad."

Mr. Armistead pulled me to a corner, away from the bustle of customers coming and going. "It's not your father I'm worried about. It's what'll become of *you* if anything happens to him."

"*Nothing* is going to happen to him!" I insisted, as desperate to persuade myself as Mr. Armistead.

He fished a half-crown from his pocket and pressed it into my palm. "For your Christmas box. I know it's early, but I may not see you again before then."

"I can't take this." I tried to give it back, even as my fingers clenched around the coin. "It's too much!"

"I can spare it." He nodded toward my father. "Better get back before he starts to worry. Just promise me one thing."

"What?" I asked, suddenly wary.

"If you ever need a friend, come find me. I'll do what I can to help."

"I told you, we'll be fine." I wanted to hurl the coin at his head for suggesting otherwise, but that small satisfaction was not worth parting with a precious half-crown.

Father proved me right that winter, bless him. He hung on then rallied with the coming of spring. But the summer yielded a poor harvest, driving prices up. People had little charity to spare for a blind beggar and his child.

We had to range farther afield and stay out later in all weathers. Days we could afford to eat at the chophouse became more and more rare. Father's cough returned with the fog and spring seemed a long time away.

"Rise and shine." I nudged him one morning after an especially late, cold night. "No one's going to come looking to give us money if we lie in bed all day."

I wished I could leave him there to rest, but that was impossible. He was the one who stirred pity in the hearts of strangers. Besides, he needed me to watch over him. I had learned that when he'd fallen one day while I was off looking for work. Since then, anywhere I went, he must go too.

"It's Sunday. Why don't we go to church?" I asked when he did not stir. "It'll be warm with the candles lit and all the people crowded in. Folks might feel charitable afterwards and slip us something."

Besides, I had a hunger even deeper than the one in my belly, to hear words from a book that spoke kindly of the poor. "Where do you fancy—St. Giles' or St. Mary-le-Strand?"

Only when I paused to await his answer did I mark how silent and still my father lay. My knees went weak. I sank down onto the edge of the bed. I didn't make a great fuss, for this was not the first I'd seen of death. Nor did I weep, though I wished I could.

For the past few years, Father had been the reason behind everything I did—keeping him fed, keeping him from harm, keeping him company. Such happiness as I'd known had come from whatever small comfort I'd been able to provide him.

Now he was gone and I was alone with nothing but my worthless dreams.

A few days after they carted Father's body away to a pauper's grave, I dragged myself up two pair of stairs to a cramped little room above a haberdasher's on Ragged Staff Court. Too tired for tears. Every feeling starved and frozen out of my heart, except one. Desperation.

I had come to an *intelligence office*. Places like this referred people seeking work to shops that were hiring or families in need of servants. I'd already been turned away from two others because I could not afford the shilling fee.

That was after I'd tried to find work at the playhouses. Neither Covent Garden nor Drury Lane was hiring, especially not a girl with no experience except at begging. I asked about selling oranges in the theatre but was told I would need a new dress, a vendor's box and a stock of fruit. How was I supposed to get those without a farthing to my name?

I paused on the threshold of the intelligence office, faint from having climbed all those stairs on an empty stomach. I'd last eaten more than a day ago—a stale penny loaf bought with the pittance a ragman had given me for Father's clothes. Hunger now gnawed at my bones as well as my belly. I squeezed into a corner of the room to wait while the stern-faced proprietress dispatched those ahead of me.

"Places for women are dreadful scarce," I heard her tell a girl who looked fresh from the country. She consulted a thick book on the table in front of her then handed the girl a scrap of paper. "But here's directions to a family on Russell Street who need a maid-of-all-work."

While she dealt with an older man who was next in line, an infant in the arms of the girl behind him began to wail.

The proprietress half-rose from her chair and jabbed a bony finger toward the door, "Be off with you and don't come back till you're rid of that brat!"

"Please, I need a job or we'll starve!" The young mother sobbed out the story of how she'd been seduced and deserted. I felt certain it would soften the old woman's heart.

But her angular features crimped into an impatient scowl. "Lose the child and I might find you a place as a wet nurse."

The girl tried to plead further but the woman next in line shoved her toward the door. "Ye should've thought of all that before ye lifted yer skirt, ye little fool. G'on now! Ye're holding up the rest of us."

On ominous grumble of agreement from the others in line drove the girl from the office in tears. I knew I should pity her, but I could not afford to. Her going put me one place further in line. Perhaps it left one job needing to be filled.

As I stood there in the airless room, listening to the drone of voices, my eyelids grew heavy. Since Father's death I'd been living on the streets, too frightened to nod off for more than brief snatches. What if I froze to death like the half-naked old woman huddled in a nearby draper's doorway, her nose gnawed off by rats? What if I was attacked by the gang of street boys I'd once seen beat a lame dog to death for sport?

It seemed only an instant after I closed my eyes that a sharp voice jolted me awake. "Find some place else to sleep, you shiftless creature! I'm not running an inn."

I rubbed my eyes and struggled to collect my scattered wits, grateful to find the office empty but for me and the proprietress. Perhaps without a crowd waiting, she would not be so quick to dismiss me.

"Begging your pardon, ma'am. I didn't mean to fall asleep. I came looking for work."

She fixed me with a doubtful glare, but extended her hand. "Make it quick. You're not the only one who's tired."

"I haven't got a shilling." I hurried on before she could stop me. "But I'll pay you the very first one I earn, I swear!"

"Fa," the woman muttered. "Nowhere I'd send you would hire such a dirty scarecrow, anyway. Folks want clean, strong country girls as servants, not thieving rooks from St. Giles!"

Part of me wanted to protest my honesty, but my wolfish hunger goaded me to make away with as many papers as I could snatch off her desk.

Before I had a chance, she pushed me out the door. "If you're not gone by the time I count three, I'll call the watch!"

Somehow I found the strength to run. Everything I'd heard of prisons and workhouses convinced me they were worse than the streets, without even the faint hope of bettering my lot.

Darkness was falling when I reached Covent Garden. The fruit and vegetable mongers were packing up their barrows and heading home, leaving the open square in front of St. Paul's church to carriages of theatre patrons, linkboys who lit their way through the dark lanes around the playhouse and harlots who accosted any man in a decent coat.

I'd stolen just enough sleep at the intelligence office to shake me from my stupor of exhaustion. Now my heart shuddered against my ribs and my empty belly quivered beneath it. Every sudden noise or movement made me jump. Danger lurked in every shadow, ready to pounce. Panic gripping me by the throat so tight I could scarcely breathe.

I bolted for a hiding place I'd found. It was behind a broken chimney, halfway down an alley that grew so narrow a body could only squeeze out the far end by turning sideways. The muddy ground was strewn with filth that gave off a sickening stench of dead things festering in sewer muck. Only the cold tamed it enough to be halfway bearable.

As I huddled in the reeking shadows, twitching with cold

and fear, two people entered the alley. I shrank back, stifling a whimper.

"Let's see yer coin," said a woman, her voice thin and scratchy. "Pay *then* play."

Silver jingled as a man asked, "How much again?"

"A shilling if ye want it here, more if we go inside."

"A shilling it is, then. And you're certain you haven't got the pox?"

"Perfect health, sir, I swear."

"Still . . ." the man sounded doubtful ". . . just as a precaution, for both our benefit . . ."

I hunched there in horrified silence, while the nameless pair flung themselves into a swift, brutal rut — panting, heaving, grunting, and moaning. How it must hurt for them to make such noises! Why would anyone pay to be pummeled and thrashed?

A few minutes later they left, their business done. Meanwhile I crouched, shivering and sickened. Many a time in the past few years, I had been cold and hungry, but never freezing or starving. A blunt, stony ache inched up my hands and feet, but my frantic efforts to warm them sent needles of ice pricking my flesh. My hunger felt like a rat had crawled up inside me and was trying to gnaw its way out.

I tried to conjure up the delightful fancies that had once sustained me, of elegant ladies in fine gowns and sparkling jewels dancing with gallant gentlemen. Now even my imagination failed me. I feared if I closed my eyes, I might never open them again.

# Chapter Two

"HOT WINKLES—BEST IN town!"

"Milk-o! Fresh, sweet milk!"

The competing cries of street vendors slapped me awake the next morning, the smells of their wares taunting my empty belly. But at least I was alive.

Bone-cold and aching, I forced myself to my feet and shuffled out of the alley. I headed for Covent Garden, determined to scavenge something for breakfast. Wilted cabbage leaves, maybe, or a piece of bad fruit tossed out to protect the rest from rot. I didn't care what it was. I would have eaten anything and I would have done anything to get it.

"Where are you bound, fair charmer?" cried a well-dressed gentleman who staggered out of the *Spotted Dog* tavern toward me.

I glanced about for the woman he must be addressing. But the only other female nearby was a pockmarked street vendor selling hot warden pears from the clay pot she balanced on her head. The smell of them made my mouth water, until the reek of spirits coming off the gentleman overpowered it.

He latched onto my arm, dispelling any doubt that his words were meant for me. "It is too cold a day to wander the streets, my dear. Come inside with me and have a hot cup of negus to warm yourself."

The invitation tempted me—to sit somewhere warm and dry and fill my belly with drink that might help me forget my desperate situation. But I knew what his hospitality would cost me. I could not bear to be used like that wretched woman in the alley last night, or find myself burdened with a child like the girl at the intelligence office.

I tried to pull away. "Forgive me, sir, I cannot tarry."

"Come girl, don't be coy." Clinging tighter to my arm with one hand, he thrust the other beneath my shawl to grope my bosom. "I need relief. Name your price."

Helpless fear engulfed me, cold and foul as the Thames oozing beneath London Bridge.

"Let me go! I'm not for hire!" I struggled to break free, but hunger and cold had sapped my strength.

"Miss Elizabeth?" Mr. Armistead's familiar voice was the most welcome sound in the world at that moment. "I know this young woman, sir. Unhand her before I call the watch!"

Giving my breast one last vicious squeeze, the drunkard spewed a curse and flung me into my rescuer's waiting arms. Then he lurched off toward Covent Garden, no doubt to seek more willing company.

Seized by a palsy of trembling, I clung to Mr. Armistead, gasping in the wholesome fragrance of dried flowers and herbs that clung to his coat. What he must have thought of *my* smell, I could only imagine but he was gallant enough to ignore it and gather me close.

"Poor lass! Did that blackguard harm you? What's your father thinking to let you wander these streets alone, even at this hour? Oh, bloody hell! He's passed on, hasn't he?"

I nodded. "Last week. I've been looking for work ever since and a place to stay."

"And a bite to eat," Mr. Armistead added. "Without much luck at any of those, by the look of you? Well, your luck's just changed." He took my hand and drew me back down the street. "I'm sorry about your father. He was always an amiable fellow in spite of his misfortunes. A rare gift, that is."

I was too overcome by relief to do anything but cling to Mr. Armistead's warm hand and follow where he led me. On the corner of Russell and Bow Streets, we slowed in front of a pie man's stall.

"One of your best pork pies for the lady." Mr. Armistead dug out thruppence and flipped it high in the air toward the vendor.

The pie man caught the coins in his meaty fist. Then he pulled a golden round of pastry from his covered barrow and tossed it to me.

I raised the steaming pie to my lips, eager to wolf it down, but Mr. Armistead shook his head. "Let it cool a bit or you'll burn your mouth. Come on, we haven't far to go."

"Where *are* we going?" I cradled the hot pie in my shawl to warm my hands. "And what did you mean about my luck changing?"

"I meant I have a job for you, if you want it, and a place to stay. We're going back to my lodgings long enough for you to eat and me to pick up a thing or two."

Where would we go then? That question had to wait upon a more urgent one. "What sort of job?"

"A hair model. All the best *friseurs* have them to show their customers the latest styles." He yanked me close to the wall to avoid being drenched by the contents of a chamber pot, emptied from a window above us. "I always thought you had lovely hair. You still have it, don't you? Haven't cut it off to sell?"

I cursed myself for not thinking to sell my hair, but only for an instant. If I had, I would have missed this golden opportunity. "It's all there still, under my cap."

"Good!" Mr. Armistead patted my hand. "Once you're groomed, fattened and dressed in a pretty gown, you'll be all the tick."

Could this be true? I wondered as I listened to him spin a rosy future for me. Someone would *pay* me to swan about in a fine gown and flaunt my handsomely dressed hair? Surely I must still be huddled in that cold, stinking alley, dreaming it!

"I can't afford to pay you much." Mr. Armistead's breath

conjured misty phantoms in the cold air. "And you'll have to share my lodgings. But you'll be warm, fed and dressed well."

Share his lodgings? A sudden chill of wariness went down my back, like the foul stream that dribbled through the gutter in the middle of the street. Did Mr. Armistead want the same thing as that drunkard outside the *Spotted Dog*? The heavy wooden signboards along Drury Lane seemed to creak a warning as they swung on their iron hinges.

"It's not very grand, my place," said Mr. Armistead, "but my landlady fancies herself respectable. So if anybody asks, say you're my wife. Mrs. Elizabeth Armistead has a nice ring."

It sounded like one of the elegant ladies I'd dreamed of being. Was this his way of saying I must behave as a wife to him? To lose my virtue would ruin me. But if I had nothing else to barter for my survival, there were worse places I might surrender it than in Mr. Armistead's warm bed.

We turned onto Wych Street, a narrow lane crowded with shops that sold lewd books and prints. From the flats above those shops came a racket of drunken singing, violent quarrels and bawling babes. The last of those rang loudest in my ears. If I got with child, I would be trapped forever in a life I was desperate to escape.

Stopping in front of a narrow door, Mr. Armistead rummaged in his pocket to retrieve a key. "There's something else I need to ask, so don't take offense. Are you a virgin?"

I understood his need for assurance that I would not give him the pox or present him with another man's child in seven month's time. Still I could not help resenting his question. "I know there are men who would sell their daughters for a cup of gin but my father was not one of them."

"That's all I needed to hear, lass." Mr. Armistead pushed the door open and beckoned me inside.

For an instant I hesitated. This was a step from which I could never turn back. But what choice did I have? I forced myself over the threshold into a narrow corridor. It had to be better than starving to death or walking the streets offering my body to strangers.

Mr. Armistead led me up two pair of steep stairs and ushered me through a door on one side of a tiny landing. After the familiar reek of the streets, I was not prepared for the cloying scent that overpowered me when I stepped into the room.

"What's that smell?"

He sniffed. "Tools of the trade—rosewater, bergamot, pomade. I never notice it anymore. Sit down and eat your pie before it gets cold. I'll just fetch a few things I need."

Before my trembling knees gave way, I sank onto a fiddle-back chair with faded upholstery and began to devour my pie. Mr. Armistead ducked into the next room. Through the door, I glimpsed a tall bed draped with brown curtains. The place was not large or well furnished, but it was tidier than I'd expected of a man living on his own. After what I'd been used to, it seemed like a palace.

I had just nibbled the last crumb of pastry from my fingers when Mr. Armistead reappeared, carrying a bulky leather satchel. "A few good hot dinners at the chophouse and you'll soon look like your old self again. Now before we go, there's one thing I need to check."

He twitched it off my linen cap and pulled the pins from my hair. "So long and thick," he murmured plunging his hands into it. "Just enough curl but not too much. And such color! It's lank and greasy now, but I can soon put that right."

I sat frozen between alarm at the liberty he was taking and the forbidden pleasure of his touch. His fingers were long and deft—not rough with calluses or limp and pudgy like the hands of some men who had given me coins over the years.

Out of the corner of my eye, I glimpsed him brandishing a quill. The next thing I knew, he began running it through my hair like a furrow, the waxy tip scraping over my scalp.

I jerked away. "What are you doing?"

"Don't fret." He pulled me back by the shoulder and continued to plow the quill through my hair. "I'm only checking for vermin. No use washing hair if it's crawling with lice."

"I have *not* got lice!" I batted his hand away. "And what did you mean about washing hair? It's the middle of winter. I'll catch my death!

"Not where I'm taking you." Mr. Armistead handed back my cap. "In case you haven't heard, there's more bathhouses within a mile of here than in the rest of the country put together."

"A bagnio?" I shook my head vigorously as I pinned my hair back up. "Father never let me near one of those places!"

The streets around Covent Garden teamed with bathhouses, bagnios and stews. All of which had come to mean *brothel*.

"Don't fret." Mr. Armistead hoisted his satchel and headed for the door, beckoning me to follow. "They're all empty at this hour. I bathe at least once a fortnight and it hasn't done me a bit of harm. I was on my way to the bathhouse when I met up with you. Now I can take you along with me."

His tone brooked no argument.

My heart was knocking against my skinny ribs by the time Mr. Armistead ducked into a crooked lane off Russell Street. I struggled to catch my breath as he stopped in front of a building that looked more prosperous than its neighbors.

"In you come!" cried the toothless old woman who answered his knock. "Quick, now, before you let a draft in!"

Mr. Armistead seemed familiar with the place. After a nod to the woman, he headed down a short hallway toward a wide door. When he opened it, a rush of warm, moist air washed over me. I tiptoed into the chamber beyond, staring about me as I'd done when Mother took me to St. Paul's. But this was no cathedral—more like a temple to some heathen goddess of pleasure!

Small colored tiles covered the floor and halfway up the walls. They also lined a sunken pool in the middle of the room. A row of smoked-glass windows across the top of the far wall let in just enough light for me to mark wisps of steam rising from the surface of the water. The sides of the room were partitioned into narrow stalls that could be made private by drawing a long red and gold curtain.

"Welcome to the world of the idle rich." Mr. Armistead dropped onto a low bench beside the door and pried off his shoes. "A man can dine here, bathe and enjoy the company of a hired nymph for six guineas."

Six guineas for one night? Father and I had lived on haypennies and farthings. To us, a shilling had been a windfall. Six guineas was wealth almost beyond my reckoning.

Once his feet were bare, Mr. Armistead rose and handed me the satchel he'd brought. "Take off your clothes and pop into the water. After you've bathed, you can change into these."

He strode toward the end of the room and entered one of the stalls, twitching the curtain closed behind him.

Undress and crawl into the water with a naked man? My breath came so fast, it threatened to run away on me. What else could I do, though? Go back onto the freezing, dangerous streets from which Mr. Armistead had just rescued me?

I ducked into a stall on the opposite end of the room. A long lounging couch took up most of the space inside. I did not have to tax my imagination to guess what *it* was used for. Battling my reluctance, I fumbled out of my mother's old gown and coarse linsey-woolsey petticoat. Then I kicked off my broken shoes and rolled down my black thread stockings riddled with holes.

Mr. Armistead was already in the water when I crept out of the retiring stall, a small linen towel barely covering my bosom and bottom. I had never felt so exposed, my legs like two long, pale sticks bared to his gaze.

But he did not seem inclined to ogle. "Pop in, lass. You won't get clean standing out there like a puppet show."

Warily I slid into the water, holding my towel in front of me until the last instant. The blessed warmth made me forget my fears. My chilled flesh soaked it up with greedy relish.

"Feels good, doesn't it?" Mr. Armistead waded toward me. "The water's cooler this time of day. By evening, when the paying customers arrive, it'll be hot as a pastry cook's oven. Now lean back and get your hair wet."

I flinched when he reached for me.

"It won't hurt, I promise." Taking hold of my hair, he forced my head back into the water.

Though panic seethed in my belly, I submitted.

Deftly, Mr. Armistead worked the water through my hair. Then he began to knead my scalp with the tips of his fingers. At first, I did not know what to make of it. But as I grew accustomed to the sensation, it felt very pleasant indeed. When he stopped, as abruptly as he'd begun, I had to bite my tongue to keep from begging him to continue.

"I could stay in here all day," said Mr. Armistead after he'd washed his own hair. "But there's work to be done. Soak a few more minutes if you like, then dry off and get dressed."

When he climbed out and wrapped a towel around his hips, I averted my eyes. But not before I glimpsed his lithe bare body. It reminded me of pictures I'd seen at Covent Garden playhouse. But those pictures had never provoked such stirrings in me.

Hearing the brass curtain rings slide over the rod, I forced myself to abandon the sultry embrace of the bath. The nip of cool air over my wet body helped quench the bewildering heat that wriggled in my loins. But I sensed it would not take much to rekindle it.

I donned the clothes Mr. Armistead had brought in his satchel, savoring the sensation of fine linen against my skin ... even as it prickled with unease. How had he come by such fashionable garments?

"Bought 'em for my first hair model," he replied when I'd worked up the nerve to ask. "I've had two before you—fine lasses, both. They've gone on to better opportunities and I reckon you will, too. A handsome, well-groomed lass going about Mayfair and Soho is bound to attract favorable notice."

Might my association with Mr. Armistead do more than save me from the cold, hunger and violence of the streets? I wondered as we made our way back to his lodgings. Could it be the first step toward the kind of life I'd only dreamed about?

While Mr. Armistead went off to work, I spent the rest of the day sitting by a small fire, combing my hair and eating some roasted chestnuts he'd bought for me.

That evening he took me to the chophouse for a hot, filling supper. It felt strange to be in those familiar surroundings without my father. Grief stung my heart like numb toes warmed too quickly. I tried to ease it by telling myself Father must be watching out for me from heaven – sending his friend to my aid. But as we walked back to Wych Street after our meal, nameless misgivings reached out of the fog with ghostly fingers to tug at the hem of my skirts.

Those fingers tightened around my throat when Mr. Armistead ushered me into his sitting room. "I've only got the one bed. I hope you won't mind sharing with a stranger."

Part of me longed to come straight out and ask if he meant to make use of me in that bed. But if he did, I would sound like a green goose for hoping otherwise. If he didn't, my question might offend him, which I could not afford.

"Not entirely strangers, are we?" I forced a weak smile.

A stew of dread churned in my belly as I followed him into the bedchamber. I had stolen a peek around it that afternoon. A large screen stood in the corner to the left of the door. Under the window, a narrow table held several ladies' wigs, all elegantly dressed and arranged on wooden stands. A large oval mirror hung on the wall next to it, above a washstand.

I caught a glimpse of myself in the glass. For the first time since a long ago day backstage at the playhouse, I beheld my own likeness. What I saw delighted and dismayed me.

A pair of large hazel eyes stared back at me, glittering with alarm. My nose was a bit long but perfectly straight, like my father's. My front teeth stuck out a bit, but did not spoil the shape of my mouth with its full lower lip. A cascade of warm chestnut hair framed my face, softening its thin hollows and lending a rosy cast to my pale skin.

No woman could be altogether sorry to find her countenance pleasing. But neither could I rejoice in it. To make my way through the world of men with such looks would be as dangerous as walking among a crowd of torchbearers, wearing a gown drenched in oil.

I let out a gasp when Mr. Armistead's face appeared in the mirror behind mine.

"See what I mean?" He lifted a lock of my hair and grazed it with his lips. "When I'm done with you, men will flock from all over London just to watch you brush that hair."

The prospect alarmed me. How many of those men would be content only to *watch?*

Mr. Armistead gave my hair a tug. Perhaps he meant to be playful, but it stung. "You'll find a chamber pot behind the screen and a bed gown."

My pulse fluttered with the urge to flee. But through the frosted window I glimpsed a few flakes of snow swirling through the fog. Nothing better waited for me out there.

Shivering from cold and nerves, I removed my new clothes with reverent care and slipped into the lace-trimmed bed gown. Arms wrapped around me, I crept out from behind the screen.

"What a time you've been," Mr. Armistead twitched down the covers beside him. "Hop in quick before you freeze."

His words shattered my hesitation. I scurried across the icy floor and slid beneath the bedclothes while he snuffed the candle and drew the curtains.

"G'night, Miss Elizabeth."

I steeled myself for his first overture—a squeeze or a grope. Instead he rolled away from me, with a drowsy chuckle. "Or should I say ... Mrs. Armistead?"

In a few moments he was snoring softly.

I lay awake, staring into the darkness, faint with relief yet strangely uneasy. I was grateful he had spared my virginity for tonight, at least. Still, I could not help wondering.

If not my body, what *did* Mr. Armistead want from me?

Over the next fortnight, my old life began to fade from my thoughts, like a disturbing but distant dream. My new life had the quality of a dream, too – one I did not want to wake from. I had all I cared to eat and more. Not just penny loaves and weak ale, but savory sausages, juicy oranges and sharp, hearty cheese. At night I slept in a snug bed, and by day I sat by a warm fire. I wore fine gowns trimmed with lace and bows. I was groomed as well any pampered gentlewoman.

For the first while, I tensed whenever Mr. Armistead approached suddenly or touched me. But he never did me any worse harm than being a bit rough-handed with his comb or smearing a disgusting plaster of oatmeal gruel in my hair. Every evening when I took off my clothes, I wondered if this might be the night he would demand payment for all he'd provided me. But he never took advantage of my presence in his bed, even after I was well washed and my figure began to fill out.

I enjoyed the mornings he spent with me, working on my hair, teaching me to walk, curtsy and speak like a lady. The warm praise he bestowed on me for my efforts made me feel all bubbly inside. As each day passed, I grew less wary of him, more grateful and eager to please him. I kept his rooms tidy and darned his stockings, blushing when he thanked me.

Before long, I found myself thinking of him as *Ned*. When I let it slip out one day in conversation, I feared he might be angry. But he accepted the familiarity without a murmur. For such a small thing, it fairly overwhelmed me with happiness.

Every evening I hovered near the window, rubbing away the fog my breath made on the cold glass. Watching people come and go in the street below, I waited with growing impatience for a glimpse of Ned's familiar figure. From the first time we'd met at the chophouse I had thought him a good-looking man. Now, as I compared him to all the others who passed beneath my gaze, I realized he was superior to them in every possible way. Men taller than him looked overgrown, shorter ones looked undersized. Darker men looked sinister, fairer ones washed-out.

When I heard Ned's swift, light tread upon the stairs, my spirits leapt to heights of happiness they had not known in years. Each day I woke wondering how soon he would pronounce me fit to begin earning my keep as his model. Then I could spend all day in his company.

"You look good enough to sit for Reynolds or Gainsborough," he announced one morning with a warm smile of approval that set my heart aglow, "which must be a sign you're ready to model for me. Go put on the blue-green polonaise I told you to save for special."

"You mean it?" I clapped my hands, giddy with excitement.

He grinned at my eagerness. "Not something I'd joke about, is it? Now off ye go. Mind ye wear the good petticoat and the clocked stockings."

What difference did my undergarments make? Surely he would not want folks distracted from admiring my well-dressed hair by a glimpse of clocking embroidery on the inside calf of my stockings. But I did not protest. If it meant I would be in Ned's company all day, I'd gladly have worn breeches!

"Will we have to walk far?" I asked when I emerged from the bedchamber to find Ned tapping his foot, his satchel all packed.

"Soho." He draped a cloak around my shoulders. "Great Marlborough Street."

It was a bit of a walk, but nothing compared to the miles I'd tramped in the past with my father. By the time we reached there, I was only a little winded. Though not far from Vinegar Alley in distance, Great Marlborough Street was a world away in character. Broad, straight and clean, it was lined on both sides with fine brick houses. There was not a print-seller's shop in sight and only a single public house.

Ned pointed to one of the houses on the north side of the street. "Lord Onslow lives there and Lord Charles Cavendish two down, with Lady Middleton beside that."

We stopped in front of a house every bit as grand as the others—three stories high and four windows wide. The brown brick front had a moulding line that stuck out a little from the second floor and several sunken panels in a row below the roof. I could scarcely believe I would be allowed inside such a place.

"Quite some'ut, isn't it?" Ned looked me over with the critical eye of a man who beautified women for a living. "You'll be fine. Just mind your manners and do as I tell you."

I followed him up a flight of stone steps to the paneled door. A man with a crooked nose and fists the size of smoked hams answered Ned's knock.

"'Morning, Enoch." Ned bowed. "Would you let Mrs. Goadby know I'm here? Tell her I've brought my new hair model."

The man beckoned us into an entry hall hung with wine-red flocked wallpaper. Then he lumbered up a wide staircase of dark polished wood.

While Ned and I waited, I stared about inhaling the aromas of perfume, well-cooked food and expensive wines. A finely woven carpet covered the floor, its vibrant pattern undimmed by dirt. On the wall opposite the stairs, a large oval mirror with an elaborate gilt frame hung above a slender table.

A pair of pictures on either side of the looking glass caught my eye. One showed a bevy of plump nymphs sporting with handsome shepherds. In the other, three naked women lay around the edge of a bathing pool, like the one Ned had taken me to.

The flesh on the back of my neck prickled.

"Fancy living in this kind of luxury," said Ned.

"Is this …?" I asked in a hesitant, horrified whisper. "Is this

... a brothel?"

I felt foolish, yet deeply relieved, when he shook his head. "A place like this is no common brothel, lass. This here is a *house of pleasure.*"

# Chapter Three

"House of pleasure?" I could scarcely summon breath to repeat Ned's words. "Dear God, I cannot stay here!"

"Why not, you little goose?" Ned stood between me and the door. Though he was not much bigger than me, I knew his wiry strength. If he refused to let me pass, I would have the fight of my life to get by him. "This is where I work to earn the brass that keeps a roof over your head and food in your belly."

"I thought you dressed the hair of ... ladies."

"So I do—ladies of pleasure." His tone hardened. "Some a good deal better bred than you!"

I flinched as if he'd struck me. This was the first cross word he'd ever spoken to me. He sounded like a different man altogether. How could I have been such a fool to give him my trust and my heart when I knew so little of him?

Before I could protest, a woman's voice floated down from behind me. "Mr. Armistead, a pleasure as always. I understand you have hired a model."

"So I have, ma'am." Ned executed a gallant bow as I spun about to catch my first glimpse of a known bawd-mistress.

What I saw was not anything I'd expected. A slender woman of middle height, Mrs. Goadby wore an olive green gown, its modest neckline draped with a crisp white fichu. Her hair was neatly dressed and she wore no jewelry. If we'd met elsewhere, I might have fancied her a housekeeper for some noble family, the widow of a prosperous merchant ... perhaps even a bishop's wife.

Ned's hand pressed into the small of my back, prodding me forward. "May I present Miss Elizabeth? My dear, this is Mrs. Goadby, one of my most valued customers."

I rearranged my slack gape into a meek smile and curtsied.

If Mrs. Goadby guessed what I was thinking, she gave no sign but descended the rest of the stairs with brisk grace until she stood before us. "A pleasure, my dear."

She reached up to cradle my chin with the tips of her fingers. Then she tilted my head this way and that, as if it were a fragile but empty casket that held neither thought nor feeling. I gave her little reason to suppose otherwise, moving as she urged me with dumbstruck obedience.

Mrs. Goadby seemed to approve my docility. "I commend you, Mr. Armistead, on your superb eye for beauty and your gift for refining it. Do come in and show me the hair."

She turned and headed down the wide corridor.

"Go on." Ned pushed me forward. "And don't be making a fool of me. You've a hell of a lot less to fear here than roaming the streets around Covent Garden."

I'd grown so used to obeying Ned's every wish that I followed Mrs. Goadby, even though reason urged me to take flight. Through a set of open double doors, I glimpsed an elegant front parlor that would have held both Ned's rooms. I could hear girlish laughter from the floor above. It seemed greatly out of place in an establishment like this. Then again, *everything* here was at odds with what I'd expected.

That did not soothe my mounting bewilderment and alarm.

Ned and I followed Mrs. Goadby past a dining room that looked grand enough for a large, wealthy family, and a back parlor as richly appointed as the front one, then through a door to the rear of the house. In a workroom on one side of the hallway, two seamstresses were busy measuring and cutting a length of shiny blue cloth.

Mrs. Goadby entered a room across the hall from them. It

was smaller than the sewing room, but warm and fragrant with the scents I'd first smelled in Ned's lodgings. It held three low-backed chairs, a tall commode with a large copper basin set in the top and a small table mounted on wheels.

Ned motioned me toward the chair in the middle of the room. "Sit down and take off your cap so Mrs. Goadby can see your hair."

I did as he bid, painfully self-conscious under the older woman's gaze.

"This has been on my mind for awhile." Ned pulled a pin from my hair, letting a lock of it fall over my shoulder. "Stiff, powdered styles are fine for formal occasions, but it's not something a man wants to run his hands through, is it?"

As if to demonstrate, he lifted my fallen curl and twisted it around his finger. "And if a lady ... exerts herself in the bedchamber, she looks a wreck by morning."

From Ned's offhand tone, he might have been talking about the weather or the price of bread. "This style can look very elegant until the pins are removed." One by one, he pulled them out, letting my hair tumble free. "Then it falls into a simple mode that's none the worse for a bit of mussing."

My cheeks glowed hot as coals in a banked fire. For a man who'd shared a chaste bed with me for so many nights, Ned talked very glib about *mussing hair* and *exertions of the bedchamber.*

"A novel idea." Mrs. Goadby gave an admiring nod as she circled around me. "These days novelty often dictates fashion. And we cater to gentlemen of fashion. I shall have Craven sent down to you at once."

Ned did not move as Mrs. Goadby marched from the room. But when her footsteps had faded down the hall, he seized me and swung me out of my chair. "This is the chance I've been waiting for, and I couldn't have done it without you, my love!"

His *love?* I melted into Ned's arms as I'd often pictured

myself doing for the past several days.

But when he let me go, I recovered a few of my wits. "Why did you not tell me you were bringing me to ... a place like this?"

"I was afraid you'd refuse to come." Ned opened his satchel and began pulling out combs, shears and curling rings, which he set on top of the wheeled table. "If I told you we were going to a pleasure house, I knew you'd picture one of those cesspits around Covent Garden. I wanted you to see that this is a whole different class of establishment."

"It's more elegant than the playhouses," I admitted. They were my only yardsticks for comparison.

"Mrs. Goadby is a canny business woman." Ned grinned. "She's got plenty of imitators now, but she was the first to open the kind of house they have in Paris for the French grandees. A doctor checks the girls to make certain they're clean and healthy. You'll not find *that* in Covent Garden."

"Is all your work in ... pleasure houses?"

Before Ned could answer, a young woman swept into the room. She looked a few years older than me, with rich red hair, a long aristocratic nose and an ample bosom. Even in my blue-green polonaise, I felt dowdy next to this stylish creature with her silver buckled shoes and gathered overskirts. I stared at her, dumbstruck with admiration.

"Delighted to see you again Mrs. Craven!" Ned bowed to her. "I trust you enjoyed your visit to Tunbridge Wells. You must be looking forward to the new Season."

"Dear Mr. Armistead, you are always such agreeable company in addition to the splendid work you do." She raised her hand and traced the line of his jaw with one long-nailed finger. "Tunbridge is a pretty place, though rather dull. I hear you mean to dress my hair in a new style that will set the fashion."

A fierce stab of envy caught me in the throat.

Ned grinned like a prize fool. "I believe my new style will set off your fiery tresses to perfection. Come Elizabeth. Let

Mrs. Craven see what I propose."

"But that is no style at all!" the haughty minx carped. "What will Lord Vane or Captain Medleycott think if I entertain them in such a careless state?"

"Not *careless*, ma'am." Ned's tone sharpened a trifle. "*Artless*. In my experience, gentlemen admire that vastly. Of course it will look ever so much better on you. Fancy each lock of hair held by a jeweled clasp to match your gown. I reckon Lord Vane might make you a present of half a dozen."

The prospect of costly presents put Mrs. Craven in a more receptive humor. "As you say, it will look far better with my brilliant hair than with that muddy color of your model."

Muddy? I wished I had a handful of Covent Garden gutter muck to grind into the harlot's sour face. Was she too vain to see that Ned only flattered her to keep his bread buttered? He had often praised the rich, warm hue of my hair.

He must have guessed my feelings, for he cupped his hands over my shoulders and gave a gentle squeeze. "I could use your help, my dear. On a peg behind the door you'll find a linen smock. Fetch it to cover Mrs. Craven's gown."

As I rose from the chair to assist Ned, Mrs. Craven sank onto it with a bewitching rustle of silk. "Work your magic, Mr. Armistead, and be quick about it. If it does not rain, I want to go for a carriage ride in Hyde Park this afternoon."

"You're a strict mistress, Mrs. Craven." His tone gave the insult an air of flattery. "It's fortunate your beauty and wit are such that your lovers take pleasure in being abused by you."

As he worked, Ned kept me busy—fetching and disposing of water, sweeping up cut hair from the floor, holding combs when his hands were full. He scarcely seemed to notice my presence, except to order me around. All his charm was lavished upon his comely customer, who flirted back in the most shameless manner.

"I'm nearly finished here." Ned glanced up at me as he laid down his scissors. "Can you go fetch Mrs. Paget?"

I was about to ask where I would find her when Mrs. Craven snapped, "Third floor. Second door on the right."

"Take the back stairs," Ned called after me.

Spotting a flight of stairs beside the sewing room, I dashed up them. When I got to the top I found the second door on the right and tapped upon it lightly. I heard a woman's voice from inside. Was she calling me to come in? I eased the door open and tiptoed into an elegant little sitting room.

Again I heard the woman's voice. It issued from an adjoining room, through a door that stood slightly ajar. "Wasn't I clever to think of this place? I've always wanted to see the inside of one. I only wish they had brothels where women could come to enjoy the company of handsome young men."

Through the narrow opening to the next room I spotted a half-dressed man and a woman standing in front of a luxurious canopied bed with golden hangings. They kissed and fondled as they fumbled the rest of one another's clothes off.

"Why would you need one of those?" asked the man as he pulled the woman's shift over her head. "You can have *me* at your service wherever and whenever you like."

I knew I had come to the wrong place and must get out at once. But shock and curiosity froze my feet to the floor. My loins were not frozen, though. A hot yearning stirred in them as it had when I spied on Ned at the bathhouse.

The man's lithe build and golden brown hair reminded me of Ned, a little. The woman looked like one of the nymphs in the paintings downstairs, with comely features and full, pink-tipped breasts.

"Wherever I like?" She gave a throaty chuckle as the man kneaded the plump lobes of her bottom and kissed her creamy white shoulders. "That is a most intriguing notion!"

The playful way this couple spoke and touched one another was nothing like what I'd glimpsed in the alley that horrible night, which now seemed so long ago. I could not help imagining myself in the woman's place, with Ned handling my body that way. My mouth watered and my cheeks burned.

"Beneath a banquet table perhaps," the man panted as he lowered his breeches, revealing his stiff upright shaft, "While the clatter of silver and glassware drowns out our mischief?"

"How wicked!" The woman squealed as her lover tipped her back onto the bed. She spread her legs. "I adore wicked men! They are far more diverting than good ones. Make haste, my dear. I have an appointment with Mr. Gainsborough at four."

The man needed little urging, scrambling eagerly onto the bed between the lady's legs and sliding into her. I thought she might cry out in pain, but instead she heaved a quivering sigh of pleasure.

"Perhaps I can bring some color to your cheeks and a sparkle to your eye for that painting." Leaning on his elbows, the man brought his open mouth down upon hers for a deep, hungry kiss. His hips began a slow thrust that soon gathered urgency.

The lady moaned and whimpered beneath him … but not in pain.

My breath was now coming so fast it made me dizzy. A flash of reason told me the lovers would not hear me now unless I slammed the door. Despite my fear of discovery, it took every ounce of will I could muster to wrest my gaze away from their twined bodies and steal out of the room.

I could not get what I had seen out of my mind. My vague fondness for Ned suddenly took on a very clear shape. That night when he undressed for bed behind the screen, I pictured him removing each piece of clothing until he was as naked as the man at Mrs. Goadby's. When he crawled into bed beside me, instead of fearing his attentions, I began to crave them.

The next few weeks passed in a blithe haze of happiness, blighted by spells of frustration, jealousy and suspicion. The constant flirting between Ned and his customers vexed me worse and worse. I dreaded Saturday evenings when he would go off without me, only to return home hours later stinking of cheap brandy and cheaper perfume.

I knew he must be visiting one of *those* women, tousling the hair he had so carefully arranged. It was a wonder my eyes did not turn as green as emeralds with the possessive way I watched him, trying to guess which one was my rival.

"Must you go out again, tonight?" I asked, one mild Saturday evening in March. "Could we not spend the evening together? Go across the river to Vauxhall? I've never been."

"Not tonight." Ned's tone warned me not to argue. Perhaps he sensed the feelings I fought to contain, for his voice softened and he offered me a crumb of hope. "I'll take you later, when all the flowers are in bloom."

I knew I should hold my tongue, but I could not. "Can I come with you, then?"

Ned paused, his hand upon the latch. "I just took you out to supper. Is that not enough?"

I could not bring myself to tell him there were too few hours in a day to allow me as much of his company as I desired. "I wouldn't be any bother. I'd sit off in a corner and be as quiet as a mouse."

"No."

"Why not? Are you going someplace dangerous?" He did not seem the type of man to seek out dodgy company. "Or someplace you're ashamed to take me."

"It's *no* business of yours!" he snapped. "Can I have no peace or privacy in my own house?"

The rage in his eyes cut me to the heart.

"Dearest Ned!" I hurled myself at him, flinging my arms around his neck. "I'm sorry to plague you. Please forgive me!"

I knew nothing about kissing, apart from an affectionate peck between family members. But I had learned a little from spying on the lovers at Mrs. Goadby's. Tilting my head so as not to bump Ned's nose, I grazed my lips over his in a provocative invitation. Then I waited for him to respond.

He raised his arms, which had fallen slack when I first

reached for him. I wanted him to slip one around me and press me closer. Would he pull my cap off with the other and plunge his fingers into the hair he had so carefully styled that morning? Or would it stray lower to fondle my bottom?

"You don't need to do this." Ned reached behind his neck and pried my arms loose. "I should have made it clear from the beginning. Your body isn't part of our bargain."

"Don't you want me? You praise my looks. You say you enjoy my company. I don't understand."

"You're a fair lass." Ned sounded sincere but he backed away from me as he spoke. "And a good-hearted one."

What was the matter, then? "We're pretending to be married. Could we not take our pretending a little farther?"

He shook his head and put more distance between us. Was he afraid I would try to force myself on him? Or was he fighting a part of himself that wanted me as much as I wanted him? "You don't know what your asking, lass."

"Of course I don't." It vexed me to admit it. "Is that why you don't want me—because I'm an ignorant, green virgin, not one of your precious *ladies of pleasure?*"

He began to laugh, which only infuriated me more.

"That's it, isn't it?" I cried. "I see the way you flirt with those wicked creatures. It's disgusting!"

Ned's laughter stopped so abruptly and his look grew so severe, it made *me* back away from him. "You *are* ignorant to sit in judgment on those women and call them wicked! They only do what they must to get by in the world. They harm nobody. That's more than I can say for some folk in this city who make a great show of being virtuous and respectable."

Reason told me he was right. How dare I question any other woman's morals when I longed to give myself to a man who was not my husband? But my injured pride and frustrated desire refused to heed reason. "How can you take *their* part against me?"

"I'm only defending them against a slur they don't deserve,

from someone who should know better. If I hadn't taken you in, you'd be a seasoned whore by now. A good many rungs down the ladder from the ladies at Mrs. Goadby's house, too."

The rough grit of his temper only whetted the edge of mine. "Do you wish I had? Then perhaps you might show me the interest of a proper man instead of pushing me away!"

"You don't know what you're talking about!" Ned grabbed his satchel and stormed off, slamming the door behind him.

As the sound of his footsteps receded down the stairs, remorse overwhelmed me. What an ungrateful wretch was I, to harass and berate the man who had done so much for me? The man I had come to ... love.

I could not wait there, eaten up with shame, for him to stagger home hours from now, too deep in his cups to listen and understand. I must go after him at once and beg his pardon before time and drink hardened his resentment!

It was impossible, though. This part of town was too dangerous for a woman to wander alone.

But what if no one knew I was a woman? I'd often heard my father speak of 'breeches' parts in plays where the heroine dressed as a boy. Such comedies were vastly popular, for they allowed actresses to show their legs in public.

Before I had time to think better of the idea, I tore off my gown and pulled on a pair of Ned's breeches, then a shirt and coat. Jamming a tricorne hat onto my head, I dashed out of the house and up Wych Street, the way I'd so often spied him go. I ran past print-sellers and pawnshops. Rounding the corner onto Newcastle Street, I peered into the distance and glimpsed Ned's familiar figure. I hurried after him, as fast as my feet would carry me. By the time the street forked, I had gained enough ground to mark which way he went.

I trailed him through a maze of lanes and courts around Lincoln's Inn. I had almost caught up with him when he slipped into an alley off Chancery Lane and entered an inn called *The White Hart*.

Was it a gambling den? Or a brothel? Though its windows were shuttered, I could hear muted sounds of music and laughter from inside. I walked to the end of the alley, wrestling with what to do next. Perhaps I should go home rather than risk making Ned angrier. But how could I turn away when I was only moments from discovering my rival for Ned's attention. The unbearable itch of curiosity threatened to overpower my remorse.

Then a massive hand landed on my shoulder and spun me about. "What are ye skulkin' about for?"

"I ... wasn't–"

A man even bigger than Mrs. Goadby's Enoch pushed me up against the building. "Ye was."

I nearly wet Ned's breeches.

"Ye one of them moral reformers?" He spat on the cobbles.

"N-never heard of them, I swear! But I've heard of *The White Hart* from my friend Armistead."

"Armistead, eh?" The ruffian's scowl softened a little. "What is it ye want at *The Hart*?"

"I have ... urgent news for Mr. Armistead."

The man's eyes narrowed. "What sort of news?"

What indeed? Lying was a sticky business, but I was in too deep to back out now. "News he wouldn't want spread about. I have no time to waste. Will you let me in or not?"

The man thought for a moment then wrapped his great hammy fist around my upper arm. "I'll do better than that. I'll take ye straight to him with yer *news*."

My bowels quaked with panic as he hauled me toward the inn. What would my reckless curiosity cost me?

My captor wrenched the door open and thrust me inside. At first I could make out nothing but shadows in the dimly lit entry. I heard the lilt of a fiddle and pipe, the rhythmic shuffle of dancing feet, high-pitched chatter and giddy laughter. The pungent scents of wine and perfume hung so thick in the air they made me gag.

"This way." My hulking escort pushed me up some steps.

Between the darkness and my trembling legs, I stumbled and might have fallen if he had not held my arm in his crushing grip. I shuddered to think of that brawny hand around my throat. It could throttle the life out of me in minutes or snap my neck like a twig. My only hope now was that Ned would protect me from harm. He would, wouldn't he?

As my eyes adjusted to the dimness, I could tell *The White Hart* was indeed a brothel – though nothing like Mrs. Goadby's elegant premises. In a large gathering hall, couples sat drinking at trestle tables ranged along the walls, while others danced in the middle of the floor. I noticed a few men in the crowd, but mostly women – the ugliest whores I'd ever seen.

A short, stout one rubbed up against me, cooing, "Who's this handsome fellow? He sets my frail heart aflutter!"

I shrank from the brazen creature. Even if I'd been a man, I could not imagine wanting anything to do with her. It would take more than a thick layer of white ceruse face paint and brightly rouged cheeks to make such coarse features attractive.

"Leave the lad be, Mistress Sweetlips," growled my captor. "He's come to see Lady Lavender."

While I puzzled what he meant, the unlikely-named woman pouted. "That is vexing. Helping herself to all the new lovelies before they even reach the dance floor. Another evening, perhaps, sir?"

A flurry of movement caught my eye from a chamber off the main one. Any words I might have spoken to Mistress Sweetlips froze in my throat. In the shadows of the other room, I glimpsed naked bodies rearing and writhing to a hushed chorus of grunts and moans. A wave of disgust made my gorge rise even as a restless hunger stirred in me.

"Time for that later." The man's grip eased a bit. Through the fabric of Ned's coat, I felt the pad of his thick thumb rub against my arm.

The sensation made my flesh crawl. Could he tell I was a

woman? Did he mean to make use of me in the room next door? I staggered the last few steps toward an open doorway.

The room beyond was smaller than the one we had just passed, or perhaps it only appeared so because it was well lit by several candles. It reminded me of the grooming room at Mrs. Goadby's, with a large looking glass on one wall behind a narrow table laden with combs, ribbons and pots of face paint.

I took all this in with a terrified glance before my gaze settled on a pair of fondling lovers. The man sat in a chair before the grooming table while a woman in a pale purple gown stood behind him. She had leaned far forward, her hand fluttering on the lap of his breeches while he rained kisses down her bare neck.

Jealousy and thwarted yearning savaged my heart.

"Ned?" I retched out his name.

Startled, the couple looked up.

I reeled back. The man in the chair was not Ned.

"Elizabeth?" That was Ned's voice. But it was coming from the woman in the purple dress.

My mouth gaped open as I recognized Ned's familiar features on her comely face. For the first time, a spark of desire heated Ned's gaze as he looked upon me in the guise of a man.

# Chapter Four

*I*T FELT AS IF I had landed in the middle of a nightmare to hear Ned's familiar voice coming from the painted lips of a harlot. "Damn it, lass, what are you doing here? What have you done?"

"What have *I* done?" Outrage trampled my bewilderment and fear. I jerked free of my captor's grip, which had gone slack. "For God sake, Ned, what have *you* done?"

I did not want or need an answer. Everything I'd seen since entering *The White Hart* spoke for itself. This was a *molly house*. I'd heard lewd jests about such places, but only dimly guessed what they were. Now the veil of my ignorance was ripped away. Seeing Ned for what he truly was forced me to see my life with him for what it was. Everything made sense now—every word, every touch, every lie.

"You used me, you filthy sod!" I ripped his hat off my head and thrashed him with it. Then I spun about and bolted.

The big man who'd brought me here made a grab to restrain me. But I sank my teeth into his hand, welcoming any outlet for the fury I could not contain. He cried out and fell back, freeing me to run. I barrelled off, lashing out at anyone in my path—tramping hard on toes, jamming my elbows into bellies, my fists into noses and throats. Every blow was meant for Ned Armistead.

I fought my way to the stairs, leaped down them and burst through the door. A man walking toward *The White Hart* recoiled in fright as I ran past him. I tore out of the alley, across Chancery Lane and down another street, not thinking where my feet were taking me, as long as it was away from that place.

I ran until I feared my lungs would burst. Then I collapsed against the side of a butcher shop, gasping in the stench of offal and rotten fish from Clare Market. I hoped it would scour away the cloying sweetness of the *molly house.*

My pulse pounded so loud in my ears, I did not hear the rush of approaching footsteps until they were almost upon me. I jerked my head up to see *Lady Lavender* rushing toward me with skirts lifted and elegant wig askew.

As I turned to flee, Ned panted, "Please, Elizabeth, you must hear me out! You owe me that, at least."

I wanted to scream that I owed him nothing, but I knew it was not true. Whatever else he'd done, Ned had saved me from the streets and brought back to life something in me that had died with my mother and Patrick. If I did not discharge that debt, I feared he would always have a hold over me.

"Very well." I could not bring myself to look him in the face. "But I will not go back to that place."

"Home, then?"

The house on Wych Street was not my home, no matter how hard I'd tried to pretend it was. Still I gave a grudging nod.

After catching our breath, Ned and I set off in silence through the darkened streets. We did not exchange a word until we were within sight of the house.

"Have you got keys?"

Ned held up his satchel. "I grabbed this before I came after you."

I had not even noticed him carrying it. "You keep your clothes in there, don't you? Your proper clothes?"

Ned did not answer but groped in his satchel for the keys and opened the door.

"And when you go out on Saturdays," I persisted, "you carry your ... other clothes in it?"

What a blind fool he must have thought me for not figuring it all out sooner.

"Quiet, for God sake!" he pleaded in a hoarse whisper. "If the landlady catches us like this, I'm done for."

"Mrs. Payne is so short-sighted, if she did see us, she'd likely think you were me and I was you."

In spite of that, I scarcely dared breathe until we were in Ned's sitting room, with the door bolted behind us. Why it felt so important to keep his sordid secret, I could not explain.

While I lit the candles, he collapsed onto the sofa like a lady swooning. "Promise me you won't tell anyone. My friends and I could be hanged. Or pilloried, which is almost as bad."

"Go change clothes and wash that damned paint off your face! I want to talk to Ned Armistead, not *Lady Lavender*." When I looked at her, I did not see the man I loved, but a hated rival who'd stolen Ned from me in a way no other woman could.

He pulled off his wig. "Like it or not, lass, *this* is who I am. When I'm kitted out in breeches, pretending to flirt with all my pretty customers, that's when I feel like I'm in disguise."

Dragging himself to his feet, he stumbled toward the bedroom.

For a moment I stood there wondering if I should change clothes, too. I didn't want to. Dressed like a man, I felt stronger and more assured, in spite of my distress. I would need all the strength I could muster to get me through this night.

A while later Ned emerged from the bedroom in his shirt and breeches, wiping the paint from his face with a damp cloth. He looked so sad and weary and frightened, part of me longed to comfort him.

Then I remembered all the times he had spurned my innocent overtures. "Your other models, did they discover your secret?"

"One never guessed." Ned sank onto the sofa again. "The other knew from the beginning but didn't care."

"And what sort of *better opportunities* did they go on to?"

Though I could well imagine, I wanted to hear the truth from his mouth for once.

"Polly's at Mrs. Hayes's pleasure house. Kitty was with Mother Mitchell, but she's now in the keeping of an alderman."

"A nice side business you have, procuring virgins for pleasure houses."

Ned shrank before my withering glare. "It's not something I set out to do. I had no choice. I needed more money than I could earn from my work."

"No doubt. Those pretty gowns of yours must be expensive."

He shook his head. "They're all second hand from my customers. Mrs. Goadby knows what I am and it suits her fine. Better to have someone like me grooming her girls than a fellow who might run off with one or give her the pox."

"To think how jealous I was of those girls flirting with you." I burst into frenzied laughter, which I only managed to stop when it threatened to collapse in sobs.

"Look, I'm sorry if I hurt you. I never meant for that to happen. You may not believe it, but I do care about you. Just not the way you need me to."

His words struck me a stinging blow to a wounded place. I could not resist stinging back. "No! You cared about me like a butcher cares about his prize beef carcass—a well-dressed slab of meat to fetch you a good price in the flesh market!"

Ned flinched. "It wasn't meant to be that way. I didn't force the other two and I wouldn't have forced you if you couldn't stomach it. I thought once you got used to the idea and saw what a fine life you could have, you'd jump at the chance."

"You truly believe they lead a fine life?" I demanded. "Or is that how you salve your conscience?"

"It *is* a fine life!" I could not doubt Ned's fierce sincerity. "Better than one woman in a thousand will ever know. Fine clothes, grand house, good food. Men fawning over you, paying top price for your favors, making love to you. My idea of heaven, that is!"

Put that way, it did sound dangerously appealing, but I could not retreat from my attack. "Why did you need the money if not for fine gowns? Lace? Jewels? Gifts for your ganymedes?"

Ned met my indignant glare. "I needed it to pay blackmail."

For the first time, I recognized the haunted, hunted air about him.

"When I was new in city," he said, "before I found the mollies club at *The White Hart*, I used to cruise the Royal Exchange looking for a partner. I met a man there. He was nice looking and seemed friendly. He led me on, tricked me to write him some … love letters then threatened to have me prosecuted. I had to get the money somehow. Do you know what they'd have done to me if I'd been tried and found guilty?"

I swallowed a choking lump in my throat as I nodded. Twice during my begging years, a cart had rattled past Father and me, bearing prisoners from the pillory back to Newgate Prison. A crowd of fishwives had run behind it, hurling rotten vegetables, fish guts and horse dung. Even on the pungent streets of the city, the sickening stench had made me ill. The creatures in those carts had scarcely looked human after hours of being pelted with filth.

When I asked Father what crime the prisoners had committed to deserve such cruel treatment, he'd shaken his head in pity. "Never you mind, Lizzie. Whatever it was, the poor buggers didn't deserve *that.*"

Outraged and humiliated as I was, I could not bear to think of Ned so brutally abused.

"Why didn't you tell me all this before?" *Before I made a fool of myself by falling in love with you.*

"You must be joking." Ned's lips twisted as if he were trying to smile while sucking on a lemon. "Tell you I was a molly who meant to sell you to a bawd mistress? You'd have run screaming straight to the magistrate."

I recoiled from his challenging stare. We both knew he was right. Much as I wanted to cast him as the villain of this sordid little tragedy, I could not. In his own way, Ned was even more a victim than I—intimidated by threats, caught in a web of secrets and lies.

"While I'm confessing," he continued, "you might as well know my models served another purpose besides making me money. You diverted suspicion."

A soft chuckle gave way to even softer weeping. I might have joined him, but I was afraid if I let my tears fall they would not stop until I drowned in them.

At last Ned composed himself and glanced up at me, a desperate plea in his eyes. "What are you going to do?"

I hoisted my shoulders. "Not run screaming to the magistrate. Apart from that, I don't know. What are *you* going to do? The neighbors will get suspicious if you bring home a fourth *wife*. Three was probably pushing your luck."

"There was never meant to be a fourth. I can't keep living like this—wondering if tomorrow's the day that leech turns me in. A friend of mine went abroad. He wrote to say it's better there. I planned to follow him."

"With the money you got for me?"

"Aye. Now, I'll have to get out of town while I can. Lay low somewhere until I can raise the brass for my passage." He sounded as dispirited as I felt.

When Ned left town, I would lose everything—job, place to live, protection. My earlier blaze of fury had burned itself out to cold, gray ashes. But it had come and gone too fast to consume the tenderness for Ned that had been growing within me for weeks. As I looked at him now, knowing he never could care for me, I still could not stifle the urge to spare him.

"I'll do it."

Ned stirred from his troubled thoughts. "Do what?"

"Go on the town. It isn't *my* idea of heaven, but if I'm likely to end up there anyway, I'd just as soon it be on my own terms. In the morning you can take me to Mrs. Goadby and collect your procuring fee. That was where you meant to sell me wasn't it?"

He looked as if I'd struck him. "She's eager to get you. Has some'ut special planned for the start of the Season, I hear. But I couldn't take the brass. Not now."

"Why not? It's what you planned. The only difference is now I know what's what."

Ned had done a great deal for me and my feelings for him had grown out of gratitude. If that obligation was discharged, perhaps I could free myself from the painful snare of love.

"It's more than I deserve." Ned spoke in a hoarse whisper, his eyes fixed on my shoes. "My life would be a hell of a lot easier if I could be the kind of man you want. But that's not who I am, love. I hope some day you won't hate me for all this."

I shook my head. "My life would be a hell of a lot easier if I *could* hate you."

Mrs. Goadby fairly glowed with satisfaction when Ned presented me to her the next morning. "Mr. Armistead tells me you wish to be considered for a place here."

Reminding myself that all my other options were much worse, I bobbed a solemn nod.

"I have a reputation for operating the most exclusive house of its kind in the country." Mrs. Goadby announced with obvious pride. "I maintain the most select circle of patrons, some of the first gentlemen of the kingdom among them."

"This young lady will be a great asset to you, ma'am." Ned looked ill at ease.

Mrs. Goadby fixed me with her shrewd gaze. "Not very lively at the moment, but that is to be expected, I suppose."

I could not bring myself to impress her with a false show of spirits.

"She'll be fine," Ned insisted, "once she settles in and gets used to the place." I wondered whether he was trying to convince Mrs. Goadby or himself. "She's amiable, obliging and eager to improve herself."

"Commendable qualities," said Mrs. Goadby. "I provide my young ladies with every opportunity to cultivate their charms." She paused for a moment then announced, "Yes. I believe she will do very well."

She took me by the arm. "Let me show you around the house. First thing tomorrow we will have you measured for some new gowns. The one you're wearing is pretty enough, but rather out of style. Here, you will wear nothing but the finest and most fashionable garments."

As she talked, she drew me into the spacious parlor. "Tell me, what name do you wish to be known by?"

I thought for a moment. Ned had explained how most of his clients took a false name when they entered the trade. They might not want to risk bringing disgrace on respectable families. Or they might not wish to be easily traced. Many took the name of their first protector.

"You may call me Mrs. Armistead." Ned had not been my lover, but he *was* responsible for launching me in this career.

I had another reason for wanting to use his name, as well. From now on, whenever I heard it, I would be reminded to keep all future dealings with men entirely in the realm of business.

My first week at Mrs. Goadby's passed in a dizzying blur of preparations for my launch on the town. I endured hours of wardrobe fittings, until I felt like a pincushion from having so many stuck into me. It was for a good cause, I decided, when I saw myself in a full-length mirror wearing the first of the finished gowns.

A peach-colored silk trimmed with brown ruching, it had a flirtatious little flounce at the hem, and a froth of white lace at the elbows. It made even the best of my old gowns look shabby. I wore it that afternoon when Mrs. Goadby took me for my first carriage drive in Hyde Park. Would any of the gentlemen who stared at me believe that, a few months ago, I had been begging from them outside Covent Garden theatre?

Their attention kindled a bewildering mixture of feelings within me. Most familiar was the qualm of fear that had been a constant companion since my father's death. Now, a hum of satisfaction joined it. Ned Armistead might not have wanted me, but there were plenty of other men who did. Desire smoldered in their gazes and their smiles.

Uncertain how I should respond, I smiled back when a particular gentleman caught my eye. Then I quickly lowered my gaze for fear of appearing too forward. But I could not resist stealing another brief glance to see if he was still watching me.

"You are a natural coquette, my dear." Mrs. Goadby patted my hand with motherly approval. "I reckon you will be vastly popular in company."

"Please, ma'am, how soon until ... I begin?"

"Not long. I have sent out invitations for a 'Banquet of Beauty' to be held next week."

Perhaps she sensed my confused reaction to her words, for she fixed me with a shrewd gaze that seemed to understand me better than I did myself. "You are anxious, naturally, wondering how it will be your first time. Every woman is, I daresay, whether she is a gently reared lady who comes innocent to her bridal bed or a less fortunate girl who must make her own way in the world."

I gave a mute nod, hungry for reassurance.

"A clever girl like you must see it is in *my* best interest to make your first experiences as pleasant as possible."

I'd been too bewildered by recent events to think of that, but it made sense.

"The gentlemen I have invited next week are all well known to me. Not only do they have ample fortunes, they are also young, agreeable looking and tender in their handling of a maiden. I expect to receive several handsome offers for the honor of your first favors." Mrs. Goadby fixed me with a doting smile. "My choice will not be determined by price alone."

"Thank you, ma'am." I clung to her reassurance.

As we drove back to Great Marlborough Street, another carriage passed us, carrying three well-dressed ladies of Mrs. Goadby's age. They glanced toward us, perhaps to check whether we might be acquaintances of theirs. Then one whispered to the others and all three turned their heads.

"Pay them no mind." Mrs. Goadby gave a sharp little laugh. "The poor creatures dare not take notice of us for fear of tainting their precious reputations. I pity them. Most are bought and sold with no more sentiment than the meanest strumpet in Covent Garden, who at least has the benefit of variety."

Her mouth compressed into a tight little purse. "My fortune is my own, to dispose of as I please. Everything they have is given and taken at the whim of a husband."

She made married women sound little better than slaves. "B-but if there is love ..."

A frost seemed to settle over Mrs. Goadby's features. "Heed me well, Armistead. Women like us are not bound by the rules that govern most of our sex. But we do have a few of our own, for our protection."

I leaned forward, intent to learn from the experience of one who had survived and made her fortune in the world I was about to enter.

"The foremost of them is this." Mrs. Goadby's flinty gaze dared me to doubt her. *"Never* fall in love."

# Chapter Five

MRS. GOADBY'S WARNING ECHOED IN my mind that evening as I played cards in her sitting room with the two other *novices*. Harriet, a pert brunette from the Midlands, had offered to teach Rose and me a game called three-card *loo*.

"What suit is trumps again?" asked Rose, a fair Kentish girl whose dimpled cheeks made her look younger than sixteen.

"Hearts." Harriet grinned. "I suppose in a place like this hearts should always be trumps."

"Diamonds, more like," I muttered under my breath, remembering my conversation with Mrs. Goadby.

"I wish we had a few coins to wager." Harriet poked at the little mound of buttons that served as our pool. "It makes the game so much more interesting."

I shrugged. "After next week, we'll have plenty of coins to wager at cards or anything else we want."

Not that I meant to gamble away my earnings. With my room, board and clothes all provided by Mrs. Goadby, I would save my money so I'd never end up back on the streets.

"I have an idea," said Harriet. "Whichever one of us takes no tricks must answer a question from the others."

"Like a forfeit?" Rose wrinkled her freckled nose.

Harriet nodded. "Forfeits are always amusing. Don't you think, Elizabeth?"

I reckoned it depended on whether you won or lost. Still, I was curious about the other two ... and I was holding good cards. "Sounds like a lark to me."

Rose took one trick in the first hand and I took the other two. After conferring in giggly whispers, we posed a fairly innocent question to Harriet. "Have you ever been in love?"

"Yes." Her curt reply only provoked my curiosity more.

I sat out the next hand on account of miserable cards.

Harriet took all the tricks and promptly asked Rose. "How did Mrs. Goadby find you?"

"At an intelligence office." Rose blushed every color of her namesake flower. "I was looking for a new place."

Hand by hand, we teased out one another's stories. We learned that Rose had been in service until the day her employer's visiting uncle molested her. She'd managed to escape with her virginity intact, but badly frightened.

"Afterward was almost worse. His lordship claimed I threw myself at him and begged him to set me up in keeping." Rose shuddered. "Rather starve, I would! But the mistress believed him and threw me out without a reference."

Harriet admitted she had not been as blameless in her conduct as Rose. Spending the winter with her aunt in Bath, she'd fallen in love with a young man who'd persuaded her to elope. On their wedding night, after putting out the candles, he'd left the room for a moment, then returned and made love to her in silence. The next morning she'd woken to find a stranger in her bridegroom's place. It turned out the marriage ceremony had been a sham and Harriet had never seen her "husband" again.

"The other man left me some money. He said Mr. Barton makes his living courting innocent girls for rich old men to deflower. My money had almost run out when Mrs. Goadby offered me a place. No doubt Mr. Barton sent her and pocketed a commission. I wish I could have denied him the income, but I was afraid I'd end up in debtor's prison. At least here I'll know what I am doing and *I* will be the one to profit from it."

Harriet glared at Rose and me as if we had taken part in

her downfall. "I suppose you think I was wicked to elope and stupid to fall for such a trick?"

"Neither." Her story made me think better of Ned Armistead. He had deceived me, but only because he was hiding a secret too dangerous to reveal. "You and Rose were used very badly."

"What about you?" asked Rose. "Did someone use you badly?"

"Only life." I was about to tell my tale when Mrs. Goadby bustled in.

"Still awake, at this hour? It will not do. We have a very full day tomorrow. I cannot have you all yawning and wilting before supper. To bed, now—at once!"

We did not hesitate, but threw down our cards and scurried into Mrs. Goadby's bedchamber to don our nightclothes.

Once we'd bedded down on sofas in her sitting room and doused the candles, Rose's whisper broke the silence. "Harriet, what's it like . . . with a man? Does it hurt *very* much?"

"It's odd, you know." Harriet sighed. "When I believed I was with Mr. Barton and we were properly married, I scarcely minded it at all. But once I found out how I'd been deceived, it felt as if I'd been torn apart."

I did not think it odd at all. I could have borne any amount of pain if Ned had wanted me that way. In spite of Mrs. Goadby's promises, I could not shake the dread of my initiation. No matter how attractive, skilled and gentle my first partner, he would not be the man I wanted . . . the one man I could never have.

As I hurried up the stairs the next evening, after a final inspection by Mrs. Goadby, I met Isabella Craven coming down.

"Enjoy your walk, Armistead." Her lip arched in a sneer. "I doubt you'll be able to tomorrow. You'd have to be daft to believe Mrs. Goadby's story about giving you to a considerate gentleman who'll go easy your first time."

My stomach took a bilious tumble.

Then another voice drifted down from the floor above, bubbling with impudent glee. "What a memory you have, Craven! I'm amazed you can recall what it's like to lose a maidenhead. Considering you lost yours so very long ago."

I glanced up to spy Nell Paget leaning over the banister.

"I'm amazed you had a maidenhead to lose!" Isabella stalked off with her nose in the air.

Nell winked at me. "Calling that one a bitch is an insult to dogs. Don't fret about tonight. Drink plenty of wine at supper, be easy and let the gentleman have his way. After a few days, you'll grow used to it and find it can feel quite pleasant. If you don't fancy the gentleman you're with, close your eyes and pretend he's someone you do fancy."

She skipped off down the stairs while I stood there wondering if my vivid imagination might finally do me some good.

Before long, Mrs. Goadby's guests arrived. The new girls had been told to wait upstairs until we were summoned. We crowded together in the hallway while a lilting mixture of music, talk and laughter wafted up from the front parlor.

Harriet was called then Rose. Time slowed to a crawl as I waited for my turn, but finally Isabella came to fetch me.

As I prepared to make my entrance, I heard Mrs. Goadby gush, "I have reserved the best for last. This young acolyte of Aphrodite hales from Greenwich, the daughter of a shoemaker who abandoned the poor child to become a Methodist preacher."

What nonsense was that? I scarcely had time to wonder before my foot caught on something and I stumbled into the room. I tried to catch myself, but with so many eyes upon me I could not seem to put a foot right. Staggering forward, I pictured myself collapsed on the floor in a humiliating heap while Mrs. Goadby's guests roared with laughter at my clumsiness.

Then a man's hand caught mine. Another wrapped around my waist, lending me the support I needed to regain my balance.

"Is it time for dancing already?" my rescuer cried. "Do permit Mrs. Goadby to finish introducing you, first, fair one."

The others laughed, but warmly in admiration of the gentleman's quick action and gallantry. "Leave it to Lyttelton to grab the prettiest girl for himself."

Lightheaded and breathless, I surrendered myself to the gentleman and sank onto the settee beside him. "Thank you for coming to my rescue, sir. I am in your debt."

I looked up into grey eyes that sparkled with adventure. "Take care about saying such things, sweet one. You might tempt me to prosecute my claim."

"Few ladies would object to serving such a sentence."

A surge of suggestive laughter made me repent my glibness. "Foul play, Lyttelton! You've made a conquest before the rest of us have been properly introduced to –. I say, Mrs. Goadby, do reveal the name of your divine young friend."

"With pleasure." Mrs. Goadby's voice betrayed no hint of vexation at my graceless entrance. "This charming addition to my house is Mrs. Armistead. My dear, may I present Captain Ayscough, Mr. Andrews, Captain O'Byrne, Mr. Barrington and Sir Francis Molyneux. You have already met Lord Lyttelton."

The other gentlemen's names jumbled together in my head. I was too much occupied with his lordship to care. His hand ranged up my side from the base of my bodice to beneath my arm.

When a servant appeared with wine, Lord Lyttelton declined. "My hands are too agreeably engaged at present to divert them."

I could not truthfully say I wanted him to. His touch sent a flutter of heat through my flesh.

"Would you care to share *my* wine, sir?" It was the least I could do to repay him for coming to my aid.

"Generous as well as beautiful." One side of his mouth arched in smile of crooked charm. "I must commend Mrs. Goadby on her newest acquisition."

"Do you visit here often, my lord?"

"Not very often. I frequent King's Place—so convenient to the clubs. I nearly begged off tonight, but my friends would not hear of it. Now I am obliged to them." He lowered his mouth to the glass, which I tipped up for him to drink.

I hoped I could tempt his lordship to bid for me. He was not Ned and we were barely acquainted, but he was attractive and attentive. I could do far worse.

The company drank and talked together for a while. Then one of the gentlemen called for dancing. Harriet joined the others to make a set of six, but Rose and I sat out. We had only begun to take dancing lessons that week.

When Lord Lyttelton urged me to try, I shook my head. "I am sorry to disappoint you. I will practice so that when you come back again I shall be able to accept your invitation."

"An excellent inducement to return." Once again his lordship lifted my hand. Rather than kissing it in the usual manner, he turned my arm and grazed his lips over the sensitive flesh of my inner wrist. I wondered if he could feel my pulse racing. "I hope you will learn quickly."

"I will try, my lord. I have so much to learn." Dancing, music, the art of lively conversation—would I ever master it all?

"I should be delighted to instruct you in one or two important subjects." His gaze flitted to my bosom, the tops of which bulged slightly above the low-cut neck of my gown. "I believe you would find me a most patient tutor."

After several dances, one of the gentlemen announced, "I have worked up a sharp appetite. How soon do we dine?"

"As soon as you wish, sir," said Mrs. Goadby. "We hope this will be a night to satisfy all appetites."

The wine had eased my nerves enough that I was able to laugh with the others. Music continued to play as our party moved to the dining room. The room looked like a scene from one of my elaborate fantasies—all gleaming glassware and polished silver, snow-white napery and vivid clusters of flowers. Steam rose from the covered serving dishes, each carrying a succulent smell. This was as far removed from Fat Joe's chophouse as I could imagine.

We heaped our plates with creamed oysters, pigeon pie, and chine of beef. I took care not to gorge. This night was too important to risk making myself ill. The gentlemen all ate and drank with lusty appetites. Now and then, one would rise and propose a toast to the ladies, Mrs. Goadby, beauty, youth, adventure or macaroni pie.

A second course followed, as lavish as the first, with veal and olives, potato pudding, duck ragout and several other rich dishes. Between courses, the gentlemen took turns excusing themselves for whispered conversations with Mrs. Goadby.

"They're bidding on you and the others," whispered Nell. "Pretty brisk, too, by the look of it."

Flushed with food, wine and the admiration of Lord Lyttelton, I lifted my glass. "Here's to the high bidder!"

His lordship reached for his wine. "What are you drinking to? I will join in the toast."

"What if I was drinking to *you*, my lord?" I did my best to mimic Nell's merry impudence.

"Do you reckon me too modest to raise a glass in my own honor?" He lifted his high then drained it in one deep draft. "I am a man of many virtues, but modesty is not among them!"

In a whiff of spicy sweetness, the dessert course arrived—little ratafia cakes, peach fritters and syllabubs.

"Just a nibble." Lord Lyttelton held a cake to my lips. "To repay you for sharing your wine with me before dinner."

I took a small bite, relishing the bitter-sweet nutty flavor. When the cake began to crumble, threatening to shower my gown with crumbs, I was forced to gobble it up, my lips and tongue grazing his fingers. He chuckled at my eagerness.

At last, when the conversation began to ebb, Mrs. Goadby rose from her chair. "Ladies, let us retire and leave the gentlemen to enjoy their port."

As I rose to leave, Lord Lyttelton drew me down to whisper. "Leave your stockings gartered until I come. I am vastly fond of helping ladies remove their stockings."

"Off to your quarters," Mrs. Goadby murmured when I emerged from the dining room. "And change clothes for private company."

Perhaps if I'd had less wine those words might have alarmed me. Instead I felt afloat in a warm, carefree haze. "Is it Lord Lyttelton I am to entertain, tonight, ma'am?"

From the way Mrs. Goadby's mouth tightened, I knew I had asked the wrong question. "You will entertain whoever I send you, Armistead. What is more, you will entertain one as well as another, without partiality."

The grim force of her displeasure shook me from my tipsy daze. "Aye, ma'am."

I raced up the stairs to find my rooms warm and softly lit, the bedding turned down. With fumbling fingers, I shed my clothes to don the loose nightshift of Irish muslin and pink brocade dressing gown that had been laid out for me.

As I was tying my dressing gown sash, I heard my sitting room door swing open. I raced out to greet the man who had bid highest for my virginity.

"Lord Lyttelton!" Sweet relief propelled me into his arms. "I was afraid it might not be you."

"Small fear of that." He kissed me full on the mouth. It was the kind of kiss I had craved from Ned, but he had not been able to give me. His lordship's lips moved against mine, as if nibbling up crumbs of spicy cake or sipping the sweet froth of syllabub. His kiss tasted of forbidden luxuries I now might share. It promised a life of ease, pleasure and plenty. How could I resist?

"You *are* an amorous creature." His lordship nuzzled my neck. "Is it true you've never lain with a man before, at your age? Why you must be every day of . . ."

"Eighteen, my lord, come July." I had lain with a man, though not in the way he meant. "Am I too forward? I swear I am a maiden. You will discover that for yourself!"

"So I shall! Do not fret over your behavior. I have no use for coy, missish whores. I can get that from any marriageable lady at a house party." He pressed another kiss upon me – more demanding, with forceful thrusts of his tongue.

I submitted to it with neither eagerness nor resistance, uncertain which he wanted. My own feelings confused me just as much. His casual mention of *whores* stung. Until now I had only heard talk of the *lady of pleasure*, the *Thais*, the *votary of Venus*, all of which served to disguise and exalt my new trade. Now I faced the truth that the only difference between me and a Covent Garden bunter was my price.

Lord Lyttelton reached under my dressing gown to fondle my breast through the light fabric of my shift. He gave it a gentle squeeze then rubbed the pad of his thumb over the nipple, which grew hard and erect. Ripples of pleasure spread through my body. Their fierce heat burned away my shame. I wriggled against his lordship, responding to his kiss and touch.

He twined his fingers in my hair. The sensation provoked such a potent reminder of Ned, my throat tightened.

No! I forced myself to concentrate on Lord Lyttelton. Ned Armistead had deceived me and used me for his own ends. His lordship wanted me with a depth of desire measured in gold guineas. I needed that now to help me forget Ned.

"Why are we sporting at the door?" His lordship chuckled. "We have two fine rooms at our disposal. For what I bid, I had better get more than a flying leap!"

"Forgive me." Once again I felt like the raw, awkward novice I was. "Come in and be comfortable. Will you have a seat on the sofa or ..." I glanced toward the bedchamber door.

He shrugged. "Might as well begin where we are sure to end up. As for my comfort, it will help to shed a few clothes."

Hoisting me in his arms, he strode toward the bedchamber. "Carrying a lady over the threshold then relieving her of her maidenhead. That's as near to a wedding night as I hope to come for good long while."

I gave a whoop of glee when he tossed me onto the bed. The lower part of my dressing gown fell open and my shift hitched up, exposing my ankles.

"Good girl!" he cried. "You remembered to keep your stockings on." Eyes glittering with desire, he stared at my legs as he removed his coat and untied his neck linen.

I pointed my toes and turned my foot in a circle. "I was worried you might not bid high enough to see them."

Lord Lyttelton let himself fall backward onto the bed. "If you knew me better, you would never have doubted."

"But you placed only one bid, early in the evening."

"That bid was for five pounds above whatever the others offered." He grasped the hem of my dressing gown and slowly pulled it up to where my garters were tied above my knees. "Poor O'Byrne was vastly put out. He was certain he had secured you. Now, about these stockings . . ."

He seized one end of the garter ribbon with his teeth and tugged it loose. Then he leaned closer and gave my inner thigh a playful nip.

I squealed and giggled.

"Did I hurt you?" His lordship feigned concern. "Then I must kiss it better."

The whisper of his lips over the sensitive flesh tickled, but it also sent shafts of heat up the inside of my leg to stoke a smoldering fire kindled by his kisses.

Hooking one finger over the top of my stocking, he pulled it down, his lips skimming over my bare leg. Then he removed my other stocking in the same leisurely, stimulating manner.

He waved it around like a trophy of conquest, while stroking my legs with the back of his hand. "If the rest of you is as lovely as the parts I can see at present, I shall not regret a penny of your price."

His lordship cast me a teasing glance as he unbuttoned his

breeches and slid them off his lean-muscled legs. "Have you ever seen a naked man before?"

Though worried the admission might make him doubt my virtue, I nodded.

To my relief, he greeted the news with his crooked grin. "You make me curious to hear the story behind that ... but not now."

In one great sweep, he pulled off his shirt and cast it aside giving me a full, close view of what I'd had only stolen glimpses of before now. His lordship's bare chest rippled with tiers of firm arched muscle and bore a light crop of brown hair. More grew down the middle of his belly to a bushy thicket on his loins. His rigid shaft strained for action.

"Your turn to undress." He gestured toward the foot of the bed. "Not too quickly, though. Let me savor the sight."

I wished *he* would take off my dressing gown and shift, as he had my stockings. If I only lay there and submitted to him, I might feel less accountable for what was about to happen. Stifling any troublesome flicker of modesty, I scrambled off the bed and stood far enough back to give his lordship a good view as he reclined upon the pillows. My dressing gown already gaped open. It took only a shrug to send it falling slowly down to pool around my feet.

Grasping the hem of my shift, I raised it inch by inch. His lordship gave a deep purr of approval when my naked thighs came into view and another when I uncovered my loins. By that time I had lifted my shift high enough to hide my blushing face. Once my breasts were exposed, I presumed there was no more need to go slowly. I pulled the shift off and tossed my head to send my hair spilling over my shoulders.

"Venus, indeed." With a cheerful leer, his lordship beckoned me. "Come, Venus. My eyes have feasted. Now other parts clamor to be satisfied."

Reluctance and eagerness battling inside me, I climbed over the foot of the bed and crawled toward him.

"Keep coming." He slid his legs under me. "A little farther. Perfect!"

By the time I got into the position he wanted me, I had one hand planted on either side of his head while my legs straddled his chest. My breasts hovered above his mouth.

He extended his tongue and flicked it over each of my nipples in turn as he raised his hands to squeeze the lobes of my bottom. "Now *this* is what I call a banquet of beauty. Just a little lower in front. That's a good girl."

I bent my elbows, bringing my nipple down to meet his puckered lips. My body ached with pleasure as he suckled my breasts and fondled my bottom. But I could not fully give myself up to it while my arms strained from bearing my weight at such an odd angle. I reminded myself that my satisfaction did not signify, only his lordship's. My pleasure would come from a full belly, fine clothes and an elegant apartment.

Then one of his hands strayed beneath me to stroke the cleft between my legs. A shudder of delight jolted through me. Only by great effort did I keep from swooning upon him.

"You are as wet and wanton as any seasoned harlot I have ever mounted. Now to discover if you truly are a maiden." He lowered his hand then raised it again ... or so I thought. But the smooth tip of flesh that pressed against my open breach was many times larger than his fingers. I knew what must be coming, but was too deep in the throes of lust to fear it.

"Before you feel his bite," Lord Lyttelton grazed my bosom with his smooth-shaven cheek, "you should taste his tickle."

The slick crown of his yard slid over my tender parts, each swipe like the rasp of a blade against the knife-grinder's stone, whetting my need to an even sharper pitch. Then the dagger of desire stabbed me, releasing a gush of pleasure so intense it overpowered my senses. I crumpled against Lord Lyttelton, shuddering with delight.

Before I could recover my wits, he rolled us both over, pinning me beneath him. He raised his hips a little to take aim. The tip of his shaft found my opening, stirring an echo of the bliss that had gripped me a moment before. His muscles clenched then released in a powerful thrust that ran me through. The pain was every bit as sharp as the pleasure that had gone before. I writhed and cried out.

He silenced me with a firm kiss. "The worst is over."

Perhaps so, but what came afterward was not a great deal better. If he had withdrawn or remained still, giving my torn flesh a chance to heal, I might have soon forgotten my hurt. But he began to thrust in and out, every stroke rubbing me raw. I bit hard on my lip, praying it would soon be over. Perhaps it was, by clock measure. But to me it seemed to go on a great while. The harsh gust of his lordship's breath in my ear kept time with the quickening movement of his hips.

Finally, when I feared I could stand it no longer, he gave a deep, rumbling growl and rammed home one last time. Spent, he crumpled on top of me. I was so consumed by the throbbing pain in my loins I scarcely noticed his dead weight.

After he rolled off of me and began to snore, I crept out of bed, leaving behind a smear of blood upon the sheets as proof of my plundered virginity. Behind my dressing screen, I found a basin and a ewer full of water. Setting the basin on the floor, I poured a measure of cool water into it. Then, with a sob of relief, I sat down in the water.

The worst was over. I no longer had a maidenhead to fret about losing. I clung to Nell Paget's reassurance that lying with a man got easier after the first time. Even for all the luxuries of life at Mrs. Goadby's, I was not certain I could bear an encounter like this every night.

What choice did I have, though? I was a whore now and there was no going back. One tiny stain on a woman's reputation was as bad as a lifetime of debauchery. I could only go forward from here and do whatever I must to survive.

# Chapter Six

*I*'D HOPED TO GIVE MY poor, battered parts time to recover before the next assault. His lordship had other ideas.

He made use of me twice more that night. Though he kissed and fondled me in the way that had brought me such delight earlier, the pain in my lower parts now dampened any sparks of pleasure. He left the next morning in high good humor after making me a present of five guineas. I thanked him sincerely and told myself my initiation might have been a good deal worse. At least his lordship had given me some enjoyment. And he had made the pain worthwhile.

I sat on the bed in my nightshift dropping gold coins from one hand to the other. They did not make a thin jingle, like farthings and haypennies, but a prosperous, robust *chink*. I doubted every gentleman I entertained would be so generous. But even if they only gave me a tenth as much, I would soon save enough to keep me in modest comfort for the rest of my life.

Abruptly the bedchamber door swung open and Mrs. Goadby strode in. "Well done, my dear! Lord Lyttelton pronounced himself vastly well entertained. One of his companions has requested you for tonight. On very generous terms, too, considering he has reason to know the state of your maidenhead."

"Another gentleman, *tonight*, ma'am?"

"Is that not agreeable?" A chill in her tone warned me to hold my tongue but the ache deep in my loins would not let me keep silent.

"It's just that I'm quite ... sore, ma'am. If I could have a little ... time for it to get better."

"Be thankful," Mrs. Goadby replied, "At least you are a woman grown and able to accommodate a man. I was not so fortunate. But I did what I had to, and so will you. The Season is a short enough time to turn a profit without girls lolling about *recovering* from their work."

I bit back a retort that would have got me tossed out onto Great Marlborough Street. "I don't mean to shirk ma'am."

"I hope not." Mrs. Goadby handed me my dressing gown. "Now, what sort of present did his lordship make you?"

I hesitated, tempted to lie, but I knew it would be no use. "Five guineas, ma'am."

"Very good." She extended her open hand.

"But this is *my* money. Didn't his lordship already pay you? He told me he'd bid a great deal."

Mrs. Goadby kept her hand extended under my nose. "Not nearly enough to cover the cost of your lodgings in a fine house like this. All those new clothes. The food you've eaten. Not to mention the money I gave Mr. Armistead."

"Money to buy me," I muttered before I could stop myself.

"I'm afraid the magistrate would not see it that way."

"Magistrate?" The very word made my belly churn. "What's he got to do with it?"

Mrs. Goadby's lips arched at the corners, but her eyes remained as cold as a January night. "A great deal, if I am forced to prosecute you for unpaid debt. Debtor's prison can be a brutal place for pretty young things like you."

"Take it, please!" I thrust the coins into her hand. "Let me work off my debt. I did not reckon how much things cost."

She stared down at me, fondling the gold. "Very well. But let us have no more talk about *your* money or taking a rest from your duties. Put on your cap and dressing gown and report to the doctor for your examination. Our livelihood depends upon our reputation for health, you know."

With that she bustled off, leaving me shaken and dispirited. How long would it take to work off my debt and be able to start putting something aside for my future?

A few minutes later, as I hobbled toward the back stairs, I met Nell Paget.

She looked tired but otherwise in good spirits. "Cheer up! You'll heal soon enough. I did."

"I wouldn't mind so much if I'd got to keep the present his lordship gave me." I knew I shouldn't complain, but my craving for sympathy was even stronger than my fear of Mrs. Goadby.

Nell cast a furtive glance behind us and lowered her voice. "None of us like it, but that's the way of things around here. Whatever you do, don't be daft enough to try and run away. One of the girls from King's Place did, and Mrs. Hayes had her arrested for *stealing* the gown she was wearing."

I was sure Mrs. Goadby would not hesitate to do the same.

"Don't fret about the money," added Nell. "Who needs it when we have the best of everything money can buy?"

I wanted to reply, but by this time we had reached the examining room. Nell hopped onto the doctor's high table as careless as if it was all a game. She bent her knees and spread her legs without the faintest blush of modesty. "Have a look, Doctor dear, and see if I am not as clean as a nun?"

The doctor chuckled and shook his head at her impudence. He was a small, slender man of middle years with a tidy wig and a kind face. His Irish brogue reminded me of my mother. "I have never inspected a nun in this fashion. But if I did, I should *hope* to find her free of the pox."

He took up an odd sort of brass lantern with a candle placed in front of a mirror. This he used to shine a strong light between Nell's spread legs.

I squirmed with embarrassment when he reached in but she only gave an exaggerated shiver. "Your hands are cold, doctor! Cold hands, warm heart, eh?"

"Perhaps so." The doctor tilted his light and his head to get a careful look. "Or perhaps your parts are too hot."

"Wicked man! Haven't you had a long enough look?" Nell's teasing tone sobered. "Nothing wrong is there? It doesn't hurt when I use the chamber pot or when the gentlemen use me."

The doctor drew back his hand. "I see nothing amiss. No secretion. No sores."

"Your turn, love." Nell scrambled down from the table. "Don't be bashful. It doesn't do in this business. Our dear doctor has seen so many women's bottoms, it's nothing to him."

I took her place and arranged myself as she had done.

"Did you try the syllabub last night?" she asked as the doctor examined me. "I could eat that three meals a day."

I flinched at the doctor's touch, but Nell made light of it. "Didn't I say his hands were cold?"

"I'll be as gentle as I can." The doctor sucked in a breath through his teeth. "You'll need some salve to soothe that and help it heal. Otherwise, everything looks healthy."

"I should hope so." Nell tugged down the hems of my garments and helped me sit up. "Can you imagine having the ill luck to catch a dose your very first time?"

I thanked the doctor when he handed me a little crock of salve, but I could not look him in the face.

"I've heard of the pox," I admitted to Nell once we were on our way back upstairs. "And I know how you get it. But is there any way to keep from getting it? I mean ... the gentlemen don't have to be examined, do they?"

"Not fair, is it?" She took my arm and led me down the hall to her rooms. "There's a few things you need to learn in a hurry if you're going to make a go of this."

We passed through Nell's sitting room to her bedchamber. She patted a place on the edge of the bed for me to sit. Opening a drawer of her night table, she pulled out a blue silk bag secured with a drawstring of darker blue ribbon.

"Nothing better for stopping the pox than these little machines."

She opened the bag and took out a slender tube, rounded at one end and secured at the other with a thin strip of ribbon, the same color as the drawstring of the bag.

I stared at the thing. "It ... looks like a sausage casing."

"Sausage casing!" Nell fell backward onto the bed in a violent fit of giggles. "Oh my, I must tell that one to Polly!"

As it dawned on me what the thing must be for, I felt like a prize fool.

"They come in three sizes." Nell wiped away the tears her hard laughter had brought on. "This middling size fits most gentlemen. But no matter which you give them, claim it's the largest. If you really want a gentleman to use one, pretend you aren't sure you have one big enough. He'll put it on just to show you how well he fills it."

I grinned at that.

Nell popped the bag back in the drawer and beckoned me toward her dressing screen in the corner. "Almost as bad as a dose is ending up with a bellyful."

She took a tall porcelain container from her washstand. Three sticks poked up from the mouth of the container, like bare flower stems from a vase. Nell lifted out one of the sticks. The end had a strip of linen wrapped around it, creating a shaft almost as thick as a man's.

"It's like a ramrod the soldiers use to tamp down powder in their muskets." Nell's dark eyes danced with merriment. "My first keeper was in the army. That's where I got the idea."

Beads of water trickled from the end of the rod. Nell pressed it against the lip of the vase to stop the dripping. "I soak 'em in vinegar that's had herbs stewed in it."

She squatted over her basin and slipped the linen-bound stick under her shift. "There's always a pot of the stuff brewing in the kitchen. One of the new girls last year thought it was tea and drank some!"

"Does it have to be vinegar?" I dreaded the sting upon my wounded flesh. "Wouldn't water work just as well?"

Nell shook her head as she scoured herself. "Vinegar is good for preserving some things, but not a man's seed."

When she'd finished, she dropped her swab into the basin and pointed to the remaining sticks in the vase. "Your turn."

I balked.

"It'll sting, but that's a small price to pay," she coaxed me. "Get it over with and we'll go down to breakfast."

I grasped one of the sticks as eagerly as I would a knife to stab myself. Clenching my teeth, I pushed the wad of wet linen up inside me. It might as well have been a flaming brand. I whimpered as it seared my raw flesh. But I kept going, picturing it scouring away the *pernicious seed*.

It seemed this new life of mine held as many dangers as luxuries. If I hoped to avoid them, I would have to learn fast.

Mrs. Goadby contrived to pass me off as a virgin long after I was not. Besides the vinegar cleansing potion, another was kept simmering in the kitchen. A thick stew of myrtle berries, and other strange ingredients boiled in wine, it had to be applied several times a day to tighten my passage and give the illusion of an unbroken maidenhead.

I knew better than to question Mrs. Goadby's orders. But I did complain to Nell on the way to our weekly examination.

She only laughed. "Do you reckon the poor dears cannot spare the fee she charges for a virgin?"

"I hate ... deceiving folks." Especially after the way Ned had deceived me.

"You're only helping them believe what they want to believe. Where's the harm in that? Besides, you've got no choice. No sense feeling guilty about what you can't help."

Was that how Ned had excused himself for lying to me?

"Still," said Nell, "I'm glad I'm done with all that. Applying that restorative is a bloody nuisance." She nudged me in the ribs with her elbow. "A *bloody* nuisance – get it?"

I believe I would have been expelled from Mrs. Goadby's

twenty times over in those first weeks if Nell had not taken me under her wing. It was she who told me how to inflate a customer's bill by getting him to order food and wine, playing cards and entertaining him with music. She also warned me Mrs. Goadby disapproved of girls drinking spirits. Like dirt and disease, drunkenness was a mark of common bawds, which we were far above. Instead, we were encouraged to drink chocolate, or boiled milk with sugar and nutmeg, to make our breath smell sweet.

"As long as ye don't get poxed or pregnant, you're safe for the first year at least," Nell told Rose and me one day as we gossiped over a cup of chocolate. "When you can't be passed off as a virgin no more, then you need to watch your step."

Though she spoke with her usual cheery impudence, Nell's words made my chocolate taste bitter. "I thought it would all get easier once we weren't such raw beginners."

Nell gave a rueful shrug. "Gentlemen like fresh ... faces."

"I have another question for you."

"You're blushing!" cried Nell. "It must be a good one. Ask away!"

"Well ... Mrs. Goadby says there's a gentleman I'm supposed to gratify *by hand*. How do I do that?"

"Easy as pie. You just wrap your fingers around him, like this." Nell went through the motions on an invisible gentleman in such a comical manner, Rose and I sputtered with laughter.

"It looks like you're milking a cow!" gasped Rose. "Only upside down!"

All three of us laughed over that until we could scarcely catch our breath. When our giddy laughter had finally settled down, I took the risk of renewing it. "Is it true Lord Winterslow will pay just to comb my hair?"

"He combed mine last week," said Rose. "Made a good job of it, too. Very gentle – didn't pull at all."

Nell nodded. "He pays well for the pleasure. It's not the strangest request we get around here. There's a gentleman who likes to wash our linen and Captain Pryce likes to dress up in a pretty gown. Mrs. Goadby had a big one made up for him after he tore a couple of the girls' trying to get them on."

"He never!" Rose cried. "I think you're telling us wild stories just to see if we'll swallow them."

Thinking back on what I'd seen at the *White Hart*, I was not so quick to dismiss Nell's account. "This Captain Pryce, is he a molly?"

"Oo!" Nell pretended to be scandalized. "So you weren't raised in a convent after all."

We speculated a bit more about Captain Pryce then Nell told us of some other *pet leches* of our customers.

"Now and then we'll get asked to birch one of them." She shook her head in disbelief at our blank looks. "You've heard of mollies, but not birching? It's flogging them on the bare bottom with a switch of birch twigs."

I winced. "I don't think I could do that—hurt somebody, even if they wanted me to."

"Don't fret. Most of that kind go to Isabella Craven. She loves flogging them to a jelly."

That did not surprise me.

"It's why Mrs. Goadby's kept her around so long. A good birching pays almost as well as a maidenhead. I often wish I had the stomach for it."

I gave Nell's fingers an affectionate squeeze. "I'm glad you don't."

Slowly my life at Mrs. Goadby's fell into a familiar pattern. I slept late in the mornings after my customer had gone. Once I'd cleansed myself, I breakfasted with Nell, often learning some new trick from her or gossiping about the performance of our departed cullies.

The afternoon hours were crammed with hair grooming, fittings for new clothes, music and dancing lessons.

"You hardly have an idle moment," Nell teased me. "I never

heard of anyone working so hard at being a lady of pleasure! If you haven't got your nose in a newspaper, you're practicing dancing or the harpsichord. It tires me just to think about."

I sensed a subtle prick of disapproval, but made light of it. "I need all the improvement I can get, don't I?"

My quip masked a sober truth. Those lessons were the only thing of lasting value I could earn at Mrs. Goadby's. Fine food was eaten and gone. Elegant gowns soon went out of style. Carriage rides and evening excursions were passing diversions. But what I could *learn* would be mine to keep. I was not about to throw away those opportunities.

Several evenings a week, Mrs. Goadby took a group of girls to the theatre, the pleasure gardens, or a masquerade at Carlisle House in nearby Soho Square. I fairly danced with excitement at my first outing to the Drury Lane playhouse.

"Remember," murmured Nell when we took our seats in a twelve-shilling box above the stage, "we haven't come to *watch* as much as to *be seen*. If you catch a gentleman looking at you, flutter your fan and glance over it at him."

I scanned the opposite boxes to see if any gentlemen were watching. But it was a lady who caught my eye. She appeared nearer thirty than twenty, yet still beautiful with fine features and a graceful neck, around which hung a string of large pearls.

"That's Nancy Parsons," Nell whispered. "She's the prime minister's mistress. Courtesans like her have it better than any other women in the kingdom. They own property and they're under no man's thumb since they have plenty of others competing for their favors. They spend more in a year than would keep most folks in comfort the rest of their days."

"Sounds fine to me." I could scarcely take my eyes off Nancy Parson's jewels. "How do we get to be courtesans, then?"

"It's more than just looks." Nell nodded toward the stage, where a finely dressed lady had begun to sing. "That's Sophia Baddeley. If I never hear another gentleman go into raptures about her it'll be too soon! She has dukes and earls bidding thousands of pounds to become her keeper, yet she's no beauty with that long face – puts me in mind of a mare."

Considering how mad most gentlemen were for hunting and racing, perhaps they admired a horsy look. Whatever secret magic had elevated Sophia Baddeley and Nancy Parsons to such dizzying heights, how I wished some of it would rub off on me!

The following week Mrs. Goadby included me in a party going to the pleasure gardens at Vauxhall. I kept up a merry chatter with Nell and Rose as our carriage trundled down Poland Street. How long ago it seemed since I had walked this route with Ned, casting envious glances at the ladies driving past.

We found Charing Cross crowded with carriages and sedan chairs. At first I wondered if they were all going to Vauxhall, but many seemed to be headed in the opposite direction.

"What a lot of soldiers!" cried Rose. "Aren't they handsome in their red coats?"

Mrs. Goadby did not look pleased by the number of soldiers on the street.

We had not gone far down Whitehall when a mounted officer stopped our carriage. "May I ask where you ladies are bound?"

"I promised my young friends a visit to Vauxhall on this fine evening, Captain." Mrs. Goadby looked every inch the respectable chaperone. "Is there some difficulty?"

"You should turn back at your first opportunity, ma'am. We've been ordered to restrict traffic across the bridges. More 'Wilkes and liberty' agitations in Southwark. I cannot answer for your safety if you venture across the Thames."

"We are obliged to you for the warning, Captain." Mrs. Goadby silenced our plaintive protests with a sharp look then directed the coachman to turn at the Admiralty.

"Wilkes and liberty," she muttered. "Wilkes the *libertine*

more like! This will hurt business, curse his hide!"

Sick with disappointment, I cursed this Wilkes person, too. How dare he prevent my first visit to Vauxhall?

"We will entertain in the back parlor this evening," Mrs. Goadby announced when we arrived back at the house. "I want no lights visible from the front. Go up to your rooms, girls, and make sure the curtains are drawn."

"What's all that about?" asked Rose as we hurried upstairs. "And what are *Wilkes and liberty agitations*?"

"Riots," said Nell. "I heard Mr. Wilkes got elected to Parliament but they won't let him take his seat on account of he wrote some bad things about the King in a newspaper. The men who voted for him say it's their right to decide who speaks for them in Parliament."

Vexed as I was about our plans for the evening being ruined, I could not stifle a flicker of sympathy for Mr. Wilkes and the voters. It sounded as if they were being treated unfairly. I knew all too well how that felt.

# Chapter Seven

ONE MORNING A FEW MONTHS later, Rose flew into my bedchamber, all in a flutter. "Have you seen Harriet?"

"I haven't seen anybody this morning." I yawned and rubbed my eyes. "What time is it?"

Rose ignored my question. "She wasn't with us in the parlor last night, remember?"

"Probably has her courses." When a girl was bleeding, she kept to her rooms and Mrs. Goadby sent her customers to be satisfied by hand or ones with *pet leches* like washing linen.

Rose shook her head. "She's not in her room. The place is empty–clothes gone, bed stripped."

"Hand me my dressing gown. Let's go ask Nell. She always knows what's what around here."

This time was no exception.

"Poor little cow." Nell shook her head. "I thought her eyes looked red when she came back from seeing the doctor. I reckon she got clapped, so dear Mother Goadby gave her the boot."

"She never said goodbye." Rose gnawed her full lower lip.

Though Harriet kept to herself more than Rose and me, a bond had grown between us new girls.

"She'd never have had a chance, love." For once Nell had no saucy quip. "The minute Mrs. Goadby discovers a girl is poxed or breeding, out they go. Same if they cause trouble or need to make room for new stock. They just disappear without any goodbyes that might upset the rest of us and spoil our company for the customers."

We spoke no more of it. What use would there have been? But I was certain we were all wondering the same thing. Which of us would be the next to go ... and when?

We were all still there a year later when a vast construction began behind Mrs. Goadby's back garden.

We soon grew to hate the constant pounding of hammers, but our mistress would hear no complaints. "It will be a place of public entertainment, many times bigger than Carlyle House, closer than Ranelagh and under a great domed roof so it will not be subject to the weather like Vauxhall. Gentlemen of fashion will flock to it. Just think of the business!"

Meanwhile, life at Mrs. Goadby's followed the movement of our wealthy customers. When the spring sitting of Parliament drew all the peers to London, she held her annual "Banquet of Beauty." After several busy months, our customers left the heat and stink of town for their country estates and we followed to the rural resort of Bath. On our way, we stopped at Oxford to help a party of graduating scholars celebrate.

A florid young lord with ginger hair led me toward a wooden dock, where several small boats were tied. "What better way to bid *adieu* to dusty books and lectures than a splendid picnic on the banks of the Cherwell with such charming company?"

"And champagne!" called one of his friends. "I mean to drink enough to make me forget everything I've learned."

The young gentlemen helped us girls into the boats along with provisions for our outing. Then they took up long wooden poles and punted us downriver to a secluded spot, shaded by several tall trees. I could not imagine heaven being any more beautiful than this soft, green place. The wholesome fragrance of wildflowers wafted on the warm breeze along with the soothing harmony of birdsong and babbling water.

We opened the hampers and feasted on cold meats, jellies, buns, cheese and fruit, all washed down with great quantities of champagne. By the time we had emptied several bottles, the whole world seemed to sparkle around me. Giggles rose to my lips like tiny bubbles, especially when my ginger-haired companion filched a kiss or his roving hands found their way under my petticoats. Since joining Mrs. Goadby's establishment, I had not often enjoyed the company of a partner so near my own age. Now I reveled in it.

"I cannot answer for the rest of you," said my companion as he fumbled with the lacing of my stays, "but I am monstrous uncomfortable in these hot, tight clothes. Who will join me for a dip in the river?"

"That sounds like a fine frolic!" Nell kicked off her slippers. "I mean to be first in and devil take the hindmost!"

Her challenge set off a mad scramble to shed clothes, with much squealing and gales of giddy laughter. Soon we were all cavorting about in the sun-dappled water like lusty young animals ... kissing ... splashing ... frisking.

Before long, I was too engrossed in the attentions of my companion to notice the others. The heat of his caresses upon my bare wet skin set me wriggling with desire. He clasped me on the bottom and lifted me up for a kiss. I wrapped my arms around his neck and my legs around his waist, rubbing my breasts against his chest. Often men had called me a nymph. Now I felt like one, in the embrace of a young satyr. Wild and wanton, I stroked his tongue with mine and squirmed to swipe my greedy breech against the head of his straining shaft.

Forgetting he had hired me for his use, I twined my fingers in his wet curls and told him, in a liquid whisper, what I would have him do to me.

"Here?" he panted. "Now? But we might drown."

"Are you afraid of *dying?*" I teased him, referring to the blissful peak of amorous sensation.

"No more than you are afraid of being run through!" With me stuck to him like an ardent limpet, he waded to a spot where the river ran waist-deep beside the bank.

Leaning back against a tuft of overhanging grass, he surrendered to my desire. Later we crawled out into a mossy nook and warmed our bodies in the most delightful manner.

Summer at Bath was like a hangover after our tipsy Oxford idyll. At least once a week, I went with Nell and Rose to the Pump Room, where we drank the foul-tasting waters that were supposed to be good for our health On other days we stewed in the hot, smelly water of Queen's Bath. The place reminded me of the Covent Garden bagnio where Ned had taken me to bathe, except that it was crowded with people, all modestly dressed in a linen gowns and caps.

We wiled away the afternoons strolling down the Grand Parade or around Serpentine Lake in Prior Park Gardens. In the evenings we attended plays and concerts at the Theatre Royal.

Business was not as brisk as in London and the gentlemen who visited us were often older or ailing, though still lusty enough to enjoy the company of pretty girls.

Being fondled and mumbled by such dotards made my skin crawl. I welcomed the harsh-tasting mineral water to purge my mouth of their foul-breathed kisses and the steaming bath to scald me clean of their lecherous touch. Though I had been a lady of pleasure for almost two years, this was the first time I truly felt like a harlot.

The bracing frosts that sent birds flying south and sportsmen taking up their guns signaled our return to Great Marlborough Street for the Little Season that lasted until Parliament recessed for the winter.

Shortly before Christmas, Nell sought me out one afternoon. "Rose and me need to slip out to run a little errand. Be a love and distract Enoch for a few minutes, will you?"

"Can I come too? I'll go barmy if I'm cooped up in here much longer." Mrs. Goadby had been ill with a cold for over a week, so there'd been no outings to the playhouses or drives in the park. "I'm beginning to feel like a prisoner in this house."

"I reckon we are prisoners." Nell sounded nothing like her carefree, impudent self. "But God save us from being set free."

"Where are you going?" I asked, suspicious of her odd manner. "How long will you be away?"

"Not long, I hope." Nell lowered her voice. "As for the other, it's better if you not know."

As she turned to rush away, I grabbed her skirt. "Then it's likely better for *you* not to *go*. This isn't the time of year you want to land in Mrs. Goadby's bad books."

Other girls had disappeared from the house in December, to be replaced by virginal novices in time for Mrs. Goadby's spring *Banquet of Beauty.*

Nell glared at me and twitched her skirt out of my grasp. "Just do as I say and we'll all stay out of trouble!"

I lured Enoch away from his post by the front door by saying I'd seen a rat in my sitting room. Later, while I was practicing my harpsichord, Isabella came into the parlor looking for Rose. I claimed she'd just missed her.

"She said something about having a cup of chocolate with Nell." I knew Isabella would sooner catch the clap than venture into Nell's sitting room. "Shall I fetch her for you?"

"Don't bother," snapped Isabella, as if my offer of help were an insult. "I'm bound to see her sooner or later."

I worried how my friends would get back in without being spotted by Enoch or Isabella but they managed somehow. Nell appeared at suppertime saying Rose had the cold, and would dine in her room.

"Shirker," Isabella muttered when Rose did not appear in the parlor that evening to receive company.

"Put a bung in it!" snapped Nell. "Rose has got *the prince*, that's all. She'll be back at it in a few days."

Isabella's eyes narrowed. "You said she had the cold."

"She has," replied Nell after a brief hesitation. "And *the prince.*

Have a little pity on someone besides yourself."

Several times the next day I tried to see Rose. I was curious to hear what she and Nell had been up to and I stood a better chance of worming it out of *her.* But whenever I stopped by her quarters, I found Nell there with a ready excuse why I could not see Rose.

"Very well, then," I snapped at last. "Keep your precious secret! See if I care."

The haunted look in Nell's eyes almost made me repent my words, but I was too vexed and hurt at being left out. When Rose appeared at supper that night, looking pale, I sat at the opposite end of the table from her and Nell. I did not speak to either of them or look their way through the whole meal.

At last Rose murmured something about not having much appetite and wanting to go lie down. I heard her rise to leave.

A gasp from one of the other girls made me look up. My gaze flew at once to a stain of vivid scarlet on the back of Rose's apple-green skirts.

She glanced over her shoulder, and our eyes met for an instant before hers rolled back and she crumpled to the floor.

I scrambled out of my chair and flew to her.

"Aha!" cried Isabella. "So that's what you were up to. I should have guessed. Enoch, fetch Mrs. Goadby!"

I clasped Rose's hand—it felt cold as a marble statue's and looked just as white. Nell knelt beside Rose, cradling the girl's head in her lap.

"Go!" She fixed me with a look of violent desperation. "Get out of here!"

When I tried to protest, she struck me hard across the face. "Go, I said!"

Reeling from the blow, I burst into sobs and groped my way upstairs. Just as I reached my sitting room, I heard a heavy rush of feet and Mrs. Goadby berating Enoch in a shrill voice.

That was the last I saw of my friends. I did not dare ask where they'd gone for fear I would disappear, too. But I overheard enough of Mrs. Goadby's grumbling and the other girls' furtive gossip to guess that Rose had gotten pregnant. Nell had tried to help her get rid of it without Mrs. Goadby finding out.

Rose bled to death that night on the hard table in the doctor's examining room, while business went on as usual in the front parlor and the bedrooms upstairs. Before Mrs. Goadby could chuck Nell out, she ran away, taking several of her best gowns.

In the weeks after that I was never so eager to welcome a new man into my bed every night. Lying beneath them, grasping some fleeting moments of physical pleasure, I was able to forget my loneliness, my grief and my regrets.

Life at Mrs. Goadby's was never the same for me after that, though outwardly the routine of the place went on as before. Behind a glittering façade of new gowns, concerts and masquerades lurked the sordid routine of cleansing swabs, examinations for the pox, catering to my customers' *pet leches* and worrying how soon Mrs. Goadby would turn me out to make room for a younger girl. Sometimes I felt like one of the ropewalkers I'd seen at Ranelagh—on top of the world, but never more than a single misstep away from disaster.

When the Pantheon finally opened, in the winter of 1772, people of fashion flocked to it, some paying as much as fifty pounds for a ticket. Afterward, so many gentlemen visited our pleasure house Mrs. Goadby could barely contain her delight. When she took me and the other girls on our first outing to the place, its vast size left me in awe. The great dome of the rotunda soared to a height of four or five stories, with two tiers of pillared walkways on either side.

I was strolling along the upper colonnade one evening the following year when Mrs. Goadby hurried toward me. Her cheeks were flushed and her lace cap had fallen askew.

"You must assist me, Armistead!" She pulled me down onto one of the many sofas that lined the colonnade.

"Of course, ma'am. What's the matter?" It must be some dire calamity to have put her in such a fluster.

"Viscount Bolingbroke." Mrs. Goadby's fan worked furiously. "I kept company with the man when we were young, but I have not spoken to him in years. Just now he latched onto me and it was all I could do to get away."

"Did he harm you?" I peered down the gallery, expecting to see some rampant bull of a man charging toward us.

During my early days at Mrs. Goadby's, details of the viscount's sensational divorce had been all the tattle. As I recalled, his wife had accused him of brutality.

"Harm? No! He is feeling ... amorous." Mrs. Goadby looked torn between vexation and embarrassment. "He wants me to entertain him tonight like I did twenty years ago. Have I not worked and saved all these years so I'm no longer obliged to jump into bed at any man's whim? Not husband or keeper and certainly not Bully Bolingbroke!"

"What has that to do with me, ma'am?"

"You must fetch him back to the house and quiet him, of course. You have a way of making men agreeable, Armistead. I believe you would have made a good wife."

There was no chance of that now, not that I cared at the moment. I was more worried about being sent to tame the beastly Lord Bully. "Please, ma'am, could we not just gather the girls and slip out the side entrance?"

"He might only follow us and make a disturbance back at the house. Something like that could cost us business. Bully is a Gentleman of the King's Bedchamber, after all."

So I must placate him by making him a gentleman of *my* bedchamber? I did not dare refuse Mrs. Goadby – not at my age. In the world of high harlotry, three-and-twenty was old.

"Jane?" a rough rumbling voice called from down the gallery. "So this is where you've been hiding."

"I don't care what you have to do." Mrs. Goadby leaped to her feet. "Just keep Bully quiet and away from me!"

She shoved me in the direction of a tall, fair man who staggered toward us. I heard an urgent rustle of petticoats as she fled in the other direction.

"Don't run off, Jane!" Lord Bolingbroke moved faster, his gaze aimed past me. "We have so much to talk over."

"I beg your pardon, my lord." I stepped into his path as eagerly as I would have a speeding carriage. "Mrs. Goadby asked me to give you a message."

I feared he might knock me to the floor. But he stopped in time to avoid a collision, ending up toe-to-toe with me. Speechless, I stared up into a pair of startling blue eyes. My chief impression of the man was one of tremendous strength and vigor. At any other time, those qualities might have appealed to me. Tonight I would have preferred a delicate, fashionable *macaroni*—my image of a royal courtier.

"Wha' message?" The whiff of spirits on his breath was almost enough to set me tipsy. "Don't stand there dumb, girl!"

Though my knees were trembling under many layers of silk, I forced myself to meet his lordship's forceful stare. I beckoned him to bend closer. I had long ago learned that a whisper could command attention better than a bellow.

As Lord Bolingbroke leaned toward me, I brought my lips within a breath of his ear. "Mrs. Goadby bid me fetch you back to the house to wait for her. Will you come with me, my lord?"

He raised his head to look at me. Glimpsing a spark of interest in his eyes, I wavered between relief and alarm.

"I have no objection to quitting this place." The viscount offered me his arm. Through the thick blue velvet of his coat sleeve, I could feel stout muscle. "The endless round of masques and assemblies grows tiresome."

"What manner of amusement *do* you find diverting, my lord?" He did not strike me as an avid patron of the theatre, except perhaps to ogle pretty actresses. "Do you hunt?"

"Waste of good horse flesh, chasing all over the countryside after a damned fox."

"You must be a racing enthusiast, then." Blacklegs, they were called, for the high black riding boots they wore almost everywhere. I had shared my bed with several blacklegs who'd been eager to talk about their passion for the turf.

"Only breed the beasts, these days." As Lord Bolingbroke gingerly patted his left leg, I realized his staggering gait was partly due to a limp. "Ever since I got this."

"I should like to watch a horserace someday. I hear they are most exciting."

"They are, especially if you wager on the outcome. I have a promising filly in training that could make me a pretty penny if she's brought along right. It takes damned deep pockets to maintain a proper stable."

All the way back to Mrs. Goadby's, he rambled on about pedigrees, stakes and The Jockey Club. But once I got him settled in my sitting room with a fresh bottle of brandy, his conversation turned in another direction.

"They were there tonight, you know. The gall of them – mixing in respectable society. Her, a proven adulteress and him a shameless seducer of another man's wife! They're only accepted in company again because her brother's a duke and Beauclerk is a great favorite of old Dr. Johnson."

So Lord Bolingbroke had seen his former wife and her new husband at the Pantheon. Was that why he'd drank so much and pursued Mrs. Goadby?

"I could have tolerated Di straying." His lordship sounded more like a sulky schoolboy than a middle-aged royal courtier. "If only she'd been discreet. But to bear a bastard who might claim my title and property if any ill befell my boys?"

"You have children." Here was a subject that interested me more than the turf. "How old are they? What are their names?"

"George is twelve and young Fred, ten." Sincere paternal fondness tempered the viscount's bitter tone. "They have felt the loss of their mother. For their sakes I gave leave she might see them whenever she wishes, which has not been often."

"You are a kind father, to put the happiness of your children ahead of your own feelings."

"*You* are kind to say so." Lord Bolingbroke stared at me over the rim of his glass. A slow-building smile lit his face, hinting at the handsome looks of his youth. "Can you forgive my bad manners in being so tardy to ask your name?"

I had learned to spot the faintest hint of lust in a man's glance or tone. There was nothing faint about his lordship's interest. "No offense taken, my lord. I am Elizabeth Armistead."

"You are a fine filly, Mrs. Armistead." He pulled me down to receive a brandied kiss. "Can you go the distance?"

His robust masculinity roused me. "With you in the saddle, my lord?"

He responded with a hearty laugh. "Spirit—a fine quality on the turf or the mattress. I'll wager you could take a man on a wild gallop."

Our horsy banter and his bold seduction fermented a heady brew of desire within me. Laughing and kissing, we stumbled into my bedchamber, leaving a trail of clothes behind us. As we stripped off each elaborate garment, our passion grew hotter. By the time we reached the bed, we were as naked as Adam and Eve. Lord Bolingbroke rubbed against me with deep growls of pleasure, nudged my knees apart and plunged in.

I was ready for him—sensing I would have a race to claim my prize before he crossed the finish line. He buried his face in my hair, his breath hissing, hot and fast against my neck. I bucked beneath him and gave a blissful squeal as pleasure coursed through me. That was all the spur my stallion needed to bound to his own victory.

He fell into a drunken doze soon after. It was all I could do to squirm out from under him. The next morning he woke in a devilish temper on account of his sore head but I managed to soothe him. He lingered the rest of the day in my bed, talking more about his horses and a scheme he had to improve his fortunes by enclosing some moorland.

I put no faith in his lordship's promise to visit me again, so I was amazed when he returned a fortnight later and again a week after that. Soon he became a regular visitor and I developed a strange, vexing fondness for him. He reminded me of an overgrown pup who chewed slippers, shed hair over everything and frightened people with his ferocious bark, but who loved to romp and often seemed starved for affection.

One night, when we were in the middle of just such a lusty romp, I heard the pounding of several fists on my sitting room door and rowdy cries of, "Bully!"

I wondered how such a party of louts had gotten past Mrs. Goadby and Enoch.

"The crowd from my club," Bully growled. "I recognize Fox's voice. No doubt Bob and Fitz are with him."

"Perhaps if we keep quiet, they'll go away," I proposed in a hopeful whisper, "or Mrs. Goadby will have them tossed out."

"Damned if I will." Bully raised his voice to a bellow that filled a brief lull in the knocking and calling. "Clear off, you daft sots! Can a man not take his pleasure in peace?"

With a violent crash, my bedchamber door burst open and several men swarmed in. The wildly flickering flames of their candles made them look like a pack of demons.

I clutched for the bed sheet to cover myself as their lewd gazes roved over my bare body.

"Where are your manners, Bully," cried one of the intruders in a slurred voice, "not inviting your club mates for a drink? What will our French guest think of us?"

Another one clucked his tongue. "A shocking lapse!"

Bully lunged out of my bed. "Damned poxy whoresons!"

I had visions of a brawl breaking out in my bedchamber, like those in the taverns around Covent Garden, with furniture flying, windows smashing and blood flowing.

What if it grew violent enough to draw the watch and get Mrs. Goadby charged with keeping a disorderly house?

If that happened, she would not blame the gentleman. I would be the one to pay.

# Chapter Eight

"GENTLEMEN, PLEASE!" I YANKED THE sheet from the foot of my bed, wrapped it around myself and launched into the fray. Though frightened and mortified, I could not cower under the covers and lose the place I'd worked so hard to keep. "This is not a prize-fighting ring!"

"What about a bull-baiting pit?" asked a tall, strapping gentleman, who seemed the most likely candidate to have kicked in my door.

"Or a Bully-baiting one?" quipped another young fellow, with a prominent chin and a contagious twinkle in his eye.

A shorter gentleman with thick dark brows tossed his hat to my naked lover. "Cover yourself, man, for God sake! Before you make the rest of us feel sorely ill-endowed."

His companions howled with laughter. There were six of them, of all shapes, sizes and coloring. The one thing they had in common was that none looked a day over five-and-twenty. I was not surprised to discover Bully had a pack of wild young rascals as friends. He often reminded me of an overgrown boy.

He snatched the hat with violent force and thrust it over his naked loins.

"Admit it Bully," said the young man with the twinkling eyes. "You'd be the first to mount this kind of raid on any of us if the tables were turned."

"Damned impudent rubbish," Bully growled, but I sensed his rage was rapidly cooling. "How in blazes did you track me here?"

"We were enjoying a friendly game of faro at the club *avec Monsieur le Duc.*" The man who'd given Bully his hat nodded toward a slender man with dainty features. "And we fell into a dispute over which city has the finest pleasure houses – Paris or London. Once we'd lost all our money, we decided to take our friend on a tour to see first hand. When we heard you were here, we could not leave without paying our compliments."

"Pretty compliments." Bully stalked back to my bed. "Now that you've done your mischief, get the hell out!"

The gentlemen bowed to me and backed out of my bedchamber, chuckling. The one with the twinkling eyes was last to go and could not resist a parting quip. "Does this mean you're not going to offer us a drink?"

He ducked out an instant before one of my pillows came hurtling through the air at him.

I was sick with dread the next day when I answered my summons to Mrs. Goadby's sitting room.

Her grim frown did not soothe my nerves. "I cannot have this, Armistead. I knew Bully would be nothing but trouble."

"It wasn't his lordship's fault." My breath was racing so fast I could scarcely gasp out the words. "It was those rowdy fellows from his club. It certainly wasn't *my* fault! You were the one who ordered me to take up with Lord Bolingbroke."

The moment I spoke, I wished I'd held my tongue.

Mrs. Goadby rose from her chair, her calm, icy dignity quite at odds with my frantic dismay. "I told you to distract Bully and keep him from creating a disturbance. I did not say to make a conquest of him."

Was there more to this than a broken door? Did Mrs. Goadby feel slighted because I'd made Lord Bolingbroke forget her? It made no sense. She'd been so anxious to escape him that night at the Pantheon. But I knew when it came to men and vanity, women's feelings often defied reason.

"I promise nothing like this will happen again, ma'am."

She shook her head. "I'm sorry, Armistead. When it comes to Lord Bolingbroke that is not a promise you can keep. I do not want that man in my house and since you are what draws him here, I have no choice but to dispense with your services."

"Please, ma'am!" Though I knew it was hopeless, I sank to my knees and clasped my hands. "I've given you five years of faithful service."

"And been well rewarded for it." Mrs. Goadby looked offended that I might suggest otherwise. "The finest gowns, lodging, food, a doctor's care, a box at the theatre, trips to the pleasure gardens – what more could a young woman require?"

"Another chance, ma'am, that's all I'm asking. I have nowhere to go. What will become of me if I lose my place here?"

At every plea, Mrs. Goadby's mouth pursed tighter, until it seemed in danger of disappearing. Her gray eyes were as cold and impenetrable as a winter fog. "I cannot afford to make that my concern. Charity is an admirable trait in a great lady with a large income, but not in a business woman who must make her own way in the world."

She held out a slender packet wrapped in paper. "This should tide you over until you find a new situation."

The money might last me until summer if I was careful. It was a bribe to get me away from here without causing a fuss and perhaps to salve her conscience, if she had one. But if I did not take it, I would have nothing.

Mrs. Goadby dangled the packet above me. I could not reach it if I stayed on my knees. So I struggled to my feet and grabbed the money before she changed her mind. I was allowed to take my clothes, perhaps because I was too tall for them to fit any of the other girls. But I had to leave the house while they were off for a drive in the park. I was not permitted to say goodbye. I disappeared, like so many others before me.

That thought might have made me weep, but I could not afford the weakness of tears just then. To survive, I must keep moving up in the world, not down. I could think of only one way to make that happen, though the odds were very long against it.

But I must take the gamble and trust to luck.

"Are ye certain this is the place ye want, ma'am?" The hackney driver nodded toward a brick building on Pall Mall, only a few steps from the narrow entry to King's Place, where many of Mrs. Goadby's competitors had premises. "A gentleman's club, they call it. Naught but a gambling den, if ye ask me."

Only a short while ago, the bells of Westminster had chimed midnight, yet lights flickered in the upstairs windows.

"This is it." I could scarcely hear myself speak for the blood pounding in my ears. "I should not be long, if you would be so kind as to wait for me."

"Aye, ma'am." He helped me down from the coach. "Ye won't be long, for ye won't get in the door. Places like these only admit members and guests, and no women on any account."

I inhaled a draft of clammy night air as if it were a potion to steel my nerve. "They will admit me."

Let Lord Bolingbroke's friends see how they liked having an intruder trespass on *their* private place in the middle of the night! I wished I had half-a-dozen others with me, including one strong enough to kick down doors. Since there was only one of me, I would have to gain entry by feminine wiles rather than manly brawn.

Pausing before the door of the club, I pulled out my handkerchief. For a moment, I imagined what would become of me if my desperate plan failed. My powers of fancy had not weakened from childhood, though they had taken a darker turn. Soon tears were streaming down my cheeks.

I rapped on the door. The moment it began to open, I threw my weight against it and launched myself into the arms of the middle-aged man inside.

"Lord Bolingbroke," I sobbed. "Please, you must take me to him! There's been a terrible ... I have urgent news for him!"

"I'll fetch him, ma'am!" The poor porter recoiled from me in horror as I'd hoped he would. In my experience, most men would rather deal with an armed highwayman than a weeping woman. "Wait here. I'll be back with his lordship in a trice."

He scrambled up the stairs at a speed that would have done credit to one of Bully's racehorses. When he had cleared the first landing, I followed, mopping my tears as I climbed.

Upon reaching the second floor, I pushed open a set of double doors that stood ajar. I strode into a large, brightly lit room furnished with a great number of tables. Around each table, playing cards lay upon the floor in deep drifts.

The place was crowded with gentlemen dressed in the oddest assortment of garments I had ever seen. Some had on coarse woollen frieze coats, while others wore their own coats turned inside out. Several had on leather sleeve guards such as footmen wore for cleaning silver. Many sported high-crowned straw hats trimmed with flowers and ribbons.

A few of the gentlemen turned to glance at me when I entered, but most kept on playing. The buzz of voices, the clink of coins and the rattle of dice filled the air, together with wine fumes and clouds of pipe smoke. I peered around anxiously for the porter. Finally, I spotted him at a nearby table speaking to a masked man.

"Mrs. Armistead?" Bully pulled off his mask as I approached. "What the deuce are you doing here? And what great calamity is this fellow blathering about?"

"Only that your friends' rowdy prank last night cost me my place at Mrs. Goadby's!" Enraged that some of them ignored me to continue playing cards, I grabbed the deck out of the dealer's hand.

That got me their attention. More masks came off to reveal what I'd suspected. Lord Bolingbroke was happily amusing himself with the very men who'd burst in on us the night before.

"Is that all?" Bully puffed out his broad lower lip. "Then I shall take you into keeping. I was getting tired of my latest mistress, anyway."

His offer surprised and touched me. But going into Bully's keeping would be a temporary solution at best. I knew about his money troubles and had no faith at all in his far-fetched enclosure scheme. Moreover, he might cut me loose at a moment's notice, like his current mistress, of whom I'd known nothing.

My best hope was to pursue my original plan. "I thank you for your generous offer, my lord. But your friends are more to blame for my situation than you are. I think it only fair they should contribute to my rescue."

They stared at me as if I was mad, in an amusing way.

"What would you have us do, ma'am?" cried one. "Set you up as our banker at *quinze?* I would not mind losing so much if it was to a beautiful woman."

His quip eased my sense of desperation. "It is a tempting offer, sir. But I have another position in mind. One I believe you can assist me to obtain, if you are equal to the challenge."

"Challenge?" Another man flicked a golden *rouleau*, worth twenty pounds, in the air and caught it again. "Good Lord, Bully, your lady friend has taken our measure to the groat!"

"Hasn't she just?" agreed the swarthy man with thick brows, whom I now recognized as the celebrated politician, Charles Fox. "The only thing we have a harder time resisting than a challenge is temptation. What are you angling for, my dear, a place in the Treasury?"

"Hardly, sir." Their amusement at my intrusion boosted my confidence. "I seek a place I am well qualified to fill."

"What a novel idea." Mr. Fox chuckled. "Giving places to people qualified to fill them, rather than those who can bring the most influence to bear. You must be a Wilkesite, madam."

Did these men take anything seriously except indulging their own reckless pleasure? I reminded myself how well that qualified *them* for my purposes.

"My aim, gentlemen, is to become the most sought-after courtesan in the kingdom. With a little assistance, I believe I can do it." I spread their cards like a fan and fluttered them in front of my face. "May I count on your support?"

"Courtesan, eh? Like the exquisite Mrs. Baddeley?"

"Better," I declared, made bold by a potent brew of hope, "for I am prettier."

"Damned if you aren't." A smile of radiant sweetness lightened Mr. Fox's swarthy features. "This challenge sounds like fine sport. Are we in, gentlemen? It seems the least we can do for the poor lady after the trouble we caused her. Would that all our scrapes could be so easily remedied."

"She must have French lessons," said one of his friends.

"And her portrait painted by Reynolds," suggested another. "Don't you agree, Charles?"

Mr. Fox nodded. "What about the stage? Have you ever acted my dear?"

They were going to do it! I wanted to toss my handful of cards in the air and dance around the room, but I managed to restrain myself. "I'm certain I could learn."

"It is settled, then," said Mr. Fox. "Bully will set her up in lodgings. Richard will find her a French master. Bob will arrange her display in gallery and I shall manage her acting debut. She will soon be all the fashion!"

His friends murmured in agreement.

"In that case," Bully plucked the cards from my hand, "can we get back to our game before my luck sours?"

The gentlemen turned their backs on me like children who had suddenly lost interest in some passing novelty.

I followed the club porter out of the gaming room, not certain whether to be elated or terrified by what I'd just done. Would Bully's friends forget our bargain as soon as I was out of their sight?

Fortunately Bully's friends seemed to take their obligation to me more seriously than their gambling debts.

The very next day, Bully found me lodgings in Piccadilly, not far from their club. My landlady had three suites of rooms she let to young women in keeping. Though they were not nearly as spacious or elegant as those at Mrs. Goadby's, I was happy with them. I felt like a songbird released from a golden cage. Though I would have to hunt for my own crumbs and beware of predators, I could now fly as high as my wings would take me.

I had no idea, then, how very high that would be.

I soon became acquainted with my new patrons as each played his part in preparing me to become a courtesan.

Not long after I had settled into my new lodgings, one of them paid me a call. He was a tall, ruggedly handsome man with the lean, muscular build and proud bearing of a soldier. I suspected he was the one responsible for kicking in my door that fateful night at Mrs. Goadby's.

"Richard Fitzpatrick at your service, ma'am." He managed a courtly bow, though his arms were full of books and magazines. "Allow me to present your French master, M. Boucher." He nodded toward a smaller man, similarly laden with reading matter.

I invited them into my sitting room and rang for chocolate.

"These are for you," said Mr. Fitzpatrick as he and the French master set the books onto my tea table. "Charles Fox and I discussed our campaign to assist you. We agreed you will need more than beauty and spirit to succeed as a courtesan."

I eyed the tottering pile of books with a mixture of interest and apprehension. "I look forward to reading them, Mr. Fitzpatrick."

"Do call me Richard," he bid me with an air of such careless charm, I could not resist, "or Fitz if you'd rather. My friends and I seldom stand on ceremony. Mind you keep up with your studies, for some of us are apt to quiz you over dinner or during a drive in the park."

"As you wish ... Richard." I stumbled over even the less casual of the two names. Despite his rakish reputation, the gentleman had a distinguished air that put me a little in awe of him.

When Lord Robert Spencer insisted I call him Bob, the informality came with ease. Everything about his looks suggested impish humor, from his shock of fair hair and ever-twinkling eyes to his wide, ready grin and long Punchinello chin. I was not surprised to discover he was known as Comical Spencer.

Bob had arranged for Sir Joshua Reynolds to paint my portrait. He accompanied me to my first sitting at the great artist's studio in nearby Leicester Fields, calming my nerves with his cheerful banter.

"So," I asked, "have you and the others been friends for a very long time?"

He nodded. "Since our school days. We all seemed to flock around Charles. He was such a friendly young rogue and full of spirits."

From what I'd seen, his character had not changed since then. Charles Fox was clearly the leader of the group, to whom his friends looked for inspiration and approval. I had never met anyone who flung himself into every activity with such gusto. The man seemed determined to squeeze the experience and enjoyment of three lives into the span of one.

"Back then," Bob continued, "we called ourselves *The Spares*, because we are all younger sons. My elder brother is the Duke of Marlborough, Richard's is the Earl of Ossory. Charles's brother Ste is the heir to Lord Holland's enormous fortune. He is also wed to one of Richard's lovely sisters, the lucky dog. But it's a fine life being a spare. We are not saddled with the responsibilities and expectations that burden our poor brothers. Yet bankers are willing to lend us money in the hope we might inherit one day, Heaven forbid!"

Even as I laughed at Bob's feigned horror, I mulled over what he'd said, trying to make sense of my clever but irresponsible patrons.

As we waited in the gallery outside Sir Joshua's studio, Bob waved a hand toward several portraits clustered together on one wall. "Sir Joshua has painted all the fashionable impures – Kitty Fisher, Nelly O'Brien, Polly Jones, Nancy Parsons. Now that I think of it, Bully has kept most of them at one time or another, so you will be in first-rate company."

Pretty faces peered out of their frames with enticing stares, unlike the well-bred ladies who cast their eyes downward or directed cool gazes off into the distance. The courtesans' direct gazes promised wicked delights to any man with the fortune to claim them. I vowed to practice such looks in my mirror as faithfully as I studied my French lessons and read the books Charles Fox had loaned me.

Mr. Fox seemed to be on Bob's mind as well. "Charles says if we are to launch you into high fashion, we must make a proper study of the subject. I volunteered to quiz the Cyprians of my acquaintance about the tricks of their trade."

"How kind of you to put yourself to so much trouble on my account." I teased.

"It was a great inconvenience and vastly tiresome, I assure you." Bob struggled to keep a sober face. "But never let it be said a Spencer shirked his duty in amusing fair ladies!"

The soufflé of his wit was spiced with flirtation. I toyed with the notion of inviting a man into my bed for no other reason than because I liked him.

"And being amused by them in turn, no doubt." I pursed my lips in a seductive challenge. I did need practice, after all.

"Naturally, if the opportunity arises." A provocative huski-ness in Bob's chuckle made the flesh on the back of my neck pucker, as if his lips had grazed over it.

Before our flirtation could progress farther, Sir Joshua appeared to summon us into his studio. He was a middle-aged man of middle height with blunt features and a cleft chin. Had it not been for the color-spattered palette in his left hand and the whiff of linseed oil that hung about him, I might have fancied him a prosperous man of business rather than a fashionable portrait painter.

He shook Bob's hand. "Good to see you getting out of the club now and then, my boy. So this is your young protégé? *Enchanté*, my dear. What a fine profile you have ... and such hair! We must make every effort to show them both to advantage."

Sir Joshua ushered us into a spacious room cluttered with almost as many props as the backstage of a playhouse. A mixture of sharp, unfamiliar smells made my nose twitch.

While he and Bob chatted about various members of the Spencer family he had painted over the years, Sir Joshua sat me down and proceeded to pose me. With brisk movements and an assured touch, he eased down the left sleeve of my gown to expose my shoulder then unpinned a lock of hair to coil over my bare neck. But the caressing warmth of his fingertips upon my skin made me wonder if his intent was as businesslike as it might appear to an onlooker.

When he finished arranging me to his satisfaction, he pulled up a chair for Bob. "Sit there, if you would be so kind, and engage the lady's attention. Otherwise, I fear she will keep looking toward me and spoil the profile."

"Only if you promise not to paint me in." Bob spread his coat tails and seated himself with a droll flourish. "I look quite sulky in that portrait you did of me after my Grand Tour."

As Sir Joshua scuttled back behind his easel, Bob grinned at me. "What should I talk about to keep you occupied?"

Perhaps he could tell me how he intended to charm his way into my bed tonight? I felt certain he meant to try. "You might relate a few of the secrets you learned about what it takes to become a successful courtesan."

Was there some new carnal act I should master? Some exotic position?

Bob flicked a furtive glance at Sir Joshua then leaned toward me. His eyes glittered with salacious intrigue.

"You must learn something ... obscene," he whispered.

"Yes?" My breath quickened.

"You must learn how to spend *obscene* amounts of money."

"Spend money? You rogue!"

A few hours after leaving Sir Joshua's studio, I nestled on Bob Spencer's lap in my sitting room and pretended to throttle him. "I thought you were going to reveal some exciting new skill of the bedchamber."

"Was that all you wanted to know?" Bob loosened my hands from around his neck and planted a kiss on each palm. "In that case, there is an amusing trick I learned from a true *courtezana* in Tuscany. I would be delighted to teach it to you."

"All in the spirit of fulfilling your obligation to me." I leaned forward as if I meant to kiss him, then changed course to nuzzle his neck instead.

"Naturally." He tugged my sleeve down to bare my shoulder, as Sir Joshua had. "Never let it be said a Spencer shirks his duty ..."

"Was it true what you told me about spending money?" I asked as I untied his neck cloth. "Or were you only teasing?"

"Would I jest about two such solemn subjects as sex and money?" He peppered my bare shoulder with tickling kisses.

"I think you would jest about anything!" I relished the novelty of toying with a man for the sheer joy of it.

"Possibly." Bob edged the low neckline of my bodice lower still. "But this time I am in earnest. I got it straight from Nancy Parsons who is the highest authority. She told me the difference between a courtesan and every other kind of harlot is that the rest are for private pleasure while the courtesan is meant to be flaunted in public."

"Indeed?" I giggled as my breasts popped free of my stays. "Do tell me more."

"Let us retire to your bed," he murmured, "and I promise you a full account of all my painstaking research."

"I doubt there was much pain involved." I arched up to graze one pert nipple over his lips. "But I should like to hear more results of your *pleasure*-staking study."

We withdrew to my bedchamber where Bob proceeded to remove my clothes and his. When his mouth was not otherwise occupied, he told me more secrets he had coaxed from the Cyprian sister-hood. His husky whispers and seductive murmurs stimulated me almost as much as the skilful play of his hands, lips and tongue.

"The sort of man who keeps a grand courtesan does not feather a little love nest for her and hide her away from the world. Quite the contrary. He squires her to the opera and the pleasure gardens, where her modish gown and expensive jewels puff his wealth and exquisite taste for all to see ... and envy."

His breath raced in a sultry hiss and his fingers slithered over me. "Lust ... pride ... avarice ... envy. A courtesan personifies the goddess of pleasure and sin."

His serpent slid home and seared me with wicked delight.

# Chapter Nine

**M**Y PORTRAIT HAD BEEN HANGING for a few weeks in Sir Joshua's "gallery of gallantry" when Charles Fox invited me to attend the premiere of a new play at Covent Garden with him and his friends. "In light of Bob's fascinating discoveries, Richard suggested we undertake a campaign that combines publicity and mystery. That should pique curiosity about you in the right quarters."

"Publicity and mystery?" I glanced around the interior of Richard's carriage at each of them, hoping to find a clue to Charles's riddle. "How will you contrive two such opposites?"

"Fiendishly clever, is it not?" Richard looked well pleased with himself. "Your portrait is a perfect example. Everyone who visits Sir Joshua's gallery sees it."

"That means everyone of consequence in London," added Bob.

"When they notice your fair likeness hanging between Kitty Fisher's and Nelly O'Brien's," Richard continued, "they know your company must be available for hire. But that is all they know. Not a name, address or background. A curious gentleman asks his friends about you. Word spreads."

"This evening should further fan the flames." Bob chuckled. "Since most people go to the playhouse as much to watch other members of the audience as the actors onstage."

I recalled my first visit to Drury Lane. My heart ached at the memory of Nell, like an old injury that had never quite healed. I hoped she had found a kind, wealthy gentleman to keep her in style. "A friend once told me the point of going to the playhouse was not to watch but to *be seen*."

Charles Fox nodded. "That could be said of most places of public entertainment."

"You will certainly be seen tonight," said Richard. "And in the company of three of the most infamous young rakes in London. We shall arrive just as the play begins and leave before the actors have finished their bows. That should set tongues wagging."

Once we had taken our seats and the play began, I was far less certain anyone would notice me. But I was so well entertained, I hardly cared. Mr. Goldsmith's new play, *She Stoops to Conquer*, soon had all the members of our party convulsed with laughter.

"That Young Marlow sounds just like you, Charles." Richard nudged his friend during the intermission. "He'll have nothing to do with women of his own class, either! Will some poor lady have to masquerade as a tavern wench to win your heart?"

"It would take more than that, my friend. *J'ai nulle inclination pour le marriage, et que rien ne m'y pourroit engager.*" Charles turned to me with a glint of mischief in his dark eyes. "What do you say to that, Mrs. Armistead?"

"You have no inclination for marriage whatsoever." I did not find the translation difficult. "And nothing could induce you to engage in it. What if a lady had a very great fortune?"

I'd heard Charles had been duped by a professional matchmaker who'd promised to find him a West Indian heiress.

I thought he might be vexed at me for alluding to his old embarrassment, but he laughed more heartily at himself than he ever did at others. "The worst of all possible reasons! Though that transient madness called *love* runs a close second. Friendship is the only real happiness in the world."

Bob and Richard nodded in vigorous agreement. Recalling my disastrous passion for Ned Armistead and Mrs. Goadby's shrewd advice, I too endorsed the sentiment.

"Charles," said Bob, "have you had any luck persuading David Garrick to give Mrs. Armistead a part in one of his plays?"

"Not so far. With two sought-after beauties in his company already, the poor man is not anxious to court trouble by introducing a younger rival."

When I could not hide my disappointment, Charles gave my hand an encouraging pat. "Do not fret. Being one more beauty among many would not show you to best advantage. I reckon you would be better off here at Covent Garden. I will have a word with Mr. Colman and see what he can do for you."

For the next few months it seemed as if Charles Fox and his friends were doing far more to keep me a secret than to publicize my existence. The theatres closed for the summer with nothing decided about my going on stage. By the time they opened again in the fall, would anyone remember or care about the mystery lady among Reynolds's many portraits?

My amusing little affair with Bob Spencer lasted no longer than the spring blossoms. Truthfully, I felt more relief than regret when it had run its brief course. I was not accustomed to sharing my bed with a man except on straightforward commercial terms. Without that tidy exchange of fee for service, relations between the partners became far more complicated. I was afraid one of us might begin to feel more for the other than either of us could afford.

When Bully asked me to accompany him to the races in Berkshire then spend the summer with him and his sons at his estate in Wiltshire, I asked if he had heard anything more about his friends' promise to me.

Bully shrugged. "Nothing can be done about it at this time of year, with polite society disbursed to the four corners of the kingdom. Besides, Charles has more important matters to occupy him than your stage debut. His parents are both dying and Lord knows what will become of him then."

"The poor man!" Though I felt a twinge of shame for being so occupied with my own interests, I reminded myself that no one else would care what became of me if I did not.

Bully seemed less concerned about the prospect of his friend's personal loss than his financial one. "For as long as I've known him, Charles has borrowed against his expectations, but he will soon have to pay the piper."

As Bully had predicted, Charles's parents died that summer within six weeks of one another. We heard Lady Holland had left him an inheritance that would have supported me in luxury for the rest of my life. But Charles seemed determined to gamble it all away before a penny ever came into his hands. Since my dearest desire in the world was a small measure of security, his actions bewildered and vexed me.

I could not stay angry with him, however. Especially not after he came all the way to Bully's estate in Wiltshire with news for me.

"My dear Mrs. Armistead." He bowed over my hand and looked sincerely delighted to see me again. "You must not suppose I have forgotten about speaking to Mr. Colman on your behalf. As it happens, he has no new plays for the winter season and hopes to satisfy his audiences' thirst for novelty by engaging a few new players. I assured him your appearance would attract a very good crowd of fashionable gentlemen."

"So it shall," declared Bully, "If we have to chase the whole company from Almack's down to Covent Garden!"

Charles nodded. "Mr. Colman desires you to call on him at your earliest convenience."

"How good of you to remember, when you have so many other matters to occupy you." I regretted thinking ill of him. What he did with his fortune was no business of mine. "I shall go to Covent Garden the moment we return to town."

"I believe you will do very well for the part of Indiana, my dear." Mr. Colman handed me a playbook of Richard Steele's

*The Conscious Lovers.* "Rehearsals begin next week with a view to opening early in October."

I had the part? No good thing in my life had ever come to me so easily. "Thank you, sir. I look forward to it. I shall work very hard to do the role justice, I promise you."

The manager smiled at me in a manner I recognized all too well. "Not so hard that you lose sleep and dim those pretty eyes, I hope."

I could tell he did not care if I was as stiff as wood on stage. He only wanted to draw a crowd of free-spending young bucks by putting me on display. Though that suited my purposes, I vowed to give a performance that would make the audience take notice and do my father's memory proud.

For the next few weeks, I applied all my energies toward learning my part and performing it well. I soon discovered playacting was far more difficult than it looked from my seat in a fashionable box.

Memorizing my part was only the beginning. I had to speak loud enough that I could be heard above the noise from the upper gallery, yet not sound as if I were shouting every word. I also had to infuse the words with feeling that suited the character and the situation. I had to accompany my lines with fitting gestures to make them more than a static recitation. By the time the curtain rose on my first performance, I had gained a new respect for even the worst of actors.

I could not say the same for the play, a comedy very scant in humor but loaded with contrivances. As for my character, the poor but virtuous heroine, her situation reminded me too much of my own with Ned Armistead. How could Indiana be so naïve not to question the motives of a man who provided her with every comfort yet claimed to want nothing in return?

How could *I* have been?

Hovering in the wings awaiting my cue, I heard the audience crow with laughter. Perhaps they recognized themselves in the description of the coxcomb's servant: "The men of pleasure of the age; the top-gamesters ... false lovers; have a taste of music, poetry, billet-deux, dress, politicks, ruin damsels ..."

I made my entrance in the next act, strolling onstage with Mrs. Kennedy, an experienced, kind-hearted actress who played the part of my aunt.

The moment I looked out into the theatre and saw so many gentlemen staring at me, I felt like I had when Bully's friends discovered us in bed together at Mrs. Goadby's—only much worse. At least then there had only been a few of them and they were on my territory. Now there were hundreds and I was at their mercy. True I was not naked, but at the moment that seemed small consolation.

My legs began to tremble violently beneath my skirts. And when I tried to speak my first line, nothing would come out.

"Truly, my dear, it wasn't as bad as you think." In his bluff, awkward way, Bully tried to comfort me as I wept tears of humiliation and failure into a sodden handkerchief.

His carriage trundled westward toward Piccadilly with Charles, Richard and Bob squeezed into the seat opposite us.

"P-please take me home," I sobbed. "Forgive me for performing so ill after the trouble you took to get me the part and persuade so many of your friends to see me. I wish I could give them their money back."

"Nonsense." Bob sounded as unruffled by my disastrous debut as he was by his own gaming losses. "Colman made a point of billing this as your first appearance on a public stage. The audience expected you to be nervous. I reckon they'd have been disappointed otherwise."

"Besides," added Richard, "a ... subdued demeanor suited a chaste, modest heroine like Indiana. If there had been more ladies in the audience, I'm certain they would have been most affected by your performance."

"The *play* was vile." Charles gave one of his infectious chuckles that tempted me to smile through my tears. "I cannot abide sentimental comedies. Give me the bawdy humor of Farquhar or the pungent wit of Congreve any night. But you were *seen*, my dear, and that was the object of the exercise, was it not?"

Even as I sniffled, I had to nod.

Perhaps in an effort to distract me, Bully abruptly changed the subject. "How goes it in Parliament, lads? Any closer to settling all this agitation in the colonies?"

For several years the news from America had been disturbing, not that I'd paid it much heed. Lately, the colonial assemblies had resolved not to trade with England and had raised a volunteer militia.

"You should have heard Charles's latest speech." Richard fairly glowed with pride in his friend. "He said Lord North's policy was 'framed on false information, conceived in weakness and ignorance and executed with negligence.' By heaven, if he had half the skill at gambling that he has at debate, he would be as rich as *nabob!*"

I had never taken an interest in politics before. In my experience, the workings of Parliament never made much difference to the lives of people like me. But hearing Charles and his friends discuss the American situation so passionately stirred my sense of fairness. It seemed the King's Ministry was treating the colonies much the way Mrs. Goadby treated her girls. We'd never had anyone to seek justice on our behalf. I was glad the exploited colonies had such an eloquent champion in Charles Fox ... even if he and his friends were far outnumbered.

"Have you seen the review of your performance?" Bob Spencer waved a copy of *Westminster Magazine* under my nose when he, Charles and Richard called at my lodgings a fortnight after my stage debut. "It says your fears subdued your powers of utterance, but it praises your lusty figure and compares your voice and profile to Mrs. Cibber, which is high flattery."

The three of them looked mighty cheerful for being so bleary-eyed and unshaven. Though it was near noon, I suspected they had just come from gambling all night at their club.

"Mr. Colman seemed tolerably pleased with my reception." I beckoned them in and rang for coffee though bowls of hot soup might have done them more good. "He asked me to play the role twice more this month and to understudy the heroine in *A Winter's Tale*. I shall have to sing a song for that, but I believe I can manage it."

"Capital!" Charles beamed. "Did you make it clear you are not to appear on the playbill under your own name?"

I nodded. "He has promised to list me as 'A Novice to the Stage' or some such. Do you reckon it still matters whether my name gets about?"

"Without a doubt. Curiosity about you has been building and the time will soon be ripe to make our move." Charles nudged Richard, who handed me sheaf of banknotes. "Fortune smiled on all three of us last night, which is a passing rare event. We agreed you should take this and have some new gowns made up to prepare for your launch."

"New gowns for me? But surely ... your creditors ..."

Charles waved away my objections. "It is the best use this money could be put to. You know if we keep it, we will only lose it again and more. This way, you will be saving us from ourselves and the tradesmen will benefit. Be sure to order a splendid costume in the character of Queen Elizabeth. There is to be a masquerade at the Pantheon early in the New Year. How better to launch you as Queen of the Cyprians than for us to portray your courtiers?"

Queen Elizabeth! I let out a squeal of delight more fitting to a novice of fifteen than a seasoned *Thais* of five-and-twenty.

"I mean to go as Sir Walter Raleigh," said Richard, "and Charles must personate Shakespeare for no one apart from Garrick knows his plays better."

"I call Francis Drake!" cried Bob. "I will look quite the dashing rogue with a ring in my ear."

"You will need no help to *be* one," I teased him, relieved that our friendship had survived a few tumbles in bed.

By the evening of the masquerade, I was aflutter with excitement and nerves. I could hardly wait to show off my costume, a splendid white satin gown in the Tudor style, trimmed with gold beads and lace. The starched lace ruff around my neck felt very strange, but it did force me to hold my chin up and keep my back straight.

"You carry yourself like a queen, my dear," Richard whispered as he and his friends escorted me through the rotunda. "More so than our present one. She cannot match you for stature and is constantly breeding, poor woman."

He glanced over at Bob. "How many cots in the royal nursery these days? An even dozen yet?"

"No more than ten, but that is still a prodigious family. With so many healthy young princes, England will not have to worry about the succession in our lifetimes."

My escorts' banter kept me in constant smiles and laughter. Thus they presented me in the most favorable manner to any gentlemen watching. And there were quite a number of those. Whenever my attention strayed for an instant, I would catch the gaze of one or another. Before long, they were not content to stare, but began to approach our party.

A very tall, fair-haired gentleman offered Charles his hand. "My dear fellow, one scarcely sees you these days. What lures you away from Almack's', tonight?"

"Good evening, Cholmondeley." Charles greeted the man as if nothing in the world could please him more than their meeting. "My friends and I could not resist this opportunity to squire the divine Mrs. Armistead. She is one queen of hearts who trumps all others!"

Richard leaned closer and whispered in my ear. "Pretend to take no notice. Laugh as if I have just made you a scandalous suggestion."

I did as Richard bid me, giving a far better acting job than

I had on the stage at Covent Garden. But I also kept one ear open for the gentleman's reply to Charles. "Indeed? This is the first I have heard of the lady."

"It may be the first you have heard of her," replied Charles, "but I doubt it will be the last. Her portrait hangs beside Kitty Fisher's in Sir Joshua's gallery and she recently appeared on stage at Covent Garden. My friends and I are altogether enchanted with her."

"Ah, *that* lady." It seemed the gentleman had heard of me, after all. "Could I persuade you to introduce me?"

"Delighted to oblige an old school chum." Charles took my hand and drew me forward. "Mrs. Armistead, allow me to present the Earl of Cholmondeley. There are few men in the kingdom with a better eye for beauty."

As I curtsied to the earl, I overheard Bob mutter, "Fewer still are better equipped to bed the beauties they spy."

"Mrs. Armistead." Lord Cholmondeley bowed low over my hand. "Might I beg the honor of a dance?"

I was about to accept when Richard stepped forward and took my arm. "You may beg all you like, old fellow, but the lady is already promised to me for this set and I must claim the honor before she is besieged with offers."

"Richard," I protested as he drew me toward the south apse, where the orchestra was striking up a minuet, "what are you playing at? Your friends spend all this time and money to launch me as a courtesan then you drag me away from the first gentleman who shows an interest. A pleasant-looking young gentleman, too."

"Never fear." Richard gave my hand a reassuring squeeze as we began the slow, graceful steps of the dance. "Cholmondeley will not lose interest in you because he perceives a little competition for your favors. Quite the contrary, in fact."

"But you are *not* competing for my favors." I sometimes wished Richard might betray that sort of interest in me, for he was by far the most attractive of my three friends. "Bob says the only women you ever seduce are other men's wives."

"What trumpery! I would never do such a thing." Richard's wide mouth twisted in a devilish grin. "But if *they* set out to seduce me, I am willing to submit. Here's a piece of advice for you. If Cholmondeley bids for your favors, charge him by the inch—the fellow is hung like one of Bully's stud stallions."

"So that's what Bob's muttered jest was about." I laughed so hard, I could scarcely catch my breath.

"Poor Cholmondeley got ragged mercilessly at school. At least until Charles put a stop to it."

That did not surprise me. I had often heard Charles spring to the defence of someone who was being abused. "How did he manage that, pray?"

Richard chuckled. "By telling all the other boys that those who tormented Cholmondeley the worst must be the ones with the greatest reason to envy him."

Schoolboys being what they were, it must have taken a special blend of charm and courage to carry off such a remark without getting beaten to a bloody pulp. More and more I was coming to understand why Charles's friends idolized him so.

The rest of the night continued as it had begun, with Charles and the others parading me about, introducing me to gentlemen of title and wealth. But the moment I received an invitation to dance or sup or retire to the card room, Bob or Richard would claim a prior commitment and whisk me away for a cup of wine or another minuet.

Was this some sort of bluff by which they intended to raise the stakes and encourage higher bids for me? I hoped I had not made a disastrous error placing my whole future in the hands of such reckless gamblers.

# Chapter Ten

I WOKE WITH A SICKENING JOLT the next day to a frantic burst of knocking on my door and the shrill cries of my landlady. "Mrs. Armistead, can you come? Please!"

I dragged myself from bed, my neck stiff and chafed from the unfamiliar ruff. My feet ached from parading about the Pantheon all night in a brand new pair of slippers. When I glanced in the looking glass above my dressing table, a pasty-faced creature with swollen eyes and tumbled hair peered back at me. She did not look like anyone a gentleman of taste would pay more than a few shillings for.

Was I mad to imagine I could become a courtesan? I wondered how much longer Charles and his friends would pursue their campaign if it did not yield results. Though I had become quite fond of all three, I knew better than to fancy them men of steady purpose, especially where women were concerned.

I longed to crawl back into bed, burrow under the covers and ignore my landlady's urgent summons. But it was no use. All my striving to make a better life for myself *might* come to nothing, but giving up *surely* would.

Dashing away a cowardly tear with the back of my hand, I pulled on my dressing gown and opened my door a crack. "I will be down as soon as I get dressed. What is wrong?"

"Not a thing in the world for you." My landlady thrust a nosegay of flowers toward me along with two boxes. "But I have three footmen sitting in my parlor awaiting whatever messages you might wish to send their masters. They are being so uncivil to one another I fear it will end in a brawl if you do not satisfy them!"

For a moment I could not grasp what was happening.

"What is all this?" I sniffed the flowers and lifted the top of one box to discover a luxurious fur muff.

"They look like tokens of admiration to me." My landlady ran her hand over the muff. "Signs of interest in bidding for your favors."

I slid my hand inside the muff. It was lined with luxurious satin and ... something else. I pulled out a sheaf of banknotes, gasping when I tallied their value.

"Something to prove the gentleman is seriously interested. And see this?" My landlady turned the nosegay of flowers upside down. Holding the stems together was not a length of ribbon, but a gold ring set with a large sparkling diamond.

"Oh, my." Suddenly light-headed, I stumbled backward and collapsed onto a footstool.

I wished Charles, Richard and Bob had been there just then, for I would have given each one a kiss he would *never* forget.

Armed with my newfound wealth, I descended upon the merchants of Mayfair like a starved child set loose in a pastry shop. My deep craving for security urged me to live frugally and save for the future. But every time I was shown a pert new bonnet, a length of fine lace or a fashion book from Paris with pictures of the latest gowns, Bob Spencer's seductive advice whispered in my thoughts. "Spend *obscene* amounts of money."

"What do you think of this one, ma'am?" The mantua-maker held up a tinted fashion plate. "It arrived just the other day from Paris. Notice the neckline – none of your sharp V's or boxy square cuts, but a soft, graceful oblong trimmed with gauze ruffles. It will show a fine bust like yours to perfection."

"Very pretty indeed, Mrs. Whitelock."

"And look at what they've done with the bodice? Rosettes

down the front instead of bows. That sort of novel detail marks a true setter of fashion."

She beckoned forward two of her assistants, girls about the age I'd been when I began working at Mrs. Goadby's. Between them they held a length of lavender-colored taffeta.

"Would the gown not look lovely made up in this fabric?" asked Mrs. Whitelock. "Trimmed with a darker shade of violet, perhaps? Or ..."

"Not lavender." Though eight years had passed, even a glimpse of that shade took me back to the night I'd discovered Ned in the molly-house. "The color does not suit me. Have you something brighter?"

Mrs. Whitelock waved her assistants away with the taffeta. "I did purchase a bolt of turquoise satin from the mercer just last week, ma'am. I'd hoped to offer it to young Mrs. Eliot, but the poor creature is being divorced by her husband for receiving the attentions of Lord Valentia. She will not be venturing out in Society for awhile, I'll warrant."

"I have read about her in the scandal magazines." Together with gossip from my friseur and mantua-maker, those publications were my chief source of information about Society.

Did I despise or pity Grace Eliot, dubbed "Dally the Tall" for her willowy height and her maiden name, Dalrymple? I could not decide. Part of me wanted to believe I would have been faithful to a husband if I'd had the luck to wed a man able to take care of me. But could I have been content with a dour little doctor, twice my age, especially with charmers like Lord Valentia and Richard Fitzpatrick offering such irresistible temptation? Perhaps I should not be too quick to judge.

"I'll take the turquoise," I cried the moment I spied the bolt of fabric in the hands of Mrs. Whitelock's helpers. "The rich, unusual color was bound to attract attention. "With gold trim, I think. And save out enough for a matching pair of slippers."

My turquoise gown made its debut in June, at a great *regatta* on the Thames. Twelve boats were to race from Westminster Bridge to London Bridge and back. Stands for spectators had been erected on both sides of the river, but the best view of the event would be from private barges moored along the banks. Seats on these were much sought after, as were tickets to the supper and ball at Ranelagh afterward.

I received several invitations. In the end, I accepted one from that notorious rake the Earl of March, because he promised me Charles Fox and Richard Fitzpatrick would be included in his party. I had been so busy parading about town on the arms of my various patrons, and spending their money with giddy abandon, that I'd scarcely seen my friends all Season. I missed their lively, clever company even more than I'd expected.

Accustomed as I had become to luxurious displays of wealth, I still could not help gaping in awe when I boarded Lord March's barge that afternoon. It was a long, shallow craft manned by eight oarsmen in splendid green and gold livery. An elaborate raised cabin with large windows occupied the rear of the barge. From atop its flat, railed roof, I could hear stately music being played on strings and woodwinds. The whole barge was adorned with gilt carvings of fantastical sea-creatures – porpoises, sea-horses, and ample-bosomed mermaids.

I entered the cabin to find Charles and Richard seated on a long bench upholstered with green and gold brocade, drinking champagne. They greeted me eagerly and interjected many flattering remarks when Lord March introduced me to his other guests. My friends insisted I sit between them to watch the race, a request I was only too happy to oblige.

"What mischief have you been up to?" I asked Richard with mock severity. "I hear your name whispered in connection with those satires in the Herald. 'Criticisms of . . . something.'"

". . . the Rolliad." He pulled a droll face. "In *dis*honor of the Right *Dis*honorable Mr. Rolle. The beggar deserves worse than the sharp edge of my pen for trying to cough down Edmund Burke's fine speech. I only regret the blockhead is not clever enough to appreciate the literary abuse I heap upon him."

"Speaking of Mr. Burke, what is the latest news from America?" I turned toward Charles. "Must it come to war?"

My question erased the look of good humor from his swarthy features. "It must not and it should not ... but I fear it will. And when it does, England will be beat. The colonists are resolute, resourceful and ... right! Meanwhile, the Ministry is not in the least prepared to undertake a fight they have done everything in their power to provoke."

"Can no one talk sense to the King?" I asked. "Bully, perhaps? Is he not a Gentleman of the Bedchamber?"

"Aye." Richard sighed. "But his salary for the post is all that keeps him afloat, so he dares not make himself any more unpopular with the King and risk losing it."

"His Majesty thinks of those colonies as England's errant children," said Charles, "who must be brought to obey by whatever means necessary."

Richard rolled his eyes. "His own brood are almost as many in number as the colonies."

"And treated little better," Charles grumbled. "I hear the poor creatures are brought up very strictly and made always to obey. Any challenge to their father's authority is met with harsh punishment. Heaven knows what the King would have thought of my father's system of child rearing."

His dark eyes suddenly misted with tears at the mention of his late father. My heart ached for him but I did not know what to say.

While Charles struggled to compose himself, Richard made a jocular effort to cheer his friend. "Lord Holland permitted his boys every liberty you can imagine—Charles most of all. If he demanded a bowl of fresh cream from the dinner table to bathe in, his father would allow it. If he insisted on smashing a valuable pocket watch to examine how it worked, Lord Holland would only say, 'If you must, you must.' I shudder to think what would have happened if Charles had ever desired to set the house on fire!"

Part of me wanted to laugh at the thought of a young Charles up to such antics, but another part worried the whole subject would only grieve him worse.

Richard's gambit seemed to work, however. Charles gave a soft chuckle that sounded a little like a sigh. "Whenever my mother protested, Father would insist nothing be done to break my spirit. I was singularly fortunate in my upbringing. I only wish the colonies had so enlightened a royal parent."

Though Charles had his faults, I felt certain his frank, generous nature proved the wisdom of his unusual rearing.

By the time Richard had entertained me with a few more stories from his friend's childhood, the race was about to begin. Twelve boats, each rowed by two oarsmen, were formed into three squadrons, with the colors red, white and blue.

"Care to place a wager?" Richard asked me. "It makes the race much more exciting to watch."

"Is that why you gamble?" I gave his wrist a flirtatious tap with my fan. "To make life more exciting?"

He lowered his voice to a husky murmur. "I do quite a number of things to make life more exciting."

The rascal was too attractive by half! "Things like bedding married women? Who is your latest conquest? I fear you will be sued for *crim con* one of these days."

Charles piped up, "All that saves his hide is the common knowledge that he has no money to pay damages. Now, about the race, I have fifty guineas on blue. Are you certain you won't wager, Mrs. Armistead?"

I shook my head so hard I almost dislodged my tiny hat, plumed with peacock feathers. "I never gamble."

Not with money and not with my heart. Living the kind of life I did was enough of a risk.

Lord March's barge was moored across the Thames from the Privy Stairs, so we had a fine view of the race's start and its exciting finish. All grew quiet for a few moments as we waited for the race to get under way. A bright flag dropped and the boats were off, rowing hard against the tide.

From the other barges and the scaffolds along the banks of the Thames, a great rumble of noise swelled. Beside me, Charles bounced in his seat, his hands working a pair of invisible oars. "Blue, hurrah! They are in front! Row, men, row!"

His fifty guinea wager did not explain such boyish enthusiasm. For I knew if he lost, he would dismiss it with cheerful indifference.

"They will fly to the finish with the current behind them." Richard seemed to take the race more calmly than his friend, though I suspected he had at least as large a wager on it.

"Damn and blast!" Charles bellowed when the lead boat plowed into one of the merchant guild barges that had slipped its moorings and strayed out into the river. "I call foul!"

Once all the boats had rounded the bend in the river, the shouting and whistling died down. My friends and I resumed our conversation and sipped our champagne. Awhile later, the noise swelled again and four boats flew toward the finish, two from the white squadron and one each from the red and blue. Though Charles shouted himself hoarse, the red squadron rowed to victory.

After the race, all the barges and boats assembled into a grand procession and sailed upriver to the Ranelagh pleasure gardens at Chelsea. Many of the other barges had musicians aboard, too, filling the evening with music.

The music continued at Ranelagh where the rotunda had been converted into an enormous supper room for the vast crowd. Charles pronounced the food bland and Richard complained of a scarcity of wine. But he managed to secure enough for me to drink a good deal more than usual. We danced minuets and cotillions until dawn.

That was one of the last truly carefree days we would have for a long time. For while London was revelling in the pleasure of its first regatta, a bloody battle was being fought across the

Atlantic at a place called Bunker Hill.

While the situation in the colonies lurched from disaster to disaster, my career as a courtesan mounted from strength to strength. Before the year was out, I had adorned the arms and warmed the beds of two dukes, a marquess and four earls.

One of those was the Earl of Cholmondeley – the very first gentleman to whom Charles had introduced me. It was he who had sent me the fur muff stuffed with banknotes. I soon discovered Richard had not exaggerated about his manly proportions.

Each new conquest brought a shower of expensive presents, invitations to the theatre, masquerades and pleasure gardens, drives in the park in his lordship's carriage. Then, in the early hours of the morning, to tumble in bed with a man whose regard for me was measured in gold and jewels – a man who had competed for the honor of *my* favors. This acted as a powerful stimulant to my desire.

Breathtaking sums of money flowed through my hands, going out almost as fast as it came in for hats and gowns in the very latest styles. A French friseur to puff, powder and pile my hair into elaborate, lofty confections. Linens, lace, ribbons and clocked stockings. Slippers trimmed with jeweled buckles or silk rosettes to match the colors of my gowns. Fans painted and trimmed to catch a gentleman's eye then flutter in graceful flirtation as I cast a seductive glance over the top.

I relished each moment to the hilt. Memories of hunger and misery made every bite of roast capon taste more succulent, every sip of wine sweeter, the heat of a gentleman's caresses more welcome. Those abundant, carefree days slipped by like a vivid, tipsy dream. Though I knew I must waken from it someday, perhaps with a vicious hangover, I refused to let that spoil my enjoyment while it lasted!

Early in the New Year, Richard called on me one afternoon.

The bristle of his unshaven face and the shadows beneath his eyes told me he hadn't slept the night before.

"When did you eat last?" I asked.

"Food?" He made a face. "I haven't the stomach for it yet. Perhaps by this evening I won't feel so vile and can tuck into supper at the club."

"At least have some coffee and rusks." I rang for my waiting woman. "You will ruin your constitution if you keep on like this. Do you want to be an old man at five-and-thirty, crippled with gout?"

His face grew even paler. "Neither of my parents saw their fortieth birthday so I do not expect to. I am determined to cram as much living as possible into the time I have. If that shortens my span a year or two, what will it signify?"

Was that why he sought the favors of married women rather than finding himself a wife? Because he did not expect to live long and could not bear to leave anyone bereft by his passing, as he had been left? My own fears for the years ahead were quite the opposite—ending up back on the streets, destitute and alone.

"It signifies to me." I suggested a happier future for us both. "I hope we shall still be friends many years from now. A stooped, grizzled gentleman, as clever and witty as ever and a plump, wrinkled old lady ..."

"... as kind and amiable as ever." A fleeting smile improved his wretched looks considerably.

"And none of the young chits and bucks seeing us chat by the fire will ever guess we spent such a dissipated youth."

"Very well, then." He surrendered with a wry chuckle. "Nourish me against my will. Prolong my dissipated life. In return, I have a present for you."

Reaching into his pocket, he produced a small white box, which he handed to me with a flourish. On closer inspection, I could see it was made of carved ivory.

"How beautiful!" I turned the box over and over, marveling

at the intricate carving. "You must have won a great deal at the tables to afford this. But I cannot accept it. You should repay the friends you have dunned, not purchase trifles for me."

"Do not fret." He waved me back when I tried to return the box to him. "I am not out a farthing for it—quite the contrary. I am only delivering it for another party."

"Indeed." Though I did not want him to have spent so much on me, I felt strangely disappointed to discover the gift was not from him. "Who is this *other party*? I did not think you had a single acquaintance that was not over his head in debt."

My waiting woman appeared with coffee then. Richard took a sip of his before answering my question. "Your gift comes from the person most of us are in debt *to*—General Smith. Have you met him?"

"Bob pointed him out to me at Newmarket. He is a nabob?"

"One of the richest." Richard took a tiny, wary bite of his biscuit. "Former Commander-in-chief of Bengal. He returned to England a few years ago with a fortune rumored to exceed a quarter of a million pounds."

In my amazement I fumbled the box. Something inside made a substantial jingle. I opened it to find half-a-dozen of the golden rouleaux my friends at Almack's used to place their wagers. The things were worth twenty guineas apiece!

Richard's eyes lit up at the sight of the rouleaux. "You might as well know, General Smith promised to forgive part of my debt if I delivered his gift and spoke to you in his favor."

"Will more of your debt be forgiven if I accept?" I asked. "This sounds like a scene from Mr. Foote's play about the nabob who threatens to ruin an indebted father unless the daughter agrees to marry him."

"There is some similarity." Richard looked as if the coffee was beginning to revive him. "But the general has made no threats, I am most certainly *not* your father and ..."

"... and General Smith is not interested in marriage."

"A rather less permanent arrangement, though with the

number of divorces coming before Parliament ..."

I put the lid back on the box. "Tell me, then, what are the general's *terms of surrender?*"

Richard laughed. "You should write *tête-à-têtes* for *Town and Country!*"

He gave me a full account of the offer, which included the lease on a house with a fashionable address, a carriage at my disposal, more servants, an account with a mantua-maker and a generous allowance on top of all that. In exchange, the general desired my exclusive company for a period of six months. It was the best offer I had received thus far in my career as a courtesan.

"What should I do?" I'd already half decided, but I hoped Richard would confirm my inclination. Strange as it might seem, I trusted his judgment.

My friend pressed the tips of his fingers together and arched them in front of him. "I reckon if you play your hand skillfully, General Smith will raise the stakes."

How high would the general be willing to bid? I wondered. Enough to grant an annuity that would save me from ending up back on the streets when I could no longer trade upon my looks and youth?

# Chapter Eleven

*I* DID END UP WITH A better offer from the general, though not the ultimate prize of an annuity I had hoped for. I *consoled* myself with the leasehold of a house on Bond Street. When my career finally ended, I could provide for myself in a modest way by letting out lodgings to younger women of the town. Yet by the time my liaison with the arrogant, demanding General Smith was over, I was satisfied I had earned that house – every blasted brick of it!

Sitting in my box at Covent Garden, surrounded by several admirers, all eager to take the general's place in my bed, I was ready to put the past six months behind me and enjoy life again.

"My word, if it isn't the celebrated Thais, Mrs. Armistead!" The affectionate mockery in Richard Fitzpatrick's voice cut through the chatter of my competing admirers. "I fear the reigning toast of the *haut ton* will not have a thought to spare for a poor ruined rakehell."

His greeting quoted some flattering lines from a recent *tête-à-tête* about me in *Town and Country*. By his tone, no one would guess he had read the part about General Smith being sent to prison on corruption charges after brazenly buying a seat in Parliament with substantial bribes.

"My dear Richard!" I sprang from my seat and threw my arms around his neck with blithe disregard for propriety. "I am too happy at seeing you again to resent your teasing. If I did forget you, it would only be because I have seen nothing of you in so long. Where have you and the others been hiding?"

During the past months I had often wished myself back in the exciting, uncertain days when a gang of young rakes had carried out their campaign to make me the most sought-after courtesan in the kingdom. If the scandal magazines could be believed, they had succeeded.

I glanced behind Richard, eager for a glimpse of Charles Fox's bushy brows or Bob Spencer's prominent chin. Instead of those dear imperfections, I encountered a face of such flawless masculine beauty it struck me dumb.

Richard's courtly manners rescued me from embarrassment, for he ignored my blatant gaping. "Hiding? Hardly! Shooting and racing always keep us out of town at this time of year, but we are back now."

He drew his breathtaking companion forward. "Allow me to present my cousin, John Frederick, Duke of Dorset. He has been mad to meet the fair one of whom he's read such glowing reports. Cuz, this is the famed Mrs. Armistead. Tell me, would you recognize her at all from that vile engraving in *Town and Country?*"

Sinking into a deep curtsy, I held out my hand to the duke, hoping it would not tremble.

"Not from the picture, to be sure." His Grace bowed low and brushed his lips over my fingers with the greatest delicacy. A pulse of heat swept up my arm and through my whole body. "The written description came nearer the mark, however. Elegant and beautiful."

Both words might have applied better to him. I could see a resemblance to his cousin in their handsome, aristocratic features. Looks must run in their mothers' family. But where Richard's had a more rugged cast, the duke's made me think of an angel. Golden strands in his fawn-colored hair gleamed like a halo, while his fine hazel eyes held a wistful luster that stirred every nurturing impulse in my heart.

"It is an honor and a pleasure to meet your Grace."

A pleasure for the eye of any discerning woman. The duke's shoulders were broad and his body had the lithe firmness of a devoted sportsman. Though he wore his clothes with casual grace, I reckoned he would look quite magnificent without them.

The Third Music concluded just then, a signal that the curtain was about to rise.

"You are welcome to join me." I wished the other gentlemen crammed into my box would all disappear. "Your cousin and I have a great deal of news to catch up on, your Grace. I am eager to hear his thoughts on the situation in America."

Richard chuckled. "I doubt the actors would appreciate competing with our spirited conversation. Besides, Dorset and I are being good brothers tonight, escorting our sisters to the play. We must not desert the ladies altogether."

I stifled a pang of disappointment even as the gentlemen's regard for their sisters endeared them to me. How different my life might have been if I had been blessed with a protective elder brother.

"For any less pressing obligation," murmured the duke, "we would most happily abandon our box for yours."

"If you plan another *petit souper*," said Richard, "we should be grateful for an invitation. I enjoyed your last one so. Few places afford such a perfect blend of privacy, informality and hospitality."

"An invitation you shall have," I promised, "before the week is out."

After Richard and his cousin returned to their own box, I resumed my seat in the midst of my admirers and strove to concentrate on the play. But it did not divert me. I found my gaze wandering to the other boxes where I quickly spotted Richard's party—three women near my own age and three pretty younger girls flanked by their handsome kinsmen.

I tried to catch Richard's eye, but his attention was fixed on the stage. When I gave up and glanced toward the duke,

I found myself the object of his pensive gaze. The playhouse suddenly felt very hot. Unfurling my fan, I waved it to cool my cheeks.

The very next day I received the gift of a magnificent new fan with sticks of carved tortoiseshell and a pastoral landscape painted on the velum leaf. Attached to the fan's string was a swanskin purse full of guineas. From any other man, I would not have been surprised to receive a bid for my favors. But why should the dashing duke propose to pay for what any woman would readily grant him?

I mentioned my amazement to Richard later that week, after my *petit souper.*

He shrugged. "My cousin is a keen sportsman. Cricket, tennis, billiards – he excels at them all. He likes to compete and he loves to win. By laying claim to the most fashionable courtesan of the day, he may feel he will win at the sport of gallantry, too."

So once again I would be the prize for a man with something to prove. The *tête-à-tête* about General Smith and me had claimed he sought my company to show that he had risen to the height of the dukes and earls who'd shared my bed before him. More and more I came to trust the wisdom Bob Spencer had culled from the notorious Nancy Parsons. The courtesan was a luxury to be savored in private *and* flaunted in public.

Perhaps I should have driven the dashing duke as hard a bargain for my favors as I had the general. But my desire for him put me in a poor position to negotiate.

"I wish I could make you a settlement, of course." The duke's expressive eyes darkened with regret. "But that requires such a great outlay of capital, and my finances will not stretch to anything like the sum you are worth, my dear Mrs. Armistead. *C'est plus triste.*"

His Grace drew off my glove and began to kiss my hand. Not the swift graze of a courteous public greeting, but a leisurely and very sensual conquest of my palm, wrist and each finger. I would defy any woman to withstand such exquisite sensations from so attractive a man and keep her proper wits about her.

I *tried*. "I have my future to consider, Your Grace, and I do have other admirers."

"George Cavendish?" Lord Dorset sighed. "The man is a cold fish like all his family. Look at his brother with that enchanting bride and still not the least sign of a Devonshire heir. For all her hectic gaiety, I do not believe the young duchess is happy with her husband."

I did not care for the caressing tone of his Grace's voice when he spoke of the Duchess of Devonshire. I had seen her at the playhouses and pleasure gardens and envied her aristocratic beauty. She would never need to worry her pretty, golden head about money. Then again, she could not take the captivating Duke of Dorset as her lover without risking ruin.

In the eyes of polite society, I was already ruined. Which meant I had very little to lose. That gave me a precious freedom beyond anything most women could imagine.

"Lord George may not be very talkative," I protested as my resistance crumbled, "but he is good-tempered and generous."

"What about another house?" The duke swiped his tongue over my forefinger then traced his lips with the moistened tip. "After all, you have only one."

He made it sound like a severe deprivation. To be sure, most of the people he knew owned two or three houses. How could he understand that for most of my life, I could not lay claim to a single room? Two houses would be double the expense, but I could rent one out to provide me with an income.

I raised my hand, drawing his Grace toward me. "When I get my new house, I shall give you a key."

"And the key to your heart?" He lowered my hand, leaving my lips unguarded.

"I believe you have stolen that already." It was not an outright falsehood, only the language of gallantry.

Many gentlemen regularly professed love for me. I was certain the duke could, too, with perfect sincerity. A more truthful term would have been 'passionate desire,' which I certainly felt for him. It would be madness to let myself feel anything more. Sooner or later, a man of his station must take a suitable wife and sire an heir to his titles and fortune.

But for the present, he wanted my company and I wanted his. After my liaison with General Smith, I was starved for everything the duke was so divinely equipped to provide.

"Shall we seal our bargain," murmured his Grace, "with a frolic in your bed?"

His skilful, seductive kiss promised even greater delights in exchange for more intimate liberties. Though it was the middle of the day and the sun shone bright outside, I readily agreed. Indeed, that was part of the reason I had surrendered with such ease. Not since my innocent passion for Ned Armistead had I been so eager to feast my eyes on a man's body.

We retired at once to my bedchamber were his Grace proceeded to remove my clothes with leisurely attentiveness that provoked my anticipation to an almost unbearable pitch. After taking off each garment, he paused to kiss and caress parts of me no other man had taken interest in.

Who could have guessed the back of my knee would prove so sensitive a spot? The flick of his tongue over it sent shafts of desire darting up my thighs to strike their carnal target. Oh, and the delightful sensation of his kisses rained down my back after he had unlaced my stays and raised my chemise. By the time he had stripped me naked of every last stitch, I was hot and wriggling with need!

Yet still he was in no hurry, my sweet tormentor.

"What a living work of art you are." He stood back to admire me, still fully clothed himself, though I glimpsed a promising bulge in his breeches. "So like the marvelous Renaissance paintings I admired on my Grand Tour."

Many men had praised my looks, but none had made me

feel so beautiful.

The duke took my hand. "Come, stand by the foot post of your bed. Your right arm raised to your face." My naked flesh tingled from his touch as he posed me. "There, your left leg crossed in front of your right. Just like Eve by Rubens!"

He unbuttoned his coat and pulled it off, all the while ravishing me with his gaze. "Now recline upon the bed, leaning back on your pile of pillows."

"Like this?" I spread my legs invitingly and gave my breasts a provocative little jiggle.

"Very good!' The duke's eyes drank me in as he removed his shoes and stockings then peeled off his waistcoat. "Now bring your right leg up, bending your knee and raise your right arm to rest upon it."

As I followed his directions, I watched him untie his neck linen and pull his flowing white shirt off over his head. The tempting sight of his tight-muscled chest brought an exquisite ache to my loins.

"Here." The duke tossed his shirt to me. "Cover your thighs with this as you let your left leg loll over the edge of the bed. Mmm. You have a much lovelier face than Correggio's Danae, I must say. I wonder if Reynolds or Gainsborough would paint you in this pose for me."

The sensation of fine linen upon my thighs, still warm from his magnificent chest and fragrant with the subtle musk of his scent made me ache with delicious longing. It was all I could do to keep from begging him to quit toying with my desire and satisfy it. But that was not my right. His Grace was paying me handsomely to gratify *his* desires.

"Just one more," he promised me in a breathless whisper. "Titian's Venus. I've wanted to make love to her ever since I first glimpsed her at the *galleria* in Florence. Recline on the pillows a little more." He grabbed his shirt by the sleeve and pulled it away. "Legs together, the left crossed over the right below the knee. And your right hand ... so."

He lifted my hand and dropped a kiss in my palm, then arranged it to rest over the cleft between my legs. I was sorely tempted to use it to bring myself the relief his Grace denied me.

"Now look up at me," ordered the duke. "Do not smile. Lower the lids of your eyes just a little and use them alone to tell me what you want."

I could never have risen so high in my profession if I had not mastered the art of communicating to a man with my eyes. But never had I felt such an urgent need to employ that skill. I looked his Grace directly in the eye with a gaze so hazy hot, I wondered it did not sear his eyebrows! I let my eyes drift lower, over his fine mouth and firm chin to his graceful neck and rippling chest, then down his flat belly to the waistband of his breeches. My eyes darted up to meet his once again, demanding to see him in all his manly glory.

"Well done!" His hands flew to attack the buttons that imprisoned him, freeing his lean hips and a bold, upright truncheon of the perfect size and shape to subdue my wanton cravings. "That is precisely the look she gave me. I almost expired of lust on the spot!"

I knew the feeling all too well.

Much as I might have liked to feast my eyes upon his excellent form, I could not delay. Abandoning the pose of high art, I assumed another, all my own, which succeeded in luring the duke to me.

With lithe grace, he mounted me and brought his lips down upon mine. I expected a crescendo of vigorous thrusting, but instead he drove me mad with slow, measured strokes that soon carried us to the brink of rapture and beyond. Though I gloried in it, I could not escape the feeling that he was using my body to fulfill his desire for someone else.

Still, His Grace's skill as a lover was everything I could have wished. It soothed any regret I might have had for not securing an annuity from him. As soon as I could have a new gown made up, he whisked me off to Vauxhall, where we paraded up and down the walks, arm in arm.

Though I had attended the pleasure gardens many times since the Wilkes Riots prevented my first visit, I still found them enchanting. I could think of few more enjoyable ways to spend an evening than strolling along the broad avenues of hard-packed gravel bordered by stately elm, sycamore and lime trees.

The statues, cascades, temples and ruins scattered about the park always made me feel as if I had entered a magical realm. That sensation redoubled when darkness fell and the hundreds of tiny lanterns scattered about the gardens twinkled their fairy light. Or when brilliant fireworks spattered the night sky with vibrant, sparkling color.

"Have you noticed how everyone we pass turns to look?" asked the Duke when we paused in the Grove around the Music Pavilion to listen to the orchestra play a spritely concerto by Vivaldi. "Then they whisper furiously to their companions. Your many admirers must be downcast that you have forsaken them."

I laughed. "I reckon the whispering comes from frustrated dowagers consoling one another that you are not inclined to settle down and marry one of their daughters."

The duke did not seem as flattered by my quip as I'd hoped. Perhaps the thought of being someone else's prize did not sit well with him. "That reminds me, I caught a glimpse of Lady Betty ... that is ... *Lady Derby* at the Chinese Temple. She came as near as any woman has to bowling me out of bachelorhood."

He spoke like the avid cricket enthusiast he was. In the short time we'd been together, I had heard enough about pitches and wickets, runs, creases and innings to make me quite an expert on the sport.

"Why did you not marry her?" Perhaps the lady had been too eager, not posing enough of a challenge to his Grace's competitive nature.

"I hated to let her get away, but what could I do?" The duke pulled a rueful face. "I was too young to settle down. I hadn't even been on my Grand Tour. She could not wait for me, of course. Nor did I expect her to. I hope she is happy with Derby. He is a good fellow."

Just then I spotted Bob Spencer in the crowd and beckoned him over. "It is good to see you out taking some fresh air instead of cooped up in that smoky gambling room at your club. I hope you brought Charles and Richard with you."

"Alas, no," said Bob. "They have gone off to Paris for a grand debauch."

"To Paris, while the House is in session?" I found that difficult to credit. "Do you know when they mean to return?"

"Not until after Christmas. Charles claims there is nothing more he can profitably say about the American situation until the administration is prepared to heed reason. And Richard wanted to go on a spree before his regiment is sent to America in the New Year. No doubt they will return home poxed and penniless but otherwise in the best of spirits."

Bob's cheerful account cast down *my* spirits for this was the first I had heard about Richard being sent to war. All Charles's efforts to end the hostilities suddenly took on much greater urgency for me.

"Welcome to Knole, Mrs. Armistead," said Lord Dorset as we drove up a broad avenue flanked by tall trees, their dark web of branches bare against the pale winter sky.

My breath fogged the window of the duke's traveling coach as I strained to catch my first glimpse of the house. I'd been flattered when His Grace had invited me to spend Christmas at his family estate in the Weald of Kent. Now, off to the left, I could make out a front of gray stonework topped by a row of Dutch gables. It looked like a line of identical narrow houses on some crowded London street, except that there were no doors, only columns of windows beneath each gable. Above the rusty-brown roof, slender plumes of smoke rose from clusters of chimneystacks.

A flash of movement startled me back into my seat. "Look, your Grace, a deer!"

The creature had been standing very still, half-hidden by one of the broad tree trunks. Now it bounded away, over the snow-crusted ground. The next thing I knew, half-a-dozen others flew into swift, graceful motion, including a stag with a great rack of antlers.

"I should hope there are deer." The duke chuckled. "This is a deer park, after all. Many country estates had them once to supply game for hunting, but they have long since gone out of style. Fortunately, Knole does not bow to the fickle breezes of fashion."

Breathless with wonder, I watched the deer until our coach drove through a gate between two stout towers. It emerged into a large snow-mantled courtyard where it rolled to a stop.

"This is the Green Court," said the duke as I climbed out of his carriage, my limbs stiff from the long, cold drive. "You must come back in summer when the place lives up to its name."

Did he mean for us to be together that long? I'd been so eager to *become* his mistress that we had never agreed upon the duration of our liaison. Though practicality and experience warned me it must end sooner or later, I hoped to delay that day as long as possible.

Clinging to the duke's arm, I stared around in the fading light. Scarlet veins of creeper ran up the gray stone walls. When they put forth leaves in the summer, it must make the Green Court look like a forest grove.

"All this is yours?" I asked. No wonder his Grace had thought I needed more than one house. Both of mine together would have been lost in this vast old mansion.

"This is only the beginning." The duke pointed toward a passageway in the far wall. Rising behind it, I could see a

slender clock tower. "There is another court beyond this one
and another beyond that again. More over that way, too." He
swept his arm toward the north. "Seven altogether. One for
each day in the week, enough staircases for every week in the
year and a room for every day of the year—not that I have
managed to count them all, myself."

Three hundred and sixty-five rooms? Most of them standing
empty for weeks and months on end, no doubt, while whole
families were crammed into a single one back in my old neighborhood. What had I done to merit my escape from all that? The
weathered walls of Knole reminded me of something experience
had proven over and over—nothing good ever lasted.

I shivered.

"We must get you inside and warmed up." The duke led me
through a massive wood-framed door. "There will be plenty
of time for a thorough tour of the house."

A year would not have been enough time for a full exploration
of Knole, I realized after the first week of my stay. The place
was more like an old walled town with whole neighborhoods of
buildings grouped around each of the seven courtyards. Some
of those neighborhoods seemed separated from one another by
centuries. When I passed through a door in the Stone Court
that led to the old banqueting room, I could not escape the
sensation that I was crossing a threshold in time.

The duke's private quarters, overlooking the south gardens,
were quite modern and fine enough that they might have been
the showpieces of a more modest estate. Yet they were nothing
compared to the gilded splendor of the ballroom with its mantel
of carved alabaster. Or the magnificent bed in the Venetian
ambassador's room with its richly embroidered hangings.

"They say the Old Pretender was born in this bed." The duke
ran the back of his fingers over the gracefully draped curtains
in a cautious caress. "Perhaps King William gave it to my
great-grandfather so he would not be reminded."

Thanks to Charles Fox, I had read enough history to have

some idea what his Grace was talking about. I loved stories about kings and queens. They harked back to the lost fancies of my childhood while reminding me that life was not always easy for the wealthy and powerful, either. At Knole, surrounded by their portraits, the chairs they'd sat in and beds they'd slept in, I felt a connection to them as real people rather than hazy characters from history books.

When his Grace took me to the oldest parts of the house, down dark wood-paneled galleries and up an ornate staircase guarded by fierce carved leopards, I felt my footsteps dogged by ghosts. Not restless, vengeful specters, but busy ghosts – so occupied with hatching courtly plots that they refused to heed such trivialities as time and death.

"See what you think of this." The duke beckoned me into a dressing room off one of the grand bedchambers.

The moment I stepped inside I felt I was being watched and appraised by several pairs of heavy-lidded, knowing eyes.

"Beauties from the court of Charles II by Lely." His Grace spoke in the fond tone of a man introducing old friends. "I don't know that I find any of them particularly beautiful, but they do look ripe for a romp in bed."

They did, indeed, with their wanton cascades of curls, loose, flowing gowns and plunging necklines that flaunted a great deal of plump, white bosom. Here and there the provocative peep of a nipple beckoned a hand to fondle.

"I should like to have lived back then." The duke gave a seductive chuckle as he approached me from behind. He slipped his hand under the short fur-trimmed cape I wore for warmth on our exploration of the state apartments and began a little exploring of his own. "Everything free and easy, devoted to a life of pleasure."

I laughed as he nuzzled my ear. How could his life be any easier or more devoted to pleasure than it was already? The ladies of King Charles's court told me a different story of their time. From their hard, jealous stares, I sensed that the pleasure of powerful men had been serious business for the women who provided it. The passage of a hundred and fifty years had not changed some things.

"Should we return to your quarters?" I asked the duke in a seductive murmur. "And warm ourselves up?"

He spun me about into his embrace, keeping his hands under my cloak. "I reckon we can warm ourselves right here. Whenever I gaze upon these luscious ladies, I find myself overcome with the most wanton urges."

"Do you, indeed?" I surrendered to his kiss, my desire piqued by the fancy that we had a silent audience for our sporting. "I am beginning to feel warmer already."

Like the practiced movement of a dance, his Grace twirled us both around, pressing me back against the closed door. "I'll wager I can make you hotter still!"

Before I had time to reply, he dropped to his knees and dove beneath my hooped skirts. I gave a startled squeal as he burrowed up under my petticoats and the hem of my chemise, his hair whispering over my bare thighs.

Muffled by layers of linen and velvet his voice emerged from under my skirts. "I have often longed to do this! It is as warm as an orangery under here and quite as fragrant!"

His hands ranged over my legs from the tops of my garters up to my hips. From there, they wandered to my backside, kneading the soft flesh while his cheek pressed against my tingling loins. He amused himself that way for some little time while waves of sultry heat pulsed through me. Then he slid his fingers between my thighs and coaxed them apart to expose my tender cleft. The moist whisper of his breath warned me his tongue would follow, but it did not prepare me for the flickering liquid fire of its caress.

Bracing myself against the door, I surrendered to the blissful sensations until I was consumed with ecstasy.

# Chapter Twelve

*A* MONTH AT KNOLE PROVIDED ME with a better education in history and art than I could have received at the finest convent school in France. Though ever anxious to improve myself, I still grew eager to return to London.

"Your Grace," I said one night as we lay tangled in one another's arms after a lusty tumble, "what would you say to my hosting a little fête on your behalf to bid your cousin Richard farewell before he goes to America?"

"A capital idea," he replied in a drowsy murmur. "No doubt our aunts will host a family gathering, which is liable to be a dreadful bore. We cannot send the poor fellow off to battle without at least one good night of drunken revelry."

By the evening of the party, I was so wrought-up I could not sit still. I arranged and rearranged the hothouse flowers so many times the petals began to fall off. The sound of my first guest being admitted to the house made me gasp and glance toward the mantel clock. The festivities were not set to begin for half an hour. Perhaps the duke had come early to help me welcome the others.

But it was not his Grace who strode into my parlor a moment later.

"Richard?" My knees went weak, as did my voice. I had not fully realized how much he meant to me until I was faced with the prospect of losing him from my life.

"Am I early?" He looked about the empty room. "Or is

my honor too dubious for anyone to dine and drink on its account?"

"You are early." I flew to him and clasped his hands. "And I am glad of it. Why did you go away to Paris without telling me your regiment was being sent to America?"

He gave a careless shrug. "Perhaps I would have done if we'd met up somewhere before I left, but my cousin was claiming so much of your time. And what would it have signified ... unless you have some influence with Lord North to prevent my going? Even if you had, I'm not certain I would want you to. I trained as a soldier and it is long past time I was tested in battle. Besides, what better way to escape my creditors?"

"How can you jest about it?" My eyes began to sting. "I shall fret for your safety the whole time you are gone!"

He opened his arms to me and pressed a soft kiss upon my forehead. It was a chaste gesture of friendship and nothing more. But some unspoken tension quickened between us. I felt as if I were teetering on the brink of a precipice, knowing I must scramble back out of danger, yet barely able to subdue a mad urge to throw myself over the edge.

Richard sensed it too, though he gave no sign but a faint hitch in his breath and a subtle tightening of his muscles. A woman of less experience might have missed the signs.

"I am touched by your concern." He pulled away from me a little too quickly, his tone a trifle too casual. "But do not weep, I beg you. My sisters are sending me off with enough tears to float my ship to New York. You must not add to the general drenching."

His quip made me chuckle in spite of my other bewildering feelings. For his sake I played the cheerful hostess that night, but I could not cast off my worries so easily. I had lost too many people I cared about to believe Richard would return unscathed.

"Did you order up this fine day, Mrs. Armistead?" asked Charles as he climbed into my carriage one a sunny afternoon, three months after Richard's farewell party. "To think I might have wasted it indoors but for your kind invitation."

His broad smile was as natural and eager as a child's. It acted upon my spirits like the sudden warmth of spring on the trees and flowers.

"Richard would want me to look after you while he is away in America." I signaled the coachman to set off for Green Park.

"Nonsense!" Charles's stout frame shook with laughter. "If Richard were still here, he and I would be companions in debauchery, going from the Commons to the club and back again with only brief detours to the playhouse and even briefer ones home to sleep, shave and change clothes. Much as I detest this war, all the marching and riding and regular hours may do wonders for my friend's constitution."

For once Charles was not able to make me laugh. "So the war may improve Richard's health if it does not kill him? Have you had any news of him?"

"None of consequence. Both armies are still in winter quarters after General Washington's Christmas present of two defeats. But why ask me? Surely Dorset has had word of his cousin, or have you tired of the splendors of Knole already?"

I was flattered by Charles's belief that *I* might lose interest in the duke rather than the other way around.

"I am still his Grace's winter mistress, but Richard has not written to him."

"Winter mistress?" Charles raised one bushy brow. "Has Dorset another *amour* for the summer? Who is she, pray?"

"His Grace's summer love is a little green." I tried to keep my lip from twitching, so Charles would not guess too soon.

"That Warren girl from Mrs. Hayes' house?"

I shook my head. "I hear she has a fine leg and keeps him much on the run."

Charles suggested a number of other names that betrayed his intimate acquaintance with the brothels of King's Place.

I could no longer stifle a giggle. "I believe she admires the use he makes of his balls and he is eager to get in her crease as often as he can!"

Charles burst into delighted laughter. "You had me going, you little minx! I should have known you meant Dorset was enamored of 'Mistress Cricket.' I used to play at school and still enjoy a friendly match now and then if it does not go on too long. I do not find it nearly as diverting as the sport a man might enjoy with his lady mistress."

How I wished the duke shared my friend's earthy good sense. But being able to amuse Charles with my jest eased the discontent I fought to hide.

"Perhaps you should find a little summer diversion of your own," suggested Charles when his laughter had ebbed. "George Colman has left Covent Garden to manage the Haymarket Opera House. I'll wager he would be delighted to put you on stage again if you had the least inclination."

"You will wager on anything," I teased him, "So that does not signify. After my sorry efforts at Covent Garden, I expect Mr. Colman would rather pay me to stay *off* his stage."

"You are too severe on yourself." Charles gave my hand an encouraging pat. "Besides, commercial entertainment depends on more than skilful acting."

"Indeed? What else does it require, then?"

"Something to draw the crowds – either novelty or celebrity. When you first appeared for Colman, you provided the former, now you are in a position to deliver the latter."

Perhaps a stage appearance or two might rekindle the duke's passion for me by encouraging some competition for my favors. "I declare, Mr. Fox, you are a dangerous man."

"You think so?" He shook his head at the absurdity of my claim. "Then I wonder you are brave enough to risk a drive in the park with me. Tell me what danger I pose and to whom?"

"Why, to anyone you choose to exercise your potent powers of persuasion upon."

His engaging smile lost some of its luster. "If that were true, I would have long since persuaded His Majesty's government against prosecuting this unnecessary war."

Before I could chide myself for putting him out of spirits, he seemed to draw refreshment from some deep spring of optimism. "But I am not beaten until I give up, and that I will not do."

I wondered if he felt a greater urgency to stop the war now that his dearest friend was facing fire from a stalwart 'enemy' they both admired.

He seemed to sense my thoughts. "I would worry less about Richard if he were serving under General Washington than Howe or Cornwallis. Then if the worst did happen, at least I could mourn him with honor for giving his life in a noble cause."

I could not let either of us dwell on that thought. "Can you tell me how I might get letters to him?"

"Give them to me," Charles offered, "and I will seal them inside my own."

"Going so soon?" I slid to the edge of the bed where Lord Dorset was seated, pulling on his boots.

In the dim light of morning, with his hair loose and spilling over his broad bare shoulders, he was a tempting sight.

"Could you not stay a little longer?" I ran my hand down his back in an inviting caress. "Then I could have Cook make you breakfast."

He twisted around to fondle my breasts and give me a quick kiss that frustrated me more than anything. "I cannot loll in bed this morning. I must ride down to Hambledon for a match. Lord, I wish there was a decent cricket pitch nearer London. Winchelsea talked of making one ... perhaps when he gets back from America."

Cricket, of course. It crossed my mind to tease the duke about his *summer mistress*, but I doubted he would laugh like

Charles had. What a shame his Grace's sense of humor was not as well developed as his muscles.

I let my hand stray to his hard, lean thigh. "Speaking of America, did I tell you I've had a letter from your cousin?"

"Indeed? How is Richard getting on? Gambling away all his pay in the officer's mess? Seducing the wives of his superior officers?"

I had to bite my tongue to keep from asking if playing some silly game for days on end was so much better use of a man's time than gambling and wenching. "He is well and sounds in good spirits. Charles Fox brought me his letter. Charles has been invited to spend the summer at Chatsworth with the Devonshires."

"Chatsworth, eh?" The duke wriggled into his shirt, ignoring my wanton touch. "I wonder what Fox will make of Lord Devonshire's pretty duchess. She likes to play cards until all hours of the night and her luck is every bit as vile as his."

The duke stood up to put on his coat, crushing my hopes of luring him back to bed. I'd wanted a quick tumble for more than its own sake. Long ago I'd learned that men were most easily persuaded of anything in the blissful haze after lovemaking. Since I did not possess Charles Fox's powers of persuasion, I had to rely on my own wiles.

"Your Grace?"

"Hmm?" He glanced back, clearly eager to be off.

"I have been asked to appear onstage at the Opera House next month. I hope you approve."

He thought for a moment. "I see no reason why not. Let me know when the performance is set and I will try to attend. But now, I must be on my way."

He strode to the bed, pressed a quick kiss on my brow and retreated again before I could detain him in an embrace.

I saw little of the duke between then and the night of the play. He did come to the performance, bringing a number of his cricketing friends, but I was far more heartened to see

Charles Fox and Bob Spencer in the audience.

Though very nervous at first, I rallied my confidence upon hearing their hearty applause for my first scene. I was determined to make them proud of me and write glowing reviews to Richard. I succeeded well enough that Mr. Colman asked me to return the following month in a farce he had written.

"What date in June?" asked the duke when I told him. "I fear I may have to miss that one. The Earl of Derby is hosting a cricket match in Surrey, and I have promised to help him organize it."

The duke called in London on his way back from Surrey and collected me for another visit to Knole. He was full of praise for Lord Derby's hospitality and Lady Derby's enthusiasm for his favorite sport.

"At first I thought Betty must be in jest when she proposed the women play a match. But they did jolly well, though their petticoats hampered them running. Betty bowled at least as well as some men I know."

"Lady Betty?" I remembered him mentioning her before. "She's the one you almost married isn't she?"

"I thought of proposing," murmured the duke gazing out the carriage window at the green Kentish countryside, "that is as far as it went."

Was he beginning to wish it had gone farther?

Stung by a barb of jealousy, I set myself to make his Grace forget all about the cricket-playing countess for the duration of our stay in Kent.

Knole, in all its summer splendor, was an entirely different place from the cold, ghostly estate of winter. Green and red climbers softened the stone walls, which took on a golden glow. Lush grass carpeted the Green Court, while the fragrance of roses and lavender wafted on every breeze.

At the duke's coaxing, I tried my hand at lawn bowling on the oval green surrounded by gardens. When the weather turned rainy, we retired to an alcove of the Leicester gallery where he tried to teach me billiards. We explored parts of the house I had not seen on my previous visit and I soaked up more art and history.

I would have been content to stay the whole summer, but the duke seemed to grow restless despite my best efforts to keep him amused. After a few weeks, he took me back to London on his way to a round of house parties in the north.

"Shall I give Charles Fox your regards when I see him at Chatsworth?" he asked when he kissed me goodbye.

"Indeed, my very fondest regards. When can I expect you back in town?"

The duke shrugged. "I go to Lord Carlisle's from Chatsworth. I may stay on there to shoot. Then there's Newmarket."

He *could* take me there if he wished. In the raffish world of horse racing, gentlemen squired their mistresses rather than their wives. But perhaps the duke did not want to come all the way to London to fetch me.

"I shall look forward to seeing you whenever you return." I bid him farewell with as bright a smile as I could muster.

Though he seemed a trifle distant, nothing in his manner suggested that a few weeks later my allowance from him would stop suddenly, without a hint of warning.

A wave of panic engulfed me when I received the news from my grim-faced banker. I knew of half a dozen men who would have leapt at the chance to assist me. But they were all dispersed to the country and not due back in London for at least two months. By then I could be rotting in debtor's prison.

"The celebrated Mrs. Armistead." Charlotte Hayes, one of the most successful King's Place brothel-keepers looked me over from head to toe. "To what do I owe the honor?"

My heart sank. I had hoped to find some deputy in charge of the house, a woman nearer my own age who might recognize how much we had in common and find a crumb of compassion in her heart. A woman like Mrs. Hayes did not rise to the top of this profession and stay there so many years if such crumbs had not been swept, or scoured, from *her* heart.

I could almost smell the gutters of Covent Garden pulling me back there.

Mrs. Hayes looked to be Mrs. Goadby's age – perhaps twice mine. Her features were too flat to ever have been truly beautiful. But there was a deceptive air of innocence about her face that would not have looked out of place on the statue of a saint. Could this be the woman who, upon discovering one of her girls intended to run away, had turned the poor creature out on the street naked?

"Ma'am." I dropped a respectful curtsey. "I have a proposition for you that I hope will benefit us both."

She nodded me toward a chair in her sitting room. "Speak your piece. But keep it short and sweet, I'm a busy woman."

Inhaling a deep breath, I rested my gloved hands in my lap to keep them from betraying my desperation. "I am presently at liberty and I thought some of your customers might like to sample a style of company they could not otherwise aspire to."

After the past few years of being able to pick and choose my patrons from among the wealthiest, highest-born men in the kingdom, it sickened me to stoop to this kind of harlotry again. I recalled something Mrs. Goadby had said that night Lord Bolingbroke accosted her in the Pantheon: *Have I not worked and saved all these years so I'm no longer obliged to jump into bed at any man's whim?* Now I knew what she meant.

But debtor's prison would be a hundred times worse and this was my only hope of avoiding it ... if I was lucky.

"Do I look daft?" Mrs. Hayes leaned back in her chair. "Give you my customers? Gentlemen may call me *Santa Carlotta* but I am not in the business of dispensing charity. If you'd come to me last month I might have been able to hire you for my 'Tahitian Feast of Venus.' Quite a night that was."

Indeed. The whole world of gallantry had been a-buzz over it. Inspired by exotic stories from Captain Cook's expedition to the South Pacific, Mrs. Hayes had invited two-dozen gentlemen of wealth and title to her carnal feast. There they'd watched and aided the initiation of a party of supposed virgins into the rites of love.

Scraps of gossip about the Tahitian orgy had both repelled and excited me. At least with Mrs. Goadby's 'Banquets of Beauty,' the coupling had taken place in private. But what if taking part in such an orgy had been my only choice to stay out of debtor's prison? How far did I dare venture down that road?

Mrs. Hayes must have sensed my thoughts. "You can't afford to be particular, now, my dear. You've been dropped by that pretty duke, haven't you?"

"How do you—?"

"It's my business to know who is keeping company with whom. You'd be surprised how often I can turn that kind of information to my advantage. You would do well to learn from my example."

"I can see that, ma'am." I might not approve of all the things she did to succeed, but I respected her well-honed talent for survival. "And I assure you I have not come to solicit charity. I thought a few of your customers might be willing to pay a higher fee for a night with a celebrated courtesan. If we split that fee, you stand to profit."

Though the woman's bland features remained passive, a hint of avarice glittered in her pale blue eyes.

"Your share would be entirely profit," I added, "for I would pay all my own expenses."

"You know how *my* business works," said Mrs. Hayes. "I'll give you that. What you need to learn is how *yours* works. Summer's always a lean time. You need to be prepared for it."

"I will be," I vowed, more to myself than to her, "if I can just get through this year. I had no warning. Everything seemed fine between us."

Mrs. Hayes rose from her chair. "What warning did you expect, you daft chit? No man will feel any obligation to you, no matter how sentimental he talks when he's trying to get into your bed. Keepers are no more faithful than most husbands, which is why a woman like you needs a settlement."

She was telling me nothing I didn't already know, though I clearly needed a reminder after the way I'd given the Duke of Dorset such dangerous power over our alliance. From now on, I would need to assume control, taking and leaving keepers on terms that were most advantageous to me.

*Take control.* That was what I needed to do now.

"Thank you for your excellent advice, Mrs. Hayes." I rose and curtsied once again. "If you are not interested in my proposal, perhaps Mrs. Windsor or Mrs. Mitchell might be. Good day to you, ma'am."

"Wait!" she cried as I strode to the door. "Do not be so hasty. Perhaps we can come to an arrangement."

The autumn session of Parliament did not open until mid November, causing my period of financial distress to go on even longer than I expected. By cutting my expenses to the bone, selling some of the trinkets I'd been given by admirers, and accepting every customer Mrs. Hayes sent my way, I managed to keep out of debtor's prison.

But the fear of it hung over me every waking moment, haunting my dreams at night. Often I woke in a cold sweat, certain I would find myself back in that wretched alley again, starved and frozen.

With no letters from Richard to assure me he was safe, my worries for him grew dark and dreadful, too. Rumors swirled in the autumn air as thick as falling leaves. Some said the British army had won an important victory over the Americans. Others claimed they had suffered a disastrous defeat. Still others muttered dire predictions that the French or the Spanish might invade England.

A few short months ago, the peace and security I craved had seemed within my grasp at last. Now I found myself beset on all sides. Was there any such thing as true security, or was it only a child's comforting illusion?

My spirits were at a low ebb one day when I heard a knock at my door. A customer referred from King's Place, no doubt.

I dragged myself to my feet and made an effort to summon a smile. Whoever he was, I owed him my best service. They were decent enough fellows, the ones I had kept company with since summer—men of business, stockbrokers, moneylenders. But they represented a dangerous slip backward on my climb to success. Anxious as I was over so many matters, it taxed my composure to pretend I was carefree and eager to entertain them.

"Greetings, Mrs. Armistead." Charles Fox strode into my sitting room, overflowing with vitality and high spirits.

At the unexpected sight of him, the brittle shell of my composure shattered. I burst into tears.

"Forgive me, my dear!" Charles rushed forward, offering me his handkerchief. "You were expecting someone else and I have disappointed you."

"There is no one I would be happier to see." I wiped my eyes, laughing at my own foolishness. "Except perhaps Richard returned from America safe and sound. Have you any news? There are so many rumors flying, I do not know what to believe."

"Let us sit." Charles held my arm as I sank to the sofa then he dropped down beside me. "I will tell you all I know, little as that may be. Late in the summer the American forces scored a victory, but I do not believe Richard's regiment was involved in the fighting."

"Will France side with the Americans and invade us?" I dried the last tears from my cheeks.

There was something solid and hopeful about Charles's

presence that steadied me. Was that why he had wagered away a fortune – to inoculate himself against worse disasters? Or was he infected with the gambler's baseless assurance that his luck would turn and his next wager was certain to win? Just then, I needed to believe the best of him.

"There is no doubt in my mind the French *want* to fight. They are still smarting from their defeats in the last war and the Americans have sent Dr. Franklin to Paris to plead their cause. He is a very persuasive old fellow."

Another man might have tried to calm me with evasions or half-truths. But I sensed Charles respected me too much for that. Though he had told me the opposite of what I wished to hear, my feelings of alarm eased.

"What the French *want*," he continued, "and what they *will do* may be very different things. They will not act while the outcome of the war is in doubt. Before then, I hope we can make the government see reason. I have long believed England would do better to abandon the colonies than conquer them."

A weight lifted from my heart. From the moment I'd met Charles Fox, I had been charmed by his joviality and high spirits. Later I had come to respect his cleverness and breadth of knowledge. Now, I admired his principles and his courage. "You can persuade the Commons. I am certain of it."

"I set great store by your confidence." He rummaged in his pocket and pulled out two letters, folded and sealed with Richard's signet. "This news of our friend is old, but it may still cheer you a little. I mean to send off a reply at once, if you have a few lines you wish to enclose."

My heart brimmed with gratitude as I clutched the letters. Not just because he had eased my fears, but because I felt like a stronger, better person for knowing him. "I will write to Richard this very night. Thank you for bringing these ... and for everything."

"A pleasure, my dear," replied Charles. "After all, what are friends for?"

# Chapter Thirteen

*C*HARLES'S VISIT HERALDED A NEAR-MIRACULOUS change in my fortunes. Buoyed by his boundless optimism, I not only wrote a long letter to Richard, but warm notes to several of my old admirers. By the end of the week, one had put a carriage at my disposal and several others had applied for the honor of sitting in my box at Covent Garden.

They were all quick to acquaint me with rumors that the Duke of Dorset had embarked on a love affair with the beautiful Lady Derby. I could not hear that woman's name without a fierce rush of resentment. She was the cause of all my recent troubles. I felt certain that ladies cricket match she'd organized had been a calculated bid to gain the duke's attention.

"Perhaps so," said Bob when I confided in him, "her mother married two dukes. How could Lady Betty be content with only one earl, even if he is the richest peer in the realm?"

A week later, in the supper room at the Pantheon, Lord Cholmondeley stopped by my table to pay his respects. I knew the well-endowed earl was not looking to renew attentions to me. I'd read in the scandal magazines that he'd taken a new mistress—Dally Eliot, the notorious divorcee my mantua-maker had told me about. She was with him tonight, an elegant, swanlike beauty who matched the earl's lofty height. The man who accompanied them looked almost dwarfed by his tall companions.

"Mrs. Armistead, always a pleasure!" Lord Cholmondeley drew his mistress forward. "May I present Mrs. Eliot?"

I doubted many men would have the assurance to introduce his current mistress to a prior one, but his lordship brought it off without the least awkwardness.

As Mrs. Eliot and I exchanged civil curtsies and polite murmurs of greeting, I sensed many eyes upon us. I wondered how long it would be before one of the scandal magazines reported us fighting a duel in the rotunda with drawn hatpins!

I cannot deny I felt a flicker of competitive jealousy toward the stylish divorcée who looked two or three years younger than me. Noting the tenderness that softened her aristocratic features when she glanced at the earl, I wondered if the rumors were true that he meant to make her his countess.

Even if I'd been a gambler, I would not have placed a wager on it. After all, what would his lordship gain by making her his wife that he did not already get from having her as his mistress? Had anyone bothered to tell young Mrs. Eliot the courtesan's cardinal rule?

While all those thoughts raced through my mind, Lord Cholmondeley introduced his male companion. "May I also present the Earl of Derby? He has been anxious for some time to meet the celebrated Mrs. Armistead."

So this was the man whose wife had stolen the Duke of Dorset from me. Though he lacked the duke's stunning masculine beauty, Lord Derby was rather attractive in a blunt, honest, thoroughly English way.

"An honor, my lord." I curtsied and held out my hand for him to bow over. "I believe I saw you from a distance at Newmarket the year before last."

I purged my mind of everything I'd learned about cricket while trying to recall all I could about the turf. "Have you any promising foals or fillies coming along for next year's races?"

The earl's face lit up at my question. "There is a young filly I have high hopes for, sired by Herod." He glanced down at the table. "May I join you?"

"I should be delighted. Lord Cholmondeley, Mrs. Eliot?"

"Another time, perhaps." Lord Cholmondeley looked relieved to be free of the earl's company. "We are expected in the card room, if you will excuse us."

As they headed off, I wondered how poor Lord Derby could bear going out in public with everyone gossiping about his wife and the Duke of Dorset. Perhaps it was better than enduring the unspoken tension at home. Or perhaps he was desperately seeking some diversion from his troubled marriage.

I vowed to do everything in my power to divert the poor man. After all, he had been hurt worse than I by Lord Dorset's affair with his wife. "Herod? I believe Lord Bolingbroke is bringing along one of his foals."

"So he is!" The earl looked pleasantly surprised at my knowledge. "Highflier won at Newmarket just last month. I reckon that horse will make Bully a great deal of money."

"What about your filly?" I asked. "What do you call her?"

"Bridget. A pretty name, don't you think?"

"Indeed." His words brought a smile to my lips for Bridget was my middle name, the only legacy from my Irish mother. "Will she be ready to race next year?"

Lord Derby shook his head. "Even with the shift to running three-year-olds, she cannot race for another year after that. She has fine form, though and great spirit. I hope she will live up to her promise."

We enjoyed a cup of arrack punch together and some very rich cakes, while I plied Lord Derby with all manner of questions about horses and racing.

"I mean to promote a race for three-year-old fillies," he told me, "At Epsom Downs over a shorter course. By the time the Jockey Club sanctions it, Bridget may be able to compete."

He went on to talk about his other favorite pastime, cockfighting. Though I shrank from the thought of such a bloodthirsty sport, I did my best to appear interested.

When we parted for the night, Lord Derby seemed sincerely reluctant to leave me. "I cannot recall when I have passed so enjoyable an evening, Mrs. Armistead. I hope you will not object to my calling upon you at your convenience."

Ridiculous as it might sound his request caught me off-guard. I'd only meant to show the earl a little kindness. I had not intended to make a conquest of him.

"You may call on Thursday," I agreed with reluctance. "I have no engagements for that evening."

When he sprouted an eager grin, I warned him, "Only so we can talk and come to an understanding, mind."

"Of course." Lord Derby did not hesitate. "As you wish."

The next day he sent me a basket of oranges from his hothouse and the day after that a present of game from one of his estates. I thanked him for both when he arrived that evening. "These will go a great way toward furnishing the menu for my next *petit souper* with my Whig friends."

"I have heard warm reports of your hospitality." Lord Derby's happiness at having pleased me was obvious.

It further stirred my sympathy for him. "You are welcome to join us if you would care to."

"Name the hour and I will be there." The earl leaned forward in his chair. "If there is anything more I can supply for your table, you have only to ask."

I shook my head. "Your company will be more than sufficient. With an extra chair filled, perhaps we will not miss Richard Fitzpatrick quite so much."

A look of doubt clouded Lord Derby's face. "I hope you will not expect me to take his part in the conversation. I could never match Mr. Fitzpatrick's eloquent wit."

"I expect nothing but that you endeavor to enjoy yourself. I only meant that you would be a welcome addition to our company."

I started back when Lord Derby flew from his chair to kneel at my feet. "And I should like to enjoy more of *your* company, Mrs. Armistead. Only tell me how I may secure you for myself and you shall have it!"

I shrank from the earl's unexpected ardor before my mind responded to his offer. Could this be my chance to obtain a dependable income so I would never again have to solicit business from the King's Place brothels?

"Please, my lord." I seized his hands to keep him from flinging his arms around me. "Do not act in haste. If I accept an offer from you, I fear it will make your situation worse."

"Worse?" He gave a growl of bitter laughter. "What can be worse than knowing the woman I meant to spend the rest of my life with can scarcely bear the sight of me? Whenever I speak to her, she looks ready to retch. If I try to touch her, even to take her hand, she cringes in disgust. Am I such a monster?"

He lowered his face to rest upon our clasped hands.

Though I tried to maintain a cool detachment that would allow me to exploit this situation to my advantage, I could not. Pity for Lord Derby softened my heart, leaving it dangerously vulnerable. "No indeed! You seem a very good sort of man."

"I thought myself the *luckiest* man in the world when Betty Hamilton agreed to marry me. And I tried to be a good husband. I was never cruel to her. Never flaunted a mistress under her nose the way Devonshire does with his duchess. I gave her everything she ever asked of me. What more could I do?"

The earl still loved his errant wife, I had no doubt of it. And the Derbys had two small children. I'd become too well known for a liaison with the earl to escape gossip, perhaps even another *tête-à-tête* in *Town and Country*. If his marriage could be salvaged, a public scandal like that would doom any hope.

"There is still one thing you can do, my lord." I feared I would live to regret what I was about to say.

He lifted his face to stare at me with haunted eyes. "What is it? Tell me!"

I longed to run my hand over his hair in a comforting caress, but I resisted the urge. "You can *wait*. Indeed, I think you must. For your family's sake, do not make matters worse by acting in haste. A reckless fancy may burn itself out as quickly as it comes."

Perhaps not on Lady Derby's part, but I had reason to know the Duke of Dorset was fickle in his affections. If the earl could only be patient, his rival might move on to a new conquest. Then the spurned countess might learn to place a higher value on kindness and constancy.

"It's rather like racing isn't it?" I added, hoping to persuade him by talking in terms familiar to him. "Some horses make a very fast start only to be beaten to the finish by the true champions who can stay the course."

Lord Derby's face brightened. "By Jove, you may be right! With the stakes so high, I ought to watch my form and not pull up prematurely. I have seen too many finishes go to a patient jockey riding a steady mount."

He pressed a firm but chaste kiss on my hand then returned to his chair. "May I still come to your *petit souper?*"

"Of course." Was I a fool to let the best prospect of my career get away? "I should like to number you among my friends."

"And if I find myself in need of a confidante? This is not the sort of thing a man can talk about with other men, and you seem to understand it all so well."

Did I? There were times I believed so. I *wanted* to observe a professional detachment in matters of the heart. That way I might influence them to my own advantage. But my folly with Lord Dorset proved that I could still fall victim to the intrigues of desire.

"I am honored that you would place me in your confidence," I replied. "My past has given me an uncommon perspective on the relations between men and women. I shall be happy to place it at your service along with my discretion."

We talked a little more then Lord Derby rose to leave.

As I handed him his hat, he announced, "I will give my wife six months to come to her senses and mend our marriage. If she persists in her folly after that, will you consider offering me something more than sympathy and advice?"

I nodded. "You have my word I will it consider it then. Though, for your sake and your children's, I hope you will not feel the need of me."

For several weeks, I questioned the wisdom of my answer to Lord Derby. I sensed he was only bearing with his marriage because of his promise to me. If I released him from it, I was certain he would be only too happy to become my exclusive patron on very favorable terms.

When I recalled how his wife had stolen the duke from me, I was sorely tempted to do just that. I was prevented less by my scruples than a reluctance to put all my eggs in one basket again. At the moment I had several patrons contributing to my support. Though it meant I was busier juggling my obligations to a number of gentlemen, I had finally been able to pay all my outstanding bills and begin to save a little. If one of my lovers tired of me, which was less likely with several competing for my favors, it would not be as great a calamity as losing my sole benefactor.

Then one evening in December, I heard some news that confirmed the prudence of my decision.

"It is folly," growled Charles Fox as he and his friends dined with me after the Commons let out, "to declare a six week holiday when the nation is in the midst of such a crisis!"

"You will find no one at this table to disagree with you, Charles," said James Hare, a celebrated wit whose chief occupation seemed to be gambling away the fortune of his poor neglected wife. He took an appreciative sip of well-aged burgundy from one of several bottles Lord Derby had brought to my last *petit souper.*

Bob Spencer drained his glass. Clearly the day's debate had left them all in need of refreshment. "Derby might gainsay you if he were here. I hope we have not frightened off your new friend with all our opposition rhetoric Mrs. Armistead."

"I hope she has not introduced a government spy into our midst," muttered Hare, who might have meant to keep the words under his breath, but the wine had loosened his tongue.

Before I could protest my innocence, Charles Fox rose from his chair. His dark eyes blazed with indignation. "For shame! That is a fine way to insult a person who has shown us such hospitality. Mrs. Armistead is above allowing politics to dictate her friendships. It is we who drag our debates into her home. If any of us has something to say that cannot be heard by all her guests, then he had better hold his tongue!"

His vigorous defence touched me. And I was not sorry to see the acerbic Mr. Hare rebuked by the man he clearly idolized.

In response to his mumbled apology, I replied, "My only motive for inviting Lord Derby was my sympathy with his situation. I hoped the poor man might find some hours of amusement among you. If you object to his company, I will invite him another time."

"Indeed not." Charles shot a pointed look at Mr. Hare. "I should be glad of a word with Derby. Perhaps *he* can give us some account of how his uncle came to surrender seven thousand troops at Saratoga. Lord knows I have not been able to wring any information out of the Ministry."

"About Lord Derby," ventured a younger member of Charles's circle, "I heard a rumor that his wife is breeding. That may be why he has not joined us tonight."

Lady Derby, pregnant? The news ambushed me with a bewildering jumble of emotions, all far too intense for my peace of mind. Perhaps the sharpest of them was envy. With each passing birthday my longing for a child had grown. But memories of that desperate young mother in the intelligence office all those years ago, and of the bloodstain on Rose's gown as she swooned to the floor, spurred me to cleanse myself after every night I entertained a man.

Bob broke the stunned hush that fell over the table. "Shall we wager whether Lady Betty will hatch a Derby bantam cock or a young Kentish cricket?"

Poor Lord Derby! Every gossip in town would be soon tattling about whether the child was his or Dorset's.

"It would be a foolish wager." I threw down my napkin, disgusted with Bob for making such a thoughtless jest at the earl's expense. "Who can know for certain?"

Lord Derby knew whose child his wife carried, or believed he did, when he visited my house a few days later. "No doubt you have heard the news and all the gossip surrounding it."

I replied with a mute nod for I did not dare ask him the one question that crowded on the tip of my tongue.

"The child is mine. Betty is too far along for it to be otherwise. I am grateful to you for persuading me to be patient. I hope this will give my wife time to consider all she stands to lose if she persists in her folly."

More likely it would give the Duke of Dorset an opportunity to stray. He did not strike me as the type of man to find a heavily pregnant woman attractive.

"If you show her kindness, now, I am certain you will make her remember where her true affections lie." Not that she deserved it after what she'd done, but I hoped everything between them would work out well for Lord Derby's sake.

I tried to ignore a stab of disappointment over what I might have gained from such a generous patron. A malicious little whisper in the back of my mind reminded me that my thirtieth birthday was approaching at a gallop.

The social season was soon in glittering parade once more, with masques and ridottos at the Pantheon, strolls along the canal in St. James Park and evenings at the opera. Yet beneath this round of pleasure, like treacherous currents under brittle spring ice, lurked the perils of war.

I did my best to ignore the danger I was powerless to avoid, pretending to believe the comforting falsehoods published in the newspapers. But I could not close my ears to the table talk of my Whig friends. Nor could I close my eyes to the periodic letters I received from Richard.

He had taken part in two important battles the previous autumn to wrest the city of Philadelphia from the Americans. But that advantage had been lost with the surrender of seven thousand British troops by Lord Derby's uncle, General Burgoyne. Though Richard was a well-trained soldier who served to the best of his ability, I sensed he had come to admire his American 'enemies' and entertained even graver doubts about the war.

Meanwhile, his friends in London continued their valiant, but badly outnumbered, fight to make the King's ministers recognize their folly.

"I wish you could have heard Charles last week, Mrs. Armistead," said Bob one evening in mid-February when they had gathered around my table again. "He managed to catch Lord North flat-footed by asking if he knew that France has signed a treaty with the Americans. North had to admit he did not. That man's only merit is that he can bear to be proven a fool again and again yet not resign his post."

Charles shook his head. "North has more merit than you suppose, Bob. He is not a bad man and he is certainly no fool. But he sees himself as a servant of the Crown and does everything in his power to fulfill that role."

That was so like Charles. He always spoke up for anyone being abused by the rest of the company, even if that person was his bitterest political foe.

"An interesting observation," said Mr. Sheridan, the Irish playwright and new manager of Drury Lane who had joined us that evening at Charles's request. "Do you *not* consider yourself and Parliament to be servants of the Crown, Mr. Fox?"

Charles cleaned the last morsel of Dover sole from his plate then washed it down with a swing from his wine glass. "Sir, I become daily more convinced that Parliament and all its Honorable Members must serve the *people*."

Further drinking and eating followed as they talked more about the war and their gambling wins and losses. Thanks to Mr. Sheridan, they also talked about what plays would be performed at Drury Lane in the coming weeks.

"Anything featuring the divine Mrs. Robinson?" asked Bob with a cheerful leer. "I hope we shall see her in a 'breeches' part soon."

So this Mrs. Robinson was fashion's new favorite? My hackles rose. The old favorite, Mrs. Baddeley, no longer appeared at the Pantheon dripping in diamonds. I wondered how soon Mrs. Robinson might take her place. Or mine?

Though I smiled and nodded and pretended to look interested in my friends' conversation, I was preoccupied for the rest of the evening. I only rallied when I had a few minutes alone with Charles after his friends had gone off to their club.

"This treaty between France and America," I asked as I handed him my latest letter to Richard, "does it put the French at war with us?"

"It is the first step." Charles pocketed my letter. "I only hope the threat of a French invasion will shake the Ministry out of its madness." He did not sound hopeful.

"By the way," he remarked as he headed for the door, "I dined with your friend Lord Derby the other night."

"I hope he is well."

Charles shook his head. "The poor fellow is a great vagabond these days, dining out all over town. And he is desperately in love with you."

Love? I hoped Charles only meant that word in the way it was most often bandied about to signify desire or fascination. I did not want Lord Derby to feel anything deeper for me because I could not return it as he deserved.

Charles soon proved right about both the French and the earl. By the time Lady Derby bore her little daughter late in April, I was no longer alone in fearing a French invasion. Regiments of militia were being raised to defend the coast, most led by young noblemen eager to play at soldiering, as if war were a massive foxhunt coupled with a vast outdoor house party, staged for their amusement.

Many went to camp in Kent, near the Duke of Dorset's magnificent estate. Lord George Cavendish, the richest of my patrons talked of spending the summer there with his brother, the Duke of Devonshire.

"You should come with me, Mrs. Armistead," he suggested one evening at Vauxhall. "A great many of the other officers have their wives or mistresses staying with them."

"Let me think on it." I did not relish the prospect of putting myself between the Dover coast and London, the most likely target of a French attack. But neither did I care to repeat my experiences of the previous summer by losing the protection of a reliable admirer.

While I struggled to make up my mind, Lord Derby appeared one afternoon to invite me for a drive in the country.

"It is six months to the day since we last spoke," he reminded me as his carriage headed toward Wembley.

"So it is, my lord. Congratulations on the birth of your daughter."

"Poor little mite." He sighed. "Her mother could scarcely wait to be rid of the burden that kept her from her *amour*. I tried to win her back with kindness, but Dorset's hold over her was too strong. While mine ... I doubt it ever existed."

I wished I could assure him otherwise, but I could not.

"She has gone to Brighthelmstone," he added in a tone of bitter irony, "to *recover from the birth*."

In recent years sea bathing had become a fashionable cure for almost everything, but who would be mad enough to spend summer at the seaside when a French invasion fleet menaced the coast? A woman *madly* in love, perhaps? Much as I despised Lady Derby, I could not dismiss the power a man like the duke could exert upon women when he chose.

I wondered how often he might venture down from Knole to visit his new mistress. It seemed he had not tired of Lady Derby, as I'd predicted. Perhaps while she kept up the charade of her marriage, she continued to pose a challenge to the competitive sportsman. Though I recalled with longing the duke's divine looks and wicked skill as a lover, I could not truly envy Lady Derby. She would soon discover he had neither heart nor conscience.

"What will you do?" I asked Lord Derby.

The earl blew out a deep breath. "During these past miserable weeks, I have often thought about our last meeting and compared your conduct with my wife's. Am I wrong to believe I deserve the company of a woman who values my better qualities and cares about my happiness?"

Though my craving for security urged me to secure a wealthy patron who was twice the man his Grace of Dorset would ever be, I hesitated. Lord Derby sounded as if he might want more from me than I was willing, or able, to give.

"Of course you do," I said at last. But could *I* be the woman he needed?

"You'll do it, then?" The sudden glow that lit Lord Derby's face almost outshone the spring sun. "You will permit me the honor of supporting your expenses exclusively?"

I wrestled with my decision, but in the end practicality won out. The arrangement he offered was just what I needed. It would provide me with security through the lean summer season without compelling me to become a glorified camp follower.

By the time Lord Derby delivered me home, we had come to an agreement. In exchange for six months' exclusive rights to my company, he would support all my expenses ... and provide me with an annuity of two hundred pounds a year. I would never have to worry about ending up back on the streets again.

"Splendid!" The earl's chest puffed out like one of his fighting cocks. "Can you pack and be ready to leave by Monday?"

"Leave?" I asked. "Where are you planning to take me?"

To his house in Epsom perhaps? Or, better yet, his estate in Yorkshire, far from the vulnerable south coast?

The earl looked surprised by my question. "To camp, of course. We Stanleys have a proud tradition of fighting for our country."

# Chapter Fourteen

ERCHED ON THE SADDLE OF a gentle old gelding, I sat in the shade of a beech tree on a low hill overlooking the Winchester militia encampment. On the open ground below, companies of volunteers marched and drilled. Behind them, row upon row of white canvas tents made the camp look like a bleach-yard. The roll of drums, the crack of musket fire and the muted thunder of marching feet charged the lazy summer air with an undercurrent of danger.

I spotted Lord Derby on horseback, reviewing his men. He noticed me, too, for he lifted his hat and waved it in the air. A few moments later, he wheeled his horse and charged up the hill toward me.

"Did you ride all the way here by yourself?" He lavished me with an admiring smile, as if I had accomplished some miraculous feat.

The warmth of his praise made me uneasy. It seemed to ask more of me than I was prepared to give. "At a very sedate walk but I did get here without falling."

"Soon you will be able to gallop along by my side." The earl's voice rang with confidence.

I gave a nervous laugh. "Do not expect too much of me. Besides learning a new skill, I have my fear to overcome."

From my unsteady perch in the saddle, the ground looked a long way down. And even the gentlest horse was still a large, powerful beast that could easily toss me from its back or run away with me. Left to my own devices, I would never have set about learning to ride at my age.

But I had not been left to my own devices. I had pledged myself to Lord Derby for six months and he was determined to make a rider out of me. What else might he want to make of me? The thought unnerved me as much as this devilish riding business.

I nodded toward the soldiers. "Your men seem to be getting on well."

"They have acquired some discipline." The earl puffed up with pride. "I reckon they will be in good order for the King to review when he comes."

"When will that be?"

"At the end of the summer, when there is less danger of invasion. I am told he and the queen plan to visit all the camps."

Playing at war, I thought, as if those men marching in the hot sun were toy soldiers without lives or feelings that mattered. Quite the opposite of Lord Derby who seemed to care a good deal about the men he commanded.

"Have you had any more trouble with the sutlers?" I asked,

Militiamen were at the mercy of dishonest peddlers of provisions, who sold them grossly overpriced food that was often inedible.

Lord Derby removed his hat and fanned his face with it. "We rounded up a few of the worst and put them in the stocks. Caught one rascal soaking old eggs in lime and water so they'd pass for fresh. A pox on him and all corrupt contractors!"

I had little doubt they would end up poxed, with all the 'laundresses' and camp followers available for hire. I pitied those women and felt fortunate that Lord Derby was so temperate in his *amours*. For the first time in years, I did not have to worry about catching a disease.

"Should I expect you for supper, my lord?"

Though he lived in camp, the earl had installed me in a pleasant little cottage not far away. At least three evenings a week, he visited to dine with me and spend the evening.

"I have no pressing duties at the moment." Lord Derby put his hat back on. "I shall escort you home and stay to dine."

We rode back at a quicker pace than I had come. I sensed Lord Derby's impatience, but to me the brisk walk felt like break-neck speed already.

"Try not to hold yourself so tense, Mrs. Armistead. Relax your body and let it move with the horse."

I could have given him similar advice about his lovemaking. His advances were so tentative and methodical, I sometimes found myself entertaining wicked fancies about the Duke of Dorset to make me more receptive to Lord Derby.

That summer away from town passed slowly, but at least England was spared an invasion. I was relieved to hear Richard Fitzpatrick had returned safely from America. I longed to see him, but he was busy caring for his sister, the young widow of Charles Fox's brother.

"I fear he is exhausting himself," said Richard's brother, Lord Ossory, whose regiment was also encamped at Winchester. "I wish I could help, but I am needed here, and he is the only one poor Mary wants. They have been close ever since our nursery days."

"Is her illness serious?"

Lord Ossory nodded gravely. "Consumption made worse by spells of fever and delirium. Her doctors do not expect her to last the year. I pity her children. Caroline is only ten-years-old and the image of Mary. My nephew is but a little fellow. He was not a year old when he lost his father. Now I doubt he will have much memory of his mother."

I knew what it was like to lose a parent at that age. The Fox children might never know the privations I had, but they would suffer a loss no amount of money could compensate.

"When you speak to your brother next," I begged Lord Ossory "please give him my fondest regards."

When the sunny days of summer gave way to the cool damp of autumn, I persuaded Lord Derby to let me return to London.

"The king and queen will be coming to review your troops soon, won't they?" I asked one night as he dressed to return to camp. The earl never lingered in bed after taking his pleasure.

"We expect them before the end of the month." He stood to tuck in his shirt and button his breeches. "I can probably find you some inconspicuous spot to watch the royal inspection."

I could not imagine anything more tiresome! "That is kind of you, my lord, but I fear my presence might be a source of embarrassment for you."

"I had not thought of that." He perched on the edge of the bed to pull on his riding boots.

"Perhaps I should return to London and get some new gowns made. Fashion changes so quickly and I want to be a credit to you if you wish to take me out in public."

Lord Derby turned and reached for my hand. "Of course I wish to take you out in public, wearing the most fashionable gowns money can buy. I will give you a draft to my banker that should furnish you the most stylish wardrobe of any lady in London."

I might have rewarded such generosity by bounding out of bed naked to offer him an appreciative kiss. But I knew that would fluster Lord Derby more than please him. The man's sense of propriety could be almost puritan at times.

So I remained in bed, with a sheet tucked under my arms to cover my breasts, and I thanked him effusively for all his kindness. He was a generous, honorable man. He would never think of seducing another man's wife, like Lord Dorset or Richard Fitzpatrick. He did not have Bully's vile temper or the insufferable presumption of General Smith. And yet ...

I quickly turned my thoughts elsewhere. I had no business thinking ill of the gentleman who had rescued me from the specter of poverty. But the sun had barely risen the next morning before I was out of bed and directing my servants to pack for our return to Clarges Street. There I indulged in an orgy of shopping, placing orders with the mantua-maker, milliner and linen draper, who were all grateful for my business.

"Too many people being careful with their money these days," grumbled Mrs. Whitelock, the mantua-maker, "so they can afford to sail off to Naples or Jamaica if the French invade. The rest of us can go bankrupt and learn how to *parlez-vous!*"

When I noticed the woeful look on the milliner's motherly face, I tried to cheer her up. "Perhaps business will improve now that the militia camps are dispersing for the winter."

"It's not that, ma'am, though orders are down and folks takin' longer than ever to pay their bills. I just got word that young Lady Holland has breathed her last, poor soul. One of my best customers she was, and always so amiable."

A soft moan escaped my lips. Poor Richard!

"Beg pardon, ma'am, did ye know the lady?"

I struggled to compose myself. "Only her brothers – how I feel for them and for her children."

Did this mean Charles Fox would be put in charge of his young niece and nephew? I had no doubt he loved them dearly, with affection as open and merry as that of one child for another. But how could he provide the kind of care children needed when he did not even take proper care of himself?

"Shall I host a *petit souper* next week?" I asked Lord Derby a few weeks later when we took our seats for a subscription concert at Carlisle House. "Perhaps we could invite your uncle. I am certain Charles Fox and the others support the general's right to a fair hearing."

I had scarcely seen anything of my Whig friends since the spring and nothing of Richard Fitzpatrick since his return from America. I craved their stimulating companionship.

"Of course they do," Lord Derby replied. "And not just because a court martial might discredit the Ministry. I never had any lofty ideals about politics, but we are Englishmen for

God's sake! There comes a time when we must do what is just and damn the consequences."

An elderly lady sitting near us cast the earl a reproachful look, while a large man with a face like a red bulldog's huffed.

"Well said, my lord," I whispered. It did not surprise me to hear him express such sentiments. In his twin passions of racing and cockfighting, fairness was vital and all classes of society mixed as equals.

"As for the supper," Lord Derby continued, "you needn't bother. Lady Melbourne and the Duchess of Devonshire have both invited the general and me to their recent salons. Anything he wished to discuss with Fox and the others was well aired there."

"I see." As a string quartet began to play the opening bars of an Albinoni concerto, I was overcome by a rush of resentment. Did the duchess and Lady Melbourne mean to steal my friends from me the way Lady Derby had stolen Lord Dorset?

"Besides," the earl whispered, "you and I have an exclusive arrangement."

"Of course we do, my lord!" I spoke louder than I intended, provoking some sharp looks from people around us. I lowered my voice to an emphatic whisper. "I was not proposing to invite them for a night of debauchery. They are my friends."

Those friendships were my only lasting personal connections. I would not let anyone take them away from me.

Lord Derby did not back down from my indignant glare. "Some on *very friendly* terms, I understand."

Did he assume I opened my arms to all the gentlemen I counted as friends? Outrage smoldered in my belly, but how could I protest otherwise after my tryst with Bob Spencer?

I made no reply until the first movement of the concerto had concluded. While the audience applauded, I leaned toward Lord Derby and spoke loud enough for him alone to hear. "As you say, my lord, we have an exclusive arrangement. I hope you trust me to keep my word."

We did not speak again until the concert had concluded and the musicians taken their bows. Then Lord Derby escorted me to the banquet room where a sumptuous buffet of pastries awaited us. On the way, he called out hearty greetings or paused engage in animated conversation with every gentleman of his acquaintance. He seemed determined to make everyone notice us.

I flattered myself that my appearance alone might have drawn a few eyes that night, for I wore a cherry-red gown of rich paduasoy silk. The overskirt, of sprigged Persian taffeta, was gathered in the back with cream colored bows. A matching one adorned the low-cut bosom of my bodice. Instead of an ordinary fan, I carried a single ostrich plume. I wanted no one who glanced at me that night to doubt Lord Derby had got the better bargain, exchanging his wife for the Duke of Dorset's mistress.

"I have been thinking," said the earl as he heaped a plate with nuggets of German gingerbread, tiny iced cakes and ring-shaped biscuits called *gimblettes*. "With winter coming, you would be better off in the country. Hampstead, perhaps. It is no more than five miles from your present address, but on higher ground where the winter air is more wholesome."

Though I tried to appear pleased with the plan, in truth, I felt as if the lavishly decorated walls of Carlisle House were closing in upon me. When Lord Derby was not parading me about the parks, assembly rooms and theatres of London, he seemed bent on keeping me cloistered away. I suppose I could not blame him. Having suffered the pain and humiliation of an unfaithful wife, why should he trust a woman who changed lovers faster than the coming and going of the seasons?

Late one afternoon in December, I glanced out the frosted window in the upstairs landing of my spacious new house in Hampstead. It was a handsome dwelling, built of golden brown brick, with pleasing proportions and large well-lit rooms.

Unlike my place on Clarges Street, this one was not squeezed promiscuously between the houses on either side, but kept a decorous distance from its neighbors behind a wrought-iron fence and a veil of trees and shrubs.

Living here would save me a pretty penny, for Lord Derby paid all the expenses of the house and stables directly, without decreasing my allowance by a farthing. Away from the shops of London, with merchandise tempting me from their display windows, I would be less apt to squander my pin money. Still, I felt as if I was being slowly suffocated with a silken pillow.

I cast a longing look toward the distant dome of St. Paul's rearing up out of the fog that blanketed the city below. A ghostly moon hung on the eastern horizon. Some days London seemed nearly as distant as the moon. Hampstead Heath had long been a favorite haunt of highwaymen so I was afraid to venture into town without Lord Derby's company.

Though I had not expected a visit from him that night, the earl arrived after dark, looking flustered. Scarcely had he shed his hat and greatcoat when he called for champagne.

"I am not certain there is any on hand, my lord." I sent the footman off to check. "Would you not prefer a cup of *smoking bishop* to warm you after your ride?"

"I am plenty warm." As if to prove it, he pulled me toward him and kissed me soundly on the mouth. "Since I celebrated the getting of my bride with a *fête champêtre*, it seems only fitting I should raise a glass to toast being rid of her."

Beneath the earl's defiant show of triumph, I glimpsed the pain he strove to hide. Sympathy overcame my growing irritation with his possessiveness. I drew him into the parlor, where a warm fire crackled in the hearth. "So you have secured the evidence you need to prosecute her for *crim con?*"

The earl gave a grim nod as he chafed his hands before the fire. "I confronted Betty with it. Told her I refuse to be a complaisant cuckold any longer. What if she bore a son next? Then, if any harm came to young Edward, all the Stanley lands and titles would go to a Sackville changeling. I cannot risk that."

The thought of such a confrontation made my stomach churn. "What did she say?"

"What *could* she say? Denial would have been a waste of breath. She has left my house. That is all I care about."

My footman appeared then, bearing two glasses and an open champagne bottle. Once he'd placed them on the table in front of the sofa, Lord Derby dismissed him and filled the glasses.

He handed one to me, then lifted his in a toast. "It may be a few weeks until the New Year, yet I say, 'Out with the old and in with the new!'"

I raised my glass and took a sip of champagne while Lord Derby bolted his. The tart little bubbles stung my mouth.

Pain and rage radiated from the earl, intense as heat from the hearth. When he refilled his glass, I feared his fierce grip might shatter the bottle. "She tried to convince me Dorset had sired little Hetty, but I am certain it is only a ruse so she can keep one of the children. Damned if I will permit it!"

I stifled a pang of sympathy for Lady Derby. She must have known she would forfeit her children if she persisted in her affair with the duke. And yet . . . plenty of *men* had affairs and kept mistresses without fear of losing their offspring. Lord Derby had not been one of those men, I reminded myself. He and his children were the wronged parties in all of this.

Setting down my barely-touched glass, I opened my arms to him. "Think no more of her tonight. She has made a foolish choice and I am certain she will repent it. This is your chance to make a fresh start. Whatever lies ahead must surely be better than what you have endured this past year."

"You talk confounded good sense!" Lord Derby tossed back his second glass of champagne with a less troubled air then surrendered to my embrace.

Perhaps the champagne was especially potent. Or perhaps Lord Derby's confrontation with his wife had fired the passions he usually kept under strict control. Whatever the cause, the result was most stimulating.

He kissed me with fierce energy, his hot tongue thrusting and probing. I feigned the slightest reluctance, as if I were a timid creature, overwhelmed yet secretly excited by his manly ardor. Indeed, I found myself entering the spirit of the part far more than I ever had on stage.

Because the hour was late and I had not expected company, I wore no hoops beneath my gown and loose, front-laced jumps instead of stays. Lord Derby took full advantage of my casual attire. Lowering me to the chaise lounge, he knelt beside it, tugging my bodice lacings open until my breasts burst free like round, ripe fruit. While he proceeded to feast upon them, I responded with little feigned gasps of alarm and sighs of pleasure, which were perfectly genuine.

He extended one arm to reach beneath my petticoats, pulling them up as his hand roved over my thighs, prying them apart with rough impatience. I offered only such token resistance as I sensed would inflame his desire. But the dewy heat that greeted his fingers when they reached the object of their search betrayed my wanton eagerness.

His breath gusting like a lathered stallion's, he unbuckled his waistband and wrenched open the foreflap of his breeches. Lowering them just enough to free his straining shaft, he mounted and "ravished" me to my vast enjoyment.

Afterward, he lay with his head on my shoulder, all tension wrung from his body. "I'd be a fool to pine for a woman who's treated me as Betty has. I have my gamecocks and my horses. I have my children and I have you. What more could I want?"

Another woman might have resented being mentioned after his precious livestock, but knowing how Lord Derby doted on them, I took it as a sort of compliment.

"I do love an early spring." I gave my parasol a twirl as I rode with Lord Derby in an open carriage toward Kensington. "Now that the Season has begun, I must open my house in town."

"What is wrong with Hampstead?" The earl cast me a sidelong look. "I thought you liked the country."

My fingers tightened around the handle of my parasol. "It is an excellent place to spend the winter–healthier than the city but not too far distant."

"Why leave it, then?" he challenged me. "There are more dangers in London than the winter fog. Why it has been scarcely a month since that mob attacked the Admiralty."

"Clarges Street is a good way from the Admiralty," I protested. "And no one can blame *me* for Admiral Keppel's court martial. I would give your Uncle Burgoyne one, if it were in my power. I have no doubt it would clear his name while exposing the Ministry's mismanagement of the war."

I'd heard a great deal on that subject during the past several weeks, for General Burgoyne was the only guest his nephew ever invited to dine with us in Hampstead. Though I found the general rather pompous and given to bragging, I welcomed the news he brought me of my Whig friends.

"I reckon Hampstead will be just as pleasant in the summer." Lord Derby pointed north. "Up in the hills, it is sure to catch a breeze while escaping the smells of the city."

"I suppose but–"

"Then perhaps you should find a tenant for your house on Clarges Street." It sounded more like an order than a suggestion.

This whole conversation took me by surprise. "You mean I should make my home in Hampstead year round?"

"Why not?" asked the earl. "If Knowsley were as near London as Hampstead I doubt I would bother keeping a house in town, no matter what the season."

Did he not realize I needed somewhere of my own–a place I could return to when our liaison ended?

When Lord Derby went to the country for a few days to look at breeding stock for his stables, I braved the road to London for a round of shopping. At the milliner's, I met up with Lord Cholmondeley's mistress, Dally Eliot, who greeted me most cordially. I wondered if she might be as lonely for a little female companionship as I sometimes found myself.

We struck up a pleasant conversation while trying on hats. After we had chatted about the unseasonably warm weather and the extravagant height of the new hairstyles, we fell to exchanging gossip about the latest Society scandals.

"There is much ado among Lady Derby's friends," Mrs. Eliot murmured, "about who will visit her now that she has left the earl. The Duke of Dorset told Lord Cholmondeley he means to marry her the moment she is free, so her friends must reckon she will soon be respectable again."

Though I still resented all the mischief Lady Derby had made, I replied tartly, "I cannot see how she is any *less* respectable than some of them, just because their husbands are more complaisant."

"I quite agree," said Dally. "But the ladies should not count their chickens, should they?"

"I beg your pardon?"

"I mean ... because Lord Derby has sworn he will never divorce her. He has told you that, surely."

Never divorce? I could only shake my head in stunned silence as I considered the consequences of such action. The countess would never be free to remarry, never allowed to have any place in society. How long would the fickle Lord Dorset be prepared to bear with her on those terms before he sought a fresh challenge?

"Forgive me!" cried Dally. "I should have held my tongue. I thought this would be good news for you."

Would it?

Flustered by my silence, she rattled on. "It must mean he has no wish to wed again. Perhaps he will make a permanent arrangement with you like Lord Sandwich has with Miss Ray."

Dally made it sound like a most desirable situation and perhaps it was. For more than fifteen years, Martha Ray had lived openly with Lord Sandwich at the Admiralty, where she acted as his hostess. He had hired masters to train her in all the accomplishments of a lady. She'd born him several children. It seemed as secure a union as a woman of our kind could hope for.

If what Dally said was true, I might soon gain the security I had craved for so long. But would it come at a higher cost than I could bear to pay?

# Chapter Fifteen

"I HAVE NEVER KNOWN APRIL TO feel so much like August," I remarked to General Burgoyne as my carriage bore us along Piccadilly Street toward Covent Garden. "I am obliged to you for escorting me this evening, sir. I hope you will not find it too hot in the theatre."

Tonight's performance would be a benefit for Margaret Kennedy, the experienced actress who had been so kind to me during my first disastrous venture on the stage. I'd wanted to support her and enjoy a rare evening out. But I knew Lord Derby would not approve of my going to the theatre while he was off spending Easter with his children, except in the company of his trusted uncle. The way I sometimes caught the general looking at me, I was less certain he could be trusted. All the same, I was grateful for his company tonight.

General Burgoyne fanned his flushed face with his hat. "This is nothing to the stifling heat my troops suffered at Ticonderoga two summers ago. Savage country, perfectly savage!"

I braced myself to hear yet another sensational account of his campaign in America—the sleepless nights and exhausting days, his army starved and unsupported by General Howe. It might be true in every particular, but I could not forget the general was a playwright as well as a soldier. He had just reached the part about being shot through the hat when my carriage came to a halt in the piazza outside the theatre.

"I shall save the rest of the story for our journey home," the general promised as he helped me out of the carriage.

If listening to his doubtful war stories was the price of a rare evening on the town, I reckoned it a cheap fare. "It gives me such confidence knowing I have a battle-tested warrior as my escort."

Strutting and preening, the general conducted me through the crowded lobby to our box.

We had barely gotten settled when a familiar voice rang out behind me, its sound sweeter than any music that could have come from the orchestra pit. "General Burgoyne, well met!"

I spun about, overjoyed to see Charles, Richard and Bob crowding into our box.

Richard fixed me with a quizzical look, his dark eyes twinkling. "Pray introduce us to your lovely companion, General. I believe we may have met before, but it is so long ago, I cannot recall her name. Can you, Bob?"

"Surely you mistake, Richard," Bob replied in so solemn a tone it sounded quite droll. "I could never forget such an enchanting creature, no matter how long she ignored our existence."

Surely they did not believe it had been my choice to avoid their company?

"Enough, you too," rumbled Charles with gruff good humor as he grasped my hand, "or Mrs. Armistead may decide she wants nothing more to do with us."

"Indeed not!" The sight of them made me feel like a starving child who'd been admitted to a banquet. "I am delighted to see you all and I could never forget you, no matter how long we are parted. But what brings you to Covent Garden? Will Mr. Sheridan not brand you traitors for abandoning Drury Lane?"

Richard chuckled. "With the crowds Mrs. Robinson draws, Sherry can spare us for one night. When we overheard General Burgoyne brag of squiring you to the theatre, we decided we must seize the opportunity to see you again."

They had taken the trouble to seek me out? I had never been so sincerely flattered in all my life.

"Besides," Bob quipped "Sherry is putting on Macbeth tonight, and we are in the mood for laughter and singing."

"So am I, now that we are together again." I clung to Richard's hand after he bowed over mine. "We have not spoken since you returned from America. It is such a relief to have you back safe among us."

I suddenly recalled part of the reason for that. "But how sorry I was to hear of Lady Holland's passing. From all accounts you were the most attentive of brothers. What a comfort you must have been to her."

The sorrow I glimpsed in Richard's eyes made me long to put my arms around him. But I refrained in case some *Town and Country* scandalmonger might be spying on us from the galleries.

Charles answered for his friend. "Dear Mary's loss is a blow for the whole family, her children most of all."

"Has it been decided who will have charge of them?" Though I had never seen either child, my heart yearned for them.

Before Charles could answer, the prompter's bell rang to signal the start of the evening's entertainment. I latched onto Richard's coat sleeve with one hand and Charles's with the other. "Join us, please. I cannot let you go again so soon!"

Who knew when I would see them next? Having lost one woman to a charming rake, Lord Derby was not apt to trust me with a whole clutch of them, even if they were his political allies. Though I understood the reasons for his possessiveness, it still vexed me beyond bearing.

Fortunately my friends' presence did not trouble General Burgoyne. "Come, gentlemen, you must not disappoint Mrs. Armistead. Besides, I have something to discuss with Mr. Fox."

He towed Charles to a seat at the back of the box, leaving the front ones free for me to sit between Richard and Bob.

An actor strode onstage and began to declaim a prologue to the evening's entertainment.

"Will you look who is here tonight, *sans* Lord Sandwich?" Bob nodded toward one of the stage boxes opposite ours.

There sat Martha Ray, the woman who'd been much in my thoughts since Dally had mentioned her to me. Miss Ray's noble patron was nowhere in sight. Instead she sat with a middle-aged woman and a man I recognized as Lord Coleraine, eldest of the three wild Hanger brothers.

As the prologue concluded, to a spatter of applause and a few orange peels pelted onstage from the upper gallery, Richard muttered, "It appears Sandwich has no better control of his mistress than he has of the Admiralty."

"Perhaps he is afraid to appear in public," said Bob, "since that mob tore the Admiralty gates off."

I recalled Lord Derby mentioning the attack when he'd suggested I stay on in Hampstead for the summer.

Charles leaned forward to whisper, "I hope the poor lady enjoys her evening out. The way public sentiment against the war is growing, we may soon secure enough votes to turn Lord Sandwich out of office."

"Do you suppose Coleraine is trying to persuade her to jump ship before *HMS Sandwich* goes down with all hands?" Bob quipped.

"The dog has a history of celebrated *amours*," Richard muttered. "We must protect Mrs. Armistead from his advances."

"Hush, you two!" I feigned a severe look at both of them. "Let Mrs. Kennedy act her benefit in peace."

I remembered how it had rattled me to hear the audience chattering while I tried to recall my lines. Fortunately, Margaret Kennedy was a seasoned player who knew how to hold her own with a rowdy crowd. Tonight she had only to display her fine legs in breeches, as she strode about playing the hero of a one-act comic opera. That could always be counted upon hold the men's attention.

Despite Mrs. Kennedy's excellent singing, I found it difficult to keep my mind on her performance. Instead, my senses responded to the presence of my friends. When Richard tapped his hand against his knee in time to the music, my heart seemed to beat with that same rhythm. I breathed deeper to inhale the familiar scent of Bob's shaving soap. A burst of hearty laughter from Charles tempted me to join in. It felt as if I had stepped into the fresh air and sunshine of spring after having been wrapped in a long winter fog.

At the same time, my gaze often strayed from the stage to the box where Miss Ray sat. She was a pleasant-looking woman, though a jutting jaw and cleft chin kept her from ideal beauty. I wished I knew her well enough that we might talk freely together. I longed to know if she was content in her life with Lord Sandwich. Did she have any regrets?

Her answers might calm my doubts about accepting Lord Derby's offer of long-term keeping. Every ounce of sense I possessed urged me to settle my future at once. The earl was a generous man, who would provide handsomely for me. He was also a constant man who would not abandon me without a thought the way Lord Dorset had. What more could I ask from life?

Freedom? Surely I'd had enough of that since leaving Mrs. Goadby's. Though it had its exciting moments, it was also fraught with risks which multiplied as I grew older.

When Richard and Bob suddenly broke into polite applause, I realized the play had ended. I joined in, clapping vigorously to make up for my tardiness.

During the entre-act music, Bob twisted about in his chair to talk politics with Charles and General Burgoyne.

Richard turned toward me. "You asked after my sister's children. Caroline has gone to my half-sister, Lady Warwick. My brother is in charge of wee Harry, but Charles and I mean to have a hand in his upbringing."

"He is a fortunate boy to have three of the cleverest men in England for his uncles," I replied. "But I pity him with all my heart, losing his mother at such a tender age."

Richard gave a sorrowful nod. "Have I ever thanked you for all the letters you sent while I was in America? I looked forward to the ones from you and Charles more than any others. When I read them, the Atlantic no longer seemed so wide and I did not feel quite so far from home."

Should I seek Richard's advice about Lord Derby? Somehow I shrank from the thought of him urging me upon another man.

Before I could make up my mind, the main piece of the evening commenced. *Love in a Village* was a popular ballad opera about two young people who ran away from home to escape an arranged marriage. Finding employment in the same household as a gardener and a serving maid, they promptly fell in love. All their problems vanished when their true identities were revealed. If only life could work out as neatly as a play!

After a final two-act pantomime, the theatre let out with the usual mad scramble for carriages.

"Can we offer you a drive back to your club?" I asked my friends, eager to remain with them a few minutes longer. "It is not out of our way."

"Another time we would be delighted to accept." Richard kissed my hand, turning his face slightly to graze my knuckles with his cheek. "But my carriage awaits us, if my creditors have not seized my horses out of their traces!"

I laughed, though his jest troubled me. I'd hoped that going to war and nursing his dying sister might have tempered Richard's passion for high play. All the same, I bid him and the others farewell with regret.

Intrepid fellows that they were, my friends did not wait under the piazza for Richard's carriage to fight its way to them. Instead they set off across the market square on foot to find it. General Burgoyne and I did not dare follow. I knew too well how dangerous this neighborhood could be after dark for people as finely dressed as we were. At least I was fortunate to have a male escort.

Through the crowd, I glimpsed Miss Ray looking anxiously about for her carriage. It did not surprise me that Lord Coleraine had deserted her just when he might have been of service. Gallantry was his game, not chivalry.

General Burgoyne had better manners. In the flickering light of oil lamps and linkboys' bobbing torches, he spotted my carriage and beckoned the coachman. As he was helping me in, a young man wearing a black cassock rushed past, jostling him.

The general barked an oath.

Shaken, I clutched the carriage door and shot a glare after the unmannerly clergyman. I was about to look away, when I spied an object in his hand. Why on earth would a priest be carrying a brace of pistols?

The sight of the weapons froze me there, half-in and half-out of my carriage, as he approached another woman preparing to enter hers. Having glanced at her so often that evening, I instantly recognized Martha Ray.

The young cleric called out to her. When she looked back, he raised one of the pistols to her forehead and fired. She fell to the cobblestones, sending a spray of blood over the shocked face of a gentleman behind her.

I screamed.

Then a vigorous push from the general hurled me into my carriage. As I huddled in my seat, struggling not to vomit, I heard him bellow at the coachman to fly.

"Should we go to the magistrate and testify?" My hands still trembled as I sat in my drawing room sipping brandy to calm my nerves.

The general shook his head. "There must have been a dozen witnesses. And I would not dare venture back to Bow Street at this hour."

I knew what he meant. In that volatile part of town, one act of violence could trigger a series of explosions.

"Let us see what the morrow brings." He tossed back his second tot of brandy, barely flinching when he swallowed it. "If our testimony is needed to prosecute Miss Ray's assailant, *then* we can decide whether to come forward."

"What would there be to decide?" I sputtered, teetering on the brink of hysterics. "That madman must not go unpunished!"

"Of course not!" The general looked as eager to escape from me as he had been from Covent Garden. "I only meant we will need to tread carefully on account of my position and yours ... and Miss Ray's."

I took another sip of brandy, determined not to break down in front of the general. "What made him do it—a man of God shooting an innocent woman?"

"Perhaps he didn't think she *was* innocent." The general poured himself more brandy. "Living so publicly for years with a married man. Some people are too moral for their own good."

Was that why Martha Ray had been shot? Had a religious fanatic decided it was his duty to punish her for the *sin* of using her God-given attractions to make a decent life for herself? If that was the case, then his pistol could just as easily have been aimed at my head.

"There." General Burgoyne flung down his empty glass with such force it made me jump, my pulse thundering in my ears. "I reckon that has steadied my nerves enough to see me home."

Without asking if *my* nerves were steady enough to bear his going, he bid me good night and hurried away.

My maid urged me to go to bed, but I could not face lying in the darkness picturing the shooting. If I did manage to sleep, I feared I would dream those wrenching moments again and again. And perhaps the man in black might turn his pistol upon me, instead.

I composed myself enough to order my servants to bed. I had only taken a few more sips of my brandy when the uneasy silence shattered with violent pounding on my front door. I shrieked and fumbled my glass, spilling what was left of the spirits over the bodice of my gown. A mad certainty possessed me that the man in black had come to finish the gruesome mission he'd started with Martha Ray.

I tried to cry out for my footman not to open the door. But I could not make a sound, any more than I had been able to cry out a warning to poor Miss Ray back at Covent Garden. As urgent footsteps thundered toward me, I cowered in my chair. Convinced I was about to die, I could only think of how I had struggled to secure a comfortable retirement I would not live to enjoy.

A man lurched through the door, his countenance as distraught as any madman's. But his clothes were not black ... they were blue.

"Richard?" I burst into a frenzy of weeping.

"Thank God you are alive!" He sank to his knees in front of my chair and grappled onto me with the strong arms of a soldier. "Someone ran into the club saying the earl's mistress had been shot outside Covent Garden playhouse. You can imagine what we thought. Charles went to the theatre. I came here."

"Miss Ray ... was shot." I spewed out the words between sobs. "I saw it! He put the pistol ... to her head."

"The poor creature!" Richard tightened his hold on me. "But at least you are alive. You are safe."

Was I? Was anyone ... ever?

I *felt* safe in Richard's embrace though I knew a different kind of danger lurked there. And yet ... he was the only person I'd ever lost from my life who had come back again.

Suddenly his lips were on mine. Or mine were on his. I did not know which of us initiated that kiss, only that we both wanted it ... desperately. It was as if we had been straining toward each other for a very long time, held back by powerful, invisible bonds. Now that those restraints had been broken, no force in the world could have stopped us.

Our mouths clashed, hot and ravenous. Our hands

ranged – stroking, groping.

How many men had I hired my body to over the years? Too many to count. Far too many to remember. This savage need went beyond anything those other men had ever stirred in me.

How long we kissed and touched, I do not know. Nor can I remember when our clothes began to fall away before the onslaught of reckless hands. By unspoken accord, we clambered to our feet and lurched up the stairs to my bed, continuing to ravish one another every step of the way.

When the last stitch of linen came off, we did not plunge at once into fierce lovemaking but pressed and rubbed our bodies together, as if *that* had been our foremost aim. Once it was accomplished, our passion slowed ... and deepened.

Hands squeezed and caressed, translating into touch the feelings we had never put into words. Or perhaps we needed to satisfy ourselves, in the most intimate way, that we were both alive and whole. For a time, we lay entwined in a fluid embrace. Then he rolled onto his back and I climbed astride him, letting him suckle my breasts and fondle my bottom until I was half-mad with need. I took my revenge with a teasing tongue until he writhed and strained.

"Enough," he gasped at last.

Raising a hand to my shoulder, he toppled me gently onto my back then thrust himself between my parted, welcoming thighs. All that ignited our earlier frenzy of desire. We romped upon my bed until I feared the feather mattress would burst, or I would from a surfeit of pleasure.

The mattress proved sturdier than I thought.

As Richard shuddered and cried out, I wondered if any of his adulterous ladies had urged him to such a peak of ecstasy.

I woke the next morning in Richard's arms. His eyes were already open, watching me with a look of affection darkened by a shadow of regret.

"My dear Mrs. Armistead." He ran the backs of his fingers over my tousled hair in a fond caress.

"Elizabeth." Not since Ned had I invited a man to call me by a name that was rightfully mine.

"Elizabeth." My name sounded so sweet upon his lips. "Last night was ..."

"Wondrous?" I suggested. "Glorious? Blissful?"

"All of those, of course. Though what I meant to say was *a mistake*. My mistake. I did not mean for it to happen, I swear. But I was so overwhelmed with relief at finding you safe."

"Hush." I planted a kiss on my fingertip then stopped his lips with it. "I am not angry with you. I did not intend what happened between us, either. But it did happen and it was good. Let us not spoil our pleasure with regrets."

He made a comical effort to talk while pretending my finger pinned his lips shut. "Nay I sveak, now?"

I lifted my finger far enough to give his nose a playful tweak. "That depends on what you have to say."

"What if I say your good sense is matched only by your generosity?"

"I should hope I have sense enough never to prevent a man from praising me."

"There is so much about you I find praiseworthy I scarcely know where to begin." The hand that had caressed my hair strayed lower to cup my breast.

"Mmm. That is as good a place as any."

"Indeed it is. How should I praise such perfection? Compose a sonnet? 'Shall I compare thee to–?'"

"I do not question your skill as a poet, but I have always thought actions speak louder than words."

"Have you?" He dipped his head to swipe his tongue over my out-thrust nipple. "Does *that* speak loud enough?"

I arched my body against his. "It is a fine beginning."

He looked up at me, and for the first time in our acquaintance, one of the most self-assured gentlemen in the kingdom seemed uncertain. "Are you certain this is what you want? We had good excuses for our actions last night. Now we have none."

"No excuses," I agreed, "but the best of reasons."

He lifted one brow in a wordless question.

I had an answer ready for him. "Because we want to."

When was the last time I had done anything purely for that best of reasons? Though the shock of what I'd witnessed last night had abated, it still haunted me. If death were to come upon me unawares, as it had Martha Ray, I knew there was nothing I *had done* in my life that would cause me more regret than things I might *not* have done.

This was one of them.

On a Monday morning, two weeks later, Richard and I sat side-by-side in my carriage near Tyburn gallows, drinking coffee as we awaited the execution of Martha Ray's killer. Compared to the disastrous American war and a threatened French invasion, the murder of one woman scarcely signified. Yet it had transfixed the country. The newspapers were full of it. Coffeehouse patrons discussed it for hours on end. It was the theme of conversation in playhouses and pleasure gardens.

What intrigued people about the case were not the events of that night, but the motives behind them. What had driven a young cleric to commit such a brutal crime? Why had he chosen Miss Ray as his victim? Readers of the scandal magazines wondered about the relationship between Miss Ray and her killer and how *that* bore on her relations with the Earl of Sandwich.

"This is a vile hour to be up and about." Richard yawned. "Especially for such a morbid event. My friend Selwyn never misses a hanging, but they hold no fascination for me. Are you certain you would rather not go home and spend the time in more amusing pursuits?"

Since that first morning, there had been no more talk between us of mistakes or regrets. Richard spent every night with me and as much time as he could each day. When we were together, I treasured each sweet, stolen moment.

"Bear with me, please." I caught his hand and nuzzled my cheek against it. "That man killed Miss Ray right before my eyes. My circumstances are so much like hers I can too easily imagine myself in her place. I reckon I understand her better than some of these men who scribble nonsense for the newspapers. If I read one more account that urges readers to pity 'the unfortunate Mr. Hackman' I will scream! Martha Ray is the unfortunate one!"

Richard caressed one corner of my mouth with the knuckle of his forefinger to coax a smile from me. "No doubt those scribblers are young men of education but slim prospects who identify themselves with Hackman."

Much as those newspaper accounts vexed me, at least they'd assured me Rev. Hackman had not murdered Miss Ray to punish her *sins*. Hopelessly in love with her for some years, he had wanted her to leave Lord Sandwich and marry him. At his trial he'd claimed he meant to do away with himself in front of her that night at Covent Garden. But in an instant of madness, he'd resolved to make her his companion in death. Though he had tried to shoot himself after killing her, the bullet only grazed his temple.

No doubt Richard was right about the newsmen imagining themselves in Hackman's place. "You, sir, are too objective by half."

"Not about everything, my dear." He stretched his arm over my shoulders and drew me close. "Not about everything."

Out my carriage window, I had a clear view of the three-cornered gallows where the murderer would soon hang for what he'd done. The nearby spectator stands were crammed with people eager to view the final act of such a highly-publicized crime. The whole proceedings had a holiday atmosphere, with food vendors doing a brisk business among the crowd.

We did not have long to wait before an open, two-wheeled

cart drove up bearing the condemned man, the hemp noose already slung around his neck like a halter. The cart also carried the hangman, a chaplain and Hackman's coffin. A company of soldiers bearing halberds marched with the cart, fanning out to surround the gallows when they reached it.

"At least the fellow is behaving with dignity," said Richard. "No swooning or wailing."

We watched the hangman secure the noose to one of the stout crossbeams while the prisoner prayed. He took such a long time at his devotions the spectators began to grow restless. But before they could express their displeasure with a hail of rotten fruit, Hackman rose and received a large handkerchief from the hangman. When he let it drop, that would be the signal to drive the cart out from under him.

My belly felt as if I had swallowed a bumper of squirming slugs, but I refused to close my eyes or look away. I owed that much to Martha Ray.

The chaplain climbed down from the cart and a moment later, James Hackman threw down the handkerchief. But instead of urging the horses forward, the hangman jumped down to retrieve the handkerchief.

"What is he doing?" I cried.

"That cloth will fetch a good price from collectors of such morbid keepsakes," said Richard. "And the hangman has the right to it. He must fear someone else will make away with it."

No sooner had Richard finished explaining than the hangman sprang back into the cart. He whipped the horses and gave a loud bellow so they bolted forward, leaving the prisoner to swing.

The sight did not horrify me as the murder had done. Instead, a sense of emptiness and futility gaped inside me.

"What do all the trunks and boxes signify?" asked Richard when we arrived back at my house after the hanging. "Are you planning a journey? I would not recommend Paris this spring.

Nor the south coast."

"I sent for my things from the house in Hampstead. They must have come while we were away. I have decided to refuse Lord Derby's offer of permanent keeping."

"Refuse Derby?" cried Richard. "You cannot mean it! I hope you are not contemplating this foolishness on my account."

"Why?" After what I had witnessed that morning, I needed Richard to fill my life and give it some purpose. "Do you want me to be with another man?"

I strode into the parlor, unpinning my hat as I went.

"I *want* you to be protected and provided for," cried Richard. "Derby has an income of £35,000 a year! He can keep you in better style that any man in the kingdom. I am not a sentimental young ass like James Hackman. I know how hard the world can be on a woman without resources. I have never thought less of you for keeping company to provide for yourself."

"I know." I shut the door behind us. "Charles is the same. Bob Spencer, perhaps. Other men may desire me, need me, yet deep down I know they despise me."

"Perhaps they fear you."

"Fear *me?*"

Richard nodded. "Their desire and need give you power over them. Most men do not yield to that easily."

"But you do?"

He thought for a moment then shrugged. "I do not claim to understand all the strange workings of the heart. My own especially. I only know I do not want to be the cause of your tossing away the opportunity of a lifetime. I cannot afford a single night with you, let alone undertake your support."

"I do not want you to keep me!" How could he think such a thing? "I told you I took you into my bed for one reason—because it was what we both wanted."

"That is all very well for a night or two," replied Richard. "But not just cause for disrupting your whole way of life. Do not abandon prudence."

I would rather abandon *anything* than let him abandon me! "You are a fine one to talk of prudence – win two thousand guineas at your club then head to Newmarket the next day to lose twice that much wagering on the horses!"

He held up his hands in mock surrender. "Perhaps it is because I lack prudence that I have always admired yours. How will you live without Derby's support?"

"The same way I lived before I had it – keep company with a number of men and let them all contribute to my expenses. George Cavendish would be happy to take me back. Then you and I could still be together ... sometimes."

It seemed a fine arrangement to me. Not as safe and certain as Lord Derby's house in Hampstead, but allowing me some measure of freedom and happiness.

Richard shook his head. "Even if I could afford you, this cannot go on. I only let it continue this long because I thought once Derby returned from Yorkshire ..."

"You do not want to be with me?" It would have cut me to the heart if I'd believed it, but I knew it could not be true. I would never forget Richard's stricken look when he'd come here the night of Martha Ray's murder.

"Of course I do!" He took a step toward me then stopped himself. "I would be mad not to. But life is not as simple as that. Do you fancy I bed married women because I am an immoral rake? Perhaps I am, but I see my reasons differently. Most marriages among the nobility are mercenary transactions that have more to do with property than affection. I provide the wife with what is missing from her marriage in return for fulfilling my carnal needs without expense or responsibility."

"Does she also fulfill your craving for risk?"

Richard gave a grunt of wry amusement. "Perhaps so. I fear you understand me far too well to be happy with me."

I held my hand out to him. "I reckon mutual understanding is an ideal basis for happiness."

"Only in sentimental plays, my dear." He made it sound as if

I were a little fool who knew nothing of the world.

Since he refused to take my hand, I pulled it back and wrapped both arms around myself. "The exchange between you and your mistresses sounds fair enough in its way. But what of their husbands? Are you not cheating them of their due?"

"By helping myself to something they do not want? Depend upon it, they do not suffer. Their wives are more content. They can trust me to be discreet—unlike my cousin Dorset. And if I happen to sire a younger child in the family, they know the offspring will be well-bred and likely a credit to them."

Was he *trying* to make me despise him? "You justify your actions very well."

Richard glared at me. "Do you never justify yours?"

I refused to back down. "Every time I take a new man into my bed. That is one of the many things I like about being with you, Richard—I do not need to work so hard to justify it."

For a moment the master of quick repartee seemed lost for an answer. But he found one at last, damn him. "It comes down to this, Elizabeth. You need wealthy men. I need married women. If I let my feelings for you continue to grow, I fear they could be my undoing and the undoing of our friendship. Gambler that I am, I cannot risk that."

I cudgeled my brains for anything I might say to hold Richard. Not forever, but one more day . . . one more hour. Could I threaten to end our friendship if he walked away? I had never been a gambler.

Richard seemed to sense my surrender. He walked slowly toward me and wrapped his arms around my shoulders. "Stay with Derby. You deserve everything he can give you."

Aching with regret, I pressed one last kiss upon his unyielding lips. "I deserve more than Lord Derby can ever give me."

I grieved the ending of our brief affair. But in the days that followed I felt an unaccountable sense of relief, too. What I felt for Richard was too much like love. I had lived too long by the courtesan's creed to abandon it now.

# Chapter Sixteen

ELLING LORD DERBY I MUST refuse his offer was one of the hardest things I'd ever done. He was a good man and he had been badly used by his wife. But I could not become to him what Martha Ray had been to Lord Sandwich. Insecure as it might be at times, my freedom meant too much to me.

"I do not understand." The earl looked so taken aback, I was tempted to recant. "I thought it was all decided. If it is a more generous settlement you want, name your price."

"This is not a bargaining ploy, my lord. Your offer is vastly generous, I am not seeking more." I hoped he would not name a figure for I was not certain my fledgling convictions could stand against the power of my old acquisitive urges. "Recent events have forced me to reconsider."

"Recent events? That murder, you mean? I do not see what that signifies to you and me."

Suddenly I felt as if I were reliving my last conversation with Richard, but from the other side. A crushing load of guilt burdened my conscience, for I knew the hurt I was inflicting.

I reminded myself I had Lord Derby's future happiness at heart, too. "All the publicity surrounding the case made me see that you deserve better than a half-life with a half-wife. Do not let your bitterness keep you from that. Free her ladyship to marry Lord Dorset if that is what they want. Then you will be free to find a wife who is worthy of your devotion."

I could see the struggle within him and for an instant I hoped he might renounce the harsh spite that was so foreign to his generous nature. But Lady Derby's betrayal was too fresh and his humiliation too deep.

"I fear that is not possible." He made a curt bow. "Good day to you, Mrs. Armistead."

For a while after he had gone, I stood there trying to sort out all my conflicting feelings. When they defied any kind of tidy order, I diverted myself by planning my next conquest.

I soon learned my relationship with Lord Derby was not the only other victim of Martha Ray's murder. The next month I read in the *Morning Post* that Dally Eliot had left Lord Cholmondeley and gone to France. I wondered if all the publicity surrounding the murder had finally made her realize the earl regarded her as a permanent mistress, like Miss Ray, rather than a future wife.

Late in October, Parliament opened once again and the great lords and ladies flocked to London from their second summer in militia camps. Charles Fox returned from a series of shooting parties in high spirits, eager to get Lord North back in his sights and blast him with a volley of pungent debate. I was delighted to host more of my supper parties at a time when my Whig friends seemed poised to succeed at last.

One night in November, Charles was as eager and talkative as ever, but his friends seemed subdued and anxious, their few witty remarks forced. Determined to find out the cause of their ill-spirits, I waylaid Bob Spencer, who was the last to leave.

"What is wrong?" I clutched the elbow of his coat sleeve and refused to let go. "Do not play me a fool by pretending all is well. Did the debate go badly in Parliament?"

I doubted that could be it. They all made a point to quip and clown in the face of political reversals as they did when luck went against them at the tables. Tonight Charles was the only one who had not looked cast-down.

"Something is wrong with Charles, isn't it?" I demanded, when Bob would not speak. "Tell me, damn you! He is *my* friend, too. I have a right to know."

Bob flinched at my words, confirming my guess. But what could ail Charles? Debt was nothing new to him. He looked healthy enough after his summer tramping the countryside.

"A duel," Bob croaked. "Mr. Adam challenged him over some hot remarks Charles made in the House. I fear for him—we all do. If you had ever seen him shoot, you would know why. Meanwhile, Mr. Adam will have a fine, large target."

I felt as if my stays had tightened until I could not breathe and my heart scarcely had room to beat. The strength drained from my fingers and I lost my grip on Bob's coat.

"Don't fret," he begged as he backed out my door. "And don't tell Charles I told you. He didn't want you worried."

What *did* Charles want? I wondered as I watched Bob flee. For me to open a newspaper tomorrow to read that he'd been shot? Harrowing memories of Martha Ray's murder returned to bedevil me. I knew trying to stop him would be useless. But if I did nothing I would go mad with worry.

Dawn found me sitting in a closed carriage on the street outside Charles's lodgings. I prayed he'd had the sense to snatch a few hours sleep and not gone to the dueling ground straight from his club. Wringing my hands inside my fur muff, I glanced at the shadowy figure of the doctor seated opposite me. It had taken some doing to secure his services at such an early hour—and the payment of a very handsome fee.

"Are you certain you have brought everything you might need?" I asked for the fifth time.

"Bandages ..." The doctor betrayed his impatience with a faint sigh, but humored me—for the sake of his fee, no doubt. "Compresses, laudanum, leeches—I am equipped for such aid as can be administered in these cases."

"Very good." I glimpsed another carriage driving past us to park in front of Charles's door. It must be Richard come to fetch him. I knew Charles would have no one else as his second.

"Such aid as can be administered," the doctor repeated. "I make no promise what I can do if your friend suffers worse than a flesh wound. A shattered bone, a vital organ pierced, a belly wound ..." He trailed off with a shudder.

"I do not expect miracles, sir." I refused to contemplate any of the horrible possibilities he mentioned. "I only want to ensure my friend gets whatever treatment will help him."

A short while later, Richard and Charles emerged from the house, climbed into the waiting carriage and set off. My coach followed through the still-dark streets of Mayfair to Hyde Park. It had rained a great deal the week before, but this morning was clear and cold, the grass whitened by a touch of frost.

The instant my carriage stopped, I scrambled out, not waiting for the doctor or coachman to help me.

"Bless me, what is this?" cried Charles when he spied me. "The only person less likely than me to be out at such an early hour."

He cast a dark look at Richard, who held up his hands. "I did not breathe a word to her, I swear it. Go home, Mrs. Armistead. A field of honor is no place for a woman."

"Honor?" I cried. "What honor can there be in such dangerous folly? Make peace with the man, Charles, however you must. Then come back to my house for a good breakfast."

"A tempting offer, my dear, but if I try to satisfy Mr. Adam, there will be no end to it. I must stand by what I said in the House, for it was true and I meant it with all my heart."

When I tried to argue further, he shushed me. "I am deeply touched by your coming here at this hour, but I must ask you to leave and not distress yourself further on my account."

The depth of my anxiety surprised me. It surpassed even my fears for Richard when he had gone to war. "How can I leave now, fearing the worst? I have brought a doctor to tend you in case you are injured. I pray you will have no need of him."

"So do we all," Richard muttered grimly. "Come, Charles, let us have this over with."

Tucking a slender wooden box under his arm, he stalked toward a pair of men waiting beneath a nearby tree.

"If you insist upon staying," Charles flashed me an impish grin, "might I have a kiss from you ... for luck?"

His request took me by surprise, though not nearly so much as my own compelling need to agree.

I leaned toward him for a brief peck. But there was something fond and sweet in the touch of his lips upon mine that made me feel like an innocent young girl with her first bashful swain. I believe he felt it, too. For when we drew apart, he inhaled a deep breath and swayed on his feet, as if made dizzy.

"Upon my word," he murmured. "You shall make me want to provoke a duel every week."

"Do that," I cried, "and I shall never speak to you again, let alone kiss you!" Then I relented a little. "But I *will* give you another if you survive this duel."

"We have a bargain." He bowed then marched off to join his opponent and their seconds, who were loading the pistols.

Trembling with dread, I backed away to stand beside the doctor. After a few moments' earnest discussion, the seconds handed Charles and Mr. Adam each one of their weapons. The men stood back-to-back then walked away from each other. Under my breath, I counted fourteen paces. I wished Charles had longer legs to make the distance between them as great as possible.

"It could be worse," muttered the doctor, who seemed familiar with such proceedings. "The number of paces is determined by the gravity of the insult."

As he spoke, the two men turned toward one another. Mr. Adam stood sideways, his pistol arm extended before him and the other tucked behind. I'd seen enough prints of duels to assume this was the proper stance. Charles did not appear to care, for he planted himself full and square to face his opponent.

"For God sake, Charles," cried Richard, "stand sideways!"

"To what purpose? I am as thick one way as the other!"

"Fire, Mr. Fox!" called his opponent.

Charles shook his head. "You think yourself injured. You fire first."

A shot rang out, startling a scream from me even though I'd expected it. That scream muted to a sob of relief when Charles remained on his feet, unharmed. He deliberately fired wide.

At that, Richard hastened to confer with Mr. Adam then with Charles. I presumed he must be enquiring if honor had been satisfied, hoping to bring the duel to a close before any blood was shed. When Charles shook his head, refusing his opponent's conditions, I longed to throttle them both!

The seconds gave each man a fresh pistol.

I clapped my hand over my mouth as Mr. Adam took careful aim and fired his second shot. I could scarcely believe my eyes when Charles did not fall or spurt blood. Instead, he calmly raised his pistol and discharged it into the air.

As the duelists came together to make peace, I approached them with trembling knees, thankful I could give Charles the kiss he had done so little to deserve.

He turned toward me. "It was thoughtful of you to bring a physician, Mrs. Armistead. I fear I have some need of him."

"Why?" I had not truly noticed the morning's chill until that moment. "You were not hit."

"The first shot caught me in the belly," he admitted in a rueful tone. "Perfectly amazing how little it hurts."

His words struck *me* like a pistol shot in the belly–one that hurt a great deal. I dropped my fur muff to the ground and seized him by the arm. "Doctor, come! Mr. Fox has been hit."

"Damn you, Charles!" Richard dropped the pistol box to grab his friend's other arm. "Why did you not speak sooner? The duel should have been concluded at first blood!"

Blood? I gazed at Charles's buff-colored waistcoat wondering why it was not stained a deadly crimson, like the back of

Rose's skirts on the night she died.

The doctor's quick examination solved that mystery. "The ball appears to have bounced off your belt buckle, Mr. Fox."

A frenzy of laughter seized Richard, bringing tears to his eyes. "Another man's buckle might not be strong enough to withstand a pistol shot. But yours must be of solid construction, Charles, to gird such a belly!"

My heart gave a fearful lurch as I pondered what might have happened if Charles had not faced Mr. Adam head-on with such careless courage.

"There is a contusion," the doctor warned, "caused by the impact of the shot. I would advise you to keep to your bed for two or three days, Mr. Fox, in case of inflammation."

Richard mastered his laughter and swiped a tear from his cheek with the back of his hand. "I shall see it done, doctor, if I have to tie him down."

"If you'd assumed a different stance," the doctor muttered as if he could not believe it, "or if the shot had hit an inch in any other direction, you would likely have died in great suffering. You are a very lucky man, Mr. Fox!"

The notion appeared to delight Charles. "It must be on account Mrs. Armistead's lucky kiss! Come, my dear, I believe you owe me another."

Vexed as I was over the frights he'd given me, I could not resist his good-natured charm. "You shall get it in three days time, provided you follow the doctor's orders."

A few weeks later, England ushered in a new decade with fervent hopes it would prove better than the old one. News of Admiral Rodney's victory over the Spanish fleet soon buoyed everyone's spirits. In February, Charles's friend, Edmund Burke, introduced a bill for economic reform with a speech my Whig friends all praised. So many counties and towns sent petitions calling for reform that even Lord North, with his solid majority, dared not oppose it.

I was rather vexed that Charles and the others no longer gathered so often at my house. Besides Devonshire House and Lady Melbourne's salon, they now frequently called upon Mr. Sheridan's protégé, Mary Robinson.

"Is there a wager in Brooks' betting book," I asked Bob Spencer one evening when he lingered in my sitting room after the others had gone, "as to which of you will make his way into her bed first? Or has Mr. Sheridan already beaten you there?"

"Why he would is beyond me," Bob leaned back in his chair with his glass of port "when his own wife is every bit as beautiful and talented. But there is a consideration more vital than either of their marriages that keeps Sherry from her bed."

"Indeed?" I replied. "And what is that, pray?"

"His greed of course. Mrs. Robinson is all the fashion – packing houses no matter what the play. Sherry will not want to risk her getting with child. He stays close to her only to keep others away. Though how long he will succeed, God knows, with so many Romeos besieging to her balcony. Did you hear she turned down an annuity of six-hundred a year from the Duke of Rutland?"

The news came as a slap in the face to me. I had struggled a good many years to gain the kind of settlement at which this haughty chit turned up her nose.

"She would need a good benefit or two to earn such a sum on the stage," I sniffed. "And there is no guarantee how long her acting career may last. This year's darling of fashion may be forgotten by next season." I knew that all too well.

"Actresses come and go," Bob shrugged. "but *you* have shown tremendous staying power, my dear. Why it must be all of five years you have reigned as Queen of the Cyprians."

He raised his glass in a toast to my success.

Thinking back over all that had happened in that time, it seemed much longer. I could retire tomorrow, I supposed, for I had gained everything I wanted. But what did I have to retire *to*?

From that night, I kept a wary eye on the doings of Mrs. Robinson. Indeed, it would have been difficult to ignore them, between her frequent stage appearances, many items in the newspapers and the gossip of our mutual admirers.

While attending a performance of *The Rival Queens*, I was so struck by the lady's frequent glances toward the royal box I could not resist remarking upon it to Charles Fox. I had always found him a reliable source of information for he was the most thoroughly truthful man I had ever met.

"It looks as if the scandal sheets have got their reports correct for once," I whispered behind the cover of my fluttering fan. "Mrs. Robinson has involved herself with the Prince's friend, Lord Malden."

I could not fathom what had possessed her to choose him over the Duke of Rutland's generous annuity.

"Malden is only the messenger," Charles muttered, "and a reluctant one at that, poor fellow."

Messenger? I stole another glance toward the royal box, where Lord Malden sat with the Prince of Wales and the Duke of York. Both Malden and the duke were watching the play with lively interest, but the prince hunched forward in his seat, a picture of rapt adoration. Suddenly, Mrs. Robinson's refusal of a mere duke made perfect sense.

"The poor young devil is besotted with her," whispered Charles. "Not that I blame him, after being all but imprisoned in his father's dull, decorous court. It's only natural for a young pup to want a frisk."

Perhaps that also explained why the prince had been drawn to Charles's merry, amiable company in recent months.

Learning that the alluring young actress had no designs on any of my particular friends eased my mind and cheered my spirits. I settled back with detached amusement to watch whether the Prince would succeed in making her his mistress.

The day after Drury Lane closed for the summer, Charles confided in me that Mrs. Robinson had gone to Windsor, where the prince had high hopes of a tryst with her. "I only tell you, because I know you are the soul of discretion, my dear. And you have taken such a warm interest in the young lovers."

I assured him I was honored by his confidence, yet I felt ashamed that my motives were not as admirable as he believed. Before the week was out, however, both Charles and I had far more serious matters to occupy us than a royal love affair.

The first I heard of it was late on Friday afternoon as I was getting my hair dressed to go to Vauxhall.

A disheveled young page arrived with a message for me. "Begging your pardon, ma'am, but Lord George Cavendish sends his regrets that he cannot escort you this evening. There's been a disturbance at Whitehall. He says you must stay at home tonight as he fears the way to Vauxhall will not be safe."

The lad's warning revived memories of the Wilkes Riots, from my early days at Mrs. Goadby's.

"What sort of disturbance? Lord George is not in any danger, is he?" If he were, what of Charles, Richard and Bob? Before the young messenger could reply, I added, "What of you, lad? Are you hurt?"

I fetched him into the parlor, made him sit down and ordered a mug of ale to revive him.

"I reckon Lord George is safe enough in the House, ma'am. The Guards have been called out to clear the precincts. I heard they ripped off the Bishop of Lincoln's sleeves and tried to carve the sign of the cross on Lord Boston's forehead."

"The Guards?"

"No, ma'am. Lord George's men – Lord George *Gordon*, I mean, not Cavendish. He led a mob from Southwark with petitions demanding ... something about Catholics, ma'am. They carried banners saying, 'No Popery.' There were hundreds of them – thousands, maybe!"

The next morning, my housekeeper returned from her marketing with news that two Catholic chapels had been looted and burned during the night.

"But everything seems quiet enough, now, ma'am," she assured me.

"I hope that will be an end to it." I reminded myself London had seen plenty of riots over the years. People blew off steam for a day or two, then arrests were made, damaged property was repaired and life returned to normal.

Richard Fitzpatrick came to call on Sunday afternoon, looking grim. "The homes of some Irish families in Moorfields have been burnt. And no one in authority is lifting a finger to stop it. This is monstrous! If it were happening in Mayfair, you can be sure the Riot Act would have been read straightaway."

I shuddered to imagine such violence erupting on Clarges Street. A house in this safer part of town was one of my most prized tokens of success. "Surely the worst is over now. Riots never last more than a day or two."

The Privy Council seemed to hold the same view, for they met on Monday but took no action. They discovered their error on Tuesday when Parliament sat. Once again, the blue-cockaded mob descended on Westminster with their demands, disrupting the debates and attacking anyone who fell afoul of them.

On Wednesday, a shaken Bob Spencer appeared at my door. "Have your carriage readied and pack what you will need for a week away. You must leave within the hour."

My trust in him was such that I mastered my alarm and relayed his orders to my servants before asking a single question. "Where are we to go? What has happened?"

"I'm to send you to my aunt's house in Chertsey. Charles's orders. He and Richard are in garrison at Rockingham House. The mob is raging all over London, looting and burning!"

I had never seen comical Bob Spencer look so agitated. That frightened me more than all the dire news I had heard so far. "But the Riot Act ..."

"Justice Hyde read it this morning. Their answer was to pull down his house. One mob has set fire to Lord Mansfield's house in Bloomsbury and now they are burning Lord George Savile's in Leicester Fields. The prisons are under attack, the Bank of England and God knows what else!"

Leicester Fields? That was only a short distance away. I did not waste any more time quizzing Bob. In short order my carriage was packed and my servants squeezed aboard.

Bob offered a final suggestion. "Some people are chalking 'No Popery' on their doors, hoping the mob will spare them."

Though it would be a great blow to me if my house were damaged, I shook my head. I could not bear the thought of those vile words on my door.

I almost changed my mind when we turned onto Piccadilly and caught a glimpse eastward. Thick, black smoke billowed into the summer sky from so many parts of the city it seemed impossible any building in London would survive. Could a French invasion have wreaked as much havoc as this foul work of English hands?

My young scullery maid whimpered.

Tempted as I was to do the same, I knew I must set an example for her and the others. "Don't fret, Letty. We will soon be safe in the country until this disturbance is brought under control. It will be as good as a holiday."

Traffic moved slowly on the Knightsbridge Turnpike, which was crowded with carriages fleeing the city. We had not gone far when we met a company of grim-faced militia, marching toward London. I hoped they would be able to quell the violence.

As we drove through Kensington, I glimpsed the towering turrets of Holland House, Charles Fox's family home. I was touched that he had thought of my safety and sent Bob to dispatch me out of harm's way. I prayed he would take better care of his own safety than he had in his duel with Mr. Adam.

Past Chiswick, we took a bridge across the Thames. I was only too glad to pay the toll and escape the worst of the traffic heading west. As my carriage rolled over Kew Bridge, Cook and I and all the maids stared in horror toward burning London.

Then suddenly, a blinding plume of flame roared high into the sky as a violent blast rent the air.

"Lord-a-mercy!" Cook crossed herself. "What do ye reckon *that* were?"

I could not find my voice to reply and when the scullery maid began to weep, I could think of nothing to say that might comfort her.

Darkness had fallen by the time we reached Chertsey. The fresh sweetness of wild roses wafted on the breeze, cleansing the reek of smoke from my nostrils. From the bottom of the garden, a nightingale called. It sounded like a song of welcome.

But looking eastward from the crest of the hill, I could see flames of madness consuming London. I prayed they would not consume my friends as well.

# Chapter Seventeen

UNLIKE IN THE AMERICAN COLONIES, a show of ruthless force soon put down the Gordon Riots. But not before they had done terrible damage and taken nearly three hundred lives. Though Clarges Street escaped damage, I lingered several weeks in Surrey with my servants, savoring the tranquil beauty of the country.

When I returned to the city, I found a letter waiting for me. Not recognizing the hand, I looked at the signature before reading another word.

"Dally Eliot?" I whispered. What could Lord Cholmondeley's former mistress want with me?

I wondered how she had fared in France for the past year. It could not be easy living in a country at war with one's own. Her letter gave me a clue even before I read it, for the paper was very fine and bore an impressive looking crest at the top. Dally must have found herself a powerful protector.

Curiosity piqued, I began to read.

*"Dear Mrs. Armistead, Forgive me the liberty of addressing this inquiry to you upon so slender acquaintance, but there is no one else to whom I can turn."*

News of the Gordon Riots had reached Paris, and Dally was anxious to hear if Lord Cholmondeley had suffered any injury or losses. Though she had parted from the earl, it was clear to me that she had not ceased to care for him. Had she hoped he might pursue her to France and offer to marry her rather than lose her?

I went to my writing desk at once and composed a reply that I hoped would set Dally's mind at rest. I assured her I sympathized with her concern and was happy to be of service.

*"Rest easy. His lordship has come through the disturbances unscathed. He attended the King's birthday ball on the 4th, which was celebrated without any regard to the riots. At that event, the Prince of Wales dispatched him to deliver a pair of rosebuds to Mrs. Robinson, who was watching the festivities from the Chamberlain's box."*

I included several other pieces of news about the earl that I thought Dally might wish to hear and gave her to understand I would welcome any further letters she cared to exchange with me.

When I scanned the newspapers to find out what had been going on in town during my absence, I discovered the riots had been all but forgotten in favor of royal gossip. *The Morning Post* reported that the Prince of Wales had succeeded in his conquest of the lovely Mrs. Robinson.

Or was it the other way around?

Not long after that, I was out for a drive in Hyde Park with Richard when I caught sight of Mrs. Robinson riding nearby. Perched on a handsome dark mount, she wore a scarlet redingote with a tiny tricorne set at a rakish angle atop her high-piled hair.

"A fair Amazon, indeed!" Richard appeared unable to take his eyes off her. "Put a sword in the lady's hand and she looks ready to gallop into battle."

A hot barb of jealousy ran me through. "I believe the lady carries her playacting skills outside the theatre. Two days ago, I saw her in St. James Park wearing a plain gown and a straw hat. She looked for all the world like an innocent country lass. The night before, she appeared at Ranelagh dressed in the highest fashion with her face painted, patched and rouged beyond description."

Richard made no effort to contradict me. "There is something to be said for variety. The fortunate fellow who wins her favors may have his pick of Juliet, Polly Peachum or Cleopatra in his bed, depending on his whim."

"The *fortunate* gentleman had better hope he does not wake to find himself in the company of Lady Macbeth." My tart quip provoked a great laugh from Richard. For a moment I had the satisfaction of drawing his attention away from the fascinating Mrs. Robinson.

The newspapers soon took to calling her Perdita, after the heroine of *A Winter's Tale*. That was the play in which the Prince of Wales had first seen her and been instantly smitten. With his coming of age approaching, the prince now flaunted his mistress all over town. Besides all the usual places of public entertainment, they attended military reviews in Hyde Park and the King's Hunt at Windsor. The prince gave a ball for her at Weltje's Club with guests among the greatest lords and ladies in the kingdom. I could not deny they made a handsome couple, both young and fair-colored with a flair for fashion.

The prince installed his mistress in a house on Cork Street, bought from the disgraced Lady Derby, who had paid dearly for her affair with the Duke of Dorset. Though shunned by polite society as if she were divorced, the countess was not free to remarry. The duke's eye had soon wandered, as I'd known it would. After he took up with an opera dancer, the humiliated and heartbroken Lady Derby had fled to Italy. I wondered if Mrs. Robinson would draw a lesson from the countess about trusting the affections of men. I certainly did.

I was growing heartily sick of "Perdita fever" when the King administered a purge of politics, dissolving Parliament at the beginning of September, just when all my Whig friends were off shooting or attending the race meetings at Newmarket.

Charles Fox was in Bath, recovering from an illness he'd contracted during the Gordon Riots. He returned at once to London and set about canvassing with all the cheerful energy he would otherwise have wasted on less worthwhile pursuits.

I saw him often about town over the next three weeks, but he seldom had time for more than an exchange of bows or a quick word.

"My dear, I would deem it a very great favor if you could put in a word for me with any of the tradesmen you patronize."

"I have been doing that for a week now," I replied. "Tell me, how do you like having to work so hard for your seat in Parliament?"

Until now, his election had been assured in a 'pocket borough' where a small number of votes were controlled by a local landlord. But last winter, when feelings for Parliamentary reform were running high, Charles had been proposed as a candidate for Westminster. Always more passionate than prudent, he'd accepted. I hoped that gamble would not cost him his seat.

"I enjoy it vastly!" A smile of sweet eagerness lightened his dark features. "Talking to people, hearing their thoughts about how the country should be run – I only wish I'd undertaken it years ago."

As I drove away, having wished him every success, I shook my head over his gambler's optimism. I had seen him every bit as blithely confident of his next horserace or his next hand of cards, though with one vital difference. Elections were not won on blind luck. I knew of no man more capable of winning the hearts of voters while enjoying every moment of the canvass.

When I said as much to Bob, one evening at Vauxhall, he sounded doubtful. "If this election were at any other time, or if the seat Charles is after were in any other part of the kingdom, his charm would give him an advantage. But with those damnable riots so fresh in the minds of Londoners ..."

"Surely people cannot blame the Opposition!" I sputtered. "You were the ones who introduced the Catholic Relief Bill. Many of your members were the targets of violence!"

"True," said Bob. "But there are some who would say, 'No bill, no riots.' Others are frightened enough to vote for whoever promises to promote security and good order. The King did not dissolve this Parliament on a whim. He knows an election at this time favors *his* friends."

"But that is not fair!"

"Perhaps not." Bob gave a rueful shrug. "But it *is* politics."

Though I had been reluctant to visit Covent Garden since Martha Ray's murder, I hastened there on the day the polls closed to hear the final result.

"With three-thousand, eight-hundred and five votes," came the cry from the hustings, "The Honorable Mr. Charles James Fox is returned for Westminster!"

The whole market square erupted in cheers. Scores of happy voters hurled their hats in the air. I caught a distant glimpse of Charles being hoisted aloft on a chair by his jubilant supporters. He shook every hand lifted to him, waving and calling to those he could not reach.

I marveled that he was able to keep his seat as the crowd 'chaired' him around the market square in triumph. He did not hang on or make any effort to keep from falling, but trusted his supporters to bear him safely. As his chair bobbed past my carriage, our eyes met for a fleeting instant.

His delighted grin widened further, a feat I would not have thought possible. Then he reached for the brim of his hat and doffed it toward me.

I was happy and proud to call him my friend, but I would have been every bit as proud if he had lost.

Despite Charles's victory in Westminster, Bob's forebodings about the election results proved true. Thanks to all the fear mongering after the Gordon Riots, Lord North's Ministry once again achieved the majority they needed to pursue their stubborn course of war upon America.

Perhaps because there was nothing new or entertaining in the world of politics, the newspapers were quick to turn their attention back to Perdita Robinson once the election concluded. The lady seemed to relish her place on the center stage of

Society—playing the role of royal mistress to the hilt.

One day she appeared in Hyde Park wearing a greatcoat and matching hat of blue and silver, driving in a blue carriage pulled by four chestnut horses and attended by a pair of liveried servants.

As she passed, I overheard one gentleman remark to another, "Yo-ho, there goes the Queen of the Cyprians!"

It was not a title most women would covet, but I did. How could I not? I had made conquests of dukes, earls, nabobs and the finest men of my generation. Moreover, I had held onto what I'd achieved while other women, more beautiful and better-bred, rose and fell from favor in a twinkling. Could I now let myself be elbowed aside by this arrogant actress who'd had the good fortune to snare a prince as her first patron?

"We shall see," I whispered, clenching my fist as I watched heads turn to stare after Perdita Robinson. "We shall see who is Queen of the Cyprians."

Queen of the Cyprians? Or court fool?

As my carriage sped along the road between Richmond Park and Wimbledon Common on that winter day, I had second thoughts about my planned tryst with the Prince of Wales. I reminded myself of the admiring gaze he'd lavished upon me when we had been introduced at a Christmas ball given by his uncle.

Charles later assured me the prince had talked of nothing else to him at the New Year's reception. "No question, my dear, the boy is quite smitten with you!"

While I was not *smitten*, I did find much to admire about the young prince. He had charming manners and dressed well. His looks reminded me of Ned Armistead, whom I had almost succeeded in forgetting after all these years.

"Are you warm enough, ma'am?" asked the prince's servant, who'd been sent to fetch me to an inn near Bushy Park. The prince was to meet us there on his way back from Kew.

"Quite comfortable, thank you," I replied.

My thick woolen cloak and fur muff kept me so in body. I wished something could have a similar effect upon my thoughts and feelings. Though I flattered myself I looked younger than my years, I had passed my thirtieth birthday that summer. The prince was only eighteen. I feared once he got a good look at me up close, he might think me too ancient for his embraces.

How would I bear the humiliation if he did? Such stories never remained secret. My bold vow not to let Perdita Robinson eclipse me suddenly seemed like ridiculous folly. Perhaps I should plead an indisposition and beg Mr. Meynell to take me home. I might have done just that, but I could not bring myself to disappoint the young man who would one day be king.

At last we reached the inn, where Mr. Meynell had engaged their best room under a false name. He ordered food and wine then departed once the table had been laid.

"My master should be here soon, ma'am." He bowed to me. "Enjoy your ... meal."

After he left I wandered about the room, which was old-fashioned but snug, with an oak-beamed ceiling, mullioned windows and a stone hearth. A large bed hung with snuff-brown curtains occupied one corner, leaving a spacious area in front of the hearth for dining.

I was beginning to consider a drink of wine to steady my nerves when I heard a hesitant tap on the door. Thinking Mr. Meynell had returned I hastened to admit him.

Instead, I wrenched open the door, startling the Prince of Wales. I gave a squeak of alarm at finding him there. That made us both sputter with laughter.

"May I come in?" he asked when he had caught his breath.

I thought the request surprising, and rather endearing, coming from the man who had paid for the room. A man who would one day be my sovereign.

"Of course." Stepping back to let him enter, I swept a deep curtsey. "I beg your pardon, Your Royal Highness."

"I hope your journey was not too tiresome." He glanced around the room as he removed his greatcoat, hat and gloves. "Do the arrangements meet with your approval?"

I assured him they did.

"You are kind to say so." The prince warmed his hands in front of the fire. "Charles Fox tells me you are the kindest woman of his acquaintance."

Those words warmed me from the inside.

Before I could answer, the prince heaved a harried sigh. "You deserve far better. I wish I could entertain you in a grand town house, furnished with every comfort. Now that I am fully of age, I should have my own establishment, my own income and the freedom to entertain whomever I please!"

"Indeed you should, your Royal Highness." I had all those things. "But do you not?"

The prince shook his head slowly, then took a step toward the table and pulled out a chair for me. "Let us eat while I give you a full account. I fear the food will grow cold if we wait upon my telling you all the deprivations I suffer.

Princely deprivation? I quelled a look of doubt as I took my seat. Had the young man ever suffered chilblains or gone to bed with hunger gnawing at his empty belly?

By the time we had eaten our fill of mutton chops, veal pie and some mild cheese, washed down by a bottle of mellow red wine, my opinion had changed entirely. Perhaps the royal children had not gone cold or hungry, but they had been starved of freedom and affection – chilled by constant criticism.

"Thank God for my brother Frederick." Prince George swirled the remains of his wine in the bottom of his glass. "I do not know how I could have borne it all without him. I remember one tutor who used to thrash us with a long whip."

"The vile man!" I reached across the table to offer the prince my hand. "If you had been a pair of 'prentice boys, he might have been charged with mistreatment."

I thought of Bully's sons, with whom I'd remained friends

ever since my affair with their father. They were the same age as the young princes and also named George and Frederick. A qualm of mild disgust gripped me at the thought of taking one of them into my bed.

But the prince? I could not deny an element of motherly concern in my feelings for him. But the prospect of a young, eager, relatively inexperienced partner held more than a little attraction for me.

The prince took my hand and lifted it to his lips. "I can see Charles was right. You are as kind as you are beautiful!"

His blue eyes were so like Ned's, yet they sparkled with desire for *me*, not Mr. Meynell or some other man.

The next thing I knew, he was on the floor beside me—the future king of England, kneeling as a devoted subject before the queen of his heart. "From the moment I first glimpsed you at the Opera House, I have not been able to get you out of my mind. Your divine face, the elegance of your form, the unaffected way you laugh, all fill me with the most inexpressible delight!"

Again and again he showered my hand with ardent kisses between extravagant praise of my every virtue—including a few I was not certain I possessed. I found the prince's efforts to express his *inexpressible* admiration amusing, yet endearing too. How could a woman who had so recently entertained doubts about her age and attractiveness fail to be flattered by such passionate declarations? Especially when they came from a fine-looking man more than ten years her junior?

At last, when the flow of words slowed, I cupped his chin in my hands and raised his lips to mine. He kissed me with eager reverence, as if I were an idol of whom he'd long dreamed. Meanwhile, his smooth, supple hands whispered over my neck, my shoulders and the top of my bosom, laid bare by my low-cut bodice. Then one strayed down to lift the hem of my petticoat and caress my legs.

"Exquisite limbs!" He nuzzled my cheek with his. "How I

have longed for a glimpse of them!"

"Then you shall have it, of course." I ran my fingers over his unpowdered hair, savoring its silky texture. "Would you care to retire to the bed, where we can gratify that desire and any others you might have?"

The prince responded to my invitation like an affectionate pup, eager to romp. For every garment he helped me remove, he showered the newly uncovered part of my body with caresses, kisses and glowing words of praise. He especially admired my breasts – fondling, suckling and proclaiming their perfection in breathless whispers.

By the time he had got astride me, he was wriggling with unsuppressed excitement. A very few thrusts was all it took to send him into spasms of ecstasy, leaving me aroused but unsatisfied. As he lay with his head nestled on my bosom, wondering aloud in a drowsy voice how he had ever lived without me, I congratulated myself that I was now a *royal mistress*.

And the fair Perdita had not usurped my Cyprian crown.

# Chapter Eighteen

ESPITE THE PRINCE'S DECLARATIONS OF devotion, I was far from certain I would see him again. I had long ago learned to doubt the things men said in the fever of lust. But three nights later I returned from a ridotto at the Pantheon to find him waiting in my parlor.

"I hope it was alright to invite his Royal Highness in, ma'am," whispered my footman as he took my cloak and hat. "Him being a prince and the night so cold."

"Perfectly right, Gerald." I stole a quick glance in the nearest looking glass then hurried to the parlor where the prince had been occupying his time with a bottle of my brandy.

Before I could execute a proper curtsy, he seized my hands and pressed kiss after kiss upon them. "Dear lady, I hope you do not mind my calling on you. I enjoyed your company so vastly the other night that I have scarcely slept a wink since, between recalling every blissful moment and yearning to see you again!"

His ardent tone and the adoring glow in his eyes assured me that he believed himself deeply in love. It made me ashamed of *my* motives for being with him.

I drew one hand away from his lips to caress his cheek. "I am sorry to have disturbed your rest."

"I would much rather think of you than waste my time sleeping ... unless I could dream about you."

"But if you do not sleep, you will make yourself ill." I tried not to sound too *motherly* in my concern.

The prince did not seem to mind. "There is one way I can be certain of a perfect night's sleep, if you will permit it?"

"And what is that?" I asked, though I could easily guess.

"By spending the night here with you, of course!"

The hour was late and I would have preferred a quiet night to myself. Besides, he had not mentioned a word about payment. "I suppose it might be possible."

"I knew you would agree. You are a perfect angel of kindness!" He snatched a jeweler's box from the table and handed it to me with a flourish. "I hope you will do me the honor of accepting this token of my admiration."

I opened the box to find a dainty bow-shaped gold brooch set with topazes.

"It is lovely!" I strove to hide my disappointment. This pretty bauble would have cost very little compared to the vast sums the prince had lavished on Perdita.

We soon retired for the night. After a pleasant romp in bed, the prince fell asleep with his cheek pressed against my bosom. I wished I found it as comfortable as he seemed to. Later that night I was jarred from a restless doze by a frantic tap upon my door.

"Mrs. Armistead!" my maid called in a loud whisper, "Lord George is here! What should I do?"

I sat bolt upright, memories flashing through my mind of a gang of young bucks kicking down my door at Mrs. Goadby's.

"Delay him as long as you can!" I scrambled out of bed and a lit a candle.

The prince yawned, "What is wrong, my sweet?"

"My patron has come." I gathered up his clothes and thrust them at him. "He mustn't find you here!"

Perhaps if I'd paused and given the matter some thought, I would not have made so much ado about a trifle. But the late hour, my weariness and those distressing memories conspired to fill me with alarm.

My distress set the prince in a panic. Or perhaps it was the deeply ingrained fear of being caught doing something of which his parents would not approve.

"Oh dear!" He bolted out of my bed with his arms full of clothes. "I mustn't be seen like this!"

"This way." I pulled open the door that led to my dressing room and beckoned the prince. "Get your clothes on then leave by the other door!"

I plucked the candle off my night table and set it in the dressing room. Then I shut the door and bounded back into bed. Only then, as I lay listening to the approach of Lord George's unsteady footsteps, did I begin to shiver from the chill of the winter night air.

"Yoo-hoo, Mrs. Armistead." The door of my bedchamber opened to spill in wavering candlelight and long wobbly shadows.

"I happened to be in the neighborhood," Lord George announced in a rather slurred voice, "and it's deucedly cold outside. I couldn't face the prospect of climbing into a cold bed when yours is always so nice and warm …"

Any other night, I might have been amused to see one of the self-possessed Cavendish brothers in his cups.

"Come in." I tried not to sound vexed and breathless. "You are always welcome here."

He lurched toward the bed crooning, "Nice and warm."

Just then a stray draft blew out his candle.

"Blasted thing!" he muttered. "Still I reckon I can find my way. Been here a time or two."

I heard shuffling footsteps then, "Hmm! What's that light under the door?"

"What light?" I asked in a loud voice, hoping the prince would hear and snuff his candle.

"Down there. See?" Lord George's voice moved away from the bed. "That's your dressing room isn't it? Dangerous business leaving lit candles near all those clothes."

"Oh, I see the light now. It is probably my maid … doing some mending."

Lord George's footsteps did not stop. "Any servant in your dressing room at this hour must be stealing from you."

"Then I shall look into it. Come to bed before you trip over something in the dark and injure yourself."

It was too late. Lord George pushed open my dressing room door. "Here is the candle. But I don't see anyone."

The prince must have made his escape!

A sigh of relief caught in my throat when Lord George muttered, "Wait, there's somebody behind the door." He picked up the candle and held it high. "Show yourself at once!"

I heard shuffling footsteps. Then I glimpsed the prince clad in nothing put his shirt, his face a guilty shade of red.

For a moment none of us said a word. Then Lord George burst into the most violent laughter I had ever heard. Unable to speak for laughing, he made a low bow to the prince and retired from my chamber.

I returned to bed, but did not sleep a wink the rest of the night. Once word of this little farce got around, I would be the laughingstock of Society. If the prince's embarrassment got the better of his infatuation, I feared my reign as royal mistress might be the briefest in history.

Fortunately, the prince did not hold the incident with Lord George against me. Twice in the next two weeks he begged the honor of escorting me to masquerades.

"I wish I could attend a masquerade *every* night," he confided as we sipped punch after dancing. "There is something so exciting and mysterious about them, don't you think?"

Before I could reply, a man in the costume of a butcher approached us and engaged the prince in conversation. By his voice and the dark stubble on his lower face, I guessed he might be our mutual friend Charles Fox.

I knew for certain when he gestured toward me and declared

in a jovial tone, "A fine heifer you have there, sir. Name your price for her and I shall pay it to the shilling!"

The prince must have guessed his friend's identity, too, for he did not take offense at the impudent jest, but replied with elaborate gallantry, "I fear we can never make a bargain, sir, for I assure you she is above all price!"

The very next morning, I read an account of the incident in *The Morning Post*. A rival paper insisted such reports were false and that Perdita was still the prince's favorite. By the middle of February, the stage was set for a public confrontation. It came one evening at the Opera House.

Until recently, the place had been a final bastion of public respectability. Its management refused to sell boxes to women like me, even though I had appeared on the Haymarket stage. They made an exception for Perdita Robinson, perhaps on the basis of her royal connections. With her usual flair for self-display, the lady took a box beside the one reserved for the Royal Family.

I took advantage of Haymarket's relaxed propriety to acquire a little bower of my own—directly *opposite* the royal box.

The first evening I took my seat there, an intense buzz of whispering broke out. I only realized the cause when I glanced across the opera house to find Mrs. Robinson glaring at me. Pretending not to notice, I busied myself unfolding my silver lorgnette, a fashionable new trinket Lord George had given me. I took care to maintain a tranquil smile for the benefit of our audience. The fair Perdita might be ten years younger than me, but her haughty sneer detracted from her beauty.

A few moments later, the Prince of Wales took his seat, accompanied by his uncle Gloucester. As the musicians began the overture to Mozart's *Mithradate*, the prince took a moment to look around the opera house. A little cough from Perdita, and the rapid flutter of her fan, drew his glance. She flashed him a coy, alluring smile that I feared would win him back with ease. But the instant he recognized her, his smile froze and he looked away.

Then he glanced over at me and his countenance thawed. Turning to his uncle, he whispered something. The Duke regarded me with a nod and a smile of warm approval.

Out of the corner of my eye, I saw Perdita wilt and lift a handkerchief to daub her cheek. She heaved a sigh so loud it almost drowned out a quiet passage of the overture. Her performance might have moved the audience to pity, but it did not shift the prince's attention, which remained riveted upon me, for all to see.

I wish I could claim I did not gloat over my petty triumph, but that would be a lie.

I soon discovered Perdita Robinson had more in common with King George than either of them would ever have imagined. Both refused to surrender anything they considered their rightful possessions without a fight—no matter what it cost them or anyone else.

Britain's fortunes fell to a new low with the capture of our entire colonial merchant fleet and the loss of several valuable possessions in the Caribbean. Taxes multiplied like fleas while the government debt swelled out of control. Yet the King refused to release his stubborn hold on America.

Newspapers in the pay of the Ministry enthused over minor triumphs while dismissing catastrophic defeats, but they fooled no one. Cannons were fired to celebrate such meager military 'victories' that people began to greet the volleys with bitter ridicule rather than rejoicing.

Mrs. Robinson seemed equally determined to regain her hold over the Prince of Wales. Before that night at the opera house, she had not taken the least notice of me when our carriages passed in the park or when we held court in adjacent supper boxes at Vauxhall. Now I became the target of her disdainful sneer whenever we met. Bearing in mind how such expressions spoiled her looks, I replied with a serene smile.

The newspapers quickly seized upon our mutual dislike and exaggerated it into a vicious rivalry. Everything one of us said, did or wore was interpreted as an insult or a challenge to the other. By spring, the Morning Post was predicting a pitched catfight between us in St. James Park!

In an effort to win back the prince's affection, Perdita besieged him with letters and took care to appear wherever he went in public. She tried to make him jealous by sleeping with his friends, Lord Malden and the Earl of Cholmondeley. I despised such ridiculous ploys. My affair with the Duke of Dorset had taught me the futility of clinging to a man once he had turned his attentions elsewhere.

When it became clear his Royal Highness would never return to her, Perdita resolved that he would pay dearly for his abandonment. First she blackmailed him for the return of some embarrassing letters he had sent her, using Lord Malden to negotiate on her behalf. When the bargaining threatened to stall, she claimed to be pregnant with the prince's child. Newspaper speculation on the subject may have alarmed the king for a time, but otherwise nothing came of it.

I saw little of my Whig friends that Season, being so occupied with juggling my obligations to Lord George and the prince. One evening in May I hosted a *petit souper* and was bitterly disappointed when only Bob Spencer appeared.

"The others begged me to convey their regrets. Sherry is busy organizing a grand fete with Seignior Vetris. Charles and Richard could find no one to take their places in the faro pulpit at Brooks'."

He must have guessed what I thought of that excuse. "Do not take it ill. They are in a very bad way for money. Richard's horses were seized right off his carriage in the middle of the street and Charles had his lodgings stripped for auction by one of his creditors. He laments nothing but the loss of his books. Some of his friends mean to attend the auction and buy back as many as possible for him."

"Why bother?" My exasperation with Charles almost got the better of my fondness for him. How could a man of such abilities still behave like an irresponsible child? "If he is gambling as much as ever, he will only lose them all again."

"But you see, he is not exactly gambling. He and Richard are holding a faro bank and *making* some money. At least Charles is—enough to begin paying the most pressing of his debts and buy a few new clothes."

"I wish he had come tonight so I could have seen them. He looked so shabby all last year, I wondered if his talk about dressing like a *Man of the People* was only making a virtue of necessity." I took Bob by the arm and drew him into the dining room. "I hope you have a good appetite, for we will have five times too much food and wine."

He looked as if he could use a good meal.

"While we are on the subject of finances," I said, "how are you fixed these days?"

I knew he'd recently been forced to declare bankruptcy and sell his collection of paintings.

Bob gave the pretence of a carefree shrug. But when I continued to stare at him, silently demanding the truth, he heaved a sigh and sank onto the chair he always occupied at my table. "I have enough friends not to go hungry, but that is the best I can say for myself. My own bloody fault of course, which is no comfort."

My footmen served up fragrant, steaming bowls of turtle soup. Bob tucked into his with such an appetite, I was afraid he would burn his mouth.

"I know one is supposed to take one's reverses all in stride the way Charles does," he said between spoonfuls of soup. "Or act the fool about it like I usually do. But, dash it all, I'm getting past the age of an irresponsible young whelp! I have a hankering to settle down in a place I can call my own."

Was it finding himself suddenly over thirty that had provoked this change? I wondered. Or had one of Bob's married mistresses finally captured his promiscuous heart?

By the time he finished his soup, Bob sounded a little more hopeful. "Charles and Richard mean to give me a share in their faro bank. If I can clear enough to allow me a comfortable living, I swear I will never touch a card again!"

Perhaps there was hope for the man after all. I wished such prudent resolution would rub off on his friends.

Bob rubbed his hands with glee when a dish of his favorite macaroni was served. "Here I am going on about myself. What of you, my dear? Has the prince promised you a title?"

I hesitated for a moment before answering. Though I usually kept my own counsel, I felt a sudden need to confide in someone. I had been friends, and more, with Bob Spencer for a good many years. Perhaps one man could advise me how best to handle another.

"He's promised me nothing. Perdita Robinson soured him on making expensive pledges he might be obliged to keep. He is a sweet boy and it is flattering to be chosen as a royal mistress, but I cannot afford him! Especially not now, with Lord George getting betrothed."

I needed a new patron or two, but other gentlemen seemed reluctant to pursue the prince's mistress.

Bob paused in his eager consumption of macaroni. "I suppose you can't very well tell the heir to the throne to push off. Have you considered retiring altogether? My aunt has had to give up that little villa in Surrey where you stayed during the Riots. I could introduce you to the estate agent, if you'd like to inquire about a lease."

In some ways the prospect of retirement attracted me. Like Bob, I often longed for a more settled life. But could I abandon the hectic gaiety of London for an isolated village where my notorious past would bar me from all respectable society?

"I don't know that I'm ready to give up all this just yet, but it would be pleasant to have a place in the country where I could go in the summer. I'm not sure my retirement would discourage the prince, however."

Bob thought for a moment. "What you need is for *him* to find someone else. Have you considered encouraging him to make up with Perdita again?"

I replied with a withering look. "I hope you mean that as a jest."

"Well then, what about someone else? Lord Craven's niece, perhaps? Or Emily Roberts? The blatant way she stares at him from her opera box, it's clear she'd be willing." Bob went on to name a few other new faces in town.

"You may be on to something, though I'm not sure a girl his own age is the answer. The prince seems to want a mistress who will mother him." We were a good match that way, for I tended to cosset my lovers.

I was still mulling over Bob's suggestion when we withdrew to my sitting room after supper. My gaze fell upon my writing desk and the latest letter I'd received from Dally Eliot in Paris. I thought she'd sounded a little homesick for England.

That gave me a brilliant idea.

A surprising amount of good came of my disappointing supper party. Bob introduced me to his brother's estate agent, whom I charmed into granting me a lease on St. Anne's Hill at very reasonable terms. And Dally responded eagerly to my letter suggesting she pay a visit to England. Her return did not go quite as I anticipated, however. It seemed my fellow courtesan had plans of her own.

No sooner had I heard she was back in town than I spied her driving in the park with Lord Cholmondeley. Neither of them took any notice of me, but seemed only to have eyes for one another. Shortly afterward I heard the earl had deserted Perdita Robinson to return to Dally.

The following week, I invited the earl and Dally to join me at the opera. While we waited for the overture to begin, Lord

Cholmondeley excused himself to speak with a friend.

I turned to Dally. "His lordship seems very pleased to have you back in London. I have not seen him in such high spirits all the time you were away. I do admire your gown. That shade of blue complements your eyes to perfection. A gift from his lordship?"

"One of many. He has showered me with gowns and jewels." Dally's voice fell to a whisper. "All but the one I want most. I'd hoped my absence might make him realize he cared for me enough to defy his meddling relatives. I would rather be his wife with a modest fortune than live in luxury as his mistress."

She lifted her elegant tortoise shell lorgnette and swept a glance toward the boxes opposite us. I doubted she could see much through the mist of tears in her eyes.

I ventured a suggestion. "Perhaps if you had resisted a little longer or cultivated a rival for your affections?"

A faint sigh escaped her. "No doubt you are right. I wish I could keep my head as well as you do where such matters are concerned. But I could not bear to think of him with that Robinson creature."

Her lorgnette was trained on Perdita's box. I never deigned to glance in that direction. "Who is her escort tonight? Lord Malden?"

"No. I believe it is the Duke of Dorset."

My lip curled. "They deserve one another."

The duke seemed bent on making a conquest of every celebrated woman in the kingdom. I wondered if he meant to collect our portraits in a room at Knole for future generations of Sackvilles to admire. Of course, if he did not soon settle down and find a respectable young wife, there might not *be* any future generations.

Just then the Prince of Wales entered his box, accompanied by Charles and Richard. I wondered who was minding their faro bank. The prince did not once glance in Perdita's direction, but stared toward me with a fond smile.

I raised my fan and behind it whispered to Dally, "What do you think of the prince? Has he not grown into a handsome man?"

Dally turned her lorgnette upon him. "Fine looking, indeed, and quite charming, I hear. I congratulate you."

"I believe he is looking at *you* with a good deal of interest. Perhaps you should lower your lorgnette so he can have a better view of you face."

She did as I bid her, but slowly, the way a mysterious beauty might lower her mask at an admirer's request. "You are not jealous of your prince's interest in another woman?"

"Of some, I might be." One in particular. "Of you, not in the least." I briefly explained my difficulty.

"Men," murmured Dally in a tone of fond exasperation. "They can be the most confounding creatures to manage."

"True," I replied as Lord Cholmondeley returned accompanied by the Earl of Derby, to whom I had not spoken since refusing to become his permanent mistress. "Yet I reckon we both find the challenge quite stimulating."

I introduced Dally to the prince that evening and sensed he found her intriguing. She had many of the same qualities he seemed to admire in me—a statuesque figure and mature beauty. Besides those, she possessed a degree of elegance and sophistication I could not claim.

While I watched the prince for his reaction to Dally, she kept an eye on Lord Cholmondeley for *his* response to the prince's interest. Then, while the three of them were talking together, Lord Derby drew me aside to ask if he might call on me the next day. Though I could not guess what he wanted, I agreed.

He appeared promptly at the appointed hour, and after some stilted conversation about the weather and his horses he worked around to the reason for his call. "I should have listened to you and got a divorce from Betty while I could."

"Because of Miss Farren?" I had seen the lady perform several roles and found her subtle style of acting vastly superior to Perdita's affected posturing.

The earl's head snapped up. "You have heard?"

"Worse—I have read in the newspapers. The latest reports claim Mrs. Robinson is doing her best to win your affections away from Miss Farren."

"What nonsense!" cried the earl, though I sensed he was secretly flattered by the report. "The lady has spoken to me on occasion, but nothing more."

I suffered a petty pang of disappointment at hearing an unflattering rumor about my rival denied. "Why are you suddenly hankering after a divorce? Would you *wed* Miss Farren if you were free?"

Lord Derby sighed. "Those appear to be the only terms upon which she would consent to be mine. And the lady does have a natural gentility of manner. She would not be a disgrace to the title of countess, which is more than one can say for some ladies of noble birth."

"If that is how you feel, what is to stop you from seeking a divorce, now?"

"It would be difficult to prosecute for *crim con* against Dorset now that he and Betty are parted. Besides, there would be all manner of speculation about my delay. I would not want Miss Farren's reputation to suffer on my account."

He *was* in love with her, poor fellow. "What will you do?"

"I see only two choices. Wait for her as long as it takes or try to forget her."

"The latter sounds wisest to me." I spoke from experience.

"I thought that was what you would advise." Lord Derby looked as though he had something more to say, but it took him several minutes to work up the nerve. "Will you help me?"

"If ... I can. In what way?"

He appeared vastly relieved that I had not refused him outright. "I am not like Dorset, changing my feelings as often as my wardrobe. I have only cared for three women in all my life—Betty, Miss Farren ... and you."

Where was this all leading?

Lord Derby did not keep me in suspense. "I say ... a man has needs, damn it!"

Was that an argument he had used with the virtuous Miss Farren? Somehow, I doubted it would persuade her. "Few women have cause to know that better than I, sir."

Recalling my passions for Ned and Dorset and Richard, I considered telling Lord Derby that women had needs, too.

"I was hoping I might persuade you to go abroad with me for the summer."

"So you might indulge those needs discreetly, without embarrassment to Miss Farren?"

He hesitated, a sheepish grin on his face. "Just so."

It sounded like a possible solution to my 'princely problem.' And I had a hankering to see a little more of the world. "How soon do you wish to leave, my lord?"

The prince sulked dreadfully over my plans to go abroad for the summer, but I pretended not to notice, insisting I would return in the fall. In truth, I meant to stay away until I was certain he had forgotten me. I doubted that would take long.

I set off for France, a trifle nervous to be traveling in a foreign country at war with my own. Dally Eliot assured me there would be no difficulty. She said French merchants welcomed free-spending English visitors, and that many aristocrats were terrific Anglophiles.

In Paris I met up with Lord Derby, as we had agreed. I found him as generous as ever but far less possessive than he had been during our first liaison. I shopped a great deal for the latest Parisian fashions as well as items to furnish my dear little villa back in Surrey.

Lord Derby took me several times to Versailles where I marveled at the formal gardens and elaborate fountains. My favorite was the spectacular *Bosquet des Rocailles*, an outdoor ballroom with a marble dancing-floor half encircled by water cascading over tiers of rockwork. For all its beauty, the magnificent chateau itself made me rather uncomfortable. I could not imagine living amid such ornate grandeur, especially when I compared it to the squalor of Paris.

The oppressive smell of the old city in high summer was worse than any I had suffered while begging on the streets of London. It reeked of violent desperation.

Lord Derby shook his head in disgust as he fanned his nose. "This is what comes of having no checks on the power of monarchy."

I inhaled from vinaigrette of lavender water. "You sound like Charles Fox. You have become a thorough disciple of his."

The earl bridled. "There are many worse men I could follow but few better."

"I quite agree, my lord. Do not mind my teasing."

"Forgive me, my dear. I did not mean to be short-tempered with you, but I am sick to death of this city. Let us quit the place and go to Spa where the air and water are clean."

The next day we set out for Liege, through the rolling meadows and scenic cathedral towns of Picardy. Whenever we stopped to eat, rest or change horses, I savored the fresh air, fragrant with the country sweetness of wildflowers and ripening crops. After my visit to Paris, I would never take such workaday blessings for granted again.

Spa reminded me so much of Bath, back in England, for the town's medicinal waters drew many ailing visitors hoping to restore their health. Also like Bath, Spa boasted a wide variety of public entertainments including a playhouse and an elegant gaming establishment. Our first few weeks there were most enjoyable and I received a number of gifts from gentlemen eager to secure my company. I gave an Austrian count and a wealthy Flemish merchant some encouragement, for I had long made it a policy to keep several strings in my bow. And yet, I could not escape a growing sense of restless discontent.

For a whole year I flitted about Europe in the company of several different lovers, constantly on the move, in search of something to fill the disturbing hollow within me. But it was only when my thoughts turned to my friends back in England and my little country villa that I felt happy and whole.

# Chapter Nineteen

*T*HE FOLLOWING SPRING I ARRIVED back in London, weary from my travels and eager to venture no farther than Surrey for some time. I meant to rest for a few days, unpack and put my household in order before undertaking any social engagements. But I'd scarcely risen from bed when my footman announced Charles Fox had come to pay his compliments.

I did what any woman of fashion would do when faced with an unexpected call from a gentleman – stole a glance at my dressing table mirror. The sight distressed me. My face was pale, my hair desperately needed the attention of a friseur, and shadows under my eyes made me look nearer forty than thirty. If my caller had been anyone but Charles, I would never have allowed him to see me in such a state.

But I'd seen him looking far worse over the years of our friendship and never thought ill of him. More than anyone else of my acquaintance, I felt I could truly be myself with him. He alone seemed to see behind the courtesan's worldly allure to the anxious, frightened girl, and to regard her with fondness.

"Mr. Secretary!" I swept into my sitting room and dropped him a deep curtsy. "This is an honor! I hope I have not taken you away from any important duties. Congratulations on forming a government at last. I was delighted to hear of it."

"There is work enough to keep me out of mischief." Charles did not look as elated as I'd expected to find him under the circumstances. "But how could I not spare a few moments to welcome you home? Your presence has been sorely missed. More than once I found myself rushing here to share good news with you, only to remember that you had gone abroad. The prince has been quite lost without you."

"So he claimed when he wrote to summon me home." I had decidedly mixed feelings about that summons. I still could not afford to entertain the prince without financial support, but neither had I dared ignore a direct royal appeal. "I hear he has managed to find *some* consolation in my absence."

On my journey home I'd read newspaper accounts of Dally's pregnancy and the birth of a daughter christened *Georgiana*. I envied her the child but not the prince's attentions.

"Fleeting amusements at best," Charles protested on his young friend's behalf.

I refused to be convinced of the Prince's *devotion*, even by so persuasive an advocate as Britain's new Foreign Secretary. "They may have amused His Royal Highness, but I gather Mrs. Eliot had the last laugh."

Charles shook his head. "Call the babe what she will, everyone knows it could just as easily be Cholmondeley's."

His innocent remark stung my conscience, for the earl had been one of my recent traveling companions in Europe.

"Enough gossip," I said, eager to change the subject. "What do such matters signify compared to *your* doings? You must be busy day and night negotiating peace with the Americans."

It was only fitting. Few men had worked so hard to prevent war and, once it had started, to end the bloodshed.

"That is my dearest wish." Charles's thick brows bristled and his features clenched in a dark scowl. I had never seen him look so fearsome. "And it is my right as Foreign Secretary! It was the chief reason I accepted the post. But that snake Shelburne is playing some deep game of his own."

I knew of Lord Shelburne, a Whig who had also opposed the war. The earl was as opposite in character to Charles Fox as a man could be. He drank temperately and never gambled.

As far as anyone knew, he'd been faithful to both his wives, the second of which was Richard's sister, Louisa. Set against those virtues, his lordship had a reputation for being secretive and devious. While Charles had a large circle of friends, Shelburne had none.

"What business is it of his?" My knowledge of government was limited to what I had learned from the supper conversation of Charles and his friends. But it did not take a genius to realize a Foreign Minister should negotiate treaties on behalf of his country.

"It hinges upon whether Britain recognizes the independence of the America states *before* a treaty is negotiated. Shelburne thinks that recognition should be granted as part of the treaty, meaning Britain would negotiate with America as a colony. Since he is Colonial Secretary, the responsibility would be his."

I beckoned Charles to have a seat and rang for coffee. "Does it matter who signs the treaty so long as peace is made?"

After all this war had cost Britain, I would have let Perdita Robinson negotiate the peace. Well, perhaps not *her*–she might have insisted the Americans make her their queen.

"It is a matter of principle," Charles insisted. "American sovereignty is not ours to grant, but theirs to claim. And they claimed it most courageously when their representatives signed that Declaration of Independence. If this government pretends we can withhold recognition as some cheap bargaining tool, we will lose the only scrap of honor we might still salvage from this sorry business!"

"In that case," I assured Charles, "I am certain you will prevail." I believed it to the depths of my heart.

A few days later, after I had rested and made myself presentable, I invited Dally Eliot for a carriage ride to Berkeley Square. There we sat under the trees eating teacakes and royal cream ice from Mr. Negri's pastry shop while we exchanged the latest gossip.

"Can you guess who Perdita has taken as her latest *amour?*"

"One of my old lovers?" I asked. "One of yours?"

"Colonel Tarleton." Dally wrinkled her aristocratic nose. "A well-matched pair, don't you think?"

"Indeed." I had driven in Hyde Park with the colonel when he'd first returned on parole from his regiment in America. Like Perdita Robinson, he was good-looking, self-promoting ... and altogether ruthless.

"He seduced her for a wager." Dally's voice seethed with contempt. "I doubt even your friend Mr. Fox would be foolish enough to lay good money on Perdita's virtue."

"Has she not discovered the truth?" If I'd been cozened like that, I would never speak to the blackguard again, let alone sleep with him!

"Oh, she discovered." Dally's brows arched to an incredible height. "I gather she raged and vowed she would have nothing more to do with him. Then a few days later, she had a carriage accident. Tarleton rushed to her side, swearing he'd truly fallen in love with her in spite of the wager. They have been inseparable ever since."

"What will they live on? I hear the money she got from the prince for his love letters did not even cover her debts. And Colonel Tarleton has no fortune."

"They can go to Newgate for all I care!" Dally sniffed. "I am sick of reading about them in the newspapers and seeing them fawn upon one another all over town. Indeed, I have had enough of London altogether. My lord du Chartres has invited me back to Paris and I mean to go before the month is out."

I would miss having another woman with whom to gossip and commiserate, but I could not blame Dally for wanting to leave London. "I am sorry matters did not work out with Lord Cholmondeley. Have you abandoned all hope of him?"

I knew I should not encourage her, but I could not help myself. Was I growing sentimental in the twilight of my career?

Dally gave a resolute nod. "I am certain he cares more for me than any other woman, but not enough to risk the wrath of his uncle by marrying me. He has taken charge of my daughter, though he knows the Prince is more likely her father."

"You will not take the babe with you?" After so many years spent taking every precaution to avoid breeding, I had lately begun to yearn for a child.

"What sort of life would it be for the poor little mite?" Dally stirred the last of her royal cream ice into a beige puddle at the bottom of her saucer. "I want better for her."

I shook my head, mystified. "I fear I could not behave so nobly in your situation."

"You might be surprised what you would do for love."

Though I knew Dally meant the remark kindly, it chilled me.

All through that turbulent spring, Charles and his friends met often at my house to discuss how they might counter Lord Shelburne's influence without tearing their party to pieces.

"Our poor government is besieged by too many enemies in Opposition." Richard pounded his fist on my dining table. "Must we abide a saboteur within our own ranks as well?"

Charles rested one dark-whiskered cheek upon his fist. "You know very well, it is *because* our majority hangs by a thread that we've had to make this devilish alliance. I have done my best to work with the man, but I cannot continue to negotiate with the Americans while he is doing everything in his power to undermine my efforts."

"Shelburne has insinuated himself so far with the King," muttered Bob Spencer "he 'out-Tories' Lord North at his worst."

No one laughed at his bitter jest but Charles answered it. "Shelburne knows he has no support in Parliament, so he curries royal favor and gets it."

"That will only grow worse," said Richard, "until Lord Rockingham recovers. *If* he recovers."

I'd heard the prime minister was gravely ill. Since taking office, he had done his best to keep Charles's nemesis, Shelburne, in check. Now my friends drank in pensive silence, contemplating an uncertain future.

At last Bob ventured to speak. "What will you do, Charles, if the King asks Shelburne to form a government?"

"Try to persuade his Majesty that the man would not carry the confidence of Parliament or the country."

"And failing that?"

Charles shrugged. "Then I must resign. I have not struggled all these years to bring down a bad Ministry, only to put a worse one in its place."

I hoped it would not come to that. England needed a man like Charles at the helm. Bob Spencer appeared to be thinking the same thing.

"We have barely held power four months," he protested. "How can you throw it all away when so much remains to be done?"

Before Charles could answer, Richard spoke. "You must know you will be accused of quitting in a huff because the King did not appoint *you* prime minister."

Charles nodded. "I dislike abuse as much as any man, but I cannot let that keep me from doing what is right."

I admired his courage. For as long as I could remember, I had worked hard to be liked and never to give offense. My career had depended upon it . . . but so did his. The politician and the courtesan were both creatures of public favor.

The next day, Charles offered his resignation. The day after that, Lord Rockingham died. Some other Whigs resigned their places but others remained, including Charles's young friend, William Pitt. I knew Charles must be hurt when the impudent pup declared his mentor had resigned out of spite over being denied the office of prime minister.

When I spotted Charles at the opera house one evening, I approached to offer him a word of support. I hesitated when I noticed a lady on his arm. I looked closer, expecting to see the Duchess of Devonshire or some other Whig hostess. My blood seemed to freeze in my veins when I recognized my rival, Perdita Robinson.

"Of course I know he is keeping company with Mrs. Robinson," said Richard when I confronted him with the news. "So does everyone in London who reads a newspaper. Is that why you summoned me? I thought you must be ill or injured."

Richard knew? He was taking it far too coolly to suit me.

"Injured?" I cried. "I am not in the habit of staging accidents to bring people running. Unlike some I could name."

"I beg your pardon?" He looked mystified.

"Have you asked yourself why that woman is amusing herself with Charles?" My voice became shriller with every word. "He is out of office. He has no money. She must be using him for some ends of her own, though I cannot fathom what she wants. You must speak to him, Richard. You're the only one he might heed."

"Speak to him? About what–keeping company with Mrs. Robinson? If I did, the only thing I would say is, 'Well done, my friend!' Why do you suddenly care about Charles's *amours?* I thought that supposed rivalry between you and Perdita was all invented by the Herald and the Post to sell more newspapers."

Why *did* I suddenly care with such an alarming depth of emotion? I struggled to come up with a reason that would satisfy Richard ... and myself.

"Would you not have worried about Charles if he'd placed his confidence in our new First Minister? That woman poses as great a danger to his heart as Lord Shelburne would to his political principles. Charles is so open and trusting in his affections. When she drops him after getting whatever she wants, I fear it will break his heart." That sounded almost reasonable. Now if only I could make myself believe it.

"Don't be ridiculous!" snapped Richard. "Mrs. Robinson

may be too passionate for her own good, but I doubt she means Charles any harm. Besides, he is not some innocent lad in the flush of calf-love. The man has bedded more women than I can count. His heart is not the fragile organ you imagine."

Was I being foolish, as Richard claimed? Charles was a man of the world and quite old enough to take care of himself. Yet when I thought of Perdita Robinson flouncing about on his arm, a rush of possessive urgency shook me to the core.

"If I did not know better," said Richard, "I would swear you were jealous."

A rush of heat suffused my cheeks. "Me—jealous of Charles Fox? Really, you talk the most preposterous nonsense sometimes."

"Do I?" He fixed me with a shrewd look I could not return.

After my talk with Richard, I tried to forget about Charles and Perdita. I vowed their affair was no concern of mine. No doubt it would end as quickly as any other between a politician and a courtesan. In spite of all my good intentions, forgetting proved easier said than done. Every time I read some sly mention of them in the newspapers or overheard a bit of gossip, I grew as restless and excitable as a terrier scenting a rat.

Perdita's parting from Colonel Tarleton had been far too quiet. He'd simply gone off to Newmarket, and she had taken up with Charles. It was not the kind of break-up one would expect from two such volatile publicity-lovers. Whatever use Perdita hoped to make of Charles, I suspected Tarleton also stood to benefit. But what did they want?

Charles was out of place, with less political power than he'd had in years. He and Richard had given up their faro bank when they'd taken office, so he had no money. All he had left was his friends. Friends that included the Prince of Wales!

I could not stand by and let that scheming pair use Charles so callously. If Richard would not help me, I would have to take matters into my own hands.

"Bless my soul, am I the first to arrive?" Charles took his

accustomed chair in my sitting room and accepted a glass of claret. "Did the others enlist you to lure me out with them? I've heard grumblings that I come too seldom to Brooks' these days. I got away from clubbing when I was so busy in office. Now I am trying to reform my habits. A man cannot play the young wastrel all his life. But it is not easy to turn from gambling when one has been at it for most of one's life."

"Perhaps you should consider settling down." Though I knew it was sound advice, it gave me a sinking feeling to picture Charles married. "Find some agreeable lady with a comfortable fortune who will see that you eat properly, make certain your socks are darned and your buttons sewn on."

I pointed to a gap where one was missing from his waist-coat. "Give it here and I will have my maid sew on another."

Charles chuckled as he handed me his blue coat and buff-colored waistcoat. "What will the others think when they arrive to find you entertaining me in a state of undress?"

"The others aren't coming this evening. You are my only guest." Taking his garments, I rang for the footman and gave instructions about the missing button. While I was at it, I ordered his coat given a thorough brushing as well.

"Your famed hospitality reaches new heights," said Charles when I returned from the door. "And I am the sole recipient of it this evening. To what do I owe the honor?"

I did not feel very honorable, sharing my sordid suspicions with a man who thought well of almost everyone. I was saved from shame by the return of my footman, announcing supper.

"Let us put off explanations until after we dine." I offered Charles my arm. "And I decree no talk of politics tonight. I fear it is bad for the digestion."

"What shall be the theme of our conversation, then?" Charles rose to take my arm. "Books? The theatre?"

"What about the fascinating Mr. Fox?" I suggested.

He laughed in that merry, infectious manner I had come to

know so well. "Don't you mean *notorious*?"

"Fascinating," I repeated. "Tell me, is it true you smashed your father's pocket watch and bathed in a bowl of cream from your parents' banquet table?"

"Preposterous stories!" Charles held my chair. "I was scarcely more than an infant when I bathed in the cream. I had some fly bites that itched like the devil. Submersion in cool fresh cream was just the remedy. And I did not *smash* Father's watch. I only wanted to take it apart to see how the mechanism worked. I had no idea it would be so hard to put back together."

In recent years I had passed some of my most entertaining evenings at this table in the lively company of Charles and his friends. Now that I had him all to myself, I realized how much of my enjoyment owed to him alone.

"What of you?" he asked. "The longest reigning and most celebrated courtesan in the kingdom – magazines full of *tête-à-têtes* and Cyprian intelligence, yet you retain your mystery. I have often wondered, was there ever a *Mister* Armistead?"

"Not in the way you mean." I had never thought of myself as mysterious ... only obscure. "I once knew a man named Armistead, but he only pretended I was his wife."

Charles's dark brows shot up. "You intrigue me further. What became of this fellow and why did you keep his name?"

"He fled to the Continent to escape a blackmailer." I told Charles all about Ned, what he'd done for me and *to* me. Old secrets I'd never confided in anyone else.

We talked on through dinner. I scarcely noticed what we ate. Afterwards we returned to the sitting room, still deep in conversation. There we found his coat brushed and the missing button on his waistcoat restored. He thanked me as warmly as if I had done the work with my own hands, but he seemed in no hurry to put the garments back on.

Instead, he strolled to the sofa, beckoning me to join him. "Now, I should say you have kept me in suspense long enough. In truth you have kept me so agreeably entertained, I have not given the matter another thought until this moment. Still, I am curious. Why *did* you invite me here tonight ... alone?"

I took the invited seat, half reluctant, half eager. The pleasant evening we had just spent left me riddled with doubt. I was partly inclined to hold my tongue, fearing I might spoil my ripening friendship with Charles. But more than ever I could not bear the thought of him being used and cast aside.

Taking his hands in mine, I stared down at them rather than into his eyes. "I wanted to talk to you ... to warn you. I hope you will not resent my meddling. I swear it is prompted entirely by a desire for your happiness."

Charles clucked his tongue. "You must know it takes a great deal to provoke my resentment. I have always been a poor hater. Speak freely, I beg you."

"It is about that Robinson woman. I fear she is only using you to gain access to the Prince." I braced for Charles's reply. I knew him better than to fear a show of temper. But a sigh of injured reproach or a gaze of sorrowful censure – I dreaded those just as much.

Instead he gave a soft chuckle. "So you doubt my personal attractions are sufficient to secure a lady's affections?"

Did I? For perhaps the first time in our long acquaintance, I judged Charles upon his looks as a desirable man. Certainly compared to Richard and Lord Dorset, he was not handsome. He stood an inch shorter than me, though the difference looked greater when I wore high slippers and a towering hairstyle. Though he'd exaggerated during his duel by telling Richard was 'as wide one way as another,' he did have a stout build. His brows were so thick and black that the Duchess of Devonshire called him "The Eyebrow." His features were much more those of an honest, earthy peasant than the royal-bred aristocrat he was. And yet ...

I had come to know and like him so well that I found myself liking his looks too, just because they were *his*. Other men seemed bland and insubstantial compared to him. But Perdita

Robinson did not strike me as the sort of woman to see Charles in that light.

"I believe you could win any woman if you set your mind to it." I looked up so he might see the sincerity in my eyes. But when my gaze met his, I glimpsed something I had not expected. Something that made me add, "You would be welcome into *my* bed for the asking."

For a moment, the great orator seemed lost for words. Then, in a voice hoarse with emotion, he asked, "Would I, truly?"

I nodded.

Would he ask? I told myself this might be the only way to sever his connection with Perdita. It would be no worse than many other reasons I'd offered my body to men over the years. But I could not bring myself to seduce Charles on that excuse or any of the others I'd given myself in the past.

"You and Mary Robinson are very different kinds of women," Charles mused, "but she is not a bad creature at heart."

"You deserve better than her."

"Do I?" He disengaged one hand from mine and raised it to my cheek. "Then perhaps I *should* seek admission to your bed."

"I shall be disappointed if you do not." Such phrases had been my stock in trade for many years. This time, the depth of true feeling behind them staggered me.

Charles traced my lips with his forefinger then leaned toward me. "I could not bear to disappoint you."

Never had I awaited a man's kiss with such ardent anticipation. It would not be the first we had shared. I remembered the kisses I'd given him before and after his duel with Mr. Adam. Even then, I'd recognized them as something unique … like the man himself.

This one began softly, almost shyly, his full lower lip whispering over mine as he inhaled my scent with doting relish. When I responded, parting my lips and moving them against his in a provocative rhythm, he grew playful, teasing me with his tongue. He lifted his hand to fondle my bosom and I felt the accustomed stirring of desire that any acceptable lover's touch might kindle. But something else stirred, too—a soft, brooding tenderness in my heart.

The sensation alarmed me. I thought of asking him to stop and sending him away with an apology. But I feared that would chase him straight back into Perdita's bed. Besides, my trysts with Bob and Richard had proven that friends could become lovers then return to being friends without any great harm.

Why should Charles Fox be different?

"Shall we retire?" I whispered at last.

"A commendable suggestion." He gave me one final kiss then rose and offered me his arm.

We climbed the stairs without a further word and undressed in awkward silence, more like a pair of eager but inexperienced newlyweds than an aging courtesan and rake.

That was how we made love, too, with murmured endearments and soft sounds of pleasure, of which there were many. Though it all felt delightfully novel, we were *not* inexperienced. We both knew just where and how to stroke ... nuzzle ... knead. Even when my whole body strained for release, as I sensed his did, we continued our caresses, reluctant for it to end. But we could not resist the urgings of nature forever.

When he slid inside me and began to move with joyous passion, I shuddered in the grip of deep ecstasy that went on and on. Just when it eased, the force of his release sent a final pulse of delight coursing through me.

As the first faint rays of dawn peeped through my bedroom window, I wondered if I *had* misjudged Perdita's motives for keeping company with Charles Fox. After many years of being bedded by other men, I felt he had truly *made love* to me.

# Chapter Twenty

"**Y**OU MAY SET YOUR MIND at rest about Perdita," Charles assured me the next morning, as we lay in one another's arms after making love again. "Our connection was more economic and political than amorous. I've been negotiating on the Prince's behalf for a fair settlement in lieu of the bond he gave her to secure her favors."

What? I had fretted and fumed over nothing?

"The Prince is to be voted his own income soon," Charles continued. "It is in everyone's interest to have the matter sorted out before then. Since I have the trust of both parties and no other occupation, it kept me from worrying about what mischief Lord Shelburne might be up to. I cannot deny Mrs. Robinson was grateful for my help and affectionate in her gratitude. But I never doubted her heart belongs to Colonel Tarleton."

"You might have told me all that last night!" Though I did my best to feign severity, I could not truly regret the circumstances that had propelled me into Charles's arms after so many years of chaste friendship.

"I would have, I assure you, but dearest Liz was making such distracting remarks about my being welcome in her bed. How could I think of anything else?"

His eyes danced with such innocent mischief, I could not resist kissing him. "I should know better than to argue with the most skilled debater in Parliament."

He caressed my cheek and warmed me with an adoring gaze. "I save my arguing and abuse for political matters in the

House. At home, I study to be a model of good temper, which is the easiest thing in the world when I am in the company of my Liz!"

Talk of my house as *home* and me as *his Liz* left me with vague misgivings, but I dismissed them as his version of idle gallantry. The prince had professed worship and devotion, but he was now sacrificing at the altar of Lady Melbourne. Other men had bandied words like love and passion, but those bright flames had soon cooled to embers ... some to bitter ashes.

I did not foresee a bitter parting from such a kind friend as Charles, so I threw myself into our brief affair with cheerful disregard for the future. And I reaped a quality of happiness I had never known before.

When shooting season commenced, he departed for his accustomed round of friends' estates in Norfolk where game birds were plentiful. I headed to Surrey to spend my first summer at my dear little villa.

The anticipation of its rustic pleasures helped ease my separation from Charles. Though he promised to write often and made plans for celebrating Christmas with me in London, I knew our delightful interlude had come to an end, as it must. He could scarcely pay his own bills, let alone mine with any regularity. I would need to enlist a new patron or two when I returned to London, though I found myself strangely reluctant.

I enjoyed a peaceful but active summer at St. Anne's Hill, arranging the house to suit me, entertaining the occasional visitor, going for solitary rambles about the countryside. Best of all, I discovered the unexpected fulfillment of plunging my hands into the warm, moist earth to plant rose bushes, bulbs and perennials that would bloom the following summer.

To my surprise, I began receiving letters from Norfolk in Charles's open, boyish scrawl. They told of the weather, his bag of birds, a tasty dish served at dinner – everything he was seeing and doing, in cheerful certainty that I would find it of interest. His letters always included an endearment or two that I cherished. Nothing as florid as the prince's romantic declarations, but simple, direct and sincere.

*"It was a very good day which could only have been improved upon by a letter from Liz."* or *"I think of you often in your little house and long to hear of all your country doings. Pray give me the happiness of writing as soon as you can."*

Reading those letters, it was impossible to doubt Charles truly loved me ... for the moment. But I knew better than to suppose it would last. Soon his letters would become less frequent and less affectionate. By the time we returned to London, we would meet as friends once again. I tried to convince myself that was what I wanted.

Late in November I returned to London. There, I found Charles waiting.

"Dearest Liz!" He hurried toward me with open arms. His face glowed with delight at seeing me again. "The country agrees with you vastly. You look lovelier than ever."

As I surrendered to his embrace, a sweet warmth engulfed me. I had known many happy moments over the years, but none quite like this. No matter how intense my elation, there had always been something missing – some new goal to strive for, some ambition left to fulfill. *This* happiness felt complete.

After a long, warm kiss, we sat together holding hands and sharing all our latest news.

"I won three thousand pounds at Newmarket!" Charles took a sheaf of banknotes from his pocket and counted off ten, which he handed me with a flourish. "I would give you the lot, but my creditors must be appeased."

"These are hundred pound notes!" I thrust them back, scarcely able to believe I was refusing money from a man. "I cannot take such a sum. I did not invite you into my bed on commercial terms." The very thought sickened me.

"Of course not!" Charles looked as if I had accused him of something heinous. "If you had, a thousand pounds would not buy a single day of such happiness as you have brought me."

"Then why …?"

"Because," he gently pressed my fingers closed over the bank-notes, "what's mine is yours. This is the first time a gambling win has brought me more than fleeting pleasure. I beg you not to lessen that happiness by refusing."

I did have expenses to meet and this windfall would allow me to postpone finding another patron until Charles's feelings for me cooled. "If you insist, then. Thank you. But you must promise me one thing."

"I would do anything in my power to oblige my Liz."

"Let this be the last time you give me money won from a wager. I could not bear to be a cause of your gambling."

He cocked his head to one side and stared at me with the most endearing, quizzical look. "Does Liz mean to reform me?"

"Not *you*, Charles. Only a few of your habits, if you will let me. I want you healthy and happy and I will not settle for the momentary elation that rests on the turn of a card."

Fearing I might have offended him, I watched for his gaze to turn cold. But it only warmed and softened, tempered with chagrin. "All my life I have been blessed with the love of family and friends who have given me whatever I desired. But this is the first time anyone has cared enough to *deny* me something for my own good."

Parliament had barely resumed after the Christmas recess when Charles came home late one night bursting with news.

"Lord North has proposed a coalition between us to defeat Shelburne's ministry!" He crawled into bed and snuggled close to me in the darkness.

"North?" Waking from a light doze, I wondered if I'd heard right. "But you have been fighting that miserable man for as long as I've known you. How can you ally yourself with him now?"

A chuckle quivered through Charles's warm, solid body.

"Lord North was never a bad man, only a weak one. Even when our political combat was at its most hostile, I trusted him a hundredfold more than Shelburne."

"I fear other people will misunderstand your motives." I cupped his cheek in a protective caress. "The way they misunderstood your resignation last summer."

The satirical pamphlets, outrageous newspaper reports and cruel caricatures that lampooned Charles filled me with helpless indignation. I hoped the press would not use his affair with me to heap more abuse upon him.

"Liz must not fret on my account. As long as she and my friends think well of me, the rest may think what they like."

"I do think well of you," I pressed my forehead against his. "Nothing anyone can say will ever change that."

After almost ten years acquaintance, I was familiar with all the flaws and contradictions of his character. But the better I came to know him, the less those mattered. He possessed the most original mind and most affectionate heart I had ever encountered. In his company, the world seemed a brighter, warmer, more hopeful place.

For the rest of that winter, it seemed a more exciting place, too, with my dining table at the very hub. In Parliament, the Fox-North coalition attacked the Ministry, forcing Lord Shelburne to resign. For more than a month, the king did everything in his power to exclude Charles from the new administration. He made overtures to all the leading politicians. None would agree. Not even young Pitt was ambitious enough to attempt to govern without Charles's support.

Meanwhile, I was having as much trouble choosing a new patron as the king was finding a prime minister. The problem was not that my favors were unsought. I had the cachet of a royal mistress, after all, and I still looked younger than my years. Besides, I had little competition with Dally in France and Perdita too besotted with Colonel Tarleton to think of taking a new lover. But none of the gentlemen who bid for my favors made me feel half so alive and adored as Charles.

When the King finally agreed to let Lord Portland govern, with Charles back as Foreign Minister, I watched his return to power with mixed feelings. I was proud to see him in the high office his talents merited but I knew his duties would keep him too busy to bother with me.

Once again, Charles surprised me. Though much occupied with government business, he always found time for me. While twenty of the finest ladies in the kingdom kept themselves disengaged in hopes of dancing with the new Foreign Secretary at Lady Hertford's ball, he came to my house instead. We celebrated his victory with a private supper before retiring early to bed.

When Parliament recessed for the summer, Charles took it for granted he would accompany me to St. Anne's Hill.

"What an altogether excellent place, Liz." He strode about the grounds, inhaling draft after deep draft of the blossom-scented air. "Such views! They might move a man to poetry."

"I am glad you approve." I tucked my arm in his and led him on a tour, my delight in my little domain heightened by his. "These are the flowers I planted last fall. This year I mean to start a kitchen garden."

"What a perfect setting for my Liz." He patted my hand. "In London, she sparkles, but in Surrey she shines. I am a fortunate man to bask in her radiance."

He leased a house in Wimbledon for official entertaining but most of the time he made his home with me. We went for long rambles in the woods and dug in the garden together. After dinner he often read to me from his favorite books.

After one flying visit to Wimbledon, he returned home looking a trifle sheepish. "I hope you do not mind that I brought a visitor. He will not take up much room. I thought a holiday here might do him as much good as it has me."

He turned and beckoned to a schoolboy who walked toward

us with a slight limp. I immediately recognized the child's dark Fox eyebrows, while his grave, intelligent eyes put me in mind of Richard Fitzpatrick's.

"Liz, may I present my nephew, Lord Holland? A fine young fellow, is he not? My boy, this is Mrs. Armistead. I'm certain you will like her almost as much as I do. And she may find it amusing to keep a pair of Foxes – a young one and an old one."

I returned the boy's shy smile. "Welcome to St. Anne's Hill, Lord Holland. I am delighted to meet you at last."

"Thank you, ma'am." He bowed over my hand with the quaint formality of a child who had spent far more time among adults than other children. "You have a very pretty place here."

"What would you say to a punt on the river before dinner?" Charles proposed. "This evening you must come down to the bottom of the garden to hear the nightingales sing."

For the next fortnight the three of us spent a jolly time together, tramping off for picnics, boating and fishing on the river, playing trap-ball, skittles and jack-stones. Those sweet summer days were the closest I had ever come to motherhood and I gloried in it, for Charles's nephew seemed to crave every scrap of maternal affection I could spare him. By the time Lord Holland departed, I was pleased to see he had gained a few pounds, while Charles appeared to have lost a few.

"Thank-you for a splendid time!" Lord Holland threw his arms around my neck. "May I come back again, please?"

"Whenever and as often as you like." I clung to him, wishing I could live the past three weeks all over again. "In the meantime, I hope you will not mind my sending you a letter now and then so you do not forget me."

"I could never do that! But I should like to get letters."

"Off to the carriage, young one." Charles bid his nephew. "I will be along in a moment."

When Lord Holland had gone, Charles pulled me into his arms. "Liz, are those tears? You heard the boy – he will be back. In the meantime, you have me. You often say I act like a child."

"So you do." He had a child's impulsiveness, a child's honesty, a child's zest for life, taking pleasure in the simplest things. "I shall miss you too."

"Nonsense!" He kissed me on one cheek then the other. "I'll be back before you have time to miss me."

That was not what I meant, but I let it go. Dashing away my tears, I waved my pair of Foxes on their way with a pretence of good cheer.

"Good Lord!" I struggled to still my trembling hands so I could finish reading the letter they held. It had just arrived from one of my servants in London, informing me that several tradesmen had called looking for payment of overdue bills.

Were my finances truly that bad? I staggered back and collapsed onto the nearest chair, gasping for air as if I were drowning. Perhaps I soon would be drowning ... in debt.

I'd tried to make the £1000 I had received from Charles last as long as possible. But keeping a carriage, servants and two houses was a costly undertaking. If I could get by for another two months I would receive my annuity payments. But what further debts would I run up in the meantime? And after I paid them, what would be left for me to live on?

"Hullo? Mrs. Armistead?"

At the sound of Richard's voice and his brisk footfall, I thrust the letter into my pocket. Rising to greet him, I tried to erase any sign of distress from my features. I might have fooled most people, but not him.

"What is the matter?" He eased me back down onto the chair and knelt beside me. "You're as pale as whey."

"The sound of your voice startled me, that's all."

"Don't lie," he snapped. "You were never that good an actress."

For years I had kept my own counsel, on this subject more

than any. Yet I longed to confide in someone and I trusted Richard's judgment. "It's about ... money. Charles—"

"Good God!" Richard cried before I could say another word. "How did you find out?"

Find out? What was he talking about? His tone chilled me.

If I wanted to learn more, I would have to bluff. "The ... same way you did, I expect."

"He *told* you?" Richard slid onto the bench beside me. "For one of the cleverest men in England, he can be a damned blockhead about women. Perhaps it is just as well you know. It might make you heed what I've come to say."

Perhaps it would, but first I had to find out what he was talking about. Something to do with a woman and money, apparently. "How much did he give her?"

My guess proved correct. "Three hundred straightaway. He sent the other five the next day, but she was gone by then."

Eight ... hundred ... pounds? That would have settled all my debts with enough left to last until my annuity payment.

"Does Charles know where she went?" I was a better actress than Richard gave me credit for. But could I lead him on long enough to learn the woman's name?

Richard shrugged. "Dover is my guess, hoping to catch Tarleton before he boarded a ship to France."

Tarleton? The name hit me like a backhand blow. While tradesmen were clamoring for money I did not have, Charles was showering eight hundred pounds on Perdita Robinson?

"What *did* you come to say, Richard?" Whatever it was, I wanted him to say it as quickly as possible then leave me to sort out what I must do.

"Just that I am concerned about this ... liaison between you and Charles. I thought it would run its course months ago."

"So did I." My thought slipped out in a rueful whisper.

"The longer it goes on," said Richard, "the harder it will be on both of you when it ends."

He was not telling me anything I didn't know already, but I flinched just the same. Had I already left it too late to break with Charles without breaking my heart?

# Chapter Twenty-One

"EVERYTHING'S PACKED, MA'AM." MY MAID handed me the key to my trunk. "When should I tell Mr. Sloan you wish to set out?"

"In an hour, if he can have the carriage ready by then." That would be long enough for one last walk about the place. "Tell Cook to feed everyone before we go. Once we get on the road, I don't want to stop except for fresh horses."

After my talk with Richard, I knew there was only one course open to me. I must go abroad to escape my creditors until I could raise the money to pay them.

And to escape my ruinous entanglement with Charles.

"What about you, ma'am?" The girl's eyes danced with excitement. This would be her first journey abroad. "Should I tell Cook to fix you a plate?"

"I am not hungry, Mary, except for fresh air. Fetch me when Sloan is ready to go."

I wandered out onto the grounds, a weight on my heart growing heavier with each step. All the fragrant blossoms had fallen from my rose bushes, petal by petal, leaving behind only thorns and sour scarlet hips. The nightingales had flown away to their winter homes in the south. Next spring they would return to sing but I would not be there to hear them.

I promised myself I would come back one day. When all my debts were discharged and Charles had found a new companion. The thought of Charles made me smile ... then sigh. I hoped he would not take it ill that I had broken my news by letter. I simply could not look him in the eye and say what I needed to say without betraying the depth of my feeling for him.

He often spoke as if he intended we should be together always. I was honored to believe he cared for me more than any other woman. That did not mean his feelings would last forever. The dealings of men and women had been my business for many years. I knew that passion, desire and love were like my roses. No matter how vivid and sweet, time would destroy them.

"Liz? Where are you?" The sound of Charles's voice stirred my heart like the touch of skilled fingers upon harp strings. The melody it played was complex, with some discordant notes and a poignant thread in the harmony.

"Here."

I had barely choked the word out when he came bounding down the path toward me. His fierce dark brows were drawn together in a look of miserable anxiety, but his eyes radiated such tenderness, I could scarcely bear it.

"Dearest Liz!" He seized my hands and pressed a kiss upon one, then the other. "You cannot imagine the relief it gives me to find you still here. I feared you might be gone. Then I would have had to resign my office, raise what funds I could, and follow you to Spa or St. Petersburg or … Samarkand if need be!"

I resisted the compelling urge to kiss him. "I am sorry to have distressed you. I thought slipping away quietly would be easiest for us both. Perhaps it was cowardly of me. We need to talk so I can make you understand why we must part."

He shook his head, the picture of sweet stubbornness. "If Liz can persuade me of that, then I must give her my seat in Parliament, for she would have greater success in the debates than I have ever had."

Despite my wretchedness, I had to grin at the outrageous notion of a woman in Parliament. "You are a man of sense. It should not be difficult to make you see reason."

I began to walk, my arms wrapped around myself. Though

the day was quite mild for early November, my bones ached with the chill of a hundred frosts. "How could I not love you, Charles? Edmund Burke was right when he said you were made to be loved. But I must make a living and I know only one way to do that."

Charles fell in step beside me, his breath coming fast. "Is that truly the life you want for yourself—with no attachments, only transactions? Are you content to be coveted for a month or a year when you could be cherished forever?"

That word brought me skidding to a halt. "Is that what you are offering me?"

He replied with a shrug and a sigh, his palms open and empty. "It is all I have. But I should be the happiest man in the world to devote the rest of my life to my Liz."

I so yearned to believe him, but half a lifetime spent in the fleeting company of different men argued otherwise.

"That could be a very long while, you know. It is a wonder we have got on so well for a year. We are as different as a man and woman can be. Your ancestors were kings. I come from Vinegar Alley. You are one of the cleverest men in the kingdom. I never even attended a dame's school. You are one of the most beloved and esteemed men of our time. I am one of the most notorious women. Must I go on?"

"Allow me." He captured my hands in his. "You are the greatest beauty ever to grace a London ballroom. I am short and round, with a face only a caricaturist could love. You have earned yourself a comfortable fortune while I have pissed away a far greater one without a thing to show for it. If we tallied all that up on a balance sheet, I reckon it would come out even. But what matter, Liz? The heart is a poor bookkeeper."

"A very pretty sentiment." I fought back with the only weapon I had left. "Perhaps *your* heart cannot tally the sum of £800 you gave Perdita Robinson. Mine can reckon it well enough and it does not add up to lifelong devotion." My voice broke in a humiliating whimper. "At least, not to me."

"Oh, Liz." He did not even have the grace to look guilty. "The poor girl turned to me as her last hope to save Tarleton from his creditors, so he would not run away to France."

Richard had mentioned Colonel Tarleton, but my suspicion and jealousy had seized upon Perdita, giving no thought to *why* she might need money from Charles.

Faced with my dazed, shamed silence he added, "I raised the money for her because I knew how I would feel in her situation—if the person I loved more than all the world were in debt and about to flee the country without me."

Something broke inside me then. Or broke free from long restraint. Whether or not Charles loved me, scarcely signified. I loved him. I could not deny it or run from it. Only by giving myself up to it and holding nothing back might I know any happiness. I cast myself on his sturdy shoulder and clung there, hiding my face.

He patted my back, crooning endearments. "May I conclude this means you will stay?"

I made myself look him in the eye. "For as long as you will have me."

Charles burst into a smile so luminous, I thought for a moment spring had returned. "Be warned, that means forever. And promise you will never leave me again. I have been more wretched these past days than ever in my life."

"I will never leave you against your wishes."

He seemed satisfied. "Then that means never at all."

I did not contradict him, though I knew my vow was not quite what he believed it to be.

Almost as quickly as it had come to power, the Fox-North coalition was overthrown by the machinations of King George. This time young Mr. Pitt did not scruple to accept the office of Prime Minister. Charles and his supporters attacked the new government, which they believed had come to power unlawfully. In the end Parliament was dissolved and an election called.

"How shall I do without my Liz?" asked Charles when I prepared to go to the country on my own. "Forty days is a vastly long time."

"Nonsense." I refused to be moved by his long face and pleading eyes. "You will be out on the hustings 'til all hours. I would only be a distraction. Besides, you do not need any worse stories about you in the press."

"Well if you must." Charles sighed. "I suppose you must."

I kissed my forefinger and transferred it to the dimple on his chin. "I will write you every day with the news from St. Anne's Hill and you must scribble me a note when you can."

I smoothed his neck linen. "Try to keep regular hours and not drink too much wine or eat too much rich food. Make sure your coat is brushed and your linen clean before you go out campaigning. A slovenly candidate is not likely to win votes."

Back at St. Anne's Hill, I threw myself into feathering our rustic nest, planting more flowers and writing encouraging letters to London. My poor dear needed all my encouragement, for the King was determined to defeat him by any means necessary. Early in the polling Charles trailed by fifty votes.

*Plenty of bad news from all quarters*, he wrote, *but I think that misfortunes when they come thick have the effect rather of raising my spirits than sinking them. There are few against which I could I can not bear up and much the greatest of those few it is in your power to prevent from ever happening.*

By Good Friday the margin had widened to almost three hundred. *I must go on*, wrote Charles, *though much against my inclination. I hope you have had some cross buns today. Oh how I do long to see my Liz.*

But after Easter his fortunes improved and he began to gain on his court-favored opponent. Though Charles never mentioned why, the newspapers reported that the Duchess of Devonshire and other Whig ladies had begun to canvass for him. Wearing foxtails in their hats, they drove voters to the polls in their carriages and even exchanged kisses for votes.

"Playing at politics the way they once played at soldiering," I muttered, throwing down a copy of *The Herald*.

But I swallowed my spleen when Charles surged forward in the polling. *Now as you see, I am twenty-one ahead! It is a great part indeed of my pleasure in my triumph to think my Liz will be pleased with it.*

In my reply, I assured him I was very proud of him, though I would be so in victory or honorable defeat.

*How I long for a visit from you*, he wrote back. *I have been quite spoiled with seeing so much of you this year and begin to grow quite restless when I am three days without you.*

Finally, after a hard-fought campaign during which many other members of the coalition went down to defeat, Charles was declared elected. Once again a jubilant crowd chaired him through the streets, after which the Prince of Wales feted him with a lavish breakfast at Carlton House.

The first moment he could tear himself away from the celebrations, Charles rode to St. Anne's Hill. I welcomed him with open arms and a festive dinner of his favorite pork roast. Afterward we retired to bed early for what my angel declared was the most delightful celebration of his election.

Fighting an election against so determined and powerful a foe cost a great deal. Though many wealthy supporters contributed, Charles's debts increased. Once he was out of office, his creditors descended upon him. I feared he might try to recoup his fortunes by gambling.

So I took a step I once could not have contemplated. I sold the leases on my houses in London along with my two annuities for a considerable lump sum. I presented the proceeds to Charles to pay the most pressing of his debts.

"But . . . Liz . . ." He looked quite bewildered when I told him what I had done. "I cannot take this from you."

"Why not?" Besides the fear I'd expected to suffer at this surrender of my worldly security, I also felt an unaccountable relief, as if I had shed some invisible burden. "You said yourself, our interests are one."

"Pray reconsider, my dearest!" His voice broke. "This is every-thing you have in the world. I cannot bear to think what would become of my Liz if anything should happen to me."

"Nor can I. Though not for any material consideration." The thought of a world without Charles was too bleak to consider. "Please accept this. Nothing could make me happier than to ease your burdens."

One thing, perhaps. I would dearly love to give him a child. Several months ago, I had thrown away the cleansing rod and solution I'd used scrupulously for so many years to ward off pregnancy. Since then I had not conceived, but perhaps now that the separation and stress of the election was over ...

"I want to make you happy, Liz. God knows I have little else to offer you. But what you offer ..."

I sought to explain why it was so important to me, though I did not fully understand. "You know how I earned this money."

"What does that signify? We have both sown our share of wild oats. But they have come a good crop at last, have they not? Besides, I have far more to reproach myself in the losing of my fortune than you have in the gaining of yours."

His complete, sincere acceptance of my past made me love him more than ever. "Perhaps so, but this would be my way of making a break from all that and committing myself to you for good and all. Is that not what you want?"

He opened his mouth to speak then shut it again. For several moments he struggled to compose himself. "And they call *me* a persuasive orator. I have no choice but to accept when Liz puts the matter in such gracious terms. Bless you, my angel!"

Poor we might have been in money, but we were rich in our devotion to each other and in the kindness of our friends.

"An altogether delicious repast, Mrs. Armistead!" declared

Bob Spencer, one day in early summer as he pushed his chair away from our dining table. "The chicken was some of the tenderest I've eaten and words cannot describe the asparagus!"

"It makes a great difference," I replied with satisfaction, "when they go straight from the garden into a pot without passing through a city market. I hope you have left room for strawberries and custard."

"Afterward," said Charles, "shall we aid our digestion with a ramble down to the river? Or is such entertainment too tame for you, Richard, after your flight in that air balloon?"

Richard shrugged, as careless of his safety as he was of his money at the gaming tables. "It was quite a sensation to fly through the air and look on the world with a bird's eye view."

"I must try it." Bob savored a spoonful of strawberries. "I reckon balloon travel will be all the fashion soon."

"I shall leave such adventures to you intrepid gentlemen," I said. "A sworn coward like me prefers to keep her feet planted safely on the ground."

"Not a coward, surely, Mrs. A." Richard spoke in a tone of friendly banter. I doubted Charles or Bob marked the coolness in his gaze. But I did and it grieved me. "After all, you keep a hungry Fox about the house. That takes some courage."

Charles glanced down at his empty bowl and began to laugh. "Liz has nothing to fear from her old Fox. He is as tame as a lapdog—eats out of her hand and always comes when called!"

Though Richard joined in his friends' laughter, I suspected it was as forced as mine. Something had changed between us after that day he'd urged me to part from his friend.

"It amazes me," said Bob, staring at Charles, "how well this place suits you. I never would have thought it. And I claim the credit for introducing Mrs. Armistead to the place."

I fished the last berry from my bowl, acutely conscious that I had slept with all three gentlemen now seated around my table.

"I owe you a debt of gratitude." Charles raised his glass to his friend without the least sign of awkwardness. "This place grows dearer to me by the day, as does its lovely tenant. Indeed, there is only one thing in the world I lament."

"The deplorable state of our political fortunes," suggested Richard, taking a deep draft of his wine.

Charles shook his head. "Buck up, old fellow! There will be other elections and honorable work in Opposition."

"Then what *do* you hanker for?" asked Bob.

Charles looked around him with a sigh. The room was cramped and ill-lit, but we had shared many happy meals there. "Only the two thousand pounds it would take to buy this little paradise from your brother. It might as well be two million for the likelihood of my raising such a sum."

I thought nothing more of it until three weeks later when an official-looking letter arrived for Charles. I hovered about while he opened it, worried it might contain bad news.

"Good heavens!" he muttered. "It's from the Duke of Marlborough's agent. His Grace is pleased to offer us the copyhold of St. Anne's Hill with its buildings, pastures, woodlands and arable for two thousand pounds."

"Yes, but you said that might as well be ..."

Charles waved his hand to shush me and continued reading. "The sum of which he will advance us for a mortgage on the property at an annual interest of a hundred pounds!"

That was less than my leasehold. And the place would *belong* to us!

Charles leaped from his chair and threw his arms around me. We danced around our little library until we fell down dizzy with happiness.

To keep our dear home safe from the last few of Charles's creditors, the purchase was made in my name. Early in September, I signed the papers making St. Anne's Hill ours. Afterward we held a little dinner party to celebrate, at which Bob Spencer was the guest of honor.

I proposed a toast to Bob and his kindness. Then Charles

raised his glass. "My friends, I hope you will all join me in drinking to the health and happiness of my very dear Mrs. Armistead – the Lady of the Hill!

The ink on the deed was scarcely dry when a passionate storm descended upon us, in the person of the Prince of Wales. He was violently in love ... again. This time the object of his affections was not a courtesan whose company he could hire, nor a fashionable married peeress eager to make a royal conquest.

Mrs. Fitzherbert was a respectable Catholic widow who took her religion and her reputation seriously. She was not willing to grant the Prince her favors on any terms less than marriage, which would be illegal on account of *his* position and *her* religion. When the Prince's attentions became too relentless, she fled to Europe, leaving him distraught.

"I cannot live without my beloved angel!" He flung himself on a sofa in our book room and sobbed for a full hour despite our best efforts to comfort and reason with him.

"I would give up every title I possess to be her lover and husband!" The prince threw himself on the floor and thrashed about in a frenzy.

"Calm yourself," I pleaded. "If she cares for you, Mrs. Fitzherbert would not wish you so distressed on her account."

"*If* she cares for me?" the Prince shrieked. "You think she does not?" He commenced to tear his hair with one hand and strike his forehead with the other.

"No, sire!" I cast a harried glance at Charles. "I am sure she must, which is why she would hate to see you take on so."

The Prince flung his arms around my neck, burying his face against my shoulder, which made Charles scowl. "I s-swear, I will abandon the c-country and forfeit the Crown for her if I must."

"But, dear boy," cried Charles. "How will you support her?"

"I shall sell all my j-jewels and my plate! Somehow I shall scrape together a c-competence to fly with my love to America, where we may be free to make a life together!"

I wondered what sort of welcome the Americans would give a son of King George!

"Do not be hasty." Charles gently loosened me from the prince's grasp. "Perhaps something can be done."

For all his hysterical declarations of devotion to Mrs. Fitzherbert, I sensed that if Charles were not there, the Prince might have sought to ease his sorrow and frustration in my bed.

"Dear Charles." The prince embraced him warmly. "You are so clever, I am certain you will find some way to assist me!"

When he had gone, I collapsed in an armchair.

"I pity the boy," muttered Charles. "How could I not? I should feel as he does if circumstances conspired to separate me from my Liz." He pulled a face. "Though I might not show it with such passionate agitation."

After that upset, we settled into a life of contented domesticity. Charles went down to London for the spring sitting of Parliament, staying in a little house we took on South Street. I made brief visits to shop and attend the theatre. I never stayed in town long, though. I feared that some gentleman, not knowing of my exclusive attachment to Charles, might try to solicit my favors.

When the weather grew warmer, Charles came home to St. Anne's Hill more frequently, often bringing his friends to share our rural pleasures. Since Eton was only ten miles away, my 'young Fox,' was able to visit often, much to our delight. His presence gave me an outlet for my maternal feelings, but also reminded me how much I longed for a little Fox cub of my own.

In high summer, St. Anne's Hill was at its best with the sun shining, all my flowers in bloom, and the birds filling the woodland with their songs. Then Charles sallied forth in a green gardener's apron to prune the fruit trees. After his frantic youth, he seemed to revel in such tranquil idleness.

With the coming of autumn, he went off to shooting parties

in Norfolk and the October race meetings at Newmarket. I stayed behind in Surrey, enjoying the harvest time in busy solitude, which made me appreciate Charles's companionship all the more when he returned.

He wrote me many letters from Norfolk, as he had during the first flush of our love affair. The affection he expressed in these messages grew even more ardent over time. *"Adieu my dearest Liz. Indeed, you are more than all the world to me!"*

In November, Charles returned for a rapturous reunion, and to celebrate his dear nephew's birthday, before heading off to Parliament again. On Christmas Day we gave the servants a holiday while we celebrated quietly with family. We hosted a livelier celebration on Twelfth Night, inviting our rural neighbors for music, dancing and twelfth cake.

As month followed month and year followed year, without even a miscarriage to suggest I *could* conceive, I slowly gave up hope of having a child with Charles. Though it was one of the few subjects we never discussed, I sensed he did, too. I knew he had a son and a daughter by different women with whom he'd briefly kept company. The boy, Harry, was deaf. He boarded with a vicar's family in Kent, who took excellent care of him.

Charles's daughter was six years old when her father asked one day, "Liz, would you mind having Harry and little Harriet come for Christmas? I think they are both getting old enough to manage a visit, if you are willing."

"Of course, my dear!" I knew from my feelings for his nephew how much I could love a child. How much more could I love Charles's own children, even if they were not mine?

I enjoyed Christmas more than ever that year. Young Harry was the very image of his father and quite clever, though he could not hear or speak. He and Charles 'talked' by making signs with their fingers. Harriet resembled none of the Fox's. She was cross-eyed, but otherwise quite pretty, and chattered away like a little magpie. After that first visit broke the ice, we brought the children to stay with us often.

When the place bustled with our merry doings, I recaptured the half-forgotten sweetness of a devoted family.

If only the rest of the world could have been as happy and peaceful as St. Anne's Hill.

Charles haled the storming of the Bastille as a great triumph over tyranny but many people in England became alarmed by the growing violence in France. They took a dim view of anyone who advocated reform. Some of Charles's friends began to distance themselves from their liberal principles.

Aided by a small number of devoted followers, Charles opposed the Aliens Bill, the Traitorous Correspondence Bill and the suspension of Habeas Corpus. Though Prime Minister Pitt claimed such repressive measures were necessary to ensure the security of the country, Charles believed their assault on civil liberties posed a far greater threat.

The press attacked him as never before, calling him a traitor to the country and comparing him to the most bloodthirsty revolutionaries in France. Though he vowed their abuse would not keep him from acting on his principles, I knew it must sting. I did my best to provide him with a small haven of happiness at St. Anne's Hill.

One June day in 1793, after a morning spent gardening, we were batting a feathered shuttlecock back and forth, counting the number of volleys we could keep it in the air. After five hundred and forty-seven, I missed a shot so we retired to the verandah to read our post over a cool glass of lemonade.

"A letter from the *young one!*" I cried, recognizing Lord Holland's handwriting. I seized it to read, for Charles had plenty of political correspondence.

"How is he enjoying Italy?" asked Charles as he glanced over his share of the mail.

Lord Holland had gone abroad on his Grand Tour, a rather restricted one considering the number of countries in Europe at war with one another.

"Very well, though he says he is bitten to death by fleas in the inns. He admires the Bologna school of painting, but he did not care for the Correggio fresco. How I wish we could be there to enjoy it all with him ... not the fleas, of course!"

"My Liz may get her wish." Charles spoke in a dazed murmur as he stared at the letter in his hand.

"Oh dear, has someone died and left you a little money?" I knew Charles would take no pleasure in that.

"No." He handed me the letter.

"Honor of informing you ..." I read the words, muttering some aloud. "... contribution raised ... well-wishers all over the country ... relief of your debts. Oh Kins, how kind!"

We later discovered several of Charles's friends, including his old dueling opponent Mr. Adam, had organized a committee to raise funds on his behalf. Many of the subscribers were tradesmen, farmers, country parsons ... the ordinary people Charles had long claimed to represent. Enough money had been raised to pay all his debts, and provide for his future support.

Charles was delighted. Not only because it eased our financial worries, but on account of the source. *I think it is the most honorable thing that has happened to anyone*, he wrote to his nephew. Others might have been too proud to accept such a gift, but Charles believed pride was the passion of little, dark, intriguing minds. He regarded those contributions as a popular endorsement for his beliefs and his efforts on their behalf.

As it turned out, we did not use any of the money to go abroad. The troubled violence of the Continent could not lure us away from the peaceful haven of our little hill. By this time, Charles and I had been together for ten years and were more in love than ever. *She is a comfort to me in every misfortune*, he wrote to his nephew in a letter I glimpsed, *and makes me enjoy doubly every pleasant circumstance of life. There is a charm and delight in her society which time does not in the least wear off. And for real goodness of heart if she ever had an equal, she never had a superior.*

My throat tightened as I read those words, for they perfectly expressed my feelings for him. Though he sometimes seemed not to hear a word I said if his thoughts were elsewhere. Though he could not carve a roast properly to save his life. Though he was blissfully immune to the fleas in foreign inns that bit me to death, I adored him with all the affection I had hoarded in my heart for so many years.

Though I was now over forty and growing rather stout myself. Though I had slept with many men, including his dearest friends. Though I could not bear him a child. Still he made me feel, for the first time in my life, secure in his love.

We were both bitterly disappointed the next year when Lord Holland wrote that he would not return from Italy in time to celebrate his coming of age. I soon devised a happy diversion, however. Charles had long wanted a little garden temple. Now that our finances were in better order, we could afford to have one built. Though the 'young one' was still abroad, we decided to celebrate his coming of age with a party. While Charles was off on his autumn round of shooting, I dispatched invitations, ordered provisions and supervised a thorough housecleaning.

A few days before Charles's return, Richard arrived one afternoon from nearby Sunninghill. He often visited us, but for the past ten years he had never come when Charles was away from home. I welcomed him warmly, but a little warily.

He handed me a sheet of paper. "The verses you requested to dedicate your *Temple of Friendship*. It is fitting you and Charles should build a temple to friendship. You both make almost a creed of it."

His light-hearted tone turned earnest. "Can you and I ever be friends again, Elizabeth? Not just the two people Charles most loves, getting on together for his sake?"

The loss of his friendship had been my only regret during these past delightful years with Charles. "That is up to you, entirely. Can you forgive me for not heeding your advice to part from him? I did try, but it was beyond my power."

"I was wrong to ask it of you. I know that now. I was afraid my feelings would poison our friendship."

Did he mean jealousy? Which one of us had he been jealous of and which friendship had he feared to destroy? Both perhaps? How might all our lives have been different if he and I had not been so afraid to risk our friendship for something deeper? I could not be sorry for the way it had all worked out.

I offered Richard my hand. For a moment, I thought he might kiss it, but instead he wrapped it in both of his and smiled. We spoke no more, but I believe we both understood.

"Even the weather favors you, Mrs. Armistead," said Bob Spencer when he arrived for our party with Mr. Sheridan in tow. "I have seen colder Augusts than this November!"

The mild weather was a great relief to me. Our guest list had grown so large, I was not certain we could cram them all inside our little villa at once. "I believe there is some magic about this place, which grants especially dear wishes. Tell Mr. Sheridan about the holy well, Lord Robert."

I turned to welcome another group of guests. William Adam bowed over my hand. "It is a credit to your generosity, ma'am, that I am admitted to a celebration of friendship. I recollect an icy glare you aimed at me one long ago morning in Hyde Park."

Though I could never look back on that day without the sinking awareness of all it might have cost me, I summoned up a smile. "I must echo the sentiment Mr. Fox expressed once in the House of Commons, sir. 'My friendships are perpetual. My enmities are not so.' You have proven yourself a staunch friend since then. A dozen years of support and respect surely outweigh a few rash moments."

Leaning closer, I whispered, "Besides, your duel was the excuse for my first kissing Mr. Fox."

So it went, my happiness increasing with each new guest welcomed, each fond greeting exchanged. When all our guests had assembled, we led them down to the garden where we received many compliments on the little brick edifice banded with stone.

"To celebrate this special birthday of our beloved Lord Holland," said Charles, "and to pay tribute to our very dear friends, we dedicate this Temple of Friendship."

I unveiled the Latin inscription, which translated: *To commemorate the birthday of Henry Richard Lord Holland, who attained the age of twenty-one on the twenty-first of November 1794, which day was happily celebrated here, Charles and Elizabeth, who though not his parents love him with parental love, built as they vowed this temple sacred to him and to friendship.*

Everyone clapped and cheered. Then Richard read the verses he had composed for the occasion, for which I led the applause and kissed him on the cheek. The brief ceremony over, we returned to the house for eating, drinking and dancing. When Charles and I exchanged a loving look across our pleasantly crowded parlor, my heart strained to contain my happiness.

Then, just when I had stopped expecting it, my happy, secure little world turned upside down.

# Chapter Twenty-Two

WITH A CONTENTED SIGH, I glanced up from the flowers I was planting around our Temple of Friendship. Fond memories engulfed me as I recalled the happy day last autumn when we had dedicated it. For a moment I could almost hear the rattle of carriages coming up the lane and the call of friendly greetings.

"Mrs. Armistead, hullo!" That one was not a memory.

I scrambled up as well as my rheumatic knees would allow and waved to Mr. Adam as he ascended from his carriage. "What a pleasant surprise, sir! I was just thinking about the last time you were here, at Lord Holland's coming of age celebration."

"Will the young man be returning soon from Italy? I look forward to seeing him take his place in the House with Mr. Fox."

"He has no definite plans at present." I tucked my work gloves in the pocket of my gardening apron. "The situation in Europe is still so unsettled. But I hope it will be soon. His uncle and I both long to see him again."

Mr. Adam's features tensed. "Is Mr. Fox at home? There is a matter I must discuss with him."

Something urgent enough to come all the way here on a lovely summer day with an anxious look in his eyes. A political situation? Not likely–Parliament was in recess until the fall. Some difficulty with the fund for Charles's support?

"I am sorry you came so far. Charles and Richard Fitzpatrick

273

left this morning for Kent to visit Lord Robert Spencer. I do not expect them back until the end of the week."

Mr. Adam's fingers did a nervous little dance around the brim of his hat. "I should have sent a message, but I so seldom hear of him straying from home in the summertime."

"I will tell Mr. Fox of your visit and have him arrange to meet with you." I started for the house. "Now, you must take some refreshment after your long drive."

"Please do not trouble yourself, ma'am. If Mr. Fox is not here, I should be on my way."

Did he think it would compromise his reputation to take tea with me? My days as a notorious courtesan were long over. Glamorous as they had been, I did not miss them. "You must stay. My conscience will bother me dreadfully if I send you away without a bite to eat."

"Very well." Though still hesitant, Mr. Adam fell in step with me. "I cannot refuse your kind invitation."

Over luncheon, I used every art of persuasion to find out what my guest wanted with Charles. With each evasion my curiosity grew, until it burst the bonds of subtlety.

"Forgive me, sir, but it is plain you are anxious to speak to Mr. Fox. Since so many matters that concern him are also of consequence to me, I must insist you tell me what is wrong."

"Do not fret, ma'am! It may be of no consequence—only a misapprehension on the part of certain persons. I thought Mr. Fox should know so he can set the matter straight before it becomes fodder for scurrilous newspapers and print sellers."

Now I *had* to know. I pleaded until the poor man gave way.

"It is Mrs. Coutts ..."

The banker's wife? My spirits sank. "What about her?"

"When I spoke with the lady yesterday—" Mr. Adam sounded relieved to get the matter off his chest "—she seemed certain there would be a happy event in the near future concerning Mr. Fox and her daughter, Miss Frances."

My nerves were strung so tight, I burst out laughing at this nonsense. "The middle one, Mr. Coutts's favorite? But she is only a child!"

"Two-and-twenty, I believe, though her delicacy makes her look younger."

"That is Lord Holland's age!" I cried. "Perhaps Mr. Fox was making inquiries on behalf of his nephew."

Miss Coutts's fortune would be a great political asset for our dear young one. The lady might be a nice match for him in temperament, too, being rather shy. But why had Charles never mentioned such plans to me? He must know how heartily I would approve.

Mr. Adam burst my hopeful fancy. "Mrs. Coutts was quite definite in naming Mr. Fox as the object of her daughter's affection. She insists the girl's feelings are returned."

"Now, *that* is absurd." Was it? Charles had been his usual affectionate self of late ... though perhaps a bit preoccupied.

"So I told Mrs. Coutts." Mr. Adam bolted a mouthful of tea but looked as if he would have liked some stronger stimulant. "She said her daughter requested a lock of Mr. Fox's hair as a token of affection and he had promised her one."

The strawberry tart in my belly turned into a clutch of seething snakes.

"I assured her it must be a misunderstanding," Mr. Adam rattled on, "but she would not listen. She said how much better it would be for Mr. Fox's political career if he led a more settled domestic life. I protested that his life is that of a married man even if some straitlaced people might think otherwise. I fear I made her angry, but I do not care. I could not stand to hear Mr. Fox spoken of as if you mean nothing to him!"

I heard all the words, which came faster and faster until I feared the poor man would tie his tongue in knots. But I only heeded certain parts. Namely that it would be better for Charles if he were married. Try as I might, I could not deny Miss Coutts might be a good match for him in many respects.

Once poor Mr. Adam made his escape, I wandered back down to the Temple of Friendship, where I sank to the ground.

This turn of events should not have surprised me. I had gone into my relationship with Charles knowing it couldn't last. That was why I'd promised not to leave him *without his consent*. I had foreseen a day when that consent might be granted.

Marriage was an important matter for men like Charles, but not a matter of love. Only a few months ago, the Prince of Wales had abandoned the woman for whom he'd once sworn to forfeit the crown. In return for wedding a Protestant princess, Parliament had agreed to pay-off his massive debts. There were already rumors his bride was pregnant with a legitimate heir to the throne, something Mrs. Fitzherbert had not been able to provide.

After decades of loose living and a pair of illegitimate daughters, Lord Cholmondeley had finally wed an heiress fifteen years his junior. Unlike poor, scandalous, flighty Dally, his bride had brought him the fortune and distinction he craved for his family. His bride had speedily presented Lord Cholmondeley with an heir, and was raising his two natural daughters.

The Duke of Dorset had not needed to marry for money. But at the age of five-and-forty, he had decided it was time to secure the Sackville succession. He had parted from Signora Baccelli, his mistress for almost as long as I had been Charles's, to wed a cherubic child less than half his age. The new duchess had swiftly borne a daughter and then an heir.

Now it was Charles's turn. Miss Coutts would bring a dowry that could only enhance his political power. A more respectable domestic life would make him less open to attacks by the press. Best of all, a young bride might give him legitimate children, who could take their places in Society and carry on his work.

Was that why he had been preoccupied – wanting to tell me, but not knowing how? Had he and Richard gone to visit Bob so he could consult with his two closest friends? Might he persuade one of them to break the news to me?

Bob would try to make a jest of it. My eyes filled with tears. Richard would find some eloquent words of comfort. My tears began to fall. Perhaps they were drawing straws at this very moment to see which of them the task would fall to.

In the little sanctuary that love had built, I broke down and wept until my heart was as parched and barren as my future.

By the time Charles returned, I was calm again, resigned to what must be. His marrying another woman would not alter my feelings for him. Indeed, by stepping aside, I was bringing that love to a kind of bittersweet fulfillment. Not without cost to myself, but not entirely without reward either.

As Charles alighted from the carriage, I greeted him with a kiss so ardent it knocked his hat off.

"Yo-ho! The old one's absence has made Liz's heart grow even fonder." Glancing about to make certain none of the servants were watching, he pressed my hand to the front of his breeches. "And she needs not doubt how happy Kins is to be home with her again. How soon is it till bedtime?"

I meant to speak with him as soon as Harriet went to bed. But I postponed it a little longer. That night we made love with a tender intensity our years together had only deepened.

"Kins?" I murmured afterwards, running my hand over the familiar thatch of hair on his chest.

"Yes, my darling wife?" He spoke the words in a tone of perfect sincerity, yet they stung.

"We both know I am not your wife. Now it is time for you to make a proper match. I want you to know I will not put any obstacles in your way. Nor demand any more from you than I need to keep on living in the simple way we have been."

I wished I could refuse to take anything from him, but I did not intend to play the martyr. I needed to live and Miss Coutts's inheritance would never miss the repayment of those annuities I had sold for Charles.

"Liz?" His hand blundered over my face in the darkness,

coming to rest on my forehead. "Have you a fever? You are talking nonsense."

"I am not feverish." I pushed his hand away. Why did he have to make this more difficult? "And I am not mad. Mr. Adam was here while you were away. He told me you have promised a l-lock of your h-hair to Miss Coutts."

He stroked my arm in an appeasing caress. "True, but what does that signify? I would shave my head bald and give it all to you if you asked. God knows it would grow back fast enough."

"Are you not listening?" I sat up in bed, my arms clasped around my bent knees. "There is no need to deny it. I will not weep or carry on or make demands. I've always known this day would come. Now it has, I will not stand in your way."

Charles sat up too. I could see his ample shadow in the darkness and feel his warmth. "You think I ought to marry... Miss Coutts? But she is a child!"

I shook my head. "She is a young woman who could *give* you children. I want that for you and all the other advantages you would gain from such a splendid match."

"Is Liz tired of the old one? Have I done something to offend her? I vow I have not touched a card this whole year and I did not drink *much* wine at Bob's."

For one of the cleverest men in England, he was being monstrously thick-witted. I'd pictured us discussing the situation quietly, with bittersweet affection. But his refusal to admit the truth and his plaintive bewilderment shook my fragile self-control.

"Of course I am not tired of you!" I flung the words like an accusation as I climbed out of bed and groped for my dressing gown. "You make me happier than I ever expected to be in this world. Far happier than I deserve, no doubt. You have done nothing to offend me. I only wish you had told me about Miss Coutts before I heard it from someone else."

"But Liz, pray listen to reason my angel!"

"I cannot listen. Not if I am to do what I must. I promise not to make our parting any more difficult for you than I can help. Can you not do me the same courtesy?"

With that I stumbled off, cursing my foolishness for bringing the matter up at such an awkward time. I groped my way to our little library where we had spent so many delightful hours. Now I spent some of the most miserable of my life.

When dawn came at last, I crept back to bed to find Charles gone. He was still not there I when woke late in the morning after a restless sleep.

Hearing Harriet at play, I rose and dressed, steeling myself to go through the motions of the day for her sake. I wondered what would become of the child, now. I hoped she might still be permitted to visit me at St. Anne's Hill sometimes. Her father was not the only one I had risked my heart to love.

"Has Mr. Fox breakfasted?" I asked my maid, when she brought my plate.

She shook her head. "I haven't seen him this morning, ma'am. Is he not sleeping late?"

"I believe he may have gone out early."

A visit to the stables revealed one of the horses missing. Where could Charles have gone at that hour? I fretted at the thought of him out in the damp night air on dark roads, perhaps accosted by highwaymen. I told myself he was no longer mine to worry about, but my anxious heart refused to heed.

Some hours later, I heard the sound of hoof beats and Harriet's cry, "Papa, where have you been?"

I hurried to the verandah where I was obliged to exercise every crumb of self-restraint to keep from flinging my arms around Charles. He looked tired, rumpled and grim.

"Come, Liz." He reached for my hand. "The carriage is being harnessed. We are going for a drive."

"Can I come too?" cried Harriet.

"Not this time," her father replied in a kind but firm tone as he whisked me into the waiting carriage.

"Where are we going?" I asked as we set off down the lane toward Chertsey. Irrational hope and grim despair waged a painful battle for possession of my heart.

"I have no idea," said Charles. "I gave orders to drive until I said stop."

"Why?"

"So you must stay and hear me out without anyone to interrupt us. You caught me so off guard last night, I hardly knew what to say. And you were in no state to be reasoned with. So I rode to Sunninghill and harried poor Richard out of bed to vent my woes."

"What did he say?" The same things he'd told me ten years ago, no doubt. Richard had seen this coming and tried to warn me.

"He said only a great fool would let a woman like you go. He said if I could not persuade you to change your mind, I might as well retire from Parliament for I had quite lost my touch."

If Richard had not loved me before, I knew he did now. I pressed my fingers to my lips to stifle a sob.

"Now," continued Charles, "Let us pretend this is Parliament and abide by its rules of order. You shall have a fair turn to speak in reply then we shall have the question."

I nodded for I was too overcome to choke out a word.

"Very good." Charles cleared his throat. "Now, I have considered the matter as much as is possible where everything is on one side and next to nothing on the other. I love you more than life itself, Liz, and I can not figure any possible idea of happiness without you."

He did not declaim his feelings as the Prince once had, with violent passion, but simply and certainly as the most fundamental of truths. "How could any trifling advantage of fortune or connection weigh a feather in the scale against the whole comfort and happiness of my life?"

He assured me he had never given Miss Coutts or her family

the slightest encouragement to think of him as a potential suitor. Indeed, he feared there must be some misunderstanding between Mrs. Coutts and Mr. Adam.

"But what signifies what was said?" he concluded. "Since I never can consent to part with you, it is time we observe the legalities and make you my wife in name as well as in practice."

Wife? I could not keep silent a moment longer, rules of order or no. "Dearest Kins, I did not offer you your freedom as a threat to make you wed me! If all you say is true – and you do persuade me it is – then I am content to continue on as we have been. If I can be sure of your always loving me and being entirely mine, I shall be the happiest woman in the world!"

"Then I am the happiest of men, Liz. But I will have my way in the matter of marriage. We have already been together through better and worse, richer and poorer, sickness and health. So what will it signify if we say so in front of a clergyman and sign a bit of paper?"

"You once told me you had no inclination for marriage and nothing could induce you to engage in it." Odd how I should recall those words so clearly when they applied to me rather than Miss Coutts.

"When did I spout such foolishness?" Charles demanded. "You must be mistaken. Why I have considered myself an old married man in all but formality for years!"

I reminded him of the long ago night at Covent Garden when he had challenged me to translate his words from the French. "You called love a transient madness. You said friendship is the only real happiness in the world."

His anxious frown blossomed into a smile of spell-binding sweetness. "But don't you see, dearest Liz? I was right, in my way, though too young and foolish to see it. Love without friendship *is* a transient madness. But love that grows out of friendship – the kind of love we have been blessed to find, can you deny it is the only true and lasting happiness in the world?"

I did not dare answer that question just then. "I would rather see you married to another woman than think of you being married to me but wishing yourself free. Besides, you must know what a scandal it will cause for you to marry a woman with my past. The newspapers and printmakers will show no mercy. The wives of your friends will not want to receive me, but not wish to offend you either."

I knew of some courtesans who had married their patrons. The pressures of society's censure had taken their toll on those unions. I could not bear for that to happen to Charles and me.

"Is that the best you can do, Liz?" He raised my hands and kissed them. "Then you are as good as wed, now. If ten years has never dimmed my love for you, but only increased it, reason dictates another ten or thirty or fifty will multiply it further . . . until it becomes too much for a living body to hold. As for the other, if you do not wish the marriage to be known, let it be unknown. We will go away to some distant parish with a discreet clergyman and have as secret a ceremony as Liz could wish for. But known or unknown, married we must be."

He gave me a few moments to digest what he had said, all the while keeping my hands clasped in his and his eyes gazing deep into mine that I might see there his love, his constancy and his resolution.

*Never fall in love,* Mrs. Goadby had told me. I had lived by that demanding rule for many years. But I had never known true happiness until I'd broken it.

"Now for the question." Charles continued. "Be it resolved that Charles James Fox and Elizabeth Armistead—"

"Elizabeth Bridget Cane." Something this important demanded my full true name.

"—and Elizabeth Bridget Cane shall be joined in lawful wedlock as soon as can be arranged to their mutual convenience. Shall we have the division?"

That was the method by which the Members of Parliament went out to signify their vote.

I shook my head. "There is no need." I crossed the floor of the carriage to sit beside him, the better to seal our decision with a kiss. "The honorable gentleman's question is carried ... unanimously!"

# Epilogue

*St. Anne's Hill, Surrey, September 1835*

COURTESAN. CYPRIAN. DEMI-REP. HARLOT. CAN you think any of those words in connection with a respectable elderly widow like me and not laugh ... or grimace ... or sigh? That was all so long ago, now, it seems like a dream. One I have relived in the telling of my story.

As Charles insisted, we were married, forty years ago this very day. As *I* insisted, we wed in secret, with only my trusted maid, Mary, to know. We savored every moment of seven more wonderfully happy years living, to all appearances, as keeper and mistress.

Then, on the eve of a trip to Paris, where he would be feted by Emperor Napoleon, Charles persuaded me to let him reveal our secret so I could properly share in all the civilities shown him. As I expected, it caused a scandal. But Charles was so well loved and so impervious to public opinion that everyone soon pretended to forget the modest, respectable Mrs. Fox had ever been the alluring, infamous Mrs. Armistead.

I had another four years with my angel until he 'died happy.' His last words were an endearment to me. Now we have been parted for more years than we were together, yet I go on loving him. Will that come to an end when I do? I trust not, for since his death I have felt his love with me as strong as ever it was in life.

Do you wonder what became of all the others – Dally, Perdita,

Dorset, Derby, Bob, Richard and the Prince? I will leave you to find out for yourself, if you care. They are all gone now, too, along with the world we once knew. If I have made it live again in these pages, then I am content.

Is there a lesson to be drawn from my story? The Victorians, among whom I now live, crave lessons, morals and tidy endings. We Georgians gloried in contradictions and reckless excess. So take away whatever lesson you choose. Or none at all. If I have only aroused and entertained you with my confessions, what better can you ask ... of a courtesan?

# Fact or Fiction?

In case the Reader wonders which parts of this story are invented and which are most closely based upon documented events, there is very little reliable information about the courtesan known as Elizabeth Armistead before she appeared as the mistress of Viscount Bolingbroke in 1774. Her real name was Elizabeth Bridget Cane and she was born on July 11, 1750. To me, her middle name suggested Irish descent, while a rumor that she had once been a dresser to the celebrated actress Miss Abingdon made me suspect a connection to the theatre. From this scant evidence, I made up her parents, an actor and an Irish theatre dresser. The notion of Elizabeth begging with her blind father was invented but it is not so far fetched. I borrowed the incident from the life of Emily Warren, another courtesan of the period.

Though Elizabeth Cane was known professionally as Mrs. Armistead, her later marriage certificate listed her as spinster and nothing was known of a Mr. Armistead. It is possible he was her first keeper, but my research on *molly* culture of 18th century London suggested an even more intriguing possibility. There are conflicting reports about the West End brothel in which Elizabeth Armistead began her career. I chose Mrs. Goadby's on Great Marlborough Street because there was quite a bit of information available about this establishment. The other girls who worked there are all products of my imagination, but their stories are drawn from true accounts and reflect the ways many young women of the time became prostitutes.

Improbable as it may seem, the story of how Elizabeth Armistead first met Charles James Fox and his friends is true as reported many years later by Lord Egremont, who claimed to have been present! Elizabeth's subsequent dismissal by Mrs. Goadby and her confrontation with the young gentlemen at their club is my own invention, though making such a wager would have been perfectly in character for them. Certainly they all became good friends and Elizabeth did make her brief foray onto the London stage soon afterward.

As she ascended the heights of notoriety, Elizabeth Armistead had many wealthy and titled lovers. I have only mentioned those who were most significant to the course of her career and life. I did considerable research to confirm the time periods of her involvement with these men as well as their family circumstances and personal characters. Most of this section is very well documented, as is Elizabeth's deepening friendship with Charles Fox and Richard Fitzpatrick.

It is not known whether Elizabeth attended the theatre on the night Martha Ray was shot, but it is entirely possible that she might have. Her reaction to the tragedy and those of her friends is my own invention, but it all coincides very neatly with her parting from Lord Derby. Though Richard Fitzpatrick was significant in his absence from the roll of Elizabeth's lovers, their relationship was so close I find it difficult to believe they were never intimate. A later estrangement and eventual reconciliation suggested there was something more between them. I thought a relationship with Fitzpatrick made an interesting contrast to that with Fox.

The transformation of Charles Fox and Elizabeth Armistead from friends to lovers to spouses is also well documented, including many touching love letters. I have sometimes incorporated lines from those letters into their dialogue. More than any specific factual details, I hope I have been able to capture the robust, bawdy flavor of the Georgian era and the emotion of its greatest love story!

# What happened to...?

RICHARD FITZPATRICK served as Chief Secretary for Ireland, Privy Counsellor and twice as Secretary at War. The Duke of Queensbury left him a substantial legacy in recognition of his fine manners. Though he lived far longer than his parents and sister, the dissolute lifestyle of his younger years caught up with him in later life. Lord Byron wrote of him: "I had seen poor Fitzpatrick not very long before – a man of pleasure, wit, eloquence, all things. He tottered – but still talked like a gentleman, though feebly." On his tombstone he asked to be remembered as "during forty years, the intimate Friend of Mr. Fox." Elizabeth planted ivy to grow on his grave.

LORD ROBERT SPENCER was true to his word. After he won enough from the faro bank at Brooks' to pay off his creditors and purchase the estate of Woolbeding in Sussex, he never gambled again. Many years spent bedding the most celebrated women in the kingdom came to an end when he fell in love with Mrs. Harriet Bouverie. After the death of her husband, they married and lived happily with her youngest daughter Diana, who was widely believed to be Lord Robert's daughter. Elizabeth and Harriet became very close friends in later life. Like Fitzpatrick, Lord Robert's epitaph records that he "lived the friend of Fox."

JOHN FREDERICK, DUKE OF DORSET was appointed Ambassador to France during the years before the French Revolution where he became a favourite of Queen Marie Antoinette. He continued to promote the sport of cricket and was one of the first members of the Marylebone Cricket Club. For many years the beautiful Italian opera dancer, Giovanna Baccelli was his mistress. At the age of forty-five, he gave her up to wed twenty-one year old Arabella Cope. His wife bore him a son and two daughters before he died in 1799.

EDWARD SMITH-STANLEY, EARL OF DERBY maintained a chaste relationship with actress Elizabeth Farren until the death of his first wife allowed them to wed. The couple had one daughter together. Lord Derby died at the age of eighty-two but was immortalized in the famous horse race that bears his name, The Derby Stakes.

GEORGE, EARL OF CHOLMONDELEY married Lady Georgiana Bertie, whose brother, the Duke of Ancaster, had been one of Elizabeth's early patrons. The countess bore her husband a daughter and two sons and brought up his two illegitimate daughters as part of the family. In 1815 his title was elevated to Marquess and he was inducted into the Order of the Garter. He died at the age of seventy-seven.

FREDERICK ST. JOHN "BULLY" VISCOUNT BOLINGBROKE lapsed into madness a few years after his affair with Elizabeth and died at the age of fifty-four. Elizabeth remained very close to his sons George and Frederick, their children and grandchildren. She was particularly attached to George's son Robert, who was the child of an incestuous affair between George and his half-sister Anne Beauclerk.

THE PRINCE OF WALES persuaded Mrs. Fitzherbert to wed him in a ceremony that was not legally binding. He later abandoned her to marry Caroline of Brunswick in exchange for Parliament discharging some of his debts. After his father became mentally unfit to rule, he was made Prince Regent and later ruled as King George IV. The Prince was notorious for his extravagant lifestyle and many mistresses. In his later years, he gave Elizabeth an annuity that was continued by his brother and his niece, Queen Victoria.

Mary "Perdita" Robinson became paralysed at the age of twenty-six following a miscarriage. No longer able to act, she supported herself as a writer, producing poetry as well as six novels, two plays and an autobiography. She and Banastre Tarleton remained together for fifteen years until he left her to marry a niece of Lord Cholmondeley's wife.

Perdita died in poverty at the age of forty-two.

Grace Dalrymple Eliot left her infant daughter Georgiana to be raised by Lord Cholmondeley. She returned to France as the mistress of the Duke of Orleans. She remained there throughout the French Revolution and was imprisoned at one point for having a letter from Charles Fox in her possession. Though many of her friends were executed, she survived and was eventually set free. Dally wrote about her experiences in *Journal of my life during the French Revolution.*

# Verses Inscribed In The Temple Of Friendship At St. Anne's Hill.

*by the Right Honourable R. Fitzpatrick.*

The Star, whose radiant beams adorn
With vivid light the rising morn,
The season chang'd – with milder ray
Cheers the calm hour of parting day.
So Friendship, of the generous breast
The earliest and the latest guest,
In youthful prime with ardour glows,
And sweetens Life's serener close.
Benignant pow'r! in this retreat
O deign to fix thy tranquil seat;
Where rais'd above the dusky vale
Thy favourites brighter suns shall hail;
And, from Life's busy scenes remote,
To thee their cheerful hours devote;
Nor waste a transient thought, to know
What cares disturb the Crowd below!

# Funeral of the late Honourable Mrs. Fox

Report from *The Windsor and Eton Express,* July 16, 1842

Yesterday the funeral of this venerable and highly respected lady, the widow of that distinguished statesman the Right Hon. Charles James Fox, took place at Chertsey church. The ceremony was intended to be private, but persons of all classes were anxious to show their respect for one who has been so long and justly beloved, and who by her urbanity, kindness, and excessive benevolence, has acquired the esteem of the inhabitants of the neighbourhood of her own residence, St. Anne's Hill. At their own request, about forty respectable tradesmen of Chertsey, who had provided themselves with hatbands and gloves, and who were attired in deep mourning, were allowed to join the procession about half a mile from Chertsey, and accompany it to the church.

So intense was the general feeling of regret at the loss of this estimable lady, that many of the inhabitants of Chertsey kept their shops partially closed from the time of her death, and yesterday the generality of them were entirely closed. At about one o'clock the mournful procession left the late deceased's residence at St Ann's Hill in the following order:- The hearse contained the body drawn by four horses and attended by pages. The coffin was a neat black one with furniture and lace in the Elizabethan style. On the coffin plate was the following inscription:- "To the Memory of the Honourable Elizabeth

Bridget Fox, obit July 8th, 1842, aged ninety two years." Then followed two mourning coaches, the first containing Colonel Fox, (the executor), Lord Lilford, Sir R.Adair, and the Rev. Charles Cotton, vicar of Chertsey; the second contained Henry St. John, Esq., D.Grazebrook, Esq., C.J.Ives, Esq.; to these succeeded the private carriages of the deceased and Col.Fox, and the procession was closed by the tradesmen of the town as above noticed. A large concourse of spectators also assembled along the line of procession.

About two o'clock the procession arrived at the church, which was completely filled with the inhabitants of the town and surrounding neighbourhood, who appeared deeply sensible of the loss they had sustained. The funeral service was very impressively performed by the reverend vicar, and the body was consigned to its last resting place in a vault at the north-east end of the church-yard.

The funeral was conducted by Mr. Waterer, of Chertsey. Lord Holland was prevented attending the funeral of his illustrious relative in consequence of his being absent from this country, we believe in Italy. During the procession a little boy was knocked down and ridden over, and much anxiety was manifested for him. He was taken to Mr. Smith's surgery, where, upon examination, he was fortunately found to have been but slightly injured; his head was somewhat lacerated, but not seriously.

# Research Sources

Barker, Hannah. *Gender in eighteenth-century England*, Longman, 1997

Bass, Robert Duncan. *The green dragoon : the lives of Banastre Tarleton and Mary Robinson,* Sandlapper Publishing, 2003

Bleackley, Horace. *Ladies Fair and Frail*, John Lane, 1925

Brewer, John. *A Sentimental Murder.* Farrar, Straus and Giroux, 2004

Byrne, Paula. *Perdita.* Random House, 2004

Cleland, John. *Fanny Hill: Or the Memoir of a Woman of Pleasure*, 1749

Davis, I.M. *The Harlot and the Statesman.* The Kendall Press, 1986

Derry, John W. *Charles James Fox.* Batsford, 1972

Drinkwater, John. *Charles James Fox.* Ernest Benn Ltd. 1928

Foreman, Amanda. *Georgiana, Duchess of Devonshire,* HarperCollins UK, 1997

Foster, Vere. *The Two Duchesses.* Blackie and Sons. 1898

Genest, John. *Some Accounts of the English Stage 1660-1830*, 1832

George, M. Dorothy. *London Life in the Eighteenth Century*, Academy Chicago Publishers, 2000

Griffin, Susan. *The book of the courtesans : a catalogue of their virtues.* Broadway, 2001

Hickman, Katie. *Courtesans.* Harper Collins, 2003

Hicks, Carola. *Improper Pursuits.* Macmillan, 2001

Jesse, John Heneage. *George Selwyn and His Contemporaries.* London, 1901

Levy, M. J. *Love and madness : the murder of Martha Ray.* HarperCollins, 2004

Linnane, Fergus. *Madams, Bawds and Brothel Keepers of London,* Sutton Publishing, 2005

Manning, Jo. *My Lady Scandalous.* Simon and Schuster, 2005

Marshall, Dorothy. *Dr. Johnson's London.* John Wiley and Sons, 1968

Rictor Norton (Ed.), *Homosexuality in Eighteenth Century England: A Sourcebook.* http://rictornorton.co.uk/eighteen/

O'Toole, Fintan. *A traitor's kiss : the life of Richard Brinsley Sheridan,* Farrar, Straus and Giroux, 1998

Priestley, J. B. *The Prince of Pleasure and His Regency.* Penguin Books, 1969

Robinson, Mary. *Memoirs of the Late Mrs. Mary Robinson.* London, 1830

Rubenhold, Hallie. *The Covent Garden Ladies.* Tempus Publishing, 2005

Russell, Lord John. Memorials and Correspondence of Charles James Fox. 1853

Sackville-West, Vita. *Knole and the Sackvilles.* Heinemann, 1934

Thorold, Peter. *The London Rich.* St. Martin's Press, 1999

Tillyard, Stella. *Aristocrats.* Chatto and Windus, London, 1994

Toynbee, Mrs. Paget. *The Letters of Horace Walpole, fourth Earl of Oxford.* Clarendon Press. 1903–1925

Trevelyn, Sir George Otto. *The Early History of Charles James Fox.* 1811

Trotter, John Bernard. *Memoirs of the Latter Years of the Right Honourable Charles James Fox.* London, 1811

White, T.H. *The Age of Scandal,* Putnam, 1950

Made in the USA
San Bernardino, CA
23 June 2017